THE OTHER EMPRESS

THE OTHER EMPRESS

A QING COURT NOVEL
BOOK ONE

AMANDA ROBERTS

Red Empress Publishing
www.RedEmpressPublishing.com

Cover Design by Cherith Vaughan
https://www.facebook.com/coversbycherith

ALSO BY AMANDA ROBERTS

FICTION

Threads of Silk

The Man in the Dragon Mask

THE QING COURT

The Other Empress

The Pearl Concubine

The French Princess

THE QING DYNASTY MYSTERIES

Murder in the Forbidden City

Murder in the British Quarter

Murder at the Peking Opera

THE TOUCHING TIME SERIES

The Child's Curse

The Emperor's Seal

The Empress's Dagger

The Slave's Necklace

AUTHOR'S NOTE

Though this story features historical events and people, this is a work of fiction. Names, characters, organizations, events, dates, and incidents are products of my imagination or used fictitiously.

CHAPTER ONE

*P*lease don't choose me. I held my chin up but kept my eyes downcast to the floor, as I'd been trained to do, which made it difficult to see the empress as she glided past me, back and forth, evaluating me and the four other girls who had made it to the final round of the selection process to find the primary consort for the emperor's eldest living son, Prince Yizhu.

While the emperor had not officially named Yizhu as his heir, only he and his half-brother, Prince Yixin, were in the position to possibly be chosen. Therefore, whoever was chosen today to be Prince Yizhu's consort would most likely be the next empress of China.

But I did not want it.

After the empress passed me for the fourth time, I heard snickering from across the room. Still, I did not look up. I knew the princes were watching us, teasing one another and making lewd jokes. Yizhu had been involved in the selection process the day before, narrowing the possibilities from over a hundred to only dozens. He would lick his lips and bare his teeth like a hungry wolf whenever he looked at me. It made me shudder,

1

and I prayed to Heaven that I would not be chosen. But I had repeated the same prayer at each stage of the selection process, and each time, I took one step closer to the throne. Clearly, I was doing something wrong.

Please don't choose me.

Now, the final decision was left to Empress Jing. Well, she was not really the empress. She was only Noble Consort Jing. But ever since the death of the last empress, she had served the role of empress—including choosing the consorts for her sons. Prince Yizhu was the son of a late concubine, while Prince Yixin was Empress Jing's son. By law, such distinctions were not supposed to be observed. All children of the emperor were also children of the empress. But in practice, such divisions were well-known and played a significant part in decision-making. There had been much gossip in the weeks leading up to Yizhu's consort selection. Would Empress Jing choose the best candidate for Yizhu, as the emperor's heir apparent? Or would she save the best for her own son, Prince Yixin?

Oh, how I hoped it would be the latter!

I knew both princes well. My mother had been a lady-in-waiting to Empress Jing and was still a dear friend to her, so I had spent much time at the palace and in the company of the empress and her children and the children of the other consorts, the sons and daughters of Emperor Daoguang.

When we were little, we often ran together down the shaded paths of the Forbidden City, or even the Summer Palace when we were lucky enough to be invited. We would swim in the lakes on hot days and catch fireflies at dusk. We would watch operas or dramas on the grand stages that would be set up when theater troupes were invited to perform for the imperial court. Together, we celebrated birthdays and festivals, and observed mourning customs when a family member passed on.

But as we grew older, we were separated more and more. The boys spent less time with their mother and more time with their father and their tutors, learning to rule this great empire of ours, while we girls were taught embroidery, hairdressing, and music. The selection process was the first time I had seen either prince in over a year. From the first sight, I was reminded of how much I feared Yizhu. If I were chosen to be his primary consort, his empress, I was unsure how I could bear it.

The empress clicked her tongue. "Go," she said to the girl at the end of the row, the daughter of her cousin. The girl gave a small curtsey to the empress, but the silver charms on her head-dress tinkled as she shook, trying to not burst into tears.

How I envied her.

She had no idea how fortunate she was to not be chosen. Of course, I was probably the only girl present who didn't want to be chosen. But none of them knew Yizhu as well as I did.

I was only a child the first time he pushed me to the ground and tried to kiss me. I could not have been eight years old. I thought we had been playing a game, as we usually did. But when he pinned me to the ground and straddled me, I could see no humor in his eyes. He bent over me, his lips pursed. I turned my head and felt wetness on my cheek.

I kicked and screamed. But we had wandered too far from our mothers, and no one heard me.

No one but Yixin.

Yixin pushed his older brother off me and pulled me to my feet. The boys then began to fight. I'd seen them quarrel in the past, as brothers do, but never before had I seen them come to blows. I was so scared, I ran away and found my mother and the other ladies. I don't know what happened after that, who found them or how they were pulled apart. I don't know what excuse they gave for the fighting, but it seemed that I was never mentioned because I was not questioned about it.

After that was when I started to see the princes less often. I missed the fun of our childhood days, but I was glad I didn't have to see Yizhu again except in passing or at formal events. But even in those brief moments, something in his stare frightened me.

When I was still young, before I became a woman, I thought he was looking at me with anger. Cruelty. As if he wanted to hurt me. I couldn't understand why. A cross word had never passed between us. But as I grew older and started to attract the attention of men, I realized that the prince had not been angry with me.

He'd been lustful.

I shuddered at the memory, the jewels on my headdress shaking slightly. The empress stopped in front of me. I could see her hands folded tightly in front of her.

Please don't choose me.

I held my breath and stilled my quaking nerves. Finally, the empress moved on. I let out only the slightest sigh of relief. I still had to stand straight and hold my chin high. I could not lower my head without losing balance, such was the weight of my headdress. I usually did not wear one so heavy as to become unsteady, but for today, my mother had insisted that I wear my best gown, my tallest shoes, and as many hair decorations as my neck could bear. As much as I did not want to become Yizhu's wife, I still had to play my part. I still had to represent my family. Had to fulfill the role I was born to play.

Please don't choose me.

I pressed my lips together tightly to keep from muttering the words out loud. But then I remembered my training and softened my lips and jaw. I did not want my features to appear hard. I heard the empress click her tongue and sigh and dismiss two more girls until only I and Lady Ayan, of the Sakda clan, the daughter of a low-ranking official, remained.

Please don't choose me.

"What do you think, my son?" Empress Jing asked. I heard the footsteps of both princes as they crossed the room toward us. "These are the best ladies our empire has to offer. Which would you choose?"

I felt sick to my stomach. I didn't know Lady Ayan well, but I feared that if the choice were left up to Yizhu, he would choose me.

"I have always been fond of Zhenxiu," Yizhu said quickly, and I didn't need to see him to feel the lust pouring from his words. He chuckled, and the empress grunted her disapproval.

It wasn't that I was opposed to lustful feelings. I had to admit that even I'd had more than a few pleasant dreams about the younger prince, Prince Yixin. But with Yizhu, there was something...intimidating about him. As I remembered how he held me down in the grass, I did not think he would be a kind or caring lover, but a brute.

"But what of Lady Ayan?" the empress asked. "Is she not so much more of a beauty?"

I took no offense at her words. If Lady Ayan were chosen because she was considered more beautiful than me, I would gladly admit to being ugly.

"They are both beautiful," Yizhu said diplomatically. "But I know Zhenxiu. We've always been friends."

I hadn't eaten for two days in nervous anticipation of the selection. Otherwise, I might have vomited. Ever since the day he pinned me down and tried to kiss me, I would not consider him a friend. I avoided him whenever possible, and I was sure he had noticed over the years.

"Hmm." The empress still seemed undecided even though the prince had made his preference clear. I wondered why she was hesitating. As much as I didn't want to be chosen, there was no reason I shouldn't be. I was the daughter of a high-ranking official, a former governor. My mother had trained me from birth to marry well. As high as possible. Was I lacking in some way that I was not aware of? Was there a reason she did not want to choose Lady Ayan? If she did not want either of us, she could have easily selected another girl. The waiting made my stomach clench and my knees shake. I did not know how much longer I could stand here.

"My sons," the empress said as she turned away and motioned for the princes to follow her. She stepped away, too far for me to hear what she had to say, but I tried to read their faces, their body language, for a clue. At one point, Yizhu smiled and said something to Yixin that made him roll his eyes. Yixin then said something to his mother that seemed to displease Yizhu.

I felt a cold touch on the smallest finger of my left hand. I glanced down and saw that Lady Ayan had wrapped her pinky finger around my own. I looked up and saw her smiling at me, as though she was giving me some of her strength. I gave her a small smile in return as I squeezed her finger back. She did not seem nearly as nervous as I was. I think she looked hopeful that she would be chosen.

Ayan was younger than me by at least a year. She could not have been more than thirteen. Though, none of us were old. Yixin and I were fifteen, and Yizhu was seventeen. In truth, it was already a bit late for the son of an emperor to be given his first consort. Most were betrothed at thirteen. But I supposed that since he was the heir apparent, his choice of wife was more important and, thus, took more time to find. He would be given his first consort now, and when he became emperor, a nation-wide selection would take place to fill the Inner Court with concubines for the emperor to choose from in order to produce as many heirs as possible.

I wondered, though, what would happen if Yizhu were passed over in favor of his younger half-brother, Yixin. It was possible—and some thought it was even likely. It was customary for the emperor not to name his heir until just before his death. And both boys had reason to think they would hold precedence. Yizhu was the eldest son, but he had been born to a concubine. Yixin was the younger son, but he was the child of his father's principal wife. I wondered if it caused any animosity between the brothers.

"Good luck," Ayan whispered, and I nodded in response. Her skin was like fine porcelain, her eyes wide and glassy as though she were near to tears, but she was smiling. I had to admit that she was prettier than me, but she was also so very young. She had not been raised near the palace as I had, but had come from the north. A Mongolian, I think she was. She had no idea what Yizhu was like and must have believed that being chosen would be a great honor. Of course, it would be. I was surely a fool to not want it. What woman didn't want to be empress? But I could not deny the sick feeling that grew in my belly whenever I imagined being Yizhu's bedmate.

I then felt a pang of guilt. If I were passed over, Ayan would be the girl given to satisfy Yizhu's lust. She was thin as the branches of a willow tree. Yizhu could surely do her great harm if he wished. Should I do something? Say something? Somehow turn the tide of the selection in my favor? But how? I was supposed to stand quietly and allow the empress to make the decision. I did not think there was anything I could do to help this poor girl except pray that I was taken in her place.

But I couldn't do it.

"And to you," I whispered. In my heart, I continued to pray, *Please don't choose me.*

The empress and princes turned to us. Ayan released my hand and returned her gaze to the ground, and I followed suit.

"Lady Zhenxiu," the empress said, and I nearly burst into tears. "You will leave."

Against my training, I looked up, sure I had not heard her correctly. Ayan gasped.

"My lady?" I said.

"Lady Ayan," the empress said, turning away from me as I

was no longer of any account, "you are to be Yizhu's primary consort."

Ayan put her hands to her mouth and a whimper escaped her smiling lips as tears of joy slid down her pink cheeks.

"Thank you, Your Majesty." She somehow bent down so low she was practically kneeling on the ground and inclined her head forward without toppling over. "May the emperor live ten thousand years!"

The empress waved her hand and two eunuch servants rushed over, each taking one of Ayan's hands and leading her from the room. Empress Jing followed after her, and I was left alone with the two princes. Yizhu watched Ayan leave, his arms crossed and shaking his head. He seemed nearly as displeased as I was relieved. I tried not to look at him.

"Please, bring my maid," I told a eunuch servant waiting nearby. He bowed and was quickly gone. The height of my shoes and the weight of my clothes made it nearly impossible for me to walk unescorted.

"Congratulations, brother," Yixin said. "She's beautiful."

"They are all beautiful," Yizhu said, as if such a quality was nothing special. Though, considering that only the most beautiful of girls could ever be part of the selection process, I supposed beauty was the bare minimum quality in a consort.

"Then why do you seem displeased?" Yixin asked. "Mother picked the best girl in the empire for you. I'm sure you won't be disappointed."

Yizhu smirked and looked at me. "What do you think, Zhen? Did the best woman win?" My full given name was Zhenxiu, but in more casual situations, most people called me Zhen.

"The empress is merely the vessel through which Heaven makes its will known," I said, repeating words my mother spoke to me over and over again as she taught me how to be a dutiful daughter-in-law one day. "Heaven decreed that Lady Ayan should be the next empress, and I am pleased for her."

Yixin chuckled, but Yizhu did not seem satisfied with my answer. He stepped closer to me, reaching up with his hand to lightly tug one of the tassels hanging from my headdress.

"Don't you want to be my empress, Zhen?"

His eyes bored into mine, and I couldn't look away. My whole body trembled, my headdress decorations tinkling.

"Heaven has another plan for me," I whispered.

Yizhu stepped back. "I suppose that could be true. Who knows, maybe as one of my concubines, you'll give birth to my sons yet still."

The idea that the empress had passed me over for consort only to make me a concubine stung. To be a second wife or concubine, even to an emperor, would be a great insult to me. Whoever I married, my father would make sure I was my husband's head wife, his first wife, I was sure of it.

The door opened and my maid shuffled across the room in her flat, silk slippers to my side. Yizhu sniffed as if being in the presence of a maid offended him and left the room quickly. Yixin, however, lingered.

"I do not think you will be a mere concubine," Yixin said, and my heart fluttered in my chest. "You might not be empress, but you will be a great lady one day."

I held my maid's hand and gave a slight bow. "His highness is too kind to me."

He chuckled and shook his head. "Always so formal, Zhenxiu."

I gave a half-smile and tilted my head to the side helplessly. We may have played together as children, but that was long in the past. As a woman, there was no other way I could act toward a man. Even if Yixin were my husband, specific protocols had to always be followed. Treating my husband with respect would be my utmost requirement as a wife.

His eyes went to my maid, who was looking at the ground, trying to appear invisible, as though she could not hear what was being said. But, of course, she could hear every word. And anything we said in her presence was not something that would remain secret. As much as I adored her, for she had been with me many years, she was still a servant, and I could never trust her completely.

Yixin looked from the maid to me, and I believed there was more he wanted to say, but he knew better. He cleared his throat and gave me a polite bow. "I am sure we will meet again, Lady Zhenxiu."

"As am I," I said, gripping my maid's hand so that I could bend my knees and incline my head forward. When I stood up again, our eyes met for a moment before Yixin tore himself away and quickly walked from the room.

Oh, those eyes! I supposed they were similar to Yizhu's in that they could pierce my soul. But Yizhu's intimidating gaze pushed me away. Yixin's, however, was kind, gentle. He made me feel safe and drew me to him. But I shook such thoughts away. It was foolish to dream of love, or even affection. Feelings played no part in marriage. Our parents would make the best marriage choices for our families or, in Yixin's case, the empire.

It was not wise to marry for affection. Affection faded. It clouded one's judgment. It flitted from one pretty or handsome face to the next. I had been lectured many times in my life about the dangers of falling in love. Marriage was about unity for a common purpose. Love shrouded that purpose in uncertainty, and there should never be uncertainty in a family.

Yixin turned and left the room without another word, and I felt the need to call out to him. I did not know what I wanted to say. Nothing would have been appropriate. Still, his absence left me feeling…incomplete.

"I am so sorry, my lady," my maid said as she led me toward the other door.

"What?" I asked her. "Whatever for?"

She looked at me, confused. "Be-because you were not chosen."

"Oh," I said, remembering that I had not been sent here to become the consort of just any prince, but the likely next emperor. To be passed over was a significant failure on my part. My parents would not be pleased. I tried to frown, or at least look serious, but it was a struggle. "Of course. I only hope Mother and Father are not too disappointed."

"I'm sure you will make a good match yet," she said.

"Yes, I'm sure I will," I replied. Father probably already had a list of suitable matches for me should I not be chosen for the emperor. Whether Yixin was on that list or not, I had no way of knowing.

My opinion on the matter was irrelevant.

CHAPTER TWO

"Y ou look stunning," I said to Lady Ayan as she studied herself in a tall brass mirror held up by one of her servants. The mirror was only one of a mountain of gifts sent to Lady Ayan and her family by Prince Yizhu, her soon-to-be husband. Well, the gifts had most likely been selected by Empress Jing and sent on the prince's behalf. I could not imagine Prince Yizhu giving a single thought to silks or combs or furs, all items sent to Lady Ayan.

I had been selected to serve the future princess as a lady-in-waiting as she prepared for her wedding. As I looked around Lady Ayan's family home, however, I was even more confused as to why she was selected as Prince Yizhu's consort and I was not. Her father was merely a fourth-rank official, while mine was a former governor of Guangxi Province and a duke. My family lived north of the Forbidden City, along Beihai Lake. It was a beautiful, park-like area where Peking's most affluent families lived. Our house was a fine, well-appointed mansion with many beautiful gardens and even a stage for musical and operatic performances.

Lady Ayan's home was far to the south of the Forbidden City. It was small and dark and so close to their neighbors you could hear when they yelled at their children or their servants argued over who had to clean the chamber pots. I could tell that many of the house's rafters were new, as was the front gate. New paving stones from the front gate to Lady Ayan's room had also been laid. This was something that the emperor—or Empress Jing—would have ordered be done if the future princess's home was not grand enough. In fact, so many of the rafters had been replaced, I wondered if the house had been very near to falling down before the emperor's carpenters had arrived.

It was not uncommon for low-ranking or even impoverished girls to be selected as consorts during a grand consort selection. Any girl with a pretty face might be chosen when the emperor was looking to fill his Inner Court with as many women as possible to provide him with sons. But this was a special case. Ayan would, most likely, be the next empress of China. Would she even know how to run a household? From what I had seen, the family had five servants at the most. Her father had only his first wife and one concubine. Lady Ayan had two brothers and a sister. What would she do when she had a hundred women to oversee, along with dozens of children and thousands of servants?

Of course, my own family was not very large. No man had as many consorts as the emperor. Still, my father had seven concubines, and I had twenty siblings. The woman who gave birth to me was my father's first concubine, not his first wife. But I was his eldest daughter, and Mother loved me as she did her own children. She had taught me how to keep servants in order and concubines happy when jealousy arose. How to ensure we had enough food in stock and order silks and furs. How to entertain guests and show honor to dignitaries. How to show discipline and love to children in equal measure. I was raised to marry a man of even higher rank than my father. A prince.

But who had Lady Ayan been raised to marry? When Lady Ayan was born, had her mother thought she would marry a minor official and nothing more? Did she not prepare her daughter for greatness?

When I met Lady Ayan at the selection ceremony, I had no idea she had been raised so poorly. She held herself with grace and poise equal to my own, I had to admit. Perhaps she'd had better training than I was giving her credit for. Perhaps her grandmother or a grand aunt had taken Lady Ayan under her wing and given her the tools to succeed as an empress.

Or perhaps there had been some truth to the rumors after all. That Empress Jing had saved the best possible candidate for her own son, Prince Yixin, and would give a woman of lesser quality to Yizhu.

I shook my head to banish such thoughts away. They were unkind and ignorant. Who was I to question the decision of the empress? How could I accuse her, even in my own mind, of having dark motives? Surely, the empress had made the best decision for Prince Yizhu and China. She must have seen something in Lady Ayan that I did not. Perhaps something that would make her a better wife for Yizhu than I would have. Lady Ayan, at least, was happy about marrying Prince Yizhu. She, in that sense, was surely a better choice for him than me.

Why did it bother me anyway? I didn't want to be chosen for Yizhu. I prayed that I would not be chosen, and my prayers were answered. I should have been grateful.

And yet, something inside of me was—dare I say it? Jealous of Lady Ayan? After all, it was almost a certainty that Yizhu would be the next emperor of China. His wife would be empress. How could Empress Jing say that Ayan would be a better empress than me? I did not want to be the wife of Prince Yizhu—but I did want to be empress.

But it did not matter now. The decision was made. Lady Ayan, whether she was prepared for it or not, would be empress. I had to push any feelings of jealousy, of envy, aside and do my duty as her lady-in-waiting and wait for my own husband to be named.

"I am so nervous," Lady Ayan said, calling me back from my wandering thoughts.

"Don't be," I said as I ran a jade comb through her hair. I was supposed to brush her hair one hundred times, but I had long ago lost count. But the repetitive motion seemed to help settle the anxious bride, so I kept brushing.

"The palanquin is approaching!" someone announced. Lady Ayan gasped, putting one hand to her mouth and one to her stomach. I feared she was going to vomit all over her red wedding gown, so I took her hands and sat down on a stool beside her while all the other ladies and servants ran from the room in a flutter of excitement to see the approaching imperial procession.

"Look at me," I said. Lady Ayan did so, her eyes glassy with tears. "Do not cry," I ordered. "You will ruin your makeup."

She nodded. "Yes, of course." She looked up to the ceiling, willing her eyes to dry.

"Are you not happy?" I asked her. "Do you not feel blessed?"

"Of course!" she replied. "I never imagined I would be married to a son of the emperor, much less Yizhu! Surely, Heaven itself has smiled down upon me."

"Indeed! Then why have you reason to feel nervous?"

Even through the thick makeup she had been painted with, I could see her cheeks flush bright red. "I...I..."

"What is it?"

She shook her head. "I feel so stupid."

"About what?"

She took a deep breath. "I know that my main role as a wife —to any man—is to provide my husband with sons."

15

I nodded.

"But…how will I do that?"

"What do you mean?"

"Just as I said. How will I fall pregnant? I do not know what to do."

It felt as though a pound of lead had dropped into my stomach. I could feel my own face flush and my heart race as the memory of Yizhu's kiss flooded my brain.

"Zhen? Zhen?" Lady Ayan prodded, shaking my shoulder. "What's wrong?"

"N-nothing," I said, taking a breath to calm myself down. "Didn't…didn't your mother explain anything to you?"

Of course, my own mother had never told me how women fell pregnant, either. I knew that, after dinner each night, my father would choose a woman to spend the night in his bedchamber. But what then happened behind closed doors was a mystery to me. I had—on very rare occasions—seen my father kiss or caress one of his women. It was not the same way he kissed his children or patted us on the heads in approval. The way a father kissed a child was not how a husband kissed a wife. I was not afraid of my father's affection. But I had been afraid of Yizhu. Somehow, I knew that Yizhu's kiss was related to what my father and his women did in his bedchamber. But what? My mother and the other women did not seem afraid of my father. So why was I afraid of Yizhu? Was I only being a silly child? An ignorant girl? I assumed my mother would tell me how a woman became pregnant the night before my wedding. But here we were, waiting for Lady Ayan's imperial sedan chair to carry her to the Forbidden City and Yizhu's bedchamber, and she still didn't know. Her mother hadn't told her.

Would my mother not tell me either?

"My mother told me nothing," Lady Ayan said, her shoulders quaking, and I feared she really would cry this time and I would not be able to stop her. "I asked her, but she only said my husband would know what to do. But how? If I don't know, how will he know? What if neither of us knows what to do? What if we never have a son? What if I am the cause of the end of the Qing Dynasty?" She was working herself into a panic.

"Don't be stupid," I said. My words were harsh, but they got the effect I wanted. Lady Ayan froze, her eyes wide. At least she wasn't crying. "When Prince Yizhu is emperor, there will be another consort selection. If you don't know how to become pregnant, one of the other consorts will surely know how to do so, right?"

"That's true," she said.

"And, if come tomorrow, after your first night with the prince, you still don't know, you can always ask Empress Jing," I went on. "She has four children. She is certainly not as ignorant as you or me. Besides, once you leave here, Jing will be your mother too. She will want the best for you. She will not let you fail. She chose you for a reason."

"I wish I knew the reason," Lady Ayan said.

"Because it is your destiny," I said. "Are not the emperor and empress chosen by Heaven? You are right where you were meant to be."

"Do you really think so?" she asked, her eyes wide with hope instead of tears this time.

"I do." I smiled and placed a hand on her shoulder. She was no longer trembling. She took long, deep breaths as she looked back at the mirror.

"I will be Empress Ayan," she said and dared to smile.

"Well, you will get to choose a new name when that happens," I said.

"Oh, of course," she said, running her hands down the front of her bright red wedding gown. "I wonder what name Yizhu will choose. Perhaps I can pick something to compliment his name."

"I'm sure he would like that," I said.

The door flew open and Lady Ayan's mother burst into the room. She gasped when she saw her daughter. "Why are you still not ready? The prince is waiting for you!"

I had forgotten that I was supposed to be styling Lady Ayan's hair. I quickly ushered Ayan into her chair in front of a fine black lacquered dressing table that had been inlaid with mother-of-pearl flowers. Another gift from the prince. Thankfully, I would not be doing a full liangbatou hairstyle, with the silk-wrapped wire headdress, since the princess's head would be draped with a heavy red veil that would only be removed when she was in the privacy of the bedchamber with her husband. Instead, I wrapped her hair around an ivory plank, a bianfeng. Another gift from the prince? I supposed so since all the other bianfeng on her dressing table were made of wood. Her father was either too poor to afford an ivory one or he did not see the need to waste money on ivory when wood would do. He perhaps did not see the value of using stronger material, even though the liangbatou headdress could be quite heavy and snap a wooden bianfeng. When I finished wrapping her hair, I then added decorative pins of red flowers and attached red tassels to each side.

"Are you ready?" I asked Lady Ayan.

She took one last long look in the mirror. "Yes," she said with an air of finality that surprised me. Her mother and I each took one side of the wedding veil and draped it over her head. I then took her hand to help her stand and led her to the waiting palanquin. With Lady Ayan's exceptionally tall pot-bottom shoes and the thick, heavy veil, it would be impossible for her to walk unassisted. Usually, a daughter would walk behind her mother, but since Lady Ayan was about to become Princess Ayan, she took precedence.

As we walked slowly and cautiously through the newly renovated house, everyone we passed kowtowed before the girl who had come from very little but would one day be an empress even though she could not see them. The only exception was her father. A father cannot prostrate himself before his child. It would be considered unfilial on a child's part to allow such a thing. Still, I could see her father's pride, his eyes glistening with unshed tears.

The palanquin was a large wooden box painted red with gold accents. It was much larger than the ones most women used on their wedding days.

I held the train of Lady Ayan's gown as she climbed up into her sedan chair. She settled on her seat and I ran my hands over her gown one more time, ensuring every seam was smooth and straight. She gripped my hand tightly and turned her head toward me. I could not see her face through the thick red veil, but by the trembling in her hands, I had the feeling that she was crying. She wanted to say something, or ask me something, but could not articulate her words through her tears. I placed a hand on her shoulder.

"Everything will be fine," I told her. "You are a princess now."

She nodded and leaned back in her seat, letting out a long exhale and placing a hand on her stomach as it growled. As was tradition, Lady Ayan had not eaten all day, and we had been awake for hours. On the day of a woman's wedding, she was not to drink anything more than water until the tea ceremony with her new in-laws, nor could she eat until she shared her first meal with her new husband. I had no idea why such rules existed. I supposed it was a way to show respect for one's new family. I had never given it much thought before. But then, I had never been by a bride's side until this moment, either.

"Just imagine the grand meal you will be eating when you are a princess," I said, and we both laughed.

She loosened her grip just enough that I was able to slip my hand from her grasp. For some reason, this made me feel guilty, as if I were abandoning her to her fate. I hesitated, looking for a way to remain by her side, but it was impossible. There was no room for me in the sedan chair.

"Zhen," I heard my mother hiss behind me. I scurried out of the sedan chair as two chair bearers closed the heavy red curtains.

"You are much too slow," Mother whispered harshly to me as we stood with our heads down. "When you are serving the princess at the palace, you must be quick and diligent in your duties."

"Yes, Mother," I replied.

Eight men, four in the front and four in the back, picked up the sedan chair at once in a single fluid movement that would not jostle their precious cargo. Horns were blasted and drums were struck. I flinched at the sudden, loud sounds, but managed not to cover my ears. Everyone stood still as a statue, even the children. The men then marched forward in unison, keeping the sedan chair balanced. I imagined it must have felt like being carried on a cloud. Musicians, councilors, and holy men made up the procession, all walking on foot.

A small cart pulled by a donkey and led by a palace eunuch stopped in front of me. Mother nodded for me to climb inside. I am afraid I did so rather inelegantly. But unlike the princess's roomy and plush sedan chair, my donkey cart was small, cramped, and hard. There was only a single small pillow for me to sit upon. I centered myself on it as best I could and crossed my legs in front of me, my ankles quickly aching from being pressed upon the hard wooden floor. The curtains were drawn shut and the cart lurched forward, nearly sending me toppling backward. I was sure my headdress would look askew by the time I arrived at the Forbidden City.

Over the sounds of the music, I could hear people clapping and cheering for the new princess—and future empress—as we traveled through the city. I could hear the rushing footsteps of children as they ran alongside the procession. I wondered if my wedding would be half as grand as Lady Ayan's. Of course, it would all depend on who I married.

It had been several months since the selection ceremony when I had been passed over for Lady Ayan, and I still had not been betrothed to anyone. It was strange. At fifteen, I was more than old enough to be married. If anything, I was already becoming too old to be a first wife. I began to wonder, once again, if something was wrong with me. If I was lacking in some way. After all, I had been passed over for Lady Ayan when I was clearly more suited for the position of future empress than she was. However, even though my mother was disappointed that I had not been selected as consort for Prince Yizhu, she did not seem angry with me. She did not point out my flaws or tell me I needed to improve in some way. At least, not any more than usual. If Mother was not unhappy with me, then I must not have done anything wrong. No, there must still be a plan for me. I simply needed to be patient and wait to see what Heaven had in store.

I nearly toppled to one side as the donkey turned the cart. I straightened myself as best I could, adjusting my headdress, which I was sure was crooked but could do nothing about. I was not supposed to, but I peeked through the silk curtains of the cart as we passed the large southern gate of the Forbidden City. Only men were allowed to enter through the south gate. The only exception was for an empress on her wedding day. But today, Ayan was only a princess. And when she became empress, she would already be married. So, she would never enter the Forbidden City through the south gate. As far as I knew, there was no one alive who remembered the last time an empress was carried through the southern gate, and it would be at least a generation before it happened again. I supposed it would be very wicked of me to wish to see the day when a woman entered through the southern gate because it would mean that the emperor would have died so young that his son was not yet married. And I could never wish such a fate upon an emperor—even Yizhu.

I did not hate Yizhu. I did not wish for bad things to befall him. I feared Yizhu, nothing more. I was grateful that I had not been selected as his consort, and I prayed fervently that he and Lady Ayan would find happiness together.

The west gate of the Forbidden City opened and we were escorted through. The sounds of the crowds died away and were replaced by bird song, rustling trees, and babbling brooks. While much of the Forbidden City was paving stones and brick buildings, the Inner Court was a veritable garden—green, lush, fragrant.

Finally, the donkey cart halted and the silk curtain was pulled back. A hand was held out to help me climb down from the cart. I swung my legs to the side and scooted forward, holding my headdress with my free hand.

"Yixin!" I exclaimed when I saw the prince. I had expected a eunuch or maid to be helping me—not the emperor's second son!

Prince Yixin chuckled at my surprise, or perhaps at my disheveled appearance. He snapped his fingers and a eunuch shuffled to my side to help straighten my gown and headdress.

"Are you not happy to see me, my lady?" Yixin asked.

"No," I said, and his smile faltered. "No!" I quickly said again. "I mean, no, it's not that. I am merely surprised. I did not expect to see you here. I thought you would be at your brother's side."

"I will be soon," he said. "But as Lady Ayan's principal lady-in-waiting, I am to accompany you inside."

He held up his arm to me, and I gingerly placed my hand upon it. My stomach quivered and my heart raced. Was this how a bride usually felt on her wedding day? So full of joy, happiness, and anticipation? Oh, how hoped so! Whoever I was supposed to marry, I could not imagine feeling happier than I did at that moment.

Prince Yixin escorted me to Lady Ayan's sedan chair. Two eunuchs pulled the curtains aside and I gave the princess my hand to help her step out. I could not see her expression as I straightened her veil and gown, but she seemed calmer than before. Perhaps she had used her time being carried to the Forbidden City to still her heart and mind.

When she was once again well-arrayed, two palace maids, women specifically chosen to serve a princess and future empress, stood on each side of her and took one of her hands in each of theirs and led Princess Ayan toward the Hall of Preserved Harmony, where the emperor and empress would be waiting to receive their new daughter-in-law and present her to their son, her new husband.

Prince Yixin offered me his arm again, and we walked behind Princess Ayan. I glanced over my shoulder and saw a long procession behind us of lords and ladies, all selected to serve the prince and his new bride.

When we entered the Hall of Preserved Harmony, Emperor Daoguang and Empress Jing sat on two golden thrones on a raised dais. This was not the throne room, where the emperor's Dragon Throne stood, but an audience hall. The empress was not permitted to sit next to the Dragon Throne. Still, the golden thrones were quite grand, each adorned with dragons and phoenixes.

The maids stepped away as Prince Yizhu approached his bride. He took her hand and kissed the back of it. I wondered if Princess Ayan felt a fluttering at the base of her spine at that. I hoped she did. Prince Yizhu was not smiling, but neither did he look angry. He looked...resigned, as if he had accepted his wife even if she had not been his choice. Few women could ask for more than that, as none of us chose our spouses. They were chosen by our parents—who were far wiser than we were. I wondered, fleetingly, how parents gained such wisdom and insight. Would I have such wisdom when it came time to choose spouses for my children? Was it a wisdom gained with age? Or through the experience of being married myself? I hoped I would find out soon. Perhaps, after Prince Yizhu was happily settled, the marriages of his brothers and other young high-ranking men would be arranged.

The prince and new princess kneeled on velvet pillows before the emperor and empress. They poured cups of tea and then held them aloft, offering blessings and thanks for having their marriage arranged. The emperor then blessed his son and daughter-in-law, wishing them joy, happiness, and fertility.

The prince then stood and helped his bride to rise. He led her to another room, which would serve as the nuptial chamber. There, behind closed doors, the prince would raise his bride's veil and see her for the first time. Well, not really. He had seen her at the selection ceremony. Most men only saw their wives on the day of the wedding, but things were a bit different when it came to choosing the wife of the next emperor.

Once the doors to the nuptial chamber were closed, there seemed to be a collective sigh of relief. The ceremony was over, and life would return to normal for everyone. Well, a new normal, I supposed. I would not return home, but would go to my new quarters here in the Forbidden City. As chief lady-in-waiting, I need to be accessible to the princess at all times. At least I would not have to sleep at the foot of her bed like a loyal dog. That was what maids were for. I wondered how many maids I would have. I was not allowed to bring my own maid with me. I would be assigned a maid from those who had been selected specifically to serve in the Forbidden City.

"What will you do now, my lady?" Prince Yixin asked me. For some reason, I felt my face flush hotly.

"I am to go to my quarters to unpack," I explained. My trunks should have already arrived. "Then I must oversee the preparations in the princess's palace before she arrives in the morning."

"Where will your quarters be?" he asked. "May I escort you?" He held out his arm to me again, and I hesitated to take it. When I took his arm earlier, it was out of duty. I was required to allow him to escort me as part of the wedding ceremony. But now, Prince Yixin was not offering me his arm out of duty, but because he wanted to. As a friend. Not as a prince and lady-in-waiting, but as a man and a woman.

I glanced around the room to see if anyone was watching us. Judging us. To see if anyone would find our actions inappropriate. But no one seemed to be paying us any mind. In fact, for the first time in my life, I saw men and women mixing freely. There were eunuchs present, of course, but also councilors, princes, and more distant imperial relatives, all speaking freely with the empress, high-ranking consorts, ladies-in-waiting, female guests, and maids. It would not be like this all the time, I was sure. Most of the male guests would leave and not return unless there was another grand event such as this. The councilors would only return when they had business with the emperor. But the eunuchs and princes—Yixin and his younger brothers—were sure to be faces I would see regularly.

The eunuchs were of no concern. They were not really men, which was why they were allowed to live and serve within the walls of the Forbidden City. But the princes were another matter. Prince Yixin was old enough to marry and establish his own household, but he would still undoubtedly visit his mother and sisters in the Inner Court often. His younger brothers would likewise be ever-present.

The idea that I would be surrounded by men who were not members of my own family was at once thrilling and unnerving. According to my mother, it was my responsibility to ensure that my reputation was never called into question. On the other hand, I had to show proper respect and deference to my betters—the princes and councilors who now surrounded me.

Prince Yixin chuckled. "What is wrong? I don't bite."

I tried to smile in response but felt my lips quiver. I placed my hand lightly upon his arm.

"So, where to?" the prince asked as we walked toward the door.

"What?" I asked dumbly. My mind was mush.

"Where will your quarters be?" he asked.

"Umm. Oh, the Hall of Elegant Submission. It should be very near Princess Ayan's palace."

"Yes, of course," he said. "I know where it is."

As we exited the audience hall, two eunuchs and three maids fell in line behind us. I realized that they must be the servants assigned to me. We had not yet been introduced, but they clearly knew who I was. I realized that I had no need to worry about my reputation or mixing with men who visited the Inner Court. One was never alone within the walls of the Forbidden City.

"So, what do you think of the new princess?" Prince Yixin asked as we walked.

"She is very sweet," I replied. "Very kind. Very…" My voice trailed off. I could not say anything about the princess that might be construed as an insult. I glanced over my shoulder at the servants trailing behind us. Their eyes were downcast, but their ears were surely pricked to attention.

"Very young," the prince offered.

"Hmm." I collected my thoughts. "She is two years younger than me, younger than I initially thought."

"Do you think she will make a good empress?"

"Hopefully that will not be for many, many years. And she has your mother to guide her, does she not? I am sure Empress Jing will ensure Princess Ayan is ready when the time comes."

"Of course, you are right," Prince Yixin said. "My mother is a thoughtful woman. She surely had her reasons for choosing Ayan. "

I could only nod in agreement. Once again, my mind wondered why she had not chosen me for Yizhu.

I did not have to wait long to find out.

When we arrived, the empress's litter was outside the Hall of Elegant Submission. Since the prince and I had walked, she had arrived ahead of us even though she had still been at the audience hall when we had left. But there were other litters present as well. The prince and I rushed inside to greet the empress and her guests. Imagine my shock when I saw my own parents sitting with her.

"Your Majesty," I said, kneeling before the three of them. "Most honorable Father and Mother."

"Lady Zhenxiu," the empress said, indicating I could rise. I lifted my head but remained on my knees. I clapped my hands and ordered the servants to bring tea and snacks for my guests. A part of me thrilled at calling the empress and my parents guests. But they were! For the first time in my life, I would be living away from home, in my own palace, with my own household. I had to make sure that I was the perfect hostess.

The prince stood, but I remained kneeling until a eunuch brought a low stool for me to sit on.

"To what do I owe such an esteemed visit?" I asked. "Surely, Your Majesty, you have more important things to attend to on such a day."

"An empress's work never stops," the empress replied. "One son is married, but now I have many more to attend to."

"But what a joyful burden to have," my mother said, patting the empress on the arm. "The emperor was surely blessed to have so many sons."

"The dynasty will be secure for another two hundred years, at least!" my father added.

"Yes," the empress said. "Heaven has blessed my husband's

reign."

I sat silently as such pleasantries were exchanged. I dared not ask the empress again why she had come to call. She was the empress. If she wanted nothing more than to sit in my chair and drink my tea, she was entitled to do so. But since my parents were present, her call must have had a specific purpose.

"The new princess is certainly a beauty," my mother said. "I can see why she was chosen. Prince Yizhu must be pleased."

I bit my lower lip to keep from smiling. My mother must have been as anxious as I was to know why the empress had summoned them.

The empress sighed and looked down into her teacup. I motioned for a maid to refill the empress's cup, but the empress waved the girl away and set her cup aside.

"The future of the empire is at stake," she said. "Either Yizhu or Yixin will be the next emperor."

My breath caught in my throat at her words. While what she said was true, I was surprised to hear her openly admit that the emperor had not officially named his heir. So, even though Yizhu was the oldest son and was now married, there was still a chance that Yixin could be named as heir. Yixin could be the next emperor. What would be the deciding factor?

"I had to ensure that both Yizhu and Yixin had the best of women as wives. Either one of them could end up as the next empress."

My heart raced so quickly, I thought I might faint. I wanted to put my hand to my chest and take a calming breath, but I dared not move. I could not risk missing a single word that was said.

"I have decided that Lady Zhenxiu, your daughter, would make a most suitable wife for Yixin."

"Your Majesty!" both my parents exclaimed, scurrying from their chairs to their knees, kowtowing before the empress. Mother dragged me down beside her before I had a chance to do so. Though, I was not sure I could have moved on my own, such was my surprise. I had thought that something was wrong with me. That I had in some way shown myself to be an unsuitable wife for a prince. But that was not the case at all. The empress had chosen me, saved me, for Prince Yixin. And there was still the possibility that I, not princess Ayan, would be the next empress of China!

I was so overwhelmed by the thought, I gave no consideration to my headdress as I put my forehead all the way to the floor in gratitude.

"Your Majesty has granted me an honor I do not deserve," I said. "I am eternally grateful."

The empress chuckled, and I heard Prince Yixin laugh as well. I supposed I looked ridiculous, but it was no laughing matter! My dream had come true. I would be married to Prince Yixin—my friend. The most handsome of the emperor's sons. The kindest and most generous prince. The prince who had protected me from his own brother's advances. He would always keep me safe. He would take care of me. We would be so happy together, have so many children.

"When is the wedding to take place?" I heard my mother ask. I realized she and my father had returned to their seats while I was still doubled over on the floor. I reached my hand out, waving over a maid to help me rise. With my other hand, I held onto my headdress, fearing it would detach from my head and fall to the floor. Indeed, as I sat up, I could feel that it had shifted a bit to one side, so I had to cock my head at an angle to keep it balanced, causing my head to ache.

"I already had the court astrologers calculate the most auspicious date for them to wed. Alas, it is about three months away."

Mother scoffed. "Surely, there is a closer date that would serve just as well."

"How I wish that were the case," the empress said, shaking her head. "So many missed opportunities for Lady Zhenxiu to provide me with a grandson. To secure the family dynasty, as Lord Muyang'a said."

I felt my face flush hot at the idea of falling pregnant. I remembered my earlier conversation with Ayan and how neither of us even knew how to become pregnant. But the empress spoke about it as if it was so very easy. Well, I would have to ask Ayan about it in the morning. She would surely know by then. I did not know why the empress was concerned about me missing a chance to fall pregnant within the next three months. Surely Ayan would be pregnant by then. She would make sure the emperor had his heir.

I shook all thoughts of heirs and pregnancy away. It would all happen in time. For now, I could take joy in the fact that I would be marrying Prince Yixin. I would be happy. I would even allow myself to love him. Surely there was no danger in falling in love with a husband after marriage. Would he love me back? As my parents and the empress spoke of weddings, dowries, and babies and ignored me, I turned my head to the side ever so slightly and looked at Prince Yixin. He was smiling at me so brightly, his teeth were practically glowing.

"Did you know?" I asked, my voice barely more than breath.

He nodded and laughed. I should have been upset at him for keeping such a secret from me all day, but I could not be angry with him. I could never be angry at him.

"We should depart," I finally heard my father say as he, my mother, and the empress stood. I stood as well, but kept my head bowed. "We have many preparations to make."

"We have more than enough time to plan a grand ceremony," Mother said. "Zhenxiu will not serve Lady— I mean, Princess Ayan for long with her own marriage to prepare for."

"Indeed," the empress said. "Lady Zhenxiu will return to your home in two months' time. But after she is married, I am sure she and Ayan will remain close friends, as only sisters-in-law can be."

CHAPTER THREE

I couldn't sleep, I was so excited. I could not wait to tell Ayan that we were to be sisters-in-law. She was sure to be pleased. I would no longer be her chief lady-in-waiting, which would make both of us sad, but I would be allowed to visit her any time I wanted. And, hopefully, our children would be very near in age. They would be cousins and the very dearest of friends. Speaking of children, I was also anxious for Ayan to return so she could tell me about her wedding night. Hopefully, she now knew how a woman fell pregnant and could tell me. I wanted nothing more than to give Prince Yixin a son right away. I hoped Ayan would not be too shy or embarrassed to tell me. I needed any information I could get!

I got out of bed while it was still dark and woke my servants, who helped me wash, dress, and style my hair. Thankfully, I would not have to wear a headdress on a daily basis, only on special occasions. My maid was able to brush and wrap my hair around an ivory bianfang and attach some simple silk flowers. I then walked the short distance to the princess's palace, the Palace of Universal Happiness. It was early, but I was dismayed to see that her servants were still sleeping. I clapped my hands to rouse them and set them to lighting braziers, preparing breakfast, and boiling water. I wanted to ensure the princess was warm and well-fed before we were summoned to see Empress Jing for the morning greeting. At home, we were expected to appear before our parents every morning to greet them and receive blessings. In the Forbidden City, the empress served as the mother of the Inner Court, so all palace ladies would be expected to appear before her.

The sun had not been up very long when I heard shuffling feet. Then, a eunuch announced the arrival of Princess Ayan. I rushed outside and saw that Princess Ayan had been brought from the prince's palace in an open-air litter carried by four men. This was unsurprising, as the smaller litters were more convenient for traveling around the Forbidden City than the cumbersome sedan chairs. No, what surprised me was that Princess Ayan was wearing her wedding veil. She was not required to wear it after her husband removed it. Was it possible that the prince had not removed her veil? Had he perhaps not…done whatever it was married people did to make sons? Surely he had. But then, why was she veiled?

The litter bearers set the princess down and one of her eunuchs rushed over and held out his hand to assist her. Princess Ayan did not move. She merely sat there, her head facing straight ahead. The eunuch looked to me for guidance. I nodded at him.

"My lady," he said softly, moving his hand closer to her. Still, she did not budge. I approached the litter, motioning the eunuch aside. I noticed that Princess Ayan held a silk handkerchief in her hands, which she was wringing tightly. Other than that, she was not moving at all.

"Princess," I said softly, but again, she did not acknowledge me. I was becoming annoyed. I knew she could not see me with her veil, but she could surely hear me. Why was she ignoring me?

"Princess!" I called out more loudly and firmly. The princess startled, as if she had only just noticed I was there. I held my hand out. "Princess, please come down. You have arrived at your new home." The princess turned her head toward me and hesitated, but finally, she stood and took my hand as I helped her out of the litter. Once she was on solid ground, I attempted to shift her hand to that of a maid, but she was gripping me far too tightly. She dared not let me go as we walked through her palace gate, through her private courtyard garden, and into her new home.

"Now, why don't we remove your veil and have breakfast," I suggested, reaching for the large, heavy piece of fabric covering her face.

"No!" she said, flinching back from me.

At this point, I half-scoffed and half-laughed at how ridiculous she was acting. "Come now, Princess. Surely you want to eat and bathe."

"Yes," she said. "Bathe, please. Send the servants away." This was even more odd, as it was the servants who would usually scrub her body clean and wash her hair. But then I remembered how she'd appeared to have grown up much more poor than I had, so perhaps she was not used to being bathed by servants. Perhaps she was used to washing herself privately.

"Fine," I said, growing exasperated. I took her hand and led her to her bedchamber, where the large copper tub had been set up. The room had warmed nicely since I'd had the braziers lit, and the servants were filling the tub with warm water from the princess's private kitchen.

"Leave us," I ordered the maids. They curtseyed and did as they were told, closing the doors behind them.

"Now, will you remove your veil?" I asked. "I'd like to get this over with. I'm starving!"

Ayan burst into tears, and I was struck dumb. I had no idea what to do or say. Why was she crying? She should be so happy.

"Princess...what is wrong?" I dared to ask.

"Oh... Zhen..." She kicked off her pot-bottom shoes so she could run to her bed unassisted, where she collapsed and continued to sob. I followed and sat on the bed near her, unsure what to say.

"Wha— Why—" my words died before a sentence could form. Finally, I decided on, "Will you at least let me take off your veil?"

She stopped crying. "Only—only promise me you won't be shocked. You won't say anything."

"What are you babbling about?" I asked, growing annoyed and reaching for her.

She shrank back and gripped her veil tightly. "Promise me!" she yelled.

"Yes, yes! I promise," I said, willing to say anything to stop her from acting so strangely. She nodded and lowered her hand. I snatched away her veil before she could change her mind.

Despite my promise, I could not help but gasp when I saw her face. Her eyes and nose were red from crying and a lack of sleep, but that was to be expected. No, what shocked me was the purple bruise on her cheek and the crack in her lip.

"What— What—" I was once again rendered speechless. Ayan pulled up the sleeves of her red wedding gown and showed me more bruises on her wrists, handprints from being held down.

"I'm sure there are more," she said softly, "only I...I cannot see—"

"He...he beat you?" I asked stupidly. It had to have been the prince, as no one else would dare lay a hand on her. And while it was a man's right to punish his wife and children as he saw fit —even I had been slapped by my father on occasion—it was shocking that Yizhu would strike his wife so hard as to leave a mark. And on their wedding night! Should they not have been enjoying one another? Getting to know each other? Trying to make a son?

"What...what happened?" I asked.

"It was my fault. I know it was," she said, pulling her sleeves down and letting out a long sigh. "I was so stupid. I didn't know what to do. What he wanted—"

"Of course you didn't," I said. "But he should have told you—"

"He did," she explained. "But then, I got so frightened. I pulled away, tried to run away. So, he grabbed me and had to hold me down as I fought back."

My mouth went dry and my heart began to race as I remembered Yizhu holding me down in the garden, pinning me down as he tried to kiss me. Was that what he had done to Ayan? Was that what he had tried to do to me? Was that what husbands did to wives to make children, hold them down?

"He...he...pulled up my gown and stabbed me between my legs. I didn't know with what. I was too scared to look. It hurt so much. I thought he was killing me. But he...he enjoyed it. His eyes rolled back and he let out a long sigh before he rolled off of me. I was terrified. I wanted to run away, but I could hear everyone outside, laughing and talking. I was so embarrassed. I knew I must have done something wrong to anger him so. I decided to simply leave him alone, to try and sleep.

"But later in the night, he came for me again. This time, though, he was naked. And he— You have younger brothers, right? You know the member between their legs?"

I nodded, my mouth too dry to speak.

"Well, his was huge and hard, like a fleshy dagger. That was what he used to stab between my legs."

I shook my head in horrified shock. So that was how a man got a child into a woman. Of course. It made sense now, but I had never thought of it before. And, of course, I had no idea it was painful. Though, now I understood why the women always looked so dejected when told my father had selected them for the night.

"After the second time," Ayan continued, "I felt...wet down there. I went to use the chamber pot. When I cleaned myself, I was...bleeding. I-I think he hurt me, but I-I cannot see..." Her eyes began to well up into tears again.

"No, no," I said, wrapping my arms around her shoulders. "Maybe it is just your monthly visitor." Of course, I had no way of knowing. Maybe he really had hurt her. But I had to hope that what he had done to her was perfectly natural. That he had not meant to hurt her. That he was trying to do his duty and get a son with her.

"My what?" Ayan asked, wiping tears and snot on her sleeve.

"You know," I said, "your monthly bleed."

"My what?" she screeched, pulling away from me in horror.

I looked at her for a moment, confused. "You— Don't you bleed every month? You know...from down there?"

"No! Do you?"

My mouth gaped at her. Of course, the first time I had my monthly visitor, I had not expected it. I did not know what was happening. I thought I was dying. But I told my maid, who, instead of fetching a doctor, fetched my mother. Mother then explained that I was no longer a girl, but a woman. My body was ready to carry and bear children. Surely Ayan, if she had been put forward for marriage, was ready to have children. But then I remembered that she was two years younger than me.

"You've never bled before?" I asked her, just to be sure. "You are certain?"

"No, never," she said. "Not before last night. Why? What is happening?"

At that moment, it all became clear to me. I now understood why Empress Jing had chosen Ayan as a wife for Yizhu and me for Yixin. She was trying to put Yixin—her natural-born son—on the throne.

Did the emperor know this? Perhaps he also wanted Yixin to inherit the throne, but he could not pass over his eldest son without reason. If Yixin were to have a child first, a son, an heir of his own, then the emperor could name Yixin as his heir without any guilt. Yixin would be the logical choice to ensure the continuation of the dynasty. That was why the empress was disappointed that my marriage to Yixin was three months away. She wanted me to get with child before Ayan. Ayan might not have had her monthly visitor yet, but she could at any time.

So, there wasn't anything wrong with me. I had to hide a smile as I began to realize that Empress Jing had not passed me over in favor of Ayan. She had saved me for her own son. She had, in fact, chosen me to succeed her as empress.

"What is it?" Ayan asked me, shaking my hand to get my attention.

I had no idea how much bliss was showing on my face, but I did my best to shake it away. I would reflect on my own good fortune later.

"It is nothing," I said. "Let's get you cleaned up. You must be starving. We need to prepare you to see the empress."

"Oh, I couldn't possibly see her now," Ayan whined, on the verge of tears again. "I can't see anyone. And what is a monthly visitor?" I tried not to roll my eyes in annoyance at this princess I now knew to be no more than a child.

"I will explain everything to you. I promise."

CHAPTER FOUR

"Oh, Zhen!" my cousin, Feiya, exclaimed as I held up an exquisite pair of shoes my mother had purchased as part of my dowry. "They are magnificent! Look at the stitching. I think I can almost smell the flowers."

I sighed as I angled the shoes in the light so that the pearls dangling around the edges shimmered. "When Mother showed them to me, I thought I would faint. Have you ever owned a pair so fine?"

"Where did she get them?" Feiya reached out to touch a fringed tassel hanging on the front, but I slapped her hand away. "They must have cost a fortune."

"I'm not sure. Mother said she purchased them from a Manchu girl whose family had fallen on hard times."

Feiya raised an eyebrow and shrugged, turning away and flopping onto my bed. "I can't believe your mother would be so cheap. You are marrying a prince!"

The way her words pained me was a surprise, but I kept my mouth shut and looked away. I ran the tassel through my fingers, though the color seemed a little less vibrant now. I sighed, put the shoes back in their box, and stacked them with the others.

I had at least a dozen pairs of new shoes, in addition to two dozen embroidered gowns, a stack of furs, several boxes of hairpins, and countless embroidered kerchiefs, all folded and packed away for my dowry. In a few weeks, all of it would be bundled together into palanquins and carried to Heshen Mansion, the home that the emperor had gifted to Yixin. As a married man, he would no longer live in the palace, but have his own estate. And as his first wife, I would be the head of my own household, my own family. The knowledge was both calming and thrilling. I would not have to live in the palace, sequestered away from the world, nor would I have to live with my mother-in-law, Empress Jing, since she would have to remain in the Forbidden City with the emperor.

I ignored Feiya, who lounged on my bed, picking through a box of ribbons she'd bought on the way to my house that day. She was merely jealous. She'd never marry a prince.

I sat at my dressing table and ran a brush through my long hair, watching Feiya in the reflection of the mirror. "I'll make a good marriage for you," I told her.

Feiya looked at me, her eyes wide. She sat up and put her box aside. "Did my mother speak to you?"

"No," I said. "But it is one of the perks of being a princess, isn't it? Being able to make good marriages for all your friends and family?"

Feiya walked behind me and ran her fingers through my hair. She divided my hair into sections and began twisting each one as she pinned them up into an elaborate style.

"It won't be the same, will it?" Feiya asked, not looking at me.

"No," I said, looking at her in the mirror, and then I smiled. "It will be better! You can come over whenever you want! We can have parties and opera performances. And when we have children, they can play together and we can dress them in the prettiest clothes."

Feiya pressed her lips together. "Are you sure? Are you sure we will still see each other?"

"Of course!" I said, turning around and taking both of her hands in mine. "Why do you think I was so pleased when I wasn't chosen to be the wife of Yizhu?"

"Pleased? I thought you were devastated. You could have been empress!"

"I had to pretend I was upset at not being chosen," I explained, "for Mother's sake. She was so disappointed I thought she would take to her bed and never rise again. But you don't know the princes like I do, Feiya. I never wanted to be Yizhu's wife. I wanted to kill myself when I was told I had to appear for Yizhu's consort selection."

"You are ridiculous," Feiya said, pulling her hands away from me and stomping her foot. "Most girls would die just for a *chance* at being selected. But you turn up your nose at it? How can you be so selfish?"

I gasped. "How can you be so mean?"

"You are so lucky! You are marrying a prince. You could have married the heir to the Dragon Throne! But you act as though you are being tortured! You've been to the Forbidden City before. You've met both princes before having to marry one of them."

I snorted. "I wish I'd never met Yizhu."

"See!" Feiya exclaimed. "How could you despise the chance to be empress?"

"Because I wouldn't have my own life," I said. "My own home. My own children. I wouldn't be able to come and go as I please. My children would be taken from me, raised by nannies and tutors in their own palaces. My husband..." I shook my head. "I would be one of a hundred women. I might never even see my husband. Do you know how many consorts and concubines die without ever spending a night with the emperor?"

"But you could have been empress!" Feiya said. "The law dictates that the emperor must spend at least one night a month with you."

"Is that what you want?" I asked. "A husband who only visits you because the law commands it?"

Feiya scoffed and crossed her arms. She returned to my bed and grabbed the ribbon box, tossing it at me, but it only fluttered to the ground, the ribbons scattering. "Prince Yixin didn't choose you either. He was ordered to marry you. What makes you think he will spend time with you? He isn't under any legal obligation to make a child with you. He might run out and get another concubine as soon as possible."

"Why are you saying these things?" I asked. "Why are you being so cruel? Prince Yixin is so handsome. And tall, and smart. Did you know he speaks English?"

"Why would I care about that?" Feiya asked. "The foreigners are pigs, tearing our country apart piece by piece. They should all be expelled."

"Yixin believes that diplomacy is a better path—"

"I am to be married!" Feiya yelled.

"What?" I asked, my mouth agape. "To whom?"

"His name is Chongqi," Feiya said, using her long sleeve to dab at her wet eyes. "He's the son of the Blue Banner chieftain."

"I know who Chongqi is," I said. It was part of my education to know about all of the important Manchu and Mongolian families. "It's quite an honor—"

"To be sent away from Peking?" Feiya asked. "To never see you again? I'll be living hundreds of li to the north." She shivered at the thought.

I forced a smile so I wouldn't cry. "Of course we will see each other again. Chongqi is an important man. I am sure he will come to Peking often. You will have to come with him when he does."

"You know it doesn't work that way," Feiya said, shaking her head. "I suppose we always knew it would come to this. Each of us married and sent away. If you had been the empress, you could have ordered Chongqi to bring me with him. Or ordered me to visit you. Who could deny an order from the empress?"

I nodded, beginning to understand why she was so upset. "But who would obey the order of a mere princess?"

"Exactly," Feiya said. "Oh, Zhen, how I will miss you."

I wanted to tell her not to worry, that we would see each other again. That we would still visit and raise our children together, but it would have been a lie. She was right—I would probably never see my dear cousin again. I opened my arms to her and held her tight.

"I will write to you daily, I promise," I said.

Feiya nodded her head but seemed unable to speak.

There was a knock at the door and my maid entered the room with her head down. "Your mother is asking for you, mistress. She says that Lady Feiya is to leave."

I couldn't help but chuckle at my mother's timing. She must have known how undignified I was acting even from several rooms away and had to put an end to it.

"Of course," I said. Feiya released me and wiped her cheeks with her sleeve.

"I should go anyway," she said. "A seamstress is coming to take my measurements for my wedding gown this afternoon."

"When is the wedding to take place?" I asked.

"The astrologers are still determining the best day, but it will be before the next full moon."

Less than two weeks away. I took a breath and pressed my lips together to keep from crying again. "I will see you again before then, I am sure."

Feiya nodded and then quickly shuffled from the room. I

turned away from the maid as I let a few of my own tears escape. Feiya and I were the same age, seventeen, and our fathers were cousins. We had all lived in the same house together when we were little. But as our families grew—both in size and prosperity—eventually, Feiya's family left to form their own household. Still, she lived only a short palanquin ride away, so we saw each other often. The idea of her being hundreds of li away broke my heart. I wanted to believe we would still see one another occasionally, but I knew I was fooling myself.

Once I collected myself, I turned and faced the maid. "Where is Mother?"

"In your father's office, my lady."

"What?" I asked. It was a rare occasion that I was summoned to see my father. "Am I to wait?"

"No, my lady," the maid said. "You are to see them both, now."

I looked in my mirror, glad that Feiya had pinned up my hair, and straightened my gown before rushing out of the room. I could hear the shuffling of the maid's feet as she tried to keep up with me. It seemed like a terribly long wait for Father to give me permission to enter his office after I knocked.

"Father," I said, kneeling as I entered the room.

"Come," my father, Lord Muyang'a, said, beckoning me toward him. I stood and then kneeled again when I reached him. I noticed that my mother was standing by his side.

"Stand up," Father said. "An empress does not bow to anyone."

I looked up at him but retained my kneeling position on the floor. "What?"

Father laughed and looked at my mother, who I noticed was beaming. "So humble. Perhaps you raised her too well, my love."

"I always knew she was meant for great things, my lord," Mother replied.

"Come, come," Father said, reaching for my hands and pulling me to standing. My legs were so weak, I thought I would crumble back to the ground. "From now on, you must only kneel to the prince, the emperor, and Empress Jing.

"Wha-what?" I asked again.

"The princess consort is dead," Mother said. "She died yesterday."

"The princess..." I could hardly breathe. "Lady Ayan? She is dead? How? Why?"

"We don't know the details," Father said. "All we know is that she is dead, so the prince requires a new consort. You, my dear."

"Me...?" My head was spinning. Ayan was dead? How? I remembered her sweet, innocent face smiling at me, wishing me luck as we stood together during the selection process. I had left her only days ago. How could she be dead? Tears came to my eyes and I thought I would faint. I felt someone tug on my arm and was led to a chair.

"What is wrong with you?" Mother asked, her face hovering in front of mine. "Do you understand what is happening? What this means?"

"No," I said. "Not at all. What happened to Ayan?"

"She's dead," Mother said again without an ounce of sympathy. "You were Empress Jing's second choice then, so you are her first choice for a replacement now."

I shook my head. "No, no, that can't be right. Empress Jing didn't want me for Yizhu."

"I think she was only being hard on you, testing you," Father said. He poured a cup of water and handed it to me. The searing hot porcelain on my fingertips seemed to awaken me from my stupor.

"No," I said, standing and setting the cup on a nearby table. "Yizhu wanted me, but the empress wanted me for Yixin. Yixin will be emperor."

"Hold your tongue," Father hissed at me, his voice low. His eyes scanned the room, making sure there were no servants present, but there were surely some hovering at the doors and windows, just waiting for any bit of information they could trade or sell. "To say such a thing could be considered treason."

I gritted my teeth and grunted in frustration. Yes, any reference to the emperor dying could be considered treason. But the emperor would die eventually, and the imperial family had to prepare for that. It was the whole reason Emperor Daoguang's sons were marrying in the first place—so they, in turn, would have sons of their own and ensure the continuation of the dynasty. And Empress Jing wanted Yixin to be the next emperor. That was why she had chosen me as his wife. She would not want me to replace Ayan. She would not want Yizhu to have a child before Yixin, securing his own place in the line of succession.

"You must speak to the empress about this," I said. "She chose me for Yixin. We are engaged. To break such an engagement would be an insult to the imperial family."

"She was consulted on the matter," Father said. "But the order comes from the emperor himself. He wants the matter settled immediately."

"Go and change," Mother said, trying to wave me off. "Pack only your most necessary items. The rest of your dowery will be sent over later."

"Wait," I said. "What do you mean? I am to go…now?"

"First thing in the morning," Mother said as she smiled.

"No!" I said, stepping back.

"No?" Father asked, narrowing his gaze at me.

"I mean, I'm already promised to Yixin. I can't marry Yizhu."

"It's all arranged," Father said. "Don't worry. Yixin will have someone else. Lady Ningxin, of the Gūwalgiya clan, I believe."

"He…he's already betrothed to someone else?" I asked, and there was a pain in my chest.

"In situations such as this, things happen very quickly," Father said.

My head was spinning again. No. Everything was wrong. I thought I had escaped life in the Forbidden City. Life in a cage. Life with Yizhu.

"But...I don't want to marry Yizhu," I dared to say.

Father stomped toward me so quickly, I was already flinching before his hand slapped my face.

"Don't!" Mother yelled, reaching for him. "We can't present her to the court with her face marred!"

I saw a flash of remorse cross Father's face before his eyes hardened again. I knew that he did not regret hitting me, only that the evidence of his anger might show on my delicate skin. I bruised easily. He shook a finger in my face.

"Never say such a thing again," he warned. "Do you know what this means for you, for all of us?"

I nodded. "Of course, Father," I tried to say without crying, but I was failing. "I'm sorry. I was in shock. I...I never imagined that Prince Yizhu would want me," I lied.

"Well, it's not up to him, not any more than it is up to you," Father said, straightening his robe. "It's all been arranged. Now, do as your mother said and go pack."

I nodded and left the room, walking down the hall in a daze. How could this have happened? How could someone so young, the future empress, die? And how could I have been taken from Yixin and given to his brother? Did Yixin know? What would he say? Had he protested?

"Is it true?"

I started when I saw Feiya in my room, waiting for me. "What are you doing here?" I asked. She held up her ribbon box.

"I left it on the floor. When I came back, all the servants were talking about it. Are you really going to marry Yizhu, the emperor's eldest son?"

I could hold it in no longer and the tears escaped my eyes.

Feiya ran to me. I held onto her to keep from falling to the ground.

"But don't you see?" Feiya asked. "This is wonderful! You will be empress! And you can order me to court. Everything will work out for the best."

I nodded. I didn't want to hurt Feiya's feelings. I knew she was terrified about being sent north and needed to believe she could return to Peking often. I couldn't tell her—tell anyone— just how afraid *I* was. Of Empress Jing. Of Emperor Daoguang. Of life in the Forbidden City.

Of Yizhu.

Of losing Yixin.

Mother had always warned me against falling in love.

Now I knew why.

CHAPTER FIVE

$\mathcal{M}$y maids and cousin helped me pack quickly. The sedan chair bearers would arrive at any moment to take me to the Forbidden City. I was to go immediately to the home of my new husband, Prince Yizhu. The very idea made me want to vomit. As I tried to pack, my hands shook so violently, I kept dropping my clothes. My head began to throb in pain, so I had to sit on my bed and wait for it to pass.

"Sit, mistress," one of the maids said. "We will take care of everything."

I supposed I would as only be in her way. Feiya came and sat next to me. She took my cold, trembling hand in her warm, calm ones.

"I thought I was comforting you," I told her, attempting a smile.

"We are here for each other," she said. "This doesn't change anything between us."

"It might change everything," I said. "If Yizhu becomes the next emperor, I'll never leave the Forbidden City again, except to go to the Summer Palace on occasion. I'd never be allowed to travel north to see you."

"I can still come to Peking with my husband," she said. "I'll come to see you. And we can still write to each other often. Daily."

While I could read and write, I knew Feiya could not. Most girls were not taught such things as they would have no use for them. But my father knew I would marry well, most likely into the imperial family, and that I would have to run a grand household, so he made sure I was taught at least the basics of reading, writing, and mathematics. Feiya would have to find a male servant to read my letters to her, and she would have to dictate her letters to me. It would be difficult to speak to her openly about my life, knowing that male servants would also read my words. And anything I said could be reported back to my husband, or even the emperor himself. I would have to be careful about the things I wrote. But I did not want to trouble Feiya further.

"I look forward to hearing what life is like for you way up there," I said. "Who would have thought you'd end up in Mongolia."

"And I look forward to hearing from you!" she exclaimed. "Oh, Zhen. By morning, you will be a princess! You will be living in the grandest palace in the world! You are almost certain to be the next empress. Oh, I know that Yizhu is not Yixin, but in many ways, is this match not better? The emperor has not named his heir, but isn't it likely to be Yizhu? Next to Empress Jing, you'll be the highest-ranking woman in China! Anything you want, you need only ask."

I could understand her excitement for me. She didn't know what life in the Forbidden City was really like. I had spent the last two months as principal lady-in-waiting to Princess Ayan. I knew what every aspect of her life was like. I knew what she endured, going to Prince Yizhu's bed every night.

I suspected someone, probably the empress, had warned him against striking his wife, for he never hit Ayan again. At least, he never struck her hard enough to leave a mark. More than a few times, she had returned with an angry red welt on her face, so I knew that Yizhu had at least slapped her. Why he did so, I wasn't sure. Ayan did not like to speak about whatever happened between herself and Yizhu. I knew their marital intercourse was still painful for her, even weeks after their marriage. Would it be the same way for me? I trembled at the thought. Every time Ayan returned from an evening with Prince Yizhu, she would ask for a hot bath and soak for an hour or more. Then, she would climb into bed, under a mountain of blankets, even though it had been summer, and lay there silently until morning. I did not know if she slept. Anytime I looked in on her, her eyes were wide open. But I did not stay with her all night, as I had my own small palace to retreat to. I was able to sleep soundly, knowing that in only a few weeks, I would be marrying Prince Yixin.

But now everything had changed. I wondered if Prince Yixin had been told that his bride-to-be had been given to his brother. Would he be as disappointed as I was? Was he, perhaps, trying to stop this from happening? Was he fighting for me? For us? Or did he not even know? Would he not be told until after it was too late? After his brother had taken me? Oh, how I wished I could speak to Yixin, tell him what was happening. But it was impossible. I could never get a message to Yixin without my parents' knowledge. Unless... I looked at Feiya.

"Cousin, could you do something for me?"

"Of course. Anything."

"Could you deliver a message to Prince Yixin at his palace? It is not far from here."

She shrank back, her face falling. "Oh, I don't know. I'm not supposed to go anywhere but here and then back home again. You know that."

"It would only take a moment," I pushed.

"The rickshaw puller will surely tell my parents," she protested.

"You would have nothing to hide," I said. "You can even tell your parents yourself. You did it for me. They can be angry at me if they wish. But I daresay I'll be at the Forbidden City by the time they find out. They could not be upset at you for running an errand for a princess, could they?"

"Well, I suppose not," she said slowly after a long moment of thought. "But why would you write to the prince? What will you say? What can he do about it?"

"Probably nothing," I admitted as I got up and walked to my dressing table. I pulled out paper, ink, and a brush. I didn't have a writing desk of my own. Father saw no need to go that far. But my dressing table worked well enough for writing the very few correspondences I sent. And really, I did not know what I was going to write. After all, this had been decided by the emperor and empress. Even my parents had no say in the decision. Still, after I was married to Yizhu and sequestered within the Inner Court, I would rarely have reason or opportunity to speak to Yixin again, and never privately. I felt that I had to let him know I did not want this. But I could never be so blunt. If my letter fell into the wrong hands, I would surely be punished for expressing unhappiness with the emperor's decision.

Prince Yixin,
I wish to convey my sincere condolences for the death of
Princess Ayan. She was a dear friend to me, and her death is a
shock and heartbreak I am not sure I will ever recover from.
That I have been selected to replace the princess as Prince
Yizhu's consort is an outcome I never could have expected. I
loved the princess and wanted nothing more than be her dear
and devoted sister-in-law. My grief at her loss is a burden I
fear I will never recover from.

My brush paused in my hand. What else could I say? I could not say that I did not want to marry Yizhu. I could not plainly ask Yixin to intercede on my behalf and ask the emperor to stop the marriage. No, marrying any imperial prince was an honor and a privilege. To speak against such a union would be a grave insult to the emperor and bring dishonor to my parents. I carried no illusions that my letter would be kept secret. It would surely be revealed that I had written a letter to my former betrothed and future brother-in-law after the death of the princess. I had to be very careful about what I said.

I shook my head and blew on the ink to dry it before rolling it up and tying it with a red ribbon. It would have to be enough. Innocent enough to carry condolences, but plain enough to Yixin that I was unhappy about what was to happen next.

I handed the letter to Feiya, and she tucked it into a pocket within a sleeve of her gown.

"Oh, Zhen, how I will miss you," she said, wrapping her arms around me.

"I know," I said, hugging her back. "I will miss you too. As soon as we are both settled, I will try to arrange for us to see each other again."

Feiya had her servant call her rickshaw driver to the front of our house. I saw her speak to her driver for a moment before she climbed in the back, and he nodded his head. My heart was racing, but I told myself I had no reason to worry. Either the prince would be unable to do anything and I would become an imperial princess, or he would be able to intercede and claim me as his own wife. The second option at least gave me some hope.

"Zhen!" Mother yelled when she saw me standing by the door. "What are you doing? You need to leave as soon as possible."

"I was only saying goodbye to Feiya."

Mother nodded. "I suppose she told you about her own betrothal."

"She did," I said, and then I dared to speak further. "I had thought that as the wife of Yixin, she and I would still have plenty of opportunities to see each other. But as the wife of Yizhu..." I let the sentence die away. She would know what I was hinting at without me having to say the words out loud.

"It wouldn't matter," she said, putting her arm around me and leading me back to my room. "The next emperor will be whoever you married, I'm sure of it."

"I cannot have such influence," I said. "I am just a woman."

"Women give birth to sons," Mother said. "If you had given Yixin a son, he would be the next emperor. But now that you are to marry Yizhu, you will bear him a son, and he will be emperor."

I shook my head. That may have been true at one time. But Yixin's new wife had already been chosen, Lady Ningxin. She was near in age to me. She would be just as likely to give Yixin a son as I was for Yizhu. Empress Jing's plan had fallen apart.

"Won't the emperor choose the son he thinks will make the best emperor to follow him? I understand what you say. I know how important it is for the emperor to ensure his family line, but the person who will be a good emperor, a strong emperor, should be the most important aspect when it comes to naming an heir, don't you think?"

"When you have children of your own, you will understand," she said. "Let us pray that everything works out as we hope and you do not end up having to compete with another woman who just happens to be more fertile than you."

I was confused by her words. How could I end up competing with another woman? But then I remembered that she was not my birth mother. I saw my birth mother so rarely, I sometimes forgot about her. But did Mother compete with her? I didn't think so. Mother was the woman at Father's side. She ran the household and made the decisions. My birth mother was summoned to Father's room at night more often, but I thought Mother preferred it that way. Indeed, I would look forward to the day when Yizhu took more wives. But what if I married Yixin? The thought of him having more wives filled me with dread.

And I considered Empress Jing. She was Daoguang's third empress. His first two empresses died without having any sons. Yizhu's mother was a concubine. Empress Jing was the mother to Yixin. I thought about how Empress Jing clearly wanted Yixin on the throne even though he was the younger son. Was it because she truly believed he would be the better emperor? Or was it because he was her flesh and blood son? I shuddered at the thought. If I ever imagined that Mother loved me less because she had not given birth to me, I would be devastated. But then again, I had to wonder. Mother had other daughters, daughters she had given birth to, but they were much younger than me. If they had been nearer in age to me, old enough to marry, would Mother have pushed me aside in favor of her own children?

I hoped not. I vowed that any children born to my husband by any wife, I would love as my own.

CHAPTER SIX

*C*hapter 6

"Do not cry," Mother ordered as we stood inside our front gate, waiting for the imperial sedan chair that would carry me to the Forbidden City and my new husband. I raised my eyes and looked to the sky, at the stars above, to Heaven, to keep the tears forming in my eyes from falling down my cheeks.

"You do not want your eyes and nose to turn red," Mother went on as she fussed with my gown. Well, *her* gown. The red gown that we had ordered for my marriage to Prince Yixin had not been completed yet. The only red gown available to me without notice was Mother's. I wondered if wearing another woman's clothes on my wedding day was bad luck. I had never seen it done before. First wives always wore a new red gown. Second wives and concubines sometimes wore red, if they could afford it. They often simply wore the nicest gown they had available to them. The fact that I was not given time to have a gown made told me how I was going to be viewed by my new family—as a second wife. Of course, I would not have to bow to or serve a first wife since she was...dead.

I could hardly force myself to think it, much less say it. How could my beautiful, dear, young Princess Ayan be dead?

I would be Yizhu's first wife in practice. I would be the mother to his children and run his household. But when it came to titles and honors, I would always be second to Princess Ayan. If Yizhu did become emperor, would I be his empress? Empress Jing was Emperor Daoguang's noble consort, the highest she could rise since there were two deceased empresses before her. Would I also be relegated to the position of consort?

Father stepped through the gate and motioned me forward. "They are here," he said.

I gripped Mother's hand tightly. She looked at me and gave me a sad smile. She held up the red veil that she had worn on her own wedding day, a covering I was not required to wear but she insisted upon. I might not be Yizhu's first wife, but my parents would pretend I was. They would not suffer the indignity of their eldest daughter being treated as little more than a concubine. I bent my head forward so that she could place the veil over my head. She then took my hand and led me to the gate.

Outside, the street was silent. I had expected to hear musicians, horses, and the stomping of many feet. I was a second wife, but I was still marrying a prince. And I was his only wife. I should have been accorded some respect.

But then I heard the most hideous sound—the braying of a donkey. I could not stop myself. I lifted my veil and was horrified to see, not a sedan chair carried by half a dozen men, but a donkey cart led by a single servant. The servant cleared his throat and spat as he pulled back the flap of the cart and lifted out a small trunk, which he placed by my father's feet.

"The emperor thanks you, my lord, for the gift of your daughter for his son, Prince Yizhu." The man gave Father the fist-in-palm salute and walked back to the cart, holding the flap open for me to climb inside.

My whole family was speechless. This small box of gold was the only gift the emperor sent in exchange for me? Me? The daughter of a duke? One of the finest young ladies in Peking? The girl who should be empress? No silks. No jewels. No furs. I felt sick. Such a small amount of gold made me feel cheap. Worthless.

"Baba," I finally managed to croak out. When he looked at me, I could see he felt the same way. He was a close, personal friend of Emperor Daoguang, but he had been greatly insulted. Yet, what could he do about it? He could not refuse the emperor.

Father cleared his throat and bowed to me. "I give my daughter to Prince Yizhu, freely and with my thanks."

I bowed in return, but I could not speak. Father then pulled the veil back down over my face and I knew I had no choice but to be taken to my new husband in the back of a stinking, rickety donkey cart.

Mother did her best to help me inside. I sat cross-legged on the single cushion. When I tried to sit up straight, I heard a small tearing sound and realized that my sleeve had snagged on a splintered board. I fidgeted with the loose string, but once the cart driver dropped the curtain, I was in complete darkness. I was thankful that the ride to the palace was not very long. Hopefully, I would arrive in one piece and my bones not shaken apart.

How could this have happened to me? One minute, I was the happiest woman alive. I was going to be a princess, married to the man that, if I had been given a choice, I would have chosen for myself. I was going to be a first wife and, hopefully soon, a mother. I would help make my husband the next emperor, and I would be his empress. We would have been so happy together. But now, what even was I? What would be my rank? My title? Even if I gave Yizhu a son, would my child come before or after a son born to Yixin by Ningxin?

Nothing made sense to me.

And how would I even give Yizhu a son? He would be required to follow the protocols for mourning his first wife. He would have to mourn her for ninety days. He would have to abstain from alcohol and…marital relations. Why was I even being rushed to the palace anyway? If Yizhu and I could not behave as a married couple, what was the point of our marriage? The emperor could have waited to send for me. Or allowed me to marry Yixin and selected another woman for Yizhu.

My brain was muddled with confusion. I could not even think about going to Yizhu's bed. Marital relations between Yizhu and Ayan had not improved in the months since their wedding night. Even if the prince no longer beat her, she dreaded going to his bed. She complained about how much it pained her, both during and after the act. Never having been with a man myself, I was at a loss for how to help her. I had suggested she speak to Empress Jing, but I had no idea what the empress told her, if anything. Things seemed to have improved after that. At least, Ayan complained less. I would have to speak to the empress as soon as possible and ask her for the same advice that she had given Ayan.

Finally, the donkey cart came to a stop. I was pitched forward but managed to catch myself. The flap was pulled open and I stepped out. A maid took my hand to assist me. Her hand felt familiar, so I knew it was the same maid who served me when I was merely a lady-in-waiting.

"Can you tell me what happened to Princess Ayan?" I whispered to her.

"You do not know, my lady?" She sounded surprised.

"No," I said. "No one has told me anything. I only know that she was healthy when I left her. Could she have succumbed to a fever so quickly?"

"No, my lady. I do not believe it was a fever."

"Was she injured? Did she fall and strike her head?"

"I don't believe so, my lady."

We walked in silence for a moment. "Do you mean to make me guess every malady I can think of before you tell me what happened?"

"Forgive me, my lady," the maid said, and I could feel her hand trembling. "But I cannot speak of such things."

"Such things?" I asked, my mouth gaping even if she could not see it. "Was her death so horrible you cannot even speak of it?"

"Quite so, my lady."

"Well, now you must tell me," I said. "I fear my mind shall run wild with imagined terrors." Was she murdered? Did Yizhu kill her? My stomach felt ill at such thoughts.

"Please, my lady," the maid said when we stopped walking. "I beg you to think on this not at all. Do not trouble yourself with such morbid thoughts."

Now, my heart was racing in my chest. Could whatever calamity had befallen Princess Ayan happen to me as well?

"Was...was she murdered?" I had to ask this one last thing. I would never be able to sleep peacefully in my new home if I thought for one moment that a killer was running around the Forbidden City—in the Inner Court, no less!

I must have caused the maid some amusement, as I heard her stifling a chuckle as she said, "No, my lady. I do not believe she was murdered."

"Well, I suppose I shall take at least a little comfort in that."

"Indeed, my lady. Trouble your heart and mind over this no longer. It will only disturb your peace."

"Wise words. I will consider them." The maid then led me to a bed and helped me sit comfortably. "Oh, am I not to see the emperor and empress first?" I asked.

"No," the maid said. "This is the emperor's bedchamber."

I wanted to jump up, but my pot-bottom shoes prevented it,

and I nearly toppled forward instead. Thankfully, the maid had not moved far off and was able to help me sit upright again.

"No," I said, or perhaps whined. "No, why? The prince must surely mourn the death of his wife first. He must abstain from such activities for ninety days."

"I was told the prince would not be observing the traditional mourning period due to the great injustice the princess inflicted upon him."

"What?" Now my head was truly spinning. "What injustice? How can the prince not honor his late wife?" The maid was pulling away from me, trying to leave me here alone. But I would not let her. I gripped her hand and arm and held on with all my strength.

"Please, my lady."

"No! Tell me what is going on!"

The door slammed open and heavy footsteps stumbled into the room.

"Leave, all of you!" I heard Yizhu bark. I was not aware that anyone besides my maid and myself were present in the room, but perhaps there were eunuchs lurking in the room as well. There always seemed to be eunuchs hiding in every dark corner of the Forbidden City.

I heard footsteps shuffle away, and then the door latching closed. I heard the prince's stumbling footsteps through the room. His gait was always noticeable, even in a crowded room. He was cursed with a heavy limp due to a fall from a horse during a hunting expedition when he was younger.

"Why are you wearing that?" the prince asked me. "You look ridiculous."

His words struck me like an arrow to the chest. Why would he say such a thing to me on our wedding day? But then, this was the same man who had struck Princess Ayan on her wedding day.

"Take it off," he commanded. I did as I was told, holding the veil in my lap as I looked down. He was now my husband, but he was still my prince.

"You were her lady-in-waiting for two months," he said as he poured himself a cup of wine.

"Yes, my lord," I said, confused as to why he wanted to speak to me about Ayan on our wedding day, and why his voice carried such venom.

"And you had no idea," he said.

"No idea about what, my lord?"

"You had no idea what she was going to do?" he asked, raising his voice.

"I don't know what you are talking about," I said, growing a little annoyed at everyone speaking to me in code. Why could they not speak plainly?

"Don't you?" he scoffed. "Well, I suppose it's possible. She did wait until you left. But maybe you and she planned it that way." He went so quiet, I wondered if he had left or fallen asleep. I raised my eyes and saw that he was staring at me intently. I should have immediately looked away and apologized for my impertinence, but I could not. Our eyes locked.

"Did you?" he asked me, swaying slightly on his feet. He was drunk.

"Did I what?" I asked, still not looking away.

"Plan it!" he yelled, stalking toward me. Well, at least as well as a lame beast can stalk.

"I don't know what you are talking about," I said slowly and clearly. Perhaps, even a bit loudly, though I didn't mean to yell. I was simply tired of repeating myself. It had to be near dawn by now and I was exhausted.

"Then, what do you know?" he asked.

"Nothing!" I was growing exasperated. "I was only told that Princess Ayan was dead and that I was to take her place as your wife."

"Is that what you wanted?" he asked.

"What?"

"Is this what you planned? Did you want to take her place?"

I scoffed. "Certainly not." Then I realized how horrible that sounded. The last thing I wanted was to insult a drunken man known to beat his wife. "She was my friend. I loved her dearly. It breaks my heart that she is dead."

"Hmm." The prince took another drink from his cup. "I wish I could say the same thing."

"Why can you not? You cannot be angry with her for dying. It was hardly her fault, I'm sure."

The prince stared at me as if I had just said something terribly stupid. Then he laughed, a loud, barking laugh I had not heard from him since we were children.

"You mean... Oh, by Heaven. You really don't know, do you?"

"Know what?" I asked, so exhausted and frustrated I was near to tears.

"Princess Ayan, how she died. You really don't know."

"No. No one has told me."

He shook his head, a piteous smile on his face. He sat beside me on the bed and took another swig of his wine. He offered me the cup, but I shook my head. "You may need it after I tell you," he said.

"Tell me what?"

"Princess Ayan committed suicide last night."

I had to close my eyes at his words as I tried to comprehend what he had just said. I must have misheard him. He could not possibly have said... No. She could not have killed herself. She would not have taken her own life. I looked at the prince for any hint that he was joking, but his face was solid as stone.

"No," I finally managed to say. "No, you are playing a terrible prank on me. No. Ayan would never—"

"Well, she did."

"Wh-why? How?"

"Well, as to the how, she hung herself in her sleeping chamber. She tied a silk scarf around the top of the bedpost and just…hung there."

I let out a small gasp. It was such a horrible thing to happen. Why was she alone? Where were her servants? I suddenly had so many more questions, but I was afraid to ask them.

"As to the why. Well, I was hoping you might be able to answer that question."

"What? Me?" I managed to squeak out.

"You were her closest friend. Her lady-in-waiting. You knew her better than anyone. Tell me, why would she do this?"

My mouth went dry and I could only shake my head. No, she couldn't have. I knew she was unhappy, of course. More than that. She was miserable. She dreaded going to the prince's bedchamber night after night. But I insisted to her that things would get better. I suspected that my father's women did not enjoy going to the bedchamber either. But they were not unhappy. In fact, when they had children, they were overjoyed. I did not know how women became pregnant before Ayan told me, but I did know about childbirth. My mother had allowed me to be present at my sister's birth when I was ten years old. I had told Ayan about it. About the signs to watch for to know she was pregnant and then what happened during childbirth. I did not want her to go into the birthing chamber as blind as she had been when she went to the bridal chamber. But she seemed terrified at the prospect of giving birth. My attempt to comfort her only seemed to have the opposite effect.

And then I remembered our last goodbye. She hugged me so tightly, it was as if she didn't want to let me go.

"I'll miss you so much," she'd said.

"And I you. But the next time we see each other, it will be as sisters-in-law."

She shook her head. "I feel we will not see each other again."

I…I was so stupid.

"Of course we will," I'd said. "I'll come and visit you as soon as I can."

She shook her head but said no more. I thought she meant I would be so happy in my new life with Prince Yixin that I would not want to leave. I was so blinded by my own joy and good fortune, I did not see the utter terror and helplessness on the face of my dear friend. I had abandoned her; she saw no way out of her misery except to take her own life. She could never have anticipated that I would be forced to take her place.

I realized that the prince was still looking at me. Still waiting for an answer. I only shook my head. I could not tell him the truth. It would be a secret I would take to my own grave.

"I don't know, my lord. She never gave me cause to think that she would do something so terrible." That was, at least, mostly the truth. There were perhaps signs, things she was trying to tell me, but I was too blind to see them. "Believe me, if I ever imagined her doing something like this, I would have done everything in my power to stop her." Another truth. I would have stopped her if she had spoken to me plainly, or if I had not been so selfish and noticed her desperation. I loved her as a sister.

Yizhu let out a heavy sigh and finished off his wine before setting the cup aside. "The one good thing to come from all this is that now I have you."

"Me?" I asked dumbly.

"Yes, you," he said, gripping my chin and turning my face to him. "You know that I wanted to marry you all along."

"Did you?" I asked. Of course I knew it, but I didn't know what else to say.

"I don't know why Mother chose Ayan anyway. She was so young and silly. Not the sort of woman who could be the next empress."

"Your mother is older and wiser than either of us," I said. "She must have seen something in Ayan that I lacked."

"I think it was only because I wanted you," he said. "She did it merely to spite me."

I shook my head. "She would never—"

He leaned over to me so close that I could smell the sour wine on his breath. "I think they are plotting against me," he whispered.

"What?"

"Empress Jing, Yixin," he said. "My father?" He chuckled to himself. "No, not him. Father wants me to be the next emperor. He told me so himself."

"Did he?" This did not surprise me. I imagined that the emperor said such things to all his sons. He wanted their devotion, their loyalty. He would promise them anything they wanted while he was alive. But he would keep his true heir a secret until his death. If he made it public who his heir was, how could he ever sleep soundly? His heir might kill him to take the throne, and his other sons would hound him every day that he was alive to change his mind. He would never know peace.

"Of course he wants me to be his heir," Yizhu insisted. "I am the most like him. He and I, we share the same vision of China's future. The foreigners—" He nearly spat the word. "—only want to make us weak. They want our money, our land. They want to enslave our people as they did the Africans."

I nodded. I had heard similar claims from my own father. Our country was still suffering the effects of the war with the foreigners that had started before I was even born. I was only a baby when Emperor Daoguang ended the war by signing the Treaty of Nanking. The emperor had to pay millions of taels in compensation to foreigners for the war and destruction of their precious opium. He also had to give them land, including the island of Hong Kong. Though, that was not much more than a worthless fishing village. Daoguang had been very lenient with the greedy and corrupt councilors over the years, allowing them to grow fat pockets. After the treaty, he imposed fines on all the men who had stolen money from the empire, leaving many previously prosperous families destitute. My family was not much affected since my grandfather and father were honest men. But we had seen many family members fall prey to opium addiction, as it was allowed to flow into the country unchecked.

"I would expel all the foreigners if I were emperor," Yizhu said. "And I have told Father as much. Yixin, he would draw closer to them. Under his rule, we would be nothing more than puppets."

"Why does Emperor Daoguang not send the foreigners away?" I asked, genuinely curious. If the foreigners were so terrible, why were they allowed to stay?

Yizhu scoffed. "He has too many old, fearful, and weak men giving him advice. They think the foreigners are too powerful to oppose. But not me. I would fight them to the bitter end."

I nodded, but I was not sure what to think. Surely, we would have done so if China were strong enough to fight back against the foreigners. But we had lost the war, which was why the emperor had signed the treaty in the first place. If we tried to fight a war again now, when we did not have as much money and so many men had fallen victim to opium, we would lose again.

"But, if we go to war again, will we win?" I asked.

"Of course we will!" he declared. "We are China, the most powerful country in the world. Don't you agree? I cannot have an empress who will not agree with me."

What could I say? I was now his wife. I had no option but to agree with and support him in everything.

"Of course I do," I said with a smile. Inside, I was deeply unsure about what sort of emperor Yizhu would be. What would happen to us if he led us toward a war we could not win?

"Good," Yizhu said, then he laid back on the bed and stretched out, reminding me of a lazy cat. "Now, remove your clothes."

I clutched at the frog clasps near my throat. "What?"

"You are my wife now. It is time for you to do your job."

"Oh." I stood up slowly, my whole body shaking. My fingers were so cold, they were almost too stiff to undo the frog clasps. I tried to remember if Princess Ayan had ever told me anything that pleased the prince, anything I could do to make him happy. He seemed to be in a good mood. He was a bit drunk, but he was not angry. He had seemed aggravated when he first came to the room, but that moment seemed to have passed.

"What is taking so long?" Yizhu asked. I did not think very much time had passed, but I was so nervous, every second seemed eternal.

"I cannot undo the clasps," I said. "I..." I needed to come up with an excuse that would not offend him. "I am not used to undressing myself." It was only a small lie. I usually did have maids help dress and undress me, but that did not mean I was so helpless that I could not do so myself. Still, I was relieved when Yizhu chuckled. He got to his feet and helped undo the small frog clasps down the front of my wedding gown. He showed a kindness, a tenderness I had not seen in him since we were children.

"You are happy to be here with me, are you not?" he asked. His question surprised me, and my words fled from my mouth. "Why are you hesitating?" His voice started to rise.

"I...I..." I stepped back and took a breath, trying to quell my rising fear. I clutched at the front of my wedding gown, desperate to hold it closed even though most of the clasps had been undone. "I am only... I feel so unprepared. I thought I was not to be married for several weeks more."

"But now that you are here, you are glad of it, are you not?"

he asked. "You are relieved that you will not have to marry my weak and worthless brother, right?"

I did my best to smile at him, but I could feel my lips shake. "It is my honor to have you as my husband." True or not, it was the correct answer, for I could see a smile on his lips once again. I could tell that my words could easily sway my new husband's moods. I had to be always cautious with what I said to him.

Yizhu took two uneven steps toward me and took my chin between two of his fingers, turning my face up to him. He closed his eyes and placed his lips on mine. I was unsure of what to do in response. It was my first kiss, after all. Even though he had tried to steal a kiss from me many years before, Yixin had saved me. But Yixin could not help me now. It was too late. I was the wife of Yizhu now, and I would have to learn to please him if I hoped to have any sense of peace in my life. I did not want to end up like Princess Ayan, a shaking, terrified version of myself. If I could become pregnant quickly, I would all but ensure that Yizhu would be emperor. I would be his empress. I would be the greatest lady in the country, like Empress Jing before me. Yizhu would be very busy with his many responsibilities, and he would be gifted with a great many consorts. I would rarely have to be his bedmate again if I could help make my husband the emperor.

I leaned into the kiss, which seemed to surprise him. He leaned back and pulled away from me, looking down in confusion.

"Did...did I do something wrong?" I asked him.

"No," he said. "It is only... You want to be with me?"

"I... You are my husband. How else should it be?"

"Yes, of course," he said. "Only... Ayan, she would pull away from me. She would try to run away. I had to force her to bed."

I nodded and my heart broke at this knowledge. Ayan did not go into all the details of her time in the prince's bedchamber with me. I suppose she was too embarrassed. But she must have been very afraid. I remembered being afraid when Yizhu tried to force a kiss on me. How much worse would it have been had he tried to do more? Even though I did not want to be Yizhu's bedmate, I knew I had no choice. It would be easier on me if I submitted.

If only Ayan had learned that lesson. How could she have felt so terrible, so hopeless, that her only option was to take her own life? I wished I had done more to help her. *Anything* to help her. I was too selfish, too focused on my own good fortune, to see just how great her suffering was. I loved her, but I did not help her. When I became empress, I would have to do a better job of caring for the women of my household. I could not let any woman succumb to such total despair under my watch again.

I felt more calm, more resigned to what was about to happen. I could not change it. Could not stop it. With calm and steady fingers, I ran my hands down the front of my wedding gown and undid the final clasps. I pulled the red silk down my shoulders and let the garment fall to the floor. Thankfully, I still was not naked, but wore a red silk shift underneath. Still, I had never stood before a man wearing so little.

Yizhu stared at me, his mouth agape. I felt a flush of heat on my face and wrapped my arms around myself. Did I do the wrong thing? Yizhu rushed toward me so quickly, I thought he would knock me down. But instead, he took me into his arms and kissed me again, hard and rough. He ran his hands over my body and bit my lower lip. He pushed me back to the bed and took off his own clothes. I was surprised, and a bit thrilled, when I saw his muscular arms and chest. I had no idea his upper body was so strong, and I felt a bit of desire grow in my belly. But when he removed his pants and I saw the fleshy member protruding from dark hair, I grew a little afraid again. It was huge, much larger than I ever imagined. I had seen my little brothers naked before, but they looked nothing like Yizhu. When Ayan told me that Yizhu stabbed her with his fleshy dagger, I did not know how he could do such a thing. My brothers' members seemed very small and soft. But Yizhu's was more like a sword, and I did not know how he could use it on me and it not cause pain.

But I would not be like Ayan. I would not run away. I would not let the pain and fear overtake me. If enduring such pain was my duty as a wife, I would do it. If this was how I became a mother, I would accept it.

Yizhu pulled up my shift, exposing my whole body to him. I closed my eyes to hide my embarrassment. He laid on top of me, spread my legs, and entered my body. I did not want to cry out, but I could not help it. The sensation and pain were so shocking to me, my response was involuntary. I felt a need to push him off me. To fight back. To run. But I forced those feelings deep inside of myself. Yizhu put his hand over my mouth to stifle my cries. I laid back and waited for it to be over.

Thankfully, it did not take long. It seemed that only a minute later, Yizhu was finished, as he fell off me with a contented sigh. He climbed up into the bed and collapsed on his pillows. I pushed my shift down, which had become bunched around my chest, and tried to cover myself. I sat up and looked around, expecting to see servants ready to take me back to my quarters, but we were still alone.

"Come here," Yizhu said. I looked over and saw him patting the bed next to him. I crawled up and laid down with my head on a pillow, facing him. "Did you enjoy it?" he asked. I wanted to laugh. How could any woman enjoy what he had just done to me? But it was obvious that he enjoyed it, for pleasure was clear on his face.

"Of course," I said, since it was clear that those were the words he wanted to hear.

He scoffed. "Ayan never did."

"I am not Ayan." As much as I loved Ayan and was heartbroken over what happened to her, I did not want to be compared to her. I would not die by my own hand out of fear. I was going to be a great lady. I was going to be empress.

Yizhu laughed. "No, you certainly are not." He crawled over to me, pushed me back, and kissed me again. By now, I was learning a little more about how to kiss and what he wanted me to do. But I was shocked when he took my hand and placed it on his member. I pulled my hand away from the hot, sticky mass. He held me down and entered me again. It was even more painful this time. My skin was dry and raw, but it did not bother Yizhu. I had no idea he would want to do this again so soon. I thought it only happened once a night. It took him much longer to reach his full enjoyment this time. I counted the seconds until he was done.

This time, when he finished, he rolled over and fell asleep. I sighed in relief. I stood up to grab my clothes, but it was hard to move. I remembered how much pain Ayan would be in after her visits to Yizhu. But I did not want to appear weak in front of my servants. I did not remember my mother or my father's other women complaining of pain after they spent the night with my father.

I wrapped my wedding gown around me and buttoned up the frog clasps. I stepped into my pot-bottom shoes and picked up my veil. I walked to the door of Yizhu's bedchamber and held my head high as I exited. Outside, the sun was shining brightly. I did not know what time it was, but I did not want to insult my new mother-in-law on the very first day after my marriage. I clapped my hands at a eunuch and ordered that a litter be brought for me. He bowed and scurried away. Only a moment later, two eunuchs carrying a bamboo litter appeared. One of the eunuchs helped me into the chair, and the two of them lifted me up and carried me away. I realized I did not tell them where to take me, but they must have known as they did not ask.

The men stopped outside Princess Ayan's palace. At first, I thought that they must have made a mistake. I had expected them to take me to the palace I had lived in before. But then I realized that I was no longer a lady-in-waiting, but a princess in my own right. I was Princess Zhenxiu.

I stepped out of the litter and looked at the palace in front of me. The servants—some of whom were my old servants and some who had served Princess Ayan—scurried outside and waited for me with their heads bowed. I knew that I needed to go inside. I needed to take a bath, change my clothes, eat, and have my makeup done and hair styled so I could greet the empress. But my feet seemed frozen to the ground. I did not want to enter the palace.

Princess Ayan—my friend—had died in there.

Two maids approached me. One took the veil from my hand, and the other offered me her hand to help me walk. They must have thought that I was not moving because I needed their assistance. But that was not the case at all. I could not live there. Princess Ayan's angry ghost would surely be walking the halls. But what could I do? I was sure I looked a mess, with unkempt hair and smeared makeup. I could not approach the empress looking like that. I would have to enter the palace, prepare myself, and then ask the empress to move me to another palace. The Forbidden City had almost a thousand rooms. There was surely space for me elsewhere.

I allowed the maid to lead me into the palace and to the bedchamber. But as soon as I entered the room, I felt a headache build. Even Ayan's bed had not been replaced. My eyes went straight to the post above her bed and I would swear that I saw her body swinging there. I let out a scream and promptly fainted.

CHAPTER SEVEN

"*J* thought you were better than this."

I opened my eyes and saw Empress Jing sitting next to me. I sat up quickly. Too quickly, because my head spun and the light streaming through the window blinded me.

"My lady," I said, trying to bow from my seated position.

"Get out," the empress said to my maids, who quickly scurried away, closing the door behind them. The empress stood and looked down at me, anger on her face. "What is wrong with you?" she hissed at me as soon as we were alone.

"I'm sorry," I said, my eyes darting around the room, making sure there were no ghosts present. Though, I'm sure even Ayan's ghost would have been terrified of the empress. "Everything was so overwhelming. Ayan died here, in this room, in this bed!" I tossed the blanket back and got to my feet, kneeling before her. "I can't stay here. Please, let me move back to my old quarters."

"That is impossible," she said. "You are a princess now, and you will live in the princess's palace."

"Can I at least get a new bed?" I asked. I lowered my voice.

"She...she is still... I saw her ghost. She was hanging—" I could not even get the words out as I shuddered.

"Oh, you did not," the empress scoffed. "You are simply letting your imagination run away with you. I thought you were better than this. Stronger. I will not have you insult and dishonor me the way Ayan did."

I stood up but still kept my chin down and my hands folded in front of me respectfully. "Did you know how unhappy she was? Did you know she was going to do such a thing?"

Empress Jing let out a sigh and sank onto a nearby chair. "She was unhappy. Of course she was. You knew it, didn't you?"

I sat on the edge of my bed. "I knew. But I thought things would get better for her. I thought that after I was also married and we were sisters-in-law..." I shook my head. I was stupid, selfish. How could my happiness at marrying someone else make her life any more bearable? "I ignored how miserable she was because I was so focused on myself. I was not a good friend to her."

Empress Jing waved my concerns off. "You are just a girl yourself. How could you have known what she was going to do? You couldn't. But I do expect more from you. Why did you faint? Yizhu cannot have another weak-willed wife."

"I was overwhelmed," I said. "I didn't expect to be...to be here." I looked up at the bedpost where Ayan hanged herself.

"But it was not because of Yizhu?" she asked, and I could see the concern on her face. She was afraid that he had hurt me the way he had Ayan. While I could not be sure if the way he took me to bed was any better or worse than what Ayan endured, he at least did not strike me. He did not seem unhappy with me. Quite the opposite, in fact.

"No. It was not because of Yizhu. I think he was satisfied with me."

Empress Jing let out a long exhale of relief. "That is good. I am glad. I would have felt terrible to see you suffer the way Ayan had. I see great things in your future."

"Thank you," I said, and I was truly flattered. How many women ever heard such kind words from an empress? "But, if I may ask, why am I here? What about my betrothal to Yixin? Why was I selected to replace Ayan when I was already engaged?"

"Yizhu is a man who…always needs a woman in his bed," the empress said. "Ayan needed to be replaced immediately or else he… Well, no matter. I was going to suggest one of the other young women from the selection ceremony, but most were already betrothed. Breaking off their engagements would be a long process that would require the approval of both families involved. But you. Well, your parents would not object, and Yixin's father is the emperor, so he gave immediate approval."

I nodded in understanding. But I still did not see why there was such a rush. What would Yizhu do if he did not have a wife? Well, I supposed it no longer mattered.

"Will…will Yizhu be the next emperor?" I asked.

"I do not know," Empress Jing said. "Things are…complicated. The emperor loves Yizhu, and I think that, were these not extraordinary times, he would name him heir without hesitation. But the foreigners…" She sighed and shook her head. "Has any emperor before had to contend with such interference from outside forces?"

I was not sure what to say to that. After all, the Han people considered us Manchu to be outsiders as well. Some even called us barbarians! But I said nothing. I surely did not understand all aspects of the matter.

"The emperor knows that Yizhu will defy the foreigners, which is what he himself wants to do. But the foreigners are powerful, and he fears they will crush us. Prince Yixin would be more willing to work with the foreigners. But Emperor Daoguang thinks that following such a course could also be the end of us. We would just become another puppet state, like India."

I just shook my head. I didn't know what she was talking about. What was a puppet state? What was India? Were these things I would need to know if I were empress? I hoped not.

"I am sorry," Empress Jing said. "I am speaking of things that need not concern you."

"What should I be concerned with?" I asked her. "I know it is my job as a wife to give my husband a son. But…" I hesitated before speaking. After all, I did not know if the empress was trying to make Yixin the emperor's heir. And I did not know if it mattered. All I knew was that I thought I would one day be the empress. Was that still my future?

"Speak," Empress Jing said. "Do not mumble your words."

"Why did you want me to marry Yixin? Why did you give Yizhu a girl who could not yet bear children?" When her eyes went wide, I put my hand to my mouth. I had certainly spoken out of turn. I should not question the will of the empress. But to my surprise, Empress Jing laughed.

"You are a clever girl, just as I always thought you were."

I smiled and let out a small laugh of my own. So, I was right.

"Well, it matters not now," the empress said. "But if you want to be empress, you should bear a son quickly, before your new sister-in-law, Lady Ningxin."

"I will do my best," I said, rubbing my stomach. Could I already be with child?

Empress Jing stood up, and I followed suit. "If you have any reason to be unhappy, please let me know. I would hate to lose you as we did Ayan."

I nodded and gave a small bow, The empress turned to leave the room, but then I remembered the bed. I was sure that the empress was simply being polite. She did not really want me to bother her with trifling matters. But I did not know how I could ever sleep in the same place where Ayan had killed herself.

"My lady?" I said hesitatingly. The empress turned back to me. "The bed? Would it be possible to have it replaced? She... Ayan... She died right there." I pointed to the post above the bed.

Empress Jing let out an annoyed sigh. "The emperor will not like the expense of a new bed when this one is perfectly functional."

"Perhaps this bed could simply be exchanged for the bed in my previous quarters. No one is living there now, correct?"

The empress considered this for a moment. "Very well. It will be done today."

"Thank you, my lady," I said, giving a deeper bow. "Thank you so much!"

I started to follow after her, but the pain between my legs was a stark reminder of what had happened mere hours ago. I ordered one of the maids to prepare a bath for me while another helped me undress. I took a rag and wiped between my legs. There was some blood, but not nearly as much as I expected, or what Princess Ayan had experienced. The hot water was relaxing and soothing. The maids scrubbed my body and washed my hair. I hated to leave the bath when it was over. By the time I was dressed, my hair styled, and my makeup done, it was the middle of the afternoon. Several eunuchs arrived to disassemble my bed and make way for the new one. I summoned a scribe so that I could dictate a letter to my cousin. I could have written it myself, but I did not know where my writing instruments were. Not all of my trunks had arrived, and the few I had were not yet unpacked. I sat in a pavilion near a pond and tossed bits of seeds to the ducks and fish that lived there.

"To my dear cousin," I started, but then hesitated. I wondered how I was going to tell her about my new life with

Prince Yizhu. She knew better than anyone how happy I was to be marrying Yixin. If I told her I was happy to be married to Yizhu, she would immediately know I was lying. But I had to be careful with my words. Who knew how many people would read my letter between now and when my cousin received it.

"Where is she?"

The scribe and I were interrupted by an angry voice. A maid rushed over and offered me her arm so we could walk quickly back to my palace. When we arrived, I was shocked to see Emperor Daoguang himself yelling at the eunuchs who were moving the bed. The eunuchs were all on their knees, cowering as if the emperor had whipped them.

I rushed forward and kneeled before the emperor. "My lord? Have I done wrong?"

"Zhenxiu," he said, his voice raspy. It sounded as though he were recovering from a cough. And he seemed thinner than the last time I saw him mere weeks ago. "I thought you were more responsible than this," he barked.

"My lord, I do not know what you mean."

"You have only arrived and think you need a new bed? Why would you think you were entitled to such an expense?"

My mouth gaped at this. The emperor had always been frugal, giving princesses like Ayan a smaller allowance than even a woman such as my mother had received when she was merely a lady-in-waiting. But how a lady spent her money was never the emperor's concern. Even if I had purchased a new bed with my allowance, it would have been my right. But I could not correct the emperor. If he wished to criticize me for my spending, I supposed it was his right to do so. But in this case, I had spent no money at all, so I had to explain that much at least.

"It is not a new bed, my lord. It is only being exchanged for a bed from another palace."

"Why would you do such a thing?" he asked.

Again, my words fled. I did not wish to speak publicly about the death of Princess Ayan.

"My lord, I lived in another building when I served Princess Ayan. I feared I would not be comfortable sleeping in another bed. Please forgive me." I did not know what I needed forgiveness for, but it seemed like the right thing to say. If the emperor was angry with me, it would surely be because I was in the wrong somehow.

"Humph," the emperor said, looking down his nose at me as if he did not believe me.

"What is going on here?"

I turned and bowed to Prince Yizhu, my husband. I never thought I would be so happy to see him.

"Your princess is quite spoiled," the emperor said, and I could not defend myself. If the emperor said something, it must be true. To argue with him would be unthinkable on my part. But perhaps I would be able to explain myself to Yizhu when we were alone.

"I am sorry to hear that, Father," the prince said. "I will speak with her."

"See that you do," the emperor said. I watched him walk away through my eyelashes, and though he was walking rather slowly, I then noticed the fact he was walking at all, and alone at that. Why did he not come in a litter? And where were his attendants?

"What happened?" Prince Yizhu asked me as soon as the emperor was out of sight.

I stood and shook my head. "I was simply exchanging the bed in this palace for the one from my old palace so I would be more comfortable. I do not know why it angered him so. He accused me of spending money frivolously, but I have spent nothing. Besides, even if I wanted to spend money, how could I? I have not received my allowance. I have not even been here a day."

Yizhu pressed his lips together and gripped my elbow, leading me inside. The eunuchs took this as a signal to resume their work.

"You will receive your allowance," the prince said, his voice low, as he led me to my sitting room. We sat across from one another at a table. I motioned for one of the maids to serve tea.

"I am sure," I said. I was not worried—"

"But it may be less than you expect."

"What do you mean?" I asked. I had not yet discussed finances with my chief eunuch. There had not been time. But I knew how much money Princess Ayan received and how much it had cost to run her household, so I was not concerned. Keeping the family budget was one of the skills my mother had taught me.

"You know how much money Princess Ayan received, yes?" Yizhu asked me. I nodded. "You should expect to receive about half that amount."

"Half?" I nearly shrieked. I slapped my hand to my mouth and felt my stomach tighten. How could I possibly run a princess's household on so little? For my station, my palace was quite large. It required several maids to merely keep it clean and tidy. I had maids to help me dress and bathe and style my hair. I had my own kitchen, with cooks and maids there as well. I had a chief eunuch to help with finances and other bookkeeping matters. I had to pay the eunuchs who carried my litter around the Forbidden City. I had to feed, clothe, and pay wages to everyone who worked for me. I had to pay for the coal used to warm my palace.

Then there was the matter of sending money to my family. My family was comfortably wealthy, but I was still responsible for sending money home to care for them. My father would not be able to work indefinitely, so all of his children would be expected to care for him, his wives, and the younger children.

Because I married so high, it would be expected for me to send a rather large sum of money home every month.

My head began to ache as I tried to think about where I could cut corners to save money, but I did not anticipate having many frivolous expenses that could be cut. I employed no tutors and would not need new clothes until next year. I was running all the figures through my head and almost did not hear what Yizhu said next.

"I think the foreigners mean to break us with the money they claim we owe them," he was saying, his teeth clenched tightly. "Millions of taels."

"What? But the war was many years ago."

A maid brought over the tea things, but Yizhu indicated he was not thirsty. I suddenly wished I had not wasted the tea leaves.

"And we are still paying for it," Yizhu continued. "The interest grows every day."

I did not know how to reply to that. I did not know what growing interest had to do with how much money was owed. My confusion must have shown on my face because Yizhu patted my cheek.

"Do not worry yourself about it. These are not the concerns of women."

"But you just told me the allowance to manage my household had been cut in half. This is of great concern to me. How can I pay my servants if I have no money?"

"You ladies are spoiled anyway," he said. "So what if you have a few fewer dresses this year?"

I let out an exhale of annoyance. "I will have no money to spend on clothes this winter, nor coal to warm my home. Shall my servants and I freeze to death to save a few coins?"

"You exaggerate," the prince said, standing and stretching. "You nearly made me forget why I came here in the first place."

I stood as well. "Forgive me. Why have you come?"

He rushed to me, taking my chin between his fingers to turn my face up to him. He kissed me, pressing my lips so hard against my teeth, I feared they would bleed. I heard a maid gasp and scurry from the room. Prince Yizhu wrapped an arm around my waist to hold me closer to him, so I could only pull my face away.

"What are you doing?" I asked, my hand on his chest to try and put some distance between us.

"You are my wife," he said. Both of his arms were around me now. I bent backward, but he still managed to nuzzle my cheek.

"Then are you not supposed to send for me tonight?" I asked, afraid someone else would see us. In all my life, I had never seen a man kiss a woman, not even my father and his women. I could not believe Yizhu would kiss and touch me when a servant could walk in at any moment.

"You are my wife. I should be able to have you any time I want."

I was horrified. Of course, I was supposed to submit to my husband in all matters, but I had no idea that any husband would expect his wife to…tend to his needs in the middle of the day. Such things only happened at night…didn't they? Did not the prince have things to do during the day? I certainly was busy. I needed to check on the progress of having my bed moved. I needed to speak with my chief eunuch about the household finances. I needed to unpack my trunks and talk to my cook.

"I…I have many things to do…" I tried to say as he kissed my cheek and neck.

"It won't take long," he said as he pulled up my gown.

"My…my bed still has not been assembled."

"We can do it right there." He backed me into the table and picked me up, trying to set me atop it. But with all my squirming, he could not lift me.

"No," I said, and I instantly regretted it. But I could not think of another excuse quickly enough.

"No?" he repeated, and I could see the fury in his eyes.

"I'm sorry," I said. "Forgive me. I only meant—"

He slapped me across the face and I froze, my words dying in my throat. I had never been hit in all my life, and now I had been struck twice in as many days, first by my father, and now by my husband. What was wrong with me? I had been taught to show the utmost respect to the men in my life. But I had failed in this one aspect so gravely I had been physically punished —*twice!*

"Never, *ever*, say no to me," Yizhu said, pointing a finger in my face. "Do you understand?"

I gave a slight nod, closing my eyes so I would not cry.

"Do you understand?" he yelled.

"Yes," I said in little more than a whisper. "Yes, my lord. I'm sorry." I didn't want to cry, but the tears streamed down my cheeks of their own accord.

"You are my wife and you will obey me."

I nodded again. "Yes, my lord." I sniffed to keep the snot from escaping my nose. Unbidden, the thought came to my mind that Prince Yixin would never have struck me.

Yizhu grabbed my arms and turned me around, bending me over the table. I thought perhaps he would lash me like a slave, but then I felt cold air on my legs as he pulled my gown up. I was so shocked that I tried to stand up, but he pushed me back on the table. I squeezed my eyes shut, praying no servants would walk in. I couldn't bear it if anyone saw me so humiliated.

"In the future, you will do as I say."

"Yes, my lord. Of course."

I could not help but scream out when he entered me. It was so painful, I knew there would be more blood. I did not understand how he could take pleasure in causing me so much pain, but he seemed to enjoy what he was doing even more than he did last night.

After a moment, the pain eased, so I simply waited for it to be over. Across the room was a painting of a fox chasing a bird. The bird had already taken flight, but still, the fox leaped after it, its maw wide open. It seemed to me that the bird would escape. But I could see how someone else might think the fox would devour the bird. It was all a matter of perspective, I supposed.

The prince grunted and then stepped back, releasing me from his grip. I stood up slowly, for every muscle in my body ached, and felt my gown tumble down to cover me. But I did not turn around. I could not face him.

"I'm sorry, Zhen," he said as he straightened his clothes. I was surprised by his words, but I could not acknowledge them. "You only made me so angry, I had to do it. You understand that, don't you?"

"Yes, my lord, of course. It is I who is sorry. I forgot my place."

"Well, let's make sure it doesn't happen again."

"Of course, my lord."

We stood in silence. It seemed he had more to say, so I kept my mouth closed. I would not dare interrupt him. Finally, I heard him limp out of the room and then out of my palace. Only when I was sure the was gone could I finally reach for a nearby chair and sit down. I winced at the pain.

"My lady?" came a small voice from the doorway.

"Yes?" I asked, my voice cracking, but I did not turn toward her. I knew my hair was disheveled and my makeup smeared.

"Can I…do anything for you?" the maid asked. The kindness in her voice undid me, and tears streamed down my cheeks. But I did not move. I dared not tremble or shake. I was a princess, possibly a future empress. I could not lose control of myself in front of a servant.

"No," I managed to say, holding my voice steady.

"Very well. The bed has been completed."

"Good. Thank you."

She shuffled away and I was left alone. I suddenly realized how alone Ayan must have felt when I left her. For the first two months of her marriage, she at least had me by her side to comfort her, bathe her, wipe away her tears. But when I left...

For the first time, I did not blame her for taking her own life. I understood why she did it. How I wished I had her ghost here to comfort me now.

I should not have sent her bed away.

CHAPTER EIGHT

I felt relieved when I saw blood on the inside of my undergarment. I knew I should not feel that way. My job as a wife was to provide my husband with sons. However, I knew that he would not be able to summon me to his bed for at least the next four days. Maybe longer if I was lucky.

Yizhu had summoned me to his bed every night for the last three weeks. And sometimes he came to my palace during the day. I had been constantly on edge because I never knew when he would come for me. For the first time since I entered the Forbidden City, I was able to feel relaxed.

I didn't know why Yizhu enjoyed making love so much. While the act was no longer painful for me, it was not enjoyable. I took no pleasure from it and counted the things around me until it was over. The paintings on the walls. The dragons on the curtains around the bed. The books on the shelf. Sometimes, I simply counted down from one hundred. And if he still wasn't finished, I counted down again. At least he had not struck me again, but I had not given him reason to. We barely spoke about anything more than his health or the weather.

When he visited me, I kept my mouth closed and my eyes downcast. He made love to me and then he would leave. When I went to see him at night, I would hardly get any sleep because I did not know if he would want to do it again. Most women go back to their own quarters after coupling with their husbands. But Yizhu often wanted to make love two or even three times a night. I looked forward to finally spending a night in my bed and getting a full night's sleep. I also looked forward to the day my husband could take some concubines for himself, though I did not know when that would be.

"Please alert the Ministry of Household Affairs that my monthly visitor has come," I told my chief eunuch. "I cannot tend to the prince's needs tonight."

"Yes, my lady," he said with a bow. "I'm sorry."

"For what?"

The eunuch blushed and stammered. "Be-because you are not with child."

"Oh, yes, of course. Well, it will happen soon, I'm sure."

"Of course, my lady."

"Do you know—" I stopped myself. I almost asked if he knew if Ningxin, Prince Yixin's wife, was yet with child. But it would be too soon. They only married last week in a fine ceremony. They came to the Forbidden City for the tea ceremony with the emperor and empress, and then they went to the prince's mansion for the feast. I barely saw either of them. I don't think Yixin even knew I was there.

The eunuch waited for me to finish my request. I cleared my throat. "Do you know...how our funds are doing for the month?"

"About the same as the last time we discussed them...yesterday," he said.

"Yes, of course. You may go."

"Yes, my lady."

I went to my dressing table and counted out the few coins I had in my purse. After paying my servants their wages and giving a budget to my cook, I had very little left. I sent away two maids and one eunuch. Though, while that might have saved me money, it wouldn't save any for the emperor. Servants in the Forbidden City were hired by the Ministry of Household Affairs and given assignments there. When I dismissed a servant, they were simply reassigned somewhere else, except in cases of gross misconduct. Then they might be sent home in disgrace, but that was rare. But where they ended up and who paid for them was not my concern. I had to save money everywhere I could so that I could afford to buy coal when winter came. My cook was already unhappy with the amount of money I gave her to feed us for the month, and I was afraid that I would have to cut my servants' wages, but I hoped it would not come to that. I knew that most of the servants did not even keep their money for themselves, but sent it home to their families.

"The emperor has arrived!" a eunuch announced from outside. I put the meager coins into the bag and shoved it into a drawer. I rushed outside to my courtyard and kneeled along with all of my servants. I heard the emperor cough as he stood in front of me.

"Thank you for gracing me with your presence, Father," I said.

"I have come to see how wasteful with your allowance you have been," the emperor said.

"I have bought nothing, Your Majesty," I said, a bit confused why he constantly seemed to think I was wasting funds that were mine by right.

"We will see about that," he said as he entered my palace. "You." He pointed to a maid. "Where is the princess's wardrobe?"

The maid stood but kept her head bowed. "Please, Your Majesty, follow me." She shuffled her way to a small room near my sleeping chamber, the emperor on her heels, and me right behind him.

I was almost embarrassed that my wardrobe was half empty. Most women of my stature would have twice as many gowns as I did, not to mention jewels and hair decorations. But in this case, I think it was in my favor for the emperor to see just how little I owned.

"What is this?" the emperor asked, pulling out a gold-colored gown. "This is very costly cloth, indeed, is it not?"

"I do not know what my mother paid for it," I said truthfully.

"Your parents must be very well off if they can afford such finery."

"I...suppose," I said, unsure what to say to appease him. "But my father is a duke and he serves you well."

"Humph," the emperor said again, tossing my gold-colored gown to the floor and then pulling out a pale blue one. "Dukes, earls, princes, councilors. Did not all of them steal from my father and then me?"

"I am very sorry that such men took liberties they should not have," I said. "But my family, like all the others, was audited, and very few discrepancies were found. My family repaid their debt in full."

"Perhaps your grandfather was better at hiding his dishonesty than others," he said as he continued pulling out gowns randomly, throwing them to the floor. I held my tongue and said nothing as the emperor maligned my family. If I spoke, I knew I would say something impertinent.

From the back of the wardrobe, he pulled out winter gowns and capes lined with soft, warm fox fur. He pulled out almost all of them, tossing them onto the pile.

"Take them away," he barked at his eunuch.

"Take them?" I asked. "Where?"

"To be sold," the emperor said, brushing past me.

"Sold? Why?" I followed closely behind him out to his litter. I then noticed a second litter behind him, full of beautiful gowns. I looked over to another palace, where I saw one of the emperor's consorts, her hand to her mouth as a maid comforted her. I then realized that the emperor must have been taking clothes from everyone.

"You ladies are spoiled," he said. "Spending money recklessly and foolishly."

"The money we receive is gifted," I said. "If the ladies wish to spend it on dresses and jewels, they are allowed to, are they not?" I knew I should not contradict the emperor's will, but I did not understand his reasoning. The emperor stalked toward me, and I kneeled down very low, to my knees, out of striking range.

"You worthless women are nothing but a drain on me and my treasury. My heirs should learn from the grief my women have caused me and only have one wife."

His words alarmed me. If I were doomed to be the only wife to Prince Yizhu, I feared I would quickly follow Princess Ayan.

"I apologize for the grief those of my fellow sex have caused you, Your Majesty," I said. "But soon it will be winter. Please, leave me the furs so I do not freeze."

The emperor seemed to consider my words before stomping back to the other litter, grabbing one of the fur-lined capes, and throwing it to the ground.

"Thank you, Your Majesty," I said, even though I was furious inside. Even if he was the emperor, how could he dare to take items gifted to me by my parents and sell them to line his own pockets or pay his debts? It was in the back of my mind to sell them myself should I grow desperate enough. But if the debt was as bad as Prince Yizhu had said, millions of taels, what difference would the sale of a dozen used gowns make? Truly, all of this was beyond my understanding.

The emperor walked over to his litter, but before he climbed in, he began to cough. One of my maids rushed over and picked up the cape so that it was not trampled on as all of his eunuchs rushed to his side.

The emperor waved the eunuchs away. "I am fine. Leave me be," he said. But his coughing did not subside. I stood and went to him myself.

"Father, what is wrong? Can I help you?"

"Leave me be, woman," he said, shrugging off my touch. His coughing subsided enough for him to crawl into his litter.

"Take him back to this palace immediately," I told his eunuchs. "Prepare some tea for him and make sure he rests."

The eunuchs bowed to me and then picked up the emperor's litter, carrying him away. I could still hear this coughing long after he was gone from view.

"THE EMPEROR IS QUITE ILL," Empress Jing said while we walked along a path in one of the Inner Court's many gardens.

"I am sorry to hear that," I said. "I was quite concerned for him after he left my palace yesterday."

The empress sighed and clicked her tongue. "I do hope he left you something to wear."

"I convinced him to leave me a fur-lined cape for winter."

The empress raised an eyebrow at me. "Did you? Well, you fared better than some of the other ladies."

"I could ask my parents to send me more clothes that I could then share with the other ladies, but I don't want to do that if there is a risk that the emperor could confiscate those as well."

"Yes, don't do that just yet. And make sure to wear only your simplest gowns and as few adornments as possible. You don't want to catch his attention and send him into a tizzy again."

"Did something happen to set the emperor off?" I asked. "I don't understand what I could have done to make him think I am wasteful with money. How could I be? I couldn't afford my servants, much less clothes or jewels."

"Don't take it personally, dear," the empress said. "He raided everyone's closets. Even mine!"

"What has happened to drive him to such extreme measures?" I asked.

"Oh, it is nothing new. The emperor has been trying to find ways to pay our debts for a decade. He recently met with some foreign ministers and… Well, things did not go well. Some of the foreign governments said that they would take more land in lieu of repayment, but that only made the emperor more angry."

I nodded, but I had no feelings on the matter one way or another. I only wanted the emperor to give me a more reasonable allowance and to stop stealing my clothes.

"Whatever the cause, I hope His Majesty feels better soon."

"That was why I came to see you. We are planning to travel to Yuanming Yuan."

"The Summer Palace?" I gasped with happiness. The Summer Palace was the most beautiful residence in Peking. The whole palace, not just the Inner Court, was a veritable park, with endless old-growth trees offering shade, lakes for swimming, fishing, and sailing, and gardens with flowers of every color. Some palaces were in a French design that made you feel like you were in another world. Many items collected by or given to past emperors were on display, like an elegant museum. Oh, how I loved the Summer Palace! But I had not been there in several years.

"Yes. The emperor thinks that the fresh air of the countryside will do him good, and I can't argue with that. Though…" The empress trailed off, but I urged her to continue. "I think simply getting away from his so-called advisors for a while will help put this mind at ease. Let me give you a bit of advice. Take notice of who your husband takes advice from."

"What do you mean?"

"Men often want to trust one another far too easily without examining their motives. When you are the wife of a great man —whether he is a prince or an emperor—you can help nudge him toward those who have the emperor's best interests at heart and not just their own."

I nodded but had no idea how I could wield such influence over my husband. After the chat Yizhu and I had on my first day in the Forbidden City, we had not spoken since. I saw him every night at the very least, and often during the day as well, but we did not speak. And ever since the arrival of my monthly visitor, I had not seen him at all. I did not think Yizhu was the type of man who would appreciate his wife needling in things that were not her concern.

"Speaking of princes," Empress Jing said, "do you perchance have one on the way for us?"

I supposed the Ministry of Household Affairs did not apprise her of such things. I shook my head. "No. I'm sorry."

"Well, it has only been a month. I am sure it will happen soon enough. But you have at least been trying, right? You understand how these things happen, don't you?"

"Yes, my lady," I said, but I didn't tell her it was only because of what I had learned from Princess Ayan. The night I was whisked away to the Forbidden City, my mother told me nothing. Though, we were all a bit stunned by the suddenness of it, so I couldn't blame her.

"Good. Though, if we are fortunate, Princess Ningxin will have news to share with us when we see her at Yuanming Yuan."

I stopped in my tracks. "Pardon? Princess Ningxin will be there?" I trotted to catch up with the empress.

"Naturally. My husband wished for all his children to be present, so their spouses will be there as well."

"What a joyous reunion it will be," I said.

"Indeed. Now, you should pack for the journey. I believe your chief eunuch has made the trek before, so he will know what all you need to take with you."

"Thank you, Your Majesty," I said with a bow as she went on her way. I walked back to my palace slowly as many thoughts swirled through my head, causing it to ache, my trip to Yuan-ming Yuan already ruined before it had even begun. I would have to see Ningxin. Or, more accurately, she would have to see me. We were nearly the same rank, as we were both married to princes, but I slightly outranked her as the wife of the elder brother. But if Yixin was named Emperor Daoguang's heir and he became the next emperor, she would be the next empress, and no one, not even Empress Jing, would outrank her. How strange the empress's position would be then. An empress in name only. An empress dowager. I supposed that if Yixin were named emperor, he would still give his mother much respect and seek her counsel. Yizhu would probably not care much for what she had to say. Was the empress still trying to put Yixin on the throne? I rather thought she was. Mother had said that whoever I married would become the next emperor. But she probably thought I would fall pregnant before Prince Yixin was married. But Ningxin was married to Yixin only two weeks after my own marriage. Was it sheer luck that an auspicious day for their marriage arrived so quickly after their betrothal? I did not think so. The empress probably paid a fortuneteller to simply pick a day. It was not Yizhu and Yixin who were racing to the throne, but Ningxin and me. Was that why Yizhu was bedding me so often? I supposed it was. Was Yixin bedding Ningxin that often? I shuddered. I didn't want to think about it. I didn't even know what Ningxin looked like. I had never met her before, and she was veiled at the wedding ceremony. I would have to welcome her to Yuanming Yuan. Take tea with her. Make small talk with her. I didn't know how I was going to suffer through it.

How could I possibly show grace to the woman who married the man who should have been mine?

CHAPTER NINE

*T*he journey to the Summer Palace was not terribly long, only a few hours, but considering the number of people and the amount of luggage we took with us, you'd think we were moving permanently.

Since the imperial family went to the Summer Palace so rarely, we would make the trip worth it and stay for several weeks, so we had to take most of our servants with us, as well as the majority of our autumn wardrobes. I'd had one of my eunuchs change what little money I had into the smallest coins possible so I could toss them to the waiting crowds from my donkey cart as we proceeded through Peking. I wished I had more to give them, but until I received my next allowance, I was, for now, as poor as the people on the street. Well, that was not completely true. My food was already paid for, and I did not have to worry about losing my home. Still, if the emperor did not find more generosity within himself, I would have to find ways to earn money on my own in order to afford coal for the winter. I could embroider handkerchiefs or socks and ask my chief eunuch to sell them for me. I would have to wait until my next allowance, though, before I could buy the items I needed to do even that. I looked down at my feet and shook the little tassels at the ends of my shoes. They were my favorite pair, and I recalled Mother saying that she had purchased them from a young Manchu woman who had fallen on hard times. I wondered if we would all fall on hard times before the empire's debt was repaid to the foreigners.

When I finally climbed out of my donkey cart in front of my new residence at the Summer Palace, I instantly felt a sense of peace and joy that I had not felt in weeks. The sky here was far more clear and blue than in Peking, where the air seemed to be choked by the dust and fumes of a million people. Already, the children who had traveled with us—the emperor's younger children and some of their cousins—laughed and played, rolling around in the grass between the palaces.

Unlike the Forbidden City, which had been built on flat ground, the Summer Palace was built on a hill next to a large lake. I did not even make it inside my palace before I felt the call of the water and fresh air. While my servants unloaded my carts and unpacked my trunks, I wandered to the end of the walkway and looked down over the blue water of Kunming Lake. In the winter, the lake would freeze over so solidly, we could walk on it. But for now, in early autumn, it would be perfect for taking a leisurely boat ride.

Some rushes shook at the water's edge, and I watched as a fox slipped from the grass to the water to steal a drink. Its ears were pricked to attention, its eyes darting back and forth. The fur on its back stood straight as it lowered its head, taking only a few quick laps before raising its head again, checking for danger, and then daring a few sips more.

"What a beautiful view!"

I looked over as a young woman I didn't recognize walked up next to me and looked out at the lake, her voice so loud, I could hear it echoing off the hillside. I gaped at her, shocked that she did not introduce herself or even acknowledge me. I looked back to where the fox had been, but it must have been startled by the young woman's voice, for it was long gone.

"Ningxin!" Prince Yixin ran up next to us, his face flushed with embarrassment. "Please excuse her, Princess Zhenxiu. She is still learning her way about such things."

"It's quite alright," I said, even though it was very much not all right. Had poor Prince Yixin been saddled with a country bumpkin?

"Oh, a princess?" Ningxin said, her eyes wide. "Are you one of Yixin's sisters?"

I was already at about my wit's end with this girl. Was she intentionally being obtuse?

"No," was all I could find in me to say, looking at Yixin and noticing the lines of frustration across his forehead.

"This is Yizhu's wife. You must bow to her."

"Oh, of course," Ningxin said, giving me half the bow I deserved. "It is a pleasure to finally meet you, Sister."

"Likewise," I said, forcing a smile. "Have you ever been to The Summer Palace before?"

"No, never," she said, her smile so stretched across her face it must have been painful. "My father was the governor of Jiangxi Province. We only relocated to Peking last year. My father has been unwell."

Country bumpkin, indeed. "Then you are sure to enjoy your visit," I said. "Prince Yixin and I used to come here all the time as children."

"Yixin promised to show me everything," she said, wrapping her arms around the prince. He made a move to push her arms away, but she must have had him in a vice-like grip.

"Zhen!" Prince Yizhu called as he approached us, his limp seeming more pronounced than usual. Being jostled in a donkey cart could not have been good for his old injury.

"My lord," I said, bowing to him. Ningxin released Yixin and copied me. At least she was capable of learning.

"I went to see you in your palace, but you were not there."

"I was just admiring the view," I said. "And then I ran into my brother- and sister-in-law. You must remember Princess Ningxin from their wedding."

"Of course," Yizhu said. "A pleasure to see you again."

Ningxin giggled, and I was able to take a good long look at her. She was thin, terribly thin, with sunken cheeks and sharp cheekbones. Her skin was dark, and even darker under her eyes. I supposed she must have spent far too much time outside when she was a girl. She was certainly not what I would call pretty, and I wondered if Empress Jing had ever seen her before selecting her. With her unflattering looks and coarse manners, I once again found myself questioning why Empress Jing thought such a girl would make a fitting empress. After my talk with her the previous day, I felt that the empress still harbored hope that Prince Yixin would be named the emperor's heir should his wife succeed in bearing a son before me.

"Well, if you'll excuse us," Yixin said, gripping his wife's arm. "We have a lot of unpacking to do."

"Of course," I said. Yixin just gave a grunt and nod of acknowledgment.

"How could you embarrass me like that?" I heard Yixin hiss to his wife as they quickly walked away.

Yizhu snorted a laugh. "Obnoxious girl."

"She will learn," I said. I saw no reason to disparage her. She would do that well enough on her own.

"How are you feeling?" Yizhu asked. For a moment, I was touched that he would show such concern for me. But then I realized that he was really asking if I had stopped bleeding.

"Oh. I am very well, my lord."

"Good. Then let us go to your bedchamber. We cannot let my brother and his new mule get with child before us."

I followed Yizhu toward my palace, not at all excited at what was about to happen, but resigned to the necessity of it.

"Your Highness," a eunuch called as we approached the palace. "The emperor requests your presence."

Yizhu sighed in annoyance. "I will send for you tonight, Zhen."

"Of course, my lord." I did my best not to sigh in relief.

THAT NIGHT, all of Emperor Daoguang's family—his empress and favored consorts, their children, the emperor's sisters and their husbands and children, and myself and Princess Ningxin —as well as a select few councilors and their families who had all made the trip with us, gathered to have dinner together. It was a rare occurrence. Other than weddings and holidays, we never ate dinner together at the Forbidden City. It was a lively event with delicious food, joyous conversation, and lively musicians. The evening was tempered, though, by the emperor's appearance.

He appeared weak, entering the banquet room slowly. His skin was sallow and his eyes were rheumy. The emperor seemed to have aged many years since I had seen him only a few days before. Though no one could have failed to notice the emperor's condition, no one dared remark upon it. The emperor was surely receiving the best care, and we had come all this way for his health. He would surely feel stronger in a few days.

"The food is delicious, is it not, Sister?" Ningxin said. I had been, unfortunately, sat beside her at dinner. As was proper, the women sat on one side of the room, the men on the other.

Ningxin chatted to me endlessly about how wonderful the food was. Indeed, it was very good. Since we were all eating together, it was the emperor's cooks who prepared the food. And the emperor did not skimp on ingredients the way I had been forced to do. But by the way Princess Ningxin enthused, you would think this was her first time eating food at all.

"And are not the musicians delightful?" she asked me. "Oh, how I wish I could play an instrument."

"You cannot play?" I asked her, surprised. All young ladies of quality were taught to play an instrument, in my experience.

Ningxin giggled as if I had told a great joke. "No. I am afraid I don't have an ear for music. I tried for many years but could never move beyond the simplest of melodies."

"What skills do you possess?" I asked, more out of polite conversation than because I cared to know.

"Mother always said I would make an excellent lady-in-waiting since I enjoy talking so much."

I could not help but smirk at that. Ningxin's mother knew her daughter well.

"I heard you do not yet have a lady-in-waiting, Sister."

I felt my face flush hot and reached for a cup of water. I could not have this chatterbox as my lady-in-waiting. Her voice was like a porcelain bowl smashing on the floor.

"Have you found a lady-in-waiting?" I asked, turning the question around.

"I have several very fine maids," she said. "Though, two abruptly quit on me when within days of my arrival. Can you believe it?"

"That is very unfortunate," I said, though I could guess the reason why.

"Well, I brought it up because—"

I was saved by the empress clapping her hands to get everyone's attention. "The emperor has generously invited an opera troupe to entertain us," she said to many excited and appreciative gasps. "They will perform on the outdoor stage in the garden by the lake. We shall all go there now."

"Oh, I do love opera! Don't you, sister?" Ningxin said, gripping my hand tightly. "We must sit together."

"Of course," I said. "But please excuse me for a moment. I must relieve myself."

"That is a good idea. I should do that too. I'll meet you at the performance."

"Of course." I didn't really need to relieve myself. I only needed a break from my dear "sister." I decided to simply slip away for a few moments. I would show up at the opera a few minutes late and then claim I was unable to find her in the crowd.

I grabbed a baozi from the table and slipped outside. It was dark, but there were plenty of lanterns glowing to give one enough light to see by. I went to a nearby pond and tore off little pieces of bread, tossing them to the koi. The fish shimmered even in the low light. I let out a sigh and stretched my neck and shoulders, enjoying the few minutes of peace by myself. I had hardly been alone since I arrived in the Forbidden City. I almost always had at least a maid with me. Tonight, the servants were waiting with the many litters that would be used to carry us back to our palaces at the end of the evening.

"What are you doing out here?"

I practically jumped out of my skin at the sound of Prince Yixin's voice behind me. I stumbled to my feet and gave an awkward curtsey.

"Good evening, Your Highness," I said. "I was just taking a break from the crowd."

"From the crowd?" he asked, taking a seat on the bench. "Or from my wife?"

"I would never say anything so rude," I said, sitting on the bench but as far away from him as possible, which wasn't very far.

"Of course you wouldn't," he said with a sigh. "You're a lady."

I felt my face blush hotly. I hoped he couldn't tell in the darkness. "She is very friendly," I offered.

"She is…eager to please," Yixin said, holding his hand open to me. It took me a moment to realize he wanted a piece of baozi to feed the fish. At least, I thought he did. I tore off a piece of baozi and handed it to him. But when our hands touched, he closed his fingers around mine. His grip was not tight, yet I didn't pull away. I couldn't look up at his face. My eyes seemed frozen on our hands. My heart was racing, yet the world seemed to have stopped moving. I couldn't think. I couldn't speak.

"I received your letter," Yixin said, his voice low. It took me a moment to remember what he was talking about. It seemed that the night I sent him the letter telling him I was to marry his brother was a lifetime ago.

"I wondered if my cousin was successful in delivering it," I finally said.

The prince released my hand and tore off a bit of baozi, tossing it to the fish. "She was," he said, "but I already knew what had happened. I had rushed to the palace as soon as I heard about Princess Ayan. I had only gone to comfort my brother. I had no idea he would steal my own wife from me as a replacement."

My eyes watered. So, Yixin had wanted to marry me as much as I had wanted to many him. My affection for him was not one-sided.

"I fought for you, I swear it," he said, turning to face me. "I fought for us."

"I believe you," I said.

"I told our parents that an engagement was as good as a marriage. That you were my wife, not merely my betrothed. But Yizhu…" He grit his teeth and had to pause before he said something treasonous. "Once Yizhu put you as an option to our father, he would not be persuaded away. The old man would deny my brother nothing. He is Father's favored son."

"Don't talk like that," I said. "Your father loves you both. He cannot choose between you. Why else has he not named an heir? You could still be emperor."

"I don't think so," he said, tearing off another bit of bread for the fish.

"Why not? If you had a son—"

"I cannot have a son," he interrupted me.

"What do you mean? Princess Ningxin is surely willing and able."

"Princess Ningxin is not the problem. Well, she is, but not for the reasons you might think."

"What do you mean?"

"I...I cannot make love to her. Because every time I try, I only think about you."

I gasped, shocked at the bluntness of his words, but also flattered by them. I had wondered many times if making love to Yixin would be as unpleasant as making love to Yizhu. But at that moment, I didn't care. I would let Yixin do whatever he wanted to me, and I knew I would enjoy it. He leaned close to me, and I followed in kind.

I knew he wanted to kiss me. I knew I wanted to kiss him back. I also knew it was wrong. Yizhu would be furious if he ever found out. But I had to try. I had to know what it was like to kiss someone I loved.

His lips touched mine, and I almost wept at the tenderness of it. I scooted closer to him on the bench so he could kiss me more deeply if he wished.

But he never had the chance.

"Prince Yixin!" a voice called. The prince pulled away from me and leaped to his feet. I stood as well and moved closer to the koi pond, nearly losing my balance and falling in.

"My prince, there you are," the eunuch said when he found us.

"Yes?" Yixin asked. "What is it?"

"It's the emperor! He's collapsed!"

CHAPTER TEN

*E*veryone was gathered outside the emperor's room, but very few were granted access. Prince Yixin was permitted inside the room, but I was not. Out in the hall, the emperor's sisters and some of his consorts were sobbing as if the emperor were already dead. And perhaps he was. I had not been present when the emperor collapsed, so I did not know what had happened. I looked around for anyone who could tell me but only saw Princess Ningxin. Our eyes locked and she elbowed her way through the crowd toward me. I instantly felt guilty. While she had been waiting for me, while the emperor had possibly been taking his last breath, I had been kissing her husband. I needed to remain calm. I could not let the guilt show on my face. If I did, Yixin and I both could get in significant trouble. What was the penalty for being unfaithful to a prince? I didn't know because I had never heard of it happening before. At the very least, Yizhu could put me aside, send me back home to my parents in disgrace. I could not let that happen.

"Zhen!" Ningxin said, gripping my arm. "Where were you?"

"I wasn't feeling well," I said as we made our way out of the crowd to the edge of the room where we could hear each other better. "My stomach."

Ningxin nodded. "Maybe that is a good sign," she said.

"What do you mean?"

"Maybe the emperor just has a bit of food poisoning and will be perfectly fine in the morning."

I nodded. "We can hope. Where is Empress Jing?"

"She was the only woman admitted to the emperor's bedchamber. She was with him when he collapsed.

"She must have been greatly distraught," I said.

"Indeed. All the color drained from her face. I thought she was going to pass out as well."

"Is my husband with his father?"

"Yes," she said. "He was looking for you. I think he wanted you to go into the room with him."

Would Yizhu be angry that he could not find me? "I don't think I would have been permitted inside," I reasoned.

"There was nothing we could have done anyway," Ningxin said. "All we can do is pray for him."

"That is a good idea," I said. Ningxin and I got down on our knees and folded our hands, praying silently. Some of the other ladies caught sight of us and followed suit. A moment later, aside from a few sniffles, the room was quiet as all the ladies focused on their prayers.

I could not believe the emperor was so near to death. I thought he was old, in his late sixties, but before today, he always seemed to be a man of vital energy. His youngest son was only four years old. He had raided my closet only days ago. His oldest sons had only just gotten married. How could an emperor not live long enough to see his first grandson?

It then occurred to me that the emperor would have to name his heir. That was surely why Prince Yizhu had wanted me present. He wanted his father to see that he was ready and willing to follow in his footsteps. Not only was he, as this father's eldest son, prepared to be the next emperor, but his strong and beautiful wife was ready to be the next empress.

I didn't know how much time had passed when the door to the emperor's chambers finally opened. I was exhausted, near to falling over. It had been a very long day. We had gotten up earlier than usual to take the trip to the Summer Palace. After unpacking, having dinner, and then waiting for news of the emperor, it had to be very late, indeed. Yizhu and Yixin both left the room, as well as the emperor's councilors. The door quickly closed behind them. The councilors grabbed their wives and left the hall. The rest of the women gathered around the princes, begging for any news.

"The emperor is resting comfortably," Yizhu said. "You should all retire to your own palaces for the time being."

The emperor's sisters seemed relieved by this and eagerly left the room. The emperor's consorts, however, appeared less comforted and resumed their prayer vigil there on the floor. Yizhu paid them no mind as he came to my side to help me stand. I grunted in pain as I did so. I'd lost all feeling in my legs. I gripped tightly to the prince's arm as blood rushed to my head, making me dizzy.

"What is wrong?" Yizhu asked, his voice irritated as he tried to rush me from the room.

"Nothing," I said, looking over my shoulder as Yixin ushered his wife out a different door. "I have only been kneeling for hours."

"Get ready to do that for a hundred days more," Yizhu mumbled.

"What?" I nearly shrieked and then slapped my hand over my mouth. "You don't mean the emperor is—"

"No," Yizhu said, leading me to a small room and closing the door behind us. "Not yet, anyway."

"What do you mean?"

"He's not dead, but he is dying. He will probably be dead by morning."

I leaned against a table, shocked by this news. "I'm sorry," I told my husband.

"Why?" he asked me.

I wasn't sure how to respond to that at first. Shouldn't he be upset at the death of his father? I knew I would be.

"It…it cannot be easy to lose a parent," I finally said.

Yizhu scoffed. "You didn't have my father for a parent."

Again, I was at a loss for words. I didn't know how a son could be so calloused toward his father, but then again, I didn't know what their relationship was like. I had only met Emperor Daoguang a few times in my life, and I didn't much care for him. He had seemed very indifferent to me, except when he was chastising me for spending money, and then he had seemed downright cruel. I certainly wouldn't miss him when he was gone. But how sad it was that his own son felt the same way about him as a worthless daughter-in-law he barely knew?

"What will happen now?" I asked. "Has he named an heir?"

"He said that he that already named one."

I waited in suspense and finally stomped my foot in annoyance when an answer was not forthcoming. "Well? Who is it?"

"I don't know," Yizhu said. "He wouldn't say. He said the name of the heir was already written on a scroll and sealed in a box in his office back in the Forbidden City. He has ordered that the box be brought there, but he does not want it to be opened until after his death. He wants all his advisors and magistrates to be present when the scroll is read."

My mouth hung open as I tried to fathom why the emperor would do such a thing, but I could come up with nothing. "Why?" I finally asked.

Yizhu shook his head. "Even now, on his deathbed, he cannot relinquish an ounce of control. He wants to ensure Yixin and I bow and scrape at his side until he is gone. He doesn't trust us both to remain filial if we know who the heir is."

"I'm sorry," I said again, and this time, I meant it. "I'm sorry your father has pitted you and your brother against each other."

Yizhu looked at me for a moment, his eyes wide with surprise.

"When your father is gone, you and Yixin will still have each other." I thought back to what Empress Jing had told me, about noting who my husband's advisors were. Perhaps this was my chance to do just that. I had no idea who the emperor's advisors were, but I knew Prince Yixin. "You will never be able to trust anyone the way you will be able to trust your brother."

Yizhu smirked. "You speak as though I am emperor already."

"I will believe you are going to be the next emperor until I am told otherwise."

Even though I had not wanted to marry Yizhu, I did want to be the next empress. I would do whatever I could to help him succeed.

Yizhu sank onto a chair. "Growing up, I always thought I would be the person to succeed my father. At least, that was what my mother raised me to believe. But after her death, it was as if my whole view of the world changed. I suddenly saw just how lacking I was when compared to my brother. I have this cursed limp. He's taller than me. Stronger than me. Did you know I was born several weeks early?"

I shook my head.

"I was so small, everyone thought I was going to die. A maid even told my mother she should abandon me in the woods to make way for a stronger baby."

"That's terrible," I said, feeling sympathy for my husband for the first time since we were children. "But she didn't. Your mother must have loved you very much. She saw how strong you were. She knew you would succeed."

"Well, you know what would secure my succession?" he asked. I shook my head. "If you were to fall pregnant."

I could almost feel myself shrinking into nothing. "I'm sorry," I said. "You know I am not."

"Still, my father could pull through. If you get with child, we can ensure that I am named heir when he falls ill next time."

I nodded. I knew I could not change his mind. I stood and walked toward the door.

"Where are you going?" he asked, grabbing my hand.

"To my palace," I said. "To my bedchamber."

"Why?" he asked, pulling me into his arms. "We can do it right here."

I froze as he kissed my cheek, then the side of my neck. "But, my lord," I said, "anyone could walk in."

"That is what makes it exciting, right?" he asked. His tone was playful, but I certainly felt no excitement—only fear. The prince continued to kiss and grope me. There was no bed in the room, only tables and chairs. I did not relish the idea of making love on the hard floor, and I shuddered as I remembered the way he bent me over a table and took me. Was that his plan now?

My mind was frantic, trying to devise an excuse to force him to wait until we got to my bedchamber. I about fell to my knees and wept joyfully when I heard someone calling my husband's name. The prince grunted as he released me and opened the door.

"What?" he barked out into the hall.

I heard someone respond, but I could not hear what was being said.

"Fine," Yizhu told the messenger before turning to me. "Father has asked to see me. The scroll of succession has arrived."

Now, even more people were in the hall outside the emperor's bedchamber. News must have already been spreading that the emperor's health was poor. Many of the people were weeping profusely. Though I had never seen them before, I wondered briefly if their grief was performative, but then I remembered that the emperor was considered by many to be the father of his people. He was the Son of Heaven. The death of an emperor was considered to be not the death of a man, but the death of a god. Of course, I knew that such beliefs were nonsense. The emperor was just a man, and not a very kind man at that. How strange that the emperor would be mourned by strangers thousands of li away, but not by his own family.

Yizhu kept hold of my arm as he entered his father's bedchamber. This time, he would have me by his side. But as soon as we entered the room, I wished he had left me outside. The room smelled horrible, as if the emperor had been sick and no one had cleaned it up. Over that was the obnoxiously sweet smell of healing herbs. The doctors must have been giving the emperor every concoction they could think of with the hope of extending his life. The air was also thick with smoke from braziers that had been lit to give the room warmth and light. To one side of the room were several Buddhist priests, chanting and waving joss sticks. The room was a dizzying concoction of smoke, light, and smells, and over all of it was the incessant wailing of Princess Ningxin.

Ningxin and Yixin were already in the room when we arrived, and I could see that this greatly irritated my husband. It was clear that he did not want to miss anything that might be said to his brother. Though, how anyone could hear anything over Ningxin's crying was beyond me. Yixin was trying to comfort his wife, but I doubted she could hear him. I thought perhaps it was my duty as her sister-in-law to escort her from the room. I went to her side and put my arm around her shoulders.

"Sister," I said, "come away so the emperor may rest."

"No!" she cried. "I cannot leave him, my dear, dear father!"

"Please, do not be so loud," I hissed to her. "You will upset him."

Ningxin fell to her knees. "He must know the depth of my love for him!"

I turned to the princes and held my hands out helplessly. Yixin was rubbing the bridge of this nose while Yizhu was staring at her with such fury, she would surely whither if she caught his gaze. But she did not look at him, she did not look at anyone even though most of the room was staring at her. While there were tears seeping down the empress's face as she stood by the emperor's side, she was showing quiet dignity. Such keening was usually reserved for after a person died, not while they were still fighting for their life.

I saw one of the councilors lean over the emperor, and the emperor raised a shaky hand.

"The emperor wishes to speak!" the councilor announced. Everyone in the room went silent, even the priests, except Ningxin, who seemed to cry ever louder. Finally, it was Yizhu who could take no more. He stomped over to his sister-in-law.

"Stop screaming!" he ordered. "Your emperor wishes to speak."

Ningxin looked up at him, her whole face red and puffy. "My...my heart is br-br-breaking," she said through hiccups before wailing again.

"You," Prince Yizhu ordered, pointing at two guards, "take her to her palace and do not let her leave without her husband's permission."

The men bowed and then each of them took one of Ningxin's arms, dragging her away.

"No!" she screamed. "I will stop. I promise." And, indeed, it did seem that her crying for the emperor had miraculously ceased. Still, Yizhu would not be persuaded, and Yixin said nothing on behalf of his wife.

"No, please! Stop!" Ningxin fought against the guards so viciously, you would think they were dragging her away to be executed instead of to an opulent palace. She even kicked off her shoes, one flying across the room and the other hitting a servant in the stomach. The whole scene would have been comical if the emperor were not lying there dying. Finally, the princess was dragged out of the room and the door was shut.

"My sons. My sons," I could hear the emperor saying, though his voice was much weaker than it had been the last time he had spoken to me. Yizhu and Yixin both rushed to their father's side.

"I am here, Father," Yizhu said.

"We are all here," Yixin said, motioning for two of the emperor's consorts to bring the younger princes over. I noticed that the emperor's daughters were all absent.

Everyone stepped closer to hear what the emperor had to say.

"Bring the scroll," the emperor said. One of the councilors unlocked the box and pulled out the scroll. The scroll was quite large, as it was his complete will, not just the name of his heir. The councilor offered the scroll to the emperor, but he was too weak to break the wax seal. The councilor did the honors.

"It is my will," the councilor read aloud, "that my second son, Yixin..."

I watched my husband closely. His face did not move in the slightest, but I could see his eyes darken. Even though I had wanted Yixin to be the next emperor, I feared my husband might take his disappointment out on me. But as the councilor continued, he said words I did not expect.

"...Yixin, should serve his brother well. My eldest son, Yizhu, is my heir and successor."

The room was silent for a moment again. I don't think

anyone knew how to react, but my husband was joyous. I could see his eyes brimming with tears, and they certainly weren't tears of grief.

As for me, I was going to be empress! At least my marriage to Yizhu had put me right where I belonged. Empress Jing lowered her head. I had to think that she was disappointed.

"It was a difficult decision," the emperor said, his voice soft and rasping. "Heaven saw fit to bless me with two strong and capable sons."

The youngest boy, Prince Chun, who was only four years old, began to cry and fidget in his mother's arms. The emperor motioned for her to take the boy away.

"Yixin," the emperor said, "you are smart and people like you very much. But you are too willing to make sacrifices in the name of peace. The years ahead will be very difficult.

"Yizhu, you have what it takes to make tough decisions. This country will need a strong ruler. But I hope you both will find ways to work together. Yixin, your brother will need your support. Do not abandon him."

"I won't, Father. I promise," Yixin said, placing a hand on his brother's shoulder.

"Thank you for believing in me, Father," Yizhu said.

"I must rest," the emperor said with a sigh.

"You should all go," the councilor said.

I bowed and took my leave. I had no reason to stay.

"I will stay with him," Empress Jing said.

"As will I," Prince Yizhu said.

The councilor seemed annoyed, but he did not argue with them. I wondered what he had wanted to say to the emperor alone. Surely it did not matter now. The heir had been named. In a few hours, only Yizhu's words would matter. I paused at the door, wondering if Yizhu would want me to stay, but he did not even look in my direction.

As I left the emperor's chambers, I could see that the sun

was just starting to rise in the distance. There was no sense in going to bed now, but I was sure I would need a nap at some point. For now, my mind was swirling with thoughts and ideas. I was going to be the empress! But what did that really mean for me? How much of my life was going to change? How would I do things differently from Empress Jing? What would stay the same? Empress Jing had been very kind to me, and she had set an excellent example. I would still go to her for advice and guidance. I would have to make sure that when I moved into her palace, she was moved not too far away from me.

"Congratulations," a voice whispered behind me.

"Prince Yixin," I said, turning and seeing a pained smile on his face. "You do not need to say such words to me. I am sorry, both for the loss of your father and for being passed over as emperor."

"It was always a possibility," he said as we walked along an outer wall, overlooking the lake. "I think if he had chosen me, he would not have had the scroll opened until after he had died, so great the upset would be."

I was surprised at his candor, given the situation. But it seemed that neither son was close to his father. I would have to try and do better for Yizhu and his sons, as soon as sons came along.

"I think your father was right, saying that you should provide counsel for your brother. I only hope he listens to you."

"I will certainly do my best. But my brother is very stubborn. If he does not like what I have to say, he will not listen to me. What about you? Do you think you will have the new emperor's ear?"

I scoffed. "Certainly not. My husband is not the sort of man to listen to the voice of a woman. Besides, other than matters of the Inner Court, I don't know what I would speak to him about. I don't know anything about the world outside the palace."

"You could learn," Yixin said, stopping and leaning on the

wall. He reached into this boot and pulled out a long tobacco pipe, which he lit with a match.

"To what end?" I asked. "I might be empress, but I am still merely a wife."

"I don t know," Yixin said, puffing on his pipe thoughtfully. "I might need an ally who has my brother's attention."

"I don't know what you are talking about," I said, crossing my arms and turning away from him. I really didn't know what he was asking me to do, but I didn't like the sound of it.

"You know the empire has almost no money," Yixin went on. I nodded but did not reply. "Our father has the same advisors today as he did ten years ago when we lost the war. How much do you want to bet that Yizhu will continue listening to those same men?"

Still, I said nothing, but I thought about Empress Jing and what she told me about paying attention to my husband's advisors.

"So, you would advise your brother differently than those men? What makes you so sure your way of doing things will be better?"

"I don't. I only know that we have to try. If we keep doing things the same way, the Qing Dynasty will not last much longer."

I sighed and tapped my fingers on my crossed arms. All of this was beyond me. Other than owing large sums of money, I had no idea what problems our country or the Dragon Throne faced. How could I make things better for my husband besides ensuring he had a son and heir?

"We are both young. How can either of us possibly know what is right for a country that is thousands of years old? Have we not withstood the test of time?"

"Countries remain," he said, "but dynasties come and go."

"I don't know if you are right, but I do trust you," I said. "I will support you, but do not expect too much from me. I am only a woman."

He smiled at me, his eyes twinkling. "You and I would have made a good team, I think."

I licked my lower lip, remembering his very light kiss. How I wished we could have been so much more than brother and sister. But while I might have dared to kiss him when I was merely a princess, as the next empress, I could not take such a risk again.

"There is no point in thinking about what might have been," I said. "We have to accept the way things are."

Prince Yixin sighed and let out a groan. "So, I am stuck with Princess Ningxin, is that what you are saying?"

I laughed. "I think we all are."

"So, you will take her as your lady-in-waiting?"

"Heaven! Never!" I said, and we laughed together at poor Ningxin's expense while she was trapped in her palace.

A eunuch shuffled toward us, his head down. Then, to my surprise, he did not merely bow to us, but kneeled. Still, he said nothing. I looked at Yixin, but his face was pale.

"What is it?" I asked him.

"The servant can no longer speak to you unless you address him first."

"Why?" I asked. I then realized what this meant.

"Go ahead," I told the servant.

"The Daoguang Emperor is dead. You are now the empress."

CHAPTER ELEVEN

*T*he death of the emperor meant a period of profound mourning for the whole country. But what that meant for each person depended on their rank. The emperor's closest family—the new emperor, the new empress, and the new empress dowager—were the chief mourners, and as such, had the longest and most stringent mourning period of one hundred days. Everyone else was only required to mourn for twenty-seven days. But it also meant we were stuck in the Summer Palace for the foreseeable future. It was against Manchu tradition for a dead body to enter a walled city, so we would have to remain at the Summer Palace with the emperor's body until it was ready to be interred in the Mausoleum of Admiration, southwest of Peking.

Not that I minded staying at the Summer Palace. To me, the Summer Palace was more luxurious than the Forbidden City. It was certainly more comfortable. Even though we were facing winter, the palaces at the Summer Palace were smaller, which were easier and less costly to heat, and closer together, which meant less time out of doors when visiting people. Even though I was now the empress, little changed for me as long as we were here. I did not change palaces, nor did I yet hold morning audiences. All of the palace ladies were older than me, consorts of the Daoguang Emperor. It seemed strange that they should have to bow to me and seek daily blessings as though from a mother. I saw no reason to change how things were until the hundred days were over. Then, after the Daoguang Emperor was interred, Yizhu and I would be ceremonially recognized as the new emperor and empress. Then, Yizhu would be able to hold a selection for new consorts to fill his Inner Court. All of Emperor Daoguang's women would be sent to different palaces for retirement. I would then preside as the empress over the new Inner Court for the rest of our days. I had decades ahead of me to serve as empress; I had no need to rush things.

The same day Emperor Daoguang died, though, Yizhu came to my chambers. We immediately sent all my servants away.

"Can you believe it, Zhen?" he asked, running over and embracing me. "I am the emperor! Me!"

"I never doubted you would be, my lord," I said. "You are very much like your father."

"Exactly," he said. "He and I shared the same vision of the future. One in which China is once again the most powerful force in the East."

I was nervous, but I remembered my promise to Prince Yixin. "Will you... Will you keep the same advisors your father had?"

"Some," he said. "Some of the older men will retire, but I will only replace them with men with a similar vision and who I know will be loyal to me."

"And Prince Yixin?" I asked.

"Well, he is my brother," he said. "I will give him a new post because I have to. He will now be known as Prince Gong—a prince of the first rank. But that doesn't mean I will have to listen to him. He might as well be talking to a stone wall." He laughed.

"Of course," I said. "As emperor, you know the best counsel to keep. But your father seemed to think it was important that you heed what your brother has to say."

Prince Yizhu—or should I say, the emperor—looked at me, his mouth a frown. "You always did prefer him to me."

"What?" I said. "That is not true." *It was true.*

"When we were little, you always preferred his company to mine."

"That was so long ago. I hardly remember any of it." *I remembered all of it.*

"You were supposed to have been *his* wife."

I held my hands out helplessly. "I had no say in the matter."

"Were you distraught when you were ordered to marry me instead?"

"Of course not." *I was completely devastated.*

"Then why do you speak to me of him now?"

"I'm sorry if my words offended you. That was not my intention."

"What was your intention?"

"My lord…" I cleared my throat, stumbling over my words. I had warned Yixin that I would not be able to speak for him to his brother. Yizhu was far too cunning, and I was just a stupid girl.

"My lord," I tried again, "I was there as your father lay dying. He loved you both. He thought that China would be stronger if both of you worked together. That is all I want for you."

"You know what would make my reign stronger?" he asked, tugging at my gown. "If I had my own son and heir."

My stomach clenched and I felt sick. "But we are in mourning."

"So?" he said with a laugh, still tugging on my clothes.

"Marital relations are forbidden! Punishable by death." Honestly, a part of me hoped I would not have to share his bed again for some time. We were forbidden from being together during mourning. And then, we would have the consort selection. My husband would surely be so enthralled with all his new ladies, he would forget all about me. Of course, the law dictated that the emperor spend at least one night a month with his empress. But I could endure that. And it would not be sudden, but scheduled, so I could prepare myself—physically and mentally. I was shocked that something like that was even on my husband's mind right now, regardless of the consequences.

"And who would carry out such a ridiculous punishment?" he asked me. "I'm the emperor. I can do whatever I want. Besides, no one will know."

"If I fall pregnant, everyone will know."

"If you fall pregnant, everyone will be too busy celebrating my son to worry about when he was conceived."

"And if it is a daughter?"

Yizhu spit on the floor. "Never say such a terrible thing! Are you trying to curse me?"

"No, of course not. I'm sorry, my lord."

Yizhu took my hand and led me to the bed. "Good, now, hurry up. I have to finish planning my father's funeral."

I removed my clothes and lay on the bed with my eyes closed. I had expected him to take me quickly, but after a moment, he still had not climbed atop me. Suddenly, I felt something wet on my toes. My eyes shot open as I jerked my feet away from whatever had been touching them. I was shocked and dismayed to see that Yizhu had been suckling on my big toe. He gripped my ankle, preventing me from pulling away.

"What are you doing?" I shrieked.

"Is it not pleasurable?" he asked, running a finger along the top of my foot.

"No!" I said. "Stop it at once."

Yizhu looked at me, his face crestfallen, as though I had hurt his feelings. He let go of my foot and sat up on the edge of the bed, facing away from me.

"Wh-why?" I asked. "Does it please you?"

"Forget it," he said, getting up and leaving my room, slamming the door behind him.

As EMPEROR, it was no longer proper for Yizhu to come to my palace to make love. At first, he summoned me to this room every night after supper, though he seemed to take little joy in the act. He still achieved his pleasure, but that was all. He seemed to want to get the act over with as quickly as I usually did. Ever since he'd tried to…pleasure my feet, things were tense between us, awkward. But I did not know what to do about it. I did not know what to say, and he seemed to have no interest in speaking to me.

I was also no longer allowed to stay the night in his room after we made love. I had to return to my own quarters. This was a great improvement for me, as I no longer had to worry about him interrupting my day, and I was able to sleep soundly in my own bed at night. After my monthly visitor came again, though, I noticed that Yizhu sent for me less often. First, it was five times a week, then four, and then three. I started to wonder if he was displeased with me. I did not wish to visit his bed more often, but I did wish to fulfill my duty as a wife and empress.

One evening, I was summoned to his room, but I did not find him ready for me. He was still working, writing away furiously at his desk. He did not even acknowledge me when I entered the room. I sat on the bed for a few minutes, but when he still did not acknowledge me, I decided to speak up.

"My lord?" I said, standing across from him in front of his desk.

"Hmm?" He did not stop writing or look up at me.

"Would you like me to go?" I asked

"No," he said.

I remained standing there for several more minutes.

"You just seem very busy," I said. "I do not wish to disturb you while you are working."

Yizhu finally put his writing brush down and rubbed his eyes. "I am sorry to keep you waiting, but I must write this edict when I am alone, and this is the only time I am not surrounded by men, all giving me their opinions."

"What is the edict?" I asked, more to make conversation than because I was interested.

"I do not want your opinion," he said sternly.

I gave a laugh. "I am sure I would not understand it. I only wished to be an ear to listen if it would ease your mind."

"I am demoting the imperial commissioner, the man who signed the Treaty of Nanking. He is the one who put us into such great debt to the foreigners, allowed their holy men into our country, and lost us Hong Kong." He practically spat out every word as though they were sour on his tongue.

"All to end the war?" I asked.

"To appease the foreigners," he said through gritted teeth. "All at the expense of our country. "

I did not know why I felt compelled to protect this man. I did not even know his name. I supposed I felt pity for anyone at the receiving end of my husband's anger.

"Hong Kong is merely a fishing village, is it not?" I asked.

"But it is *my* fishing village. They have no right to take it."

"And just because foreigners are allowed to share their beliefs, that does not mean people will listen. Surely our people are smarter than that."

He shook his head and scoffed. "You are a little fool, do you know that?"

I would have agreed that I was ignorant about the issues facing my husband, but his words still stung. "I am sorry," I said.

Yizhu stood up and walked around his desk toward me. "A rebellion has broken out in the south, and it has spread like fire. The leader claims he is the brother of Jesus Christ. Do you know who that is?" I shook my head. "He is the son of the foreigners' god."

Yizhu was speaking seriously, and I think he meant to be intimidating, but I could not control myself and burst out laughing. "What? He thinks he is the son of a foreign god? Born here?" I put my hand to my mouth to try and calm my laughter, but it was so ridiculous, I could not control myself.

Yizhu seemed shocked at my reaction. At first, I was afraid I had angered him, but soon, he laughed too.

"Come to bed," I said. "Don't worry yourself over much about such things."

"I wish my life were as easy as yours," he said. "That I could laugh and forget about such things. But I cannot. Stupid as it may be, people believe this rebel. More people join him every day. And he is not the only one. Rebellions are breaking out in the west as well. I believe most, if not all, of these rebellions are being stoked by the foreigners who have been let into this country.

"First, I am going to get rid of everyone who had a hand in supporting the foreigners' cause here in this country during my father's reign. Then, I am going to stomp out the rebellions, one by one."

"What about your brother?" I asked. "What does Prince Yixin think?"

"Prince Yixin is lucky he is my brother, or he would be first demoted."

This alarmed me, but I tried not to show it on my face.

"I will be sending my dear brother west, to fight the rebels. If we are lucky, he won't come back."

"You cannot mean that," I finally said, unable to hold back. "You love your brother, and he is loyal to you."

"Maybe," he said, taking my hand. "But right now, I need to surround myself with people I can trust. Can I trust you?"

I almost laughed again at such a question, but I saw only sincerity in his eyes. I suddenly felt guilty for agreeing to help Yixin. Why did I even do it? I knew nothing of politics or foreigners. I had no idea who was right or who was wrong. My only needed to support my husband.

"Of course," I said. "Have I upset you in some way?"

He pushed my hair behind my ear. "Why would you think that?"

I gulped. "Well, because you have not been sending for me as often. I was worried I might have displeased you."

"You have not displeased me," he said. "If anything, you are the one thing in my life that has remained constant."

"What do you mean?"

"I think you might have been the only person who wasn't surprised I was selected as my father's heir. I think many people had been courting Prince Yixin's favor in anticipation of him being the next emperor. Suddenly, everyone has time for me and needs favors. Men who hardly ever even spoke to me when I was only a prince."

"Maybe they were only surprised at the suddenness of the emperor's death. They didn't realize they needed to be courting your favor while you were still so young."

Yizhu smirked. "You are far too kindhearted. You think the best of everyone. But that is why women cannot be emperors. You don't have the stomach to make hard choices."

"I'm sure you are right," I said. After all, I had no desire to rule. I only wanted to help my husband and be the mother to the next heir. "Come to bed." I tugged on his hand so he would follow me. When we made love that night, he was almost tender. He was not nearly as rushed as usual, nor did he cause me as much pain. I still did not feel pleasure in it, but I wondered if one day I might.

Dear Cousin,

I have heard of the death of the Daoguang Emperor and wanted to send my condolences on your loss. I am sure the whole of your family is deep in mourning. Even here in Mongolia, all of us kneeled before a giant portrait of the emperor and kowtowed from dawn until dusk.

We have also been informed that the late emperor named Yizhu as his heir just before his death. Despite the great sadness at losing the emperor, I know that the future of China will be strong with such a man as Yizhu on the throne, and you by his side as our new empress.

Much love,

Feiya

CHAPTER TWELVE

$\mathscr{F}$inally, we were heading back to Peking. The emperor had been laid to rest in the Mausoleum of Admiration alongside his own father. His empresses who had died before him were disinterred from where they had been buried in the Eastern Mausoleums and reinterred alongside their husband. Only women who preceded their husband in death would be buried with him. Empress Jing, who was still alive, would be buried in the Eastern Mausoleum, and that was where she would stay for eternity. My husband posthumously appointed his own mother as an empress and had her interred with his father as well. This was one of the many symbolic ways my husband demonstrated his place as emperor to the people.

There were still rebellions breaking out around the country, including the south, where the Taiping rebels, as I found out they were called, continued to spread. Since their leader said he was the son of a god, many foolish peasants thought he was the Son of Heaven, in direct opposition to the emperor. Thus, my husband took every opportunity to demonstrate his authority over the people.

When we left the mausoleum and arrived in Peking, we held

a grand ceremony, officially appointing Yizhu as the Xianfeng Emperor—the Emperor of Universal Prosperity. I was given the name Empress Xiaozhenxian, which meant "faithful to the memory of one's husband." The implication was that even if my husband preceded me in death, I would never remarry. As was only proper. I did not know a single woman who had remarried after her husband's death.

I had wanted to arrange a consort selection for my husband as soon as we entered the Forbidden City. I had been married for three months and had not yet fallen pregnant. While I had once looked forward to my monthly visitor because it meant that Yizhu would not take me to his bed for a week, I now dreaded it. Every month it came was another month I had failed my husband, my emperor, and my country. Though, it was not my fault that my husband called me to his bed so infrequently. He would send for me once a week, if I were lucky. And even then, he usually achieved his pleasure quickly, after only a few minutes, and then sent me on my way. He rarely spoke to me anymore. He was always busy, always in a hurry, always needed elsewhere. Even though he did not say it, I knew I had disappointed him. So, the sooner I could fill the Inner Court with beautiful consorts and concubines for him, the sooner he would have a son with one of them and then, perhaps, he would be happy with me again.

"We cannot have a consort selection right now," Yizhu told me when I brought up the topic after we had been in the Forbidden City for a few weeks.

"Why not?" I asked.

"We cannot afford it."

I scoffed, which I immediately regretted. But I did not know how it could be so. Even though I was now the empress and received a higher allowance than as a princess, it was not nearly as much as it should have been. I should have had ten maids, but I only had four. None of us were eating meat since butchering had been banned during the mourning period for Emperor Daoguang. We had lived at the much more affordable Summer Palace for four months. With all these cost-saving measures, how could we not have enough money for more consorts for the emperor?

"That was why I came to see you today," Yizhu said as he paced my sitting room. "I need all of your gold jewelry and ornaments."

"What?" I asked, horrified. I had not even received my empress's jewels yet. They were still in the possession of Empress Dowager Jing. Any gold jewelry I had was gifted to me by my parents.

"I need you to collect all the gold jewelry from my father's consorts as well."

"Me?"

"You are the empress," he said. "You are the head of the Inner Court, not that other woman. It is you who will carry out my orders."

I did not realize until then how much my husband detested his stepmother. I knew he did not love her, but I thought he still respected her. To hear him speak now, I almost thought he despised her.

"Yes, my lord," I said. "Of course. But...all of it? All the gold jewelry? Will we get it back? What is to become of it?"

The emperor shook his head. "It will be melted down and turned into taels."

"But why? Where will the money go? To the foreigners?" All these money-saving measures were to pay the debts we owed the foreigners. Were we still paying that despite the many sacrifices we'd made?

"It is to pay for the army. Mounting a war is expensive."

"We are at war?" I asked, alarmed.

"It feels that way sometimes. I am assaulted on all sides, even in my own court."

"I am sorry to hear that," I said. "Surely all anyone wants is peace."

"Peace is not profitable enough for some people. I have sent for someone, Viceroy Ye, from Canton. He hates the foreigners as much as I do. He will help me put them in their place."

"I hope it will work out as you wish, my lord."

"I'm sure it will. Prince Yixin's mourning period for our father is at an end. I will send him west into battle soon."

"But...will he be safe?"

Yizhu laughed at me. "Do you not know what a battle is?"

"Of course. I only meant that you lost your father so recently. I am sure you would be devastated if you lost your brother too."

The emperor walked over and cupped my cheek. "You are a kind girl and a good wife, always looking out for my best interests."

"Of course, my lord," I said.

He walked toward the door. "But right now, what I need from you is money. Collect the gold, and be quick about it."

"Yes, my lord," I said. I handed my maid a basket as we went into my dressing room. I did not have much gold, only a few necklaces, some earrings, and a few hairpins. I mostly had items carved out of jade or embellished with precious stones. I knew the emperor would be disappointed to learn I had so little to contribute to his cause. But the empire had been facing a financial crisis even before I entered the Forbidden City, so I had never received much gold.

I went to see Empress Dowager Jing. Of all the women in the Inner Court, she would have the most gold. A eunuch announced my arrival at Empress Dowager Jing's palace, which would one day be my palace. I did not have the heart to kick her out just yet. In truth, I had hoped she would volunteer to leave, since she knew it was the right thing to do. But she had not done so yet.

When I entered Empress Dowager Jing's palace, she curtsied to me, but not as low as she should have. I overlooked it.

"Daughter," she said, "how kind of you to visit me. Shall I send for tea?"

"There is no need, Mother," I said. "I am here on business for my husband. He has asked that all members of the Inner Court donate their gold jewelry to help support the many battles he is fighting to keep us safe."

Empress Dowager Jing chuckled and took a seat. "Yes, I heard that the imperial treasury was already running low thanks to that spendthrift."

My mouth dropped open at her words. I could not believe she would say such a thing, no matter what she thought. And to me! The empress and wife of the man she was disparaging. I cleared my throat and regained my composure.

"Retaining an army is expensive. We must all do our part. Please." I motioned my maid forward with her measly basket of gold. "My maid will help you collect the gold."

The empress dowager made no move to get up. She only stared at me. I did not know what else to say. I had conveyed a direct order from the emperor. Why was she acting so defiant toward me? I had hoped that she would help me, not fight me.

"Please, Mother," I said. "The emperor commands it."

The empress dowager sighed and reached up to remove her earrings, which she tossed into the basket. I waited, but she made no movement to remove the large necklace she wore, the many rings, or the long nail guards on her fingers.

"Prince Yixin believes there are many cheaper and easier ways to end the rebellions," she finally said.

"Like what?" I asked.

"The people out west have been suffering from a drought. They don't want war. They want food."

"I am sure that the emperor is dealing with this problem the best way he knows how," I said.

The empress dowager scoffed. "Is he sending relief?"

"He is sending Prince Yixin."

Now, it was my mother-in-law's turn to gape. "What? That cannot be."

"The emperor told me so himself. Now that the prince's mourning is ending, he will be sent to lead the western armies."

"I don t believe you!" she said, jumping to her feet. "I will ask him myself." She stomped past me without asking for leave, but I let her go. I took my maid to Empress Dowager Jing's wardrobe and raided her jewelry store myself. As I suspected, the empress had amassed a great collection of jewelry during her thirty years in the Forbidden City. I took only the gold and still managed to fill my basket halfway. As I was leaving the palace, I saw her being carried back to the palace by half a dozen eunuchs. It appeared that she had fainted. I supposed my husband must have put her in her place, which brought me more than a little joy.

As I visited the other ladies of the Inner Court, they gave up their gold jewelry with much less fuss than the empress dowager had. By the end of the day, my basket was full of gold.

Prince Yixin had once remarked how he and I would have made a good team. But now, I wondered if it were Yizhu and I who had made the team we were meant to make.

CHAPTER THIRTEEN

or the first time in my life, I stood in front of the Dragon Throne. The emperor had several audience halls, which he would use depending on the occasion. I had only ever seen emperors—my husband and his father before him—in the smaller audience halls where the tea ceremonies were held for marriages.

The Dragon Throne sat on a dais three levels high. It stood alone, as no empress or councilor was equal to the emperor. Above the throne hung a great brass dragon that held a large pearl in its mouth. Legend stated that if a usurper ever sat on the Dragon Throne, the guardian dragon would drop the pearl, crushing the usurper. I wasn't sure I believed it, but I would not want to challenge Heaven by sitting on the throne. I could have, though, since I was alone in the massive room.

I had never been summoned here before, but my husband had requested my presence for some reason. I had arrived early so I could take in the full grandeur of the room in private. It was unlike any other room in the Forbidden City. A red carpet ran from the Dragon Throne, down the steps of the dais, and all the way to the doors. The entire ceiling was painted with auspicious animals, such as dragons, monkeys, rats, and tigers. Windows lined each wall and, since it was spring and the air was light, the shutters had been opened, letting a cool breeze freshen the room. Standing in such a grand space made me feel important and truly fortunate. I could only imagine how powerful it must have made a man feel to sit on the Dragon Throne itself, many feet over the heads of everyone else.

The two main doors to the room opened, and dozens of men—councilors, grandees, princes—filed into the room. The emperor's chief eunuch saw me and directed me to stand beside the dais. The empress dowager entered as well and stood next to me, along with two of the emperor's sisters. We had all been instructed to wear our most formal garments. For me, that meant wearing a gown of imperial yellow embroidered with a flying phoenix.

"Do you know why we have been summoned?" I asked Empress Dowager Jing. I had never been summoned to a formal audience before, so I wondered why today was different.

"I heard that Prince Yixin has returned," she said, barely containing her excitement at seeing her son. "But that is all I know."

I nodded, but it did not really answer my question. I was glad that Prince Yixin had safely returned from fighting the rebellions out west, but why we had been asked to attend the audience for his return was still unclear to me.

"The emperor has arrived!" a eunuch announced. All the men kowtowed as my husband entered the room through the main doors while all of us ladies bowed. Once the emperor was seated on the throne, we were allowed to rise, but we could not look directly at the emperor, which was a pity. I would have liked to have been allowed to fully appreciate my husband at the height of his power.

"Bring in the prince," the emperor announced. Everyone looked toward the doors again.

"The Xianfeng Emperor is now admitting Prince Yixin," a eunuch announced. "Prince Gong of the First Rank, son of the Daoguang Emperor, Wielder of the White Rainbow Sword, Minister of the Grand Council, Banner Commander, Right Director of the Imperial Clan Court, and Head of the Imperial Clan Court."

As Prince Yixin entered the room, everyone bowed to him nearly as low as they would toward the emperor. He looked incredibly handsome in his military attire. Even though he had only been gone a few months, he seemed older, more mature, his body stronger. He held his head up and I thought he was suppressing a smile. The prince had not only returned to us alive, but victorious, and he was proud.

Behind him, the prince was leading four men in chains. They were filthy, their hair matted, and their clothes little more than rags. They wore no shoes, and their feet were covered with bloody blisters. I wondered if the men had been forced to walk all the way from wherever they had been apprehended.

"My Lord Emperor," Prince Yixin said, his voice loud and clear. "I have successfully put down two peasant rebellions against your illustrious name. As requested, I have brought back some of their leaders in chains to do with as you will."

The rebels were pushed forward, and all four of them fell to their knees and kowtowed before the emperor.

"You have done well, Prince Yixin," the emperor said. Then he addressed the rebels. "Well, what do you have to say for yourselves?"

The men only cowered, saying nothing.

"Speak!" the emperor yelled, even making me jump.

"Y-Your Majesty," one of the men said, raising his face from the floor but keeping his eyes downcast. "We humbly apologize for our foolish acts against you and throw ourselves upon your mercy.

"You ask for mercy?" the emperor said. "You led thousands of men in revolt against me and my name."

"Only hundreds," the man said. "A few inconsequential villagers."

"It may have started out that way," Prince Yixin said, "but by the time I arrived, half the province had taken up arms against us."

"Farming tools," the man said, and I noticed he was no longer shaking. He seemed to be growing in strength. "Where would people like us get weapons?"

"Still, you killed several provincial-level officials, did you not?" the emperor said.

"Because he would not open the food stores even though we were starving. Our families. Our children."

"You were given relief supplies," Prince Yixin said.

"Only after the deaths had already reached into the hundreds," the man said. "Only after my whole family was dead!"

"You did not only demand food," the emperor said. "You claimed the drought was divine will. That it showed Heaven was displeased with me, your emperor."

The man hesitated. "You are the Son of Heaven. If Heaven does not provide for us, is it not because you have displeased the gods?"

Prince Yixin stepped forward and kicked the man in the back. "Watch your mouth, you worthless dog!"

The emperor held out his arms. "Look around you. Do you think Heaven is displeased with me?"

I suddenly realized why we ladies were present. This was all a show, a demonstration of the emperor's wealth and power. But why my husband felt the need to flaunt his wealth to people who were so poor they were starving was beyond me.

"What good is it for Heaven to rain down gold if we die of thirst?" the rebel said, and his words touched me. I thought about all the gold I had collected from the palace ladies, how that money was used to clothe, arm, and feed soldiers when it could have been used to feed and clothe children.

"Isn't it true that you accepted food from Christian missionaries?" the emperor asked.

"I did, such was my desperation," the man said.

"Isn't it also true that these missionaries say that I am not the Son of Heaven? That praying to the ancestors was heresy? That you should only bow to their God?"

"I do not know what all they teach," the man said. "I only know that they offered me rice and I took it."

"Is it not true," the emperor went on, "that when you entered new villages, you slaughtered men who refused to take down their ancestor tablets?"

Everyone in the room, even I, gasped at this accusation. The man's head dropped.

"I thought that if I pleased the foreign God, he would make it rain."

I shook my head. The man had done wrong, truly, but how could I do anything but pity him? He had lost so much and was clearly acting out of desperation.

"All of you spoke out against me, your emperor. All of you are guilty of treason. Therefore, all of you shall be sentenced to death by a thousand cuts."

The prisoners cried out, one fainting, while the emperor, his guests, the councilors, and the grandees, cheered. The ladies were mostly silent aside from clapping, but I felt nauseous. Death by a thousand cuts was the most brutal and barbaric form of execution. I had heard of it, of course, but I did not think it had been used in my lifetime. I thought it was a thing of the past.

The emperor stood up. "The sentence is to be carried out immediately."

The men were dragged out of the audience hall by their chains. It seemed that they no longer had the strength to stand.

"Let this serve as a warning to all those in my realm," the emperor said. "Anyone found guilty of treason—by revolt or mere words—whether they be Chinese or foreigner, will face the ultimate punishment."

The men in the room cheered again, and many of them began filing out of the room. I could hear the prisoners screaming as their punishment was carried out, right there in front of the emperor's throne room. I was glad that there were other exits from the building because I could not stomach seeing such actions carried out.

The emperor climbed down the stairs of the dais and went to his brother. The two clasped arms in greeting.

"Welcome back, brother," my husband said to Prince Yixin.

"It is good to be back," the prince replied. He then looked at me, giving a bow. "Sister."

I stepped forward, standing next to my husband. "We are grateful for your safe return," I said.

"We will have a grand feast tonight in your honor," the emperor said.

I usually looked forward to celebratory banquets, but as the men continued to scream in pain outside, I did not think I would have the stomach for it.

"Thank you," the prince said.

"You will have to bring your lovely wife," I said. "I am surprised she was not here to greet you."

"I am sorry to say that she will not be able to come," he said.

"Is she unwell?" I asked.

"She is in confinement," he said. "She is with child."

"Oh," I said, my voice shaking, afraid I was now truly going to vomit.

"I'm sorry," I said.

The prince let out a small, awkward laugh. "Excuse me?"

"I mean, I'm sorry that I didn't know," I said. "No one had told me."

"She only told me last night when I returned home. She, apparently, didn't want me to read about it in a letter, so she had kept the news quiet. It was quite a surprise to come home to."

"I'm sure it was," the emperor said, but some of the warmth had left his voice. "Congratulations."

"Yes, congratulations," I said.

"Thank you both. If you'll excuse me, I need to see my mother. She will be delighted by the news as well."

"Of course," I said, standing by and watching him go to the empress dowager. She hugged him tightly and then led him away, probably to her palace to ply him with tea and cakes.

"How is that worthless cow pregnant and you are not?" the emperor growled at me, gripping my arm tightly. I looked at him and saw his hard, glaring eyes.

"I'm sorry," I said. "Have I not been available to you at every opportunity?"

The emperor let out an annoyed sigh. "Yes, I suppose you have. I'm sure it is not your fault."

"I am just as disappointed as you are, I assure you," I said.

"I think it is time we held a selection for new consorts," he said.

"Really?" I asked, growing excited. "Are you sure? Can the throne afford it?"

"Since Yixin was able to put down some of the uprisings, we can redirect a portion of the military funds back to the court."

"There are still more uprisings?" I asked.

"The rebellion in the south, the Taiping, still rages," he said. "But after this demonstration—" he said, walking toward the open door where the screams had died down. "Hopefully, the rebels will see the folly in their ways and back down."

I hoped he was right. I did not wish for anyone else to suffer in such a horrific way.

"Make all the arrangements," the emperor said. "Fill the Inner Court with beautiful maids and, hopefully soon, plenty of healthy sons."

"Yes, Your Majesty, of course. I am anxious to get started."

The emperor smiled and kissed me on the cheek before leaving through the main doors, perhaps anxious to see the work of his executioners. I left through a side door, excited to make the arrangements for the consort selection. Finally, I would be able to fill the Inner Court with ladies my own age. I would one longer be lonely. I would no longer have to satisfy my husband's lusts alone. I would finally be a proper empress, overseeing a family of ladies of my choosing. And then soon, very soon, children would come.

And whether I gave birth or not, I would finally be a mother.

CHAPTER FOURTEEN

inally, the day had come! I had set the date. I had made sure announcements were sent out to all the best families in the country and that signs were posted. I had made sure to hire enough new maids and eunuchs. I had made arrangements with the Ministry of Household Affairs regarding how many women would be selected, where they would live, and what their cash, food, and silk allowances would be. I set the framework for how each family would be compensated, depending on their rank. I had handled almost every aspect of selecting new consorts and concubines for my husband.

"Stand aside, dear," Empress Dowager Jing said to me as we waited in the dim light of early morning for the arrival of the candidates.

"Excuse me?" I said in surprise. Until then, Empress Dowager Jing had shown no interest in the consort selection. But now that the time had come, she was asking me to stand to the side, as if I were not the empress but only one of her maids.

"I have been part of several consort selections, including your own," she said sweetly. "This is only your first time. Yizhu is so young, you will probably oversee a dozen consort selections by the end. Why don't you stand back and see how it is done this time?"

Of course, she was right. I had only been part of my own consort selection, and that had been a very small and short affair compared to what we were now facing. At least a thousand young women were lining up in the square in front of the Hall of Supreme Harmony. It was a daunting task that would take several days. Of course Empress Dowager Jing's experience would be very useful, and I valued her input. But I had been looking forward to this day for months. I knew the process and had worked with several departments within the Forbidden City to ensure it would succeed.

More than that, I knew my husband. I knew what he liked and what sorts of women would please him. Yizhu had never liked small, young girls like Ayan. He naturally liked girls who were humble and demure, but he also liked them to be more mature in years and more confident in their bearing. He would not like girls who were frightened and would shrink away from his touch. My husband was quite rough and demanding in the bedchamber. He would need girls who were willing and eager for his advances. While I would have no way of knowing how the girls would act in his bed, I could at least find young ladies with more eager and outgoing personalities. But I did not know if Empress Dowager Jing would be looking for the same qualities in candidates that Yizhu and I would be. After all, Empress Dowager Jing had selected Ayan and Ningxin as consorts for her sons, both completely unsuitable women for their positions, in my opinion. I did not know why she had selected them or to what end, and I wasn't sure I trusted her judgment now. But what could I do? What could I say? I was the empress, but I had to show respect to my mother-in-law.

"I appreciate your help, Mother," I said. "But I believe it is my place to stand here, next to the emperor. Perhaps you can stand to one side so that there is no confusion."

The empress dowager stood still, staring ahead as if she had not heard me. But that was impossible. I knew my voice had been quite clear.

"The emperor approaches!" a eunuch announced. Still, the empress dowager did not move. I did not know what to do. I could not force her aside. I took a calming breath and stood on her other side, opposite from the emperor. When Yizhu took his place, he raised an eyebrow at me quizzically, but I did not respond. I pretended everything was going according to plan.

When we were ready, musicians played drums and cymbals and the large doors of the Hall of Supreme Harmony were opened. We stepped forward and were greeted by a thousand voices. "May the emperor and empress live for ten thousand years!" I could not help but smile as I looked down on a sea of silk in every color.

We walked down the flight of stairs, the empress dowager and I assisted by our maids. I started on the west side, the empress dowager went down the middle, and the emperor went down the east side. It was a beautiful early summer day. In the Inner Court, where there were ample trees, the day was sunny but comfortable. But here, in the large stone square, the sun beat down. A maid followed beside me, carrying an umbrella high to shade my face. I was also followed by a eunuch who would take notes, answer questions, and collect cards from the girls I selected to move to the next stage of the selection process. While the girls did their best to remain elegantly poised, some did not fare well under the sun. Any girl who sweated profusely, I dismissed. Any girl who appeared younger than her fourteen years, I dismissed. Any girl who was not smiling, I dismissed. If I asked a young lady a question and she was too nervous to answer, she was dismissed.

At the end of the first day, I noticed I had dismissed far

more girls than the emperor or empress dowager had. I wondered if I had been too harsh in my selection process. But in the end, only thirteen out of nearly a thousand girls would be chosen. Day by day, the process would grow increasingly stringent. There was no reason not to be as strict as I liked from the beginning.

The emperor, empress dowager, and I were not involved in the process for the following two days as the girls underwent physical examinations. Their hands, feet, and bodies would be checked for any marks or disfigurements. Then they would be inspected by doctors to make sure they were free of diseases and were, in fact, virgins.

When the three of us next gathered to observe the girls, fewer than two hundred were left. It was abundantly clear to me which ladies from the first day had been approved by the empress dowager. She had chosen only the youngest, smallest, and most humble-looking girls. Girls I did not think would enjoy my husband's attentions nor bring him pleasure. We were supposed to listen to the women speak and observe how they walked and moved. An imperial consort should have a pleasant voice and an elegant bearing. But it was clear that the empress dowager and I had different ideas about what those qualities looked like.

Of course, any girl who the emperor praised was asked to stay, but any girl I praised, the empress dowager quickly found flaws with and sent home. After a while, it seemed that my presence was doing more harm than good, as many elegant ladies who I thought would make excellent companions for my husband were dismissed. I excused myself and went for a walk. I sat on a bench along the side of the building and closed my eyes, praying for calm and remembering my Confucian teachings. No matter how much in error I thought my mother-in-law was, it was my duty to show her honor and respect. She was much older and wiser than me. Perhaps she saw qualities in the young ladies I did not. I needed to be patient. After all, she was right that I would surely oversee many more consort selections in my life. Most emperors held a consort selection every decade.

"Your shoes are quite beautiful," a voice said. I opened my eyes and saw a young woman who looked about my age kneeling in front of me. I looked down and shook the tassels hanging from my toes.

"Thank you," I said. "They are my favorite pair."

"Really?" the woman said, her face beaming. "I made them!"

I looked from her to my shoes and back to her again. "Are you sure? How can you tell?"

She rose and sat next to me on the bench. "See the eyes on the phoenix feathers? I always put a little star in the very center. See?"

I took one of the shoes off and examined the embroidery closely. She was right. In the very center of every eye was a small collection of yellow thread. It was so delicate, you would miss it if you didn't know it was there, as I had done many times. But once you knew to look for them, the stars were obvious.

"That is quite lovely," I said, putting the shoe back on. "You are very talented."

"You are too kind, Your Majesty," she said.

"My mother bought these as part of my dowry. She said your family had fallen on hard times."

The young woman nodded. "The emperor said my great-grandfather had stolen money from the throne when he had served as an imperial keeper of the silver reserve. I don't know if that was true or not. He's long dead, after all. But my family was ordered to pay back the money. So, I did embroidery work to help raise money."

"It is amazing that you were able to work to support your family," I said. "That is quite enterprising of you."

"Thank you for saying so," she replied. "We lost many friends when our fortunes changed. If I am chosen as one of the emperor's consorts, I hope he will forgive the remainder of the debt."

This young woman continued to surprise me. She was hardworking, open, and honest. She loved her family and would do anything to help them. She was smart. She was also beautiful. She had full, red lips and her eyes were so deep, I felt I could get lost in them. I knew that she would be an excellent companion for my husband. And I had a feeling we would get on well as friends. I had to find a way to help her advance in the selection process.

"What is your name?" I asked her.

"Lanhua, of the Nala clan."

"May I have your card?" She handed it over gladly. Each young lady had received a leather card with her information stamped on it. They were given their cards each morning, and as they passed to the next stage of the selection process, their cards were collected.

"You do not need to present yourself to the emperor and empress dowager today, Lanhua of the Nala clan. You have made it through this round. I will see to it."

"Really?" she asked. "Oh! Your Majesty!" She dropped down and performed a kowtow to me. It was not required of her during this process, as it was necessary to see her face, but also, it was a very difficult task to perform in such high pot-bottom shoes and with such a large headdress. But Lanhua performed the action with ease, such was her poise. One more way she was able to impress me.

"It is my pleasure," I told her, indicating she could stand. "Please, enjoy the rest of your day. Tonight, you will have to impress the empress dowager. That will be no easy task, and I will be unable to help you. My only recommendation is to not sleep at all."

"I will do my best," she said as we stood. "If Heaven wills it, we will meet again tomorrow."

"I will see you tomorrow, then," I said. She gave a bow and then stood with the other girls who had been fortunate enough to make it through the day.

I went back inside and handed Lanhua's card to the chief eunuch, then I took my place next to the empress dowager. For the rest of the day, I let my mother-in-law have her way. I saw no reason to argue with her or to let myself worry. I was sure that by the end of this process, I would have at least one dear friend, and that was at least more than I had now.

By the end of the day, there were about fifty contenders left. They would all sleep in a large room with the empress dowager that night. If any one of them snored, made night wind, or walked or talked in her sleep, she would be dismissed. It was tradition for the emperor's mother to oversee this part of the selection process, so I did not feel slighted by being left out. There was also nothing I could do to help Lanhua. I only prayed to Heaven that she would sleep quietly and peacefully, if she slept at all.

That evening, I was surprised when Yizhu came to my palace. He appeared to have been out for a stroll, a cup of wine in his hand.

"I think the selection is progressing well," he said.

"I am glad you are pleased."

"You were awfully quiet today."

"The empress dowager is more experienced in this process than I am," I said, "as she has repeatedly reminded me."

"I noticed that she was contradicting you quite a bit. But I value your opinion on this matter, Zhen."

My heart warmed. Yizhu had offered me very few compliments during our marriage thus far, so I lapped up his praise like a starving dog.

"I will do my best to be more assertive, my lord." Then, I did something I never thought I would do. I invited my husband to stay the night with me.

FINALLY, the last day of the consort selection arrived. The emperor, empress dowager, and I sat in the Hall of Heavenly Purity, and the final contenders were all brought in and lined up before us. I was surprised to see thirty-three women present. I had expected the empress dowager to send home more than that during the night. I was thrilled to see that Lanhua was among the finalists, but she was placed near the back of the group. I would have to point her out to the emperor if she had any hope of being seen by him.

"The emperor will now choose three noble consorts," the chief eunuch announced.

Yizhu chose two girls quickly and easily. They were quite pretty with warm smiles. They were standing toward the front, and I had a feeling they had caught the emperor's attention from early on. Yizhu made a move to select a third girl, but the empress dowager, who was sitting next to him, got his attention.

"Why not this young woman?" she said, indicating a thin girl with a sour face. "Her father is a nobleman from Shanghai."

"Very well," Yizhu said, though he did not seem very enthused about the choice, and the girl seemed greatly distraught.

"The emperor will now choose ten concubines," the eunuch announced.

The emperor chose five more girls quickly and easily, without giving me or the empress dowager time to interject.

"Son," the empress dowager finally said. "I think you have overlooked some other rather fine candidates." She indicated three of her choices. To my surprise, the emperor did not immediately agree with her.

"I would like to hear the empress's opinion," he said. I was so surprised, I could hardly speak and my eyes watered.

"My son," the empress dowager said, "I think you will greatly benefit from my long years of experience."

"Of course. Thank you, Mother," he said. "But I also value my wife's opinion, and I have barely heard from her."

"Thank you, my lord," I finally said, clearing my throat. I pointed out three young ladies, making special note of Lanhua. "She is kind and industrious. She would make an excellent addition to our family."

"How can you possibly make such a determination?" the empress dowager asked me.

"I have spoken to her," I said.

"You spoke to her? When? About what?"

"Privately," I said.

"Privately?" the empress dowager scoffed. "This is not a time for games. The emperor should have only the best, and her family is dirt poor."

"Which is why she has worked hard to support them," I said.

"She has worked?" the dowager empress nearly screeched. "What, in a factory? Does she have the hands of a laundry maid? How did she even make it this far? Send her away at once."

"No," I said, looking to Lanhua, who appeared completely undisturbed by the scene. My head began to ache, but I avoided rubbing my temple. I could not allow myself to look weak in front of the empress dowager or the new consorts.

"Enough," Yizhu said. "Mother, you are embarrassing me and this court."

"How dare you?" she said to him. There was snickering from the back of the room. "Silence!" the empress dowager snapped. "Is this what you want?" she asked Yizhu. "An Inner Court full of rude and snickering workhorses? Or an Inner Court full of elegant and refined young ladies?"

"Since it is the empress who will have to manage them, I will defer to her opinion," the emperor said. He then indicated his acceptance of the three young ladies I had selected, including Lanhua.

"The emperor may select two more concubines," the eunuch announced.

"What do you think, Zhen," Yizhu asked me.

I picked two more young ladies toward the middle of the room. The emperor nodded his approval. The ladies were then dismissed. They would all return to their homes for now, but each one who had been chosen as a consort or concubine would return to consummate her marriage when an auspicious date had been chosen. The empress-dowager stood up and nearly stomped from the room. As the emperor and I stood at nearly the same time, he came to my side.

"You did well," he said.

"You are pleased?" I asked.

"Very much so. I am sure you will soon have your hands full with far too many children to handle."

"I pray that Heaven shows us such grace," I said.

The emperor then kissed my cheek and took his leave.

"You should speak up for yourself more often."

I looked over and saw Lanhua peeking out from behind a curtain. Apparently, she had not left the room with the others.

"You should not still be here," I chided her, but I could not find it in me to be mad at her.

"I couldn't leave without saying thank you," she said. "You changed my life today. You saved my family. I will always be grateful to you."

I shook my head. "I meant what I said. You will be an asset to this family. I know it."

"Well, you must ensure our palaces are close together," she said. "I cannot wait until we are sisters."

"Sisters," I said, nodding. She hugged me and then went on her way. I remembered the last time I had a sister in the palace and how badly that ended. Poor Ayan. She had trusted me, and I had failed her. I would not let that happen again. Whatever happened, I would be sure to protect Lanhua. I would always be there for her.

And I was sure that she would be there for me too.

CHAPTER FIFTEEN

ay by day, one by one, my husband's new consorts
moved into the palace. I eagerly awaited the day
Lanhua would return, but her auspicious day ended up being
one of the last, over a month after the consort selection was
held. At least I had plenty to keep me busy until then.

Having an Inner Court full of ladies for the emperor was a
very different life from when I had been my husband's only
woman. Now, I had to help the chief eunuch from the
Ministry of Household Affairs manage my husband's nightly
calendar. Now, rank mattered. The higher a woman's rank, the
more nights she was guaranteed to spend with the emperor.
As the empress, I would spend every full moon with my
husband. The nights before and after the full moon were for
consorts of the next three levels. The rest of the month was for
the remaining women, all ranked as concubines who were
divided into a further four levels, with those of ranks five and
six holding precedence. It was a complicated system, but not
too difficult to manage since my husband only had fourteen
consorts, including myself. Ideally, every lady would spend
two nights a month with the emperor, which seemed rather

fair and balanced to me. I wondered how the emperors of the past handled their schedules when they had sixty or even eighty ladies of the Inner Court. My husband was still quite young, only twenty-one years old. If he lived as long as his father and held to the tradition of holding a consort selection every decade, he could become the emperor with the largest Inner Court in Qing Dynasty history. But those were concerns for the future. For now, I was tasked with welcoming each lady and making sure she understood the rules of the Inner Court.

I discovered that many of the young ladies were not ladies at all, but were from very poor and low-class families. How they managed to make it so far in the selection process when so much of it was based on poise and decorum was beyond me. Though, many of them were quite beautiful, which, I was sure, was all it took to please my husband. However, I learned that some of the ladies were relatives of Empress Dowager Jing, many nieces and cousins. It occurred to me that this was why the empress dowager pushed forward the candidates she did, even when I thought they were unsuitable. She was still, even now, trying to secure her dominance in the Inner Court. Those ladies would be loyal to her, not me. And should they fall pregnant, Empress Dowager Jing would be blood kin to the next emperor. If Yizhu would not listen to her, surely the next emperor would.

I decided to confront Empress Dowager Jing and put her in her place at last.

"Mother," I said one day after her morning audience with the Inner Court. "May I speak with you?"

"Of course, dear," she said. "But do be quick, my schedule is quite full."

"Then you will be relieved to know that I plan to help alleviate some of your burdens," I told her as we strolled toward her palace, which should have been my palace, but I did not quite have the heart to kick Empress Dowager Jing out of her home.

"Is that so?" the empress dowager asked.

"Now that my husband's new consorts are filling the Inner Court, I thought now was the opportune time for me to start holding morning audiences."

Empress Dowager Jing laughed. "Oh, my dear, don't be silly. There is no need for that. As you well know, the senior member of the Inner Court holds morning audiences."

Of course, she was wrong about that. The empress was the head of the Inner Court, no matter how long she had been there. Besides, if one went by seniority, Empress Dowager Jing still would not be head of the Inner Court. There were retired consorts of previous emperors who still lived in the Inner Court, though they pretty much kept to themselves. I knew at least half a dozen of Emperor Daoguang's consorts still lived, some older than Empress Dowager Jing, and I'd heard rumors that even one of the Jiaqing Emperor's consorts still lived. However, she would have to be very ancient if she lived at all. But Empress Dowager Jing clearly did not want to step aside and allow me to assume my rightful place if she was willing to state such a blatant falsehood. At the same time, she had put me in a precarious position. I could not outright call my mother-in-law a liar.

"That may be so, Mother," I said, "but as the empress, it is something that I would like to do. And, as I said, it would help ease the burden of your busy schedule."

"You don't need to worry about my schedule," she said, her voice more firm. "I am sure you have enough responsibilities of your own."

"The Inner Court certainly is more lively than before," I said.

"And it will only get busier," she said. "More ladies means children are sure to follow. After all, Princess Ningxin is already with child. I am sure it will be a boy. A little prince for the Qing Dynasty."

I had to grit my teeth at that. I was glad she was not looking at me. Of course, if something dreadful happened and Yizhu were to die without a son of his own, his brother's son would be an obvious candidate for the throne. But how could Empress Dowager Jing even think of such a thing right now? Yizhu had come to the throne less than a year ago. He'd only held his first consort selection, and not even all of them had arrived yet. Yizhu was young, healthy, and strong. Surely a son of his own, if not many sons, would come soon.

"My husband has diligently been doing his duty by all the new consorts," I said. "Surely, in a month, we will be inundated with good news."

"Yes, well, I don't suppose you have any good news to share?"

Her words pained me, which was surely her intent. "I have no news to impart at this moment," I said. I tried not to worry about the fact that I had not fallen pregnant. Of course, we had been married for well over a year, and Yizhu had called me to his bed often, though less often lately. Now that the consorts and concubines were arriving, he would go from summoning me to his bed at least every week to only once a month. My chances of falling pregnant now would drop significantly. But, hopefully, my husband's chance of conceiving an heir would grow. Of course, the emperor had much on his mind. The rebellions around the country, especially in the south, continued to grow. I did not want to put undue stress on my husband by insisting that he summon me to his bed more often. But now that he had so many ladies, and a schedule to keep, I hoped the activity in his bedchamber would increase.

"Well, it seems you have enough duties of your own to deal with," Empress Dowager Jing said. "Allow me to help you by continuing to hold the morning audiences."

"Thank you, Mother," was all I could say. "That is very kind of you." I let the empress dowager go on her way without getting what I wanted. Empress Dowager Jing was an imposing personality. I did not know how I would ever be able to put her in her place.

"My lady," a eunuch said, approaching me. "Consort Lingrong has been settled in her palace. Would you like to see her?"

"Yes, of course," I said. Consort Lingrong had arrived the night before. When the ladies arrived, they were taken directly to the emperor's quarters, not unlike my own wedding night. But the fact that Consort Lingrong did not attend the morning audience and was only just now settled in her palace meant that she must have stayed with the emperor rather late into the morning. He must have been pleased with her.

When I saw her, I knew why. Consort Lingrong had been one of the most beautiful ladies at the consort selection. She was tall, with pale skin, bright eyes, and full lips. She also had elegant poise and knew at least the basics of court protocol. She did not look directly at me at first, and bowed when I entered.

"You may stand," I told her, which also meant she could also now look at me. "How was your night with the emperor?"

"It went well, Your Majesty," she said. "The emperor seemed pleased.

I nodded. "Do you have any questions or concerns?" I asked her. Considering my and Lady Ayan's experiences with the emperor, I wanted to ensure his new ladies knew they could come to me if there were any problems. It had surprised me that, so far, none of the ladies had reported any concerns. It could have been that they were just being polite. They surely did not want to disparage the emperor on their first night in the Forbidden City. But I at least wanted the ladies to know that my door was open to them should they ever develop concerns later on.

"None at this time, my lady," she said.

"Well, life here in the Inner Court can be challenging," I said. "I want you to know that you can always come to me with your concerns."

"You are too kind."

"Have you been apprised of your monthly allowance?" I asked her.

"Yes, my lady."

"Have you ever had to manage a household budget before?"

"No, my lady."

I nodded. "Very well. Your chief eunuch will teach you how to keep a daily ledger of your expenses. He will also teach you basic math should you require it. But for the first month, I will also review your daily ledger to ensure it is appropriately managed. You also have a food allowance and allowance for silk.

"Every day, your maids will rouse you at the hour of the dragon. You are to have bathed, dressed, prepared your hair and makeup, and eaten your breakfast before you greet the empress dowager at morning audiences at the hour of the snake."

"The empress dowager?" she asked, as so many before her also had. "Not you?"

"I will be there as well," I said. The empress dowager did, at least, let me sit beside her. She said it was because she was training me to be empress, so I could observe her closely.

Consort Lingrong waited for me to explain further, and when I did not, she replied politely, "Very well, my lady."

I liked this girl. She was gracious, courteous, and, as far as I knew, unrelated to the empress dowager. Of course, I was eagerly awaiting the return of Lanhua. But until that day, perhaps Consort Lingrong would be a good companion for me.

"Would you like to join me for tea?" I asked her.

She seemed surprised and flattered by my invitation, which helped to ease some of the formality between us. I decided we would walk to my palace so we could get to know one another a little better. I discovered that her father was a high-ranking literary scholar, so he had taught his daughter to read and write, typically uncommon skills for prominent Manchu girls.

"If the emperor had not chosen me, my father would have given me to an educated man like himself," she explained over tea.

"Are you disappointed?" I asked her jokingly.

She giggled, hiding her mouth behind her hand. "Certainly not. After all, no one is as well-educated as the emperor."

She was almost right about that. All of Emperor Daoguang's sons were highly educated, spending more than ten years being educated in the Confucian texts. Not that Yizhu ever spoke with me about such things. His only business with me was to provide him with a son and manage his Inner Court. From the few interactions Yizhu and I'd had as a married couple, I wouldn't even know he was educated. If Consort Lingrong was looking for a husband who would share deep and meaningful discussions with her, I was afraid she was going to be sorely disappointed.

"We talked about his love for opera," she said, surprising me.

"You talked?"

"Of course," she said. "He said he wanted to get to know me a little before…you know."

"Oh, yes, of course," I said, but I had no idea what she meant. Yizhu never spoke to me before or after lovemaking.

"I'm not particularly interested in opera. It is a rather common pastime, don't you think, my lady?"

"I know little of opera myself. But many people of all classes seem to enjoy it."

Consort Lingrong continued on, but I was somewhat distracted. I was simply surprised at the level of conversation Consort Lingrong and Yizhu shared. Was this something Yizhu was doing with all his new ladies, or only Consort Lingrong?

Was she already his favorite? He had seemingly chosen her at random to be a consort instead of a concubine, allowing her to enter the Forbidden City at a higher rank than most, with more privileges. But hopefully, I could use Consort Lingrong to my advantage. I would have to send her to Yizhu's bed more often than the girls who were related to the empress dowager. If Consort Lingrong fell pregnant with the emperor's first son before any of Empress Dowager Jing's favorites, she would certainly be more loyal to me. Of course, I had hoped that Lanhua or I would be the ones to fall pregnant, but I couldn't wait for Lanhua's arrival before urging my husband toward a favorite of my choosing and away from the ladies Empress Dowager Jing had selected. I needed to act quickly, and Consort Lingrong seemed the perfect candidate.

"Would you like to see the emperor again tonight?" I asked her.

"So soon?" she asked, her eyes wide.

"Too soon?" I replied, wondering if perhaps she wasn't as keen to return to the emperor's bed as I thought.

"I didn't mean that," she said, blushing. "I was only surprised. He has so many ladies to choose from, I thought it would be weeks before I saw him again.

"Well, we have no new ladies entering the palace tonight, so the emperor may have his pick. I thought perhaps you might like to see him again. I do have some sway over his evening schedule."

"Your Majesty, that would be so very kind of you. Thank you."

"It's my pleasure. And if you ever need anything at all, do not fail to ask. The happiness of all the ladies of the Inner Court is my chief concern."

"I must say, I am very surprised."

"By what?"

"At the general…geniality of you and the whole Inner Court.

You eagerly put other women ahead of yourself in the emperor's bed. You share responsibilities with your mother-in-law. This is not what I was told to expect."

"What were you told to expect? And by whom?"

She bit her lower lip, as though weighing her words. "I must tell you something. My mother was not my father's first wife. She wasn't even his first concubine. But when she joined Father's family, she was his favorite. Life at home was…very contentious for my father's women. I was told that life in the Inner Court would be significantly worse. That I would have to fight for every moment I wanted to spend with the emperor. But after spending just a few minutes with you, I can already tell that life here will be quite…refreshing compared to the family I grew up in."

I had to give her a small smile as I sipped my tea. I appreciated the compliment, but I was sure she would soon discover that life here was not as peaceful as it first appeared. I harbored no jealousy of my husband's consorts. But as for the consorts themselves, I was sure that jealousy would crop up eventually, especially among the girls from lower classes. Girls like that were often not taught the benefits of a husband having many concubines. Consort Lingrong had also not yet met Empress Dowager Jing and seen that I did not willingly yield my authority to her. Empress Dowager Jing simply refused to let go of authority that had died with her husband. Still, I would do my best to keep the Inner Court as calm and happy as possible. Heaven knew that the emperor had enough stress from outside forces. He did not need the women of the Inner Court causing him more strife.

I bid Consort Lingrong a good afternoon and sent a note to the Ministry of Household Affairs, asking that Consort Lingrong be sent to the emperor's bed again that night, along with a generous gift to make sure it happened. I knew that ladies often bribed the ministry officials to ensure their names were put forward to the emperor. It was a practice I did not condone and often warned against. I felt it was a waste of money and favored the girls from wealthy families or were ranked higher and already had more opportunities with the emperor. Of course, as the empress, I never had to compete for Yizhu's attention and already had him all to myself for almost a year. I didn't understand the pressure the ladies were under. But if I needed to simply outbid them until they were all broke —which I could do since my allowance as empress was significantly more than the next highest-ranking consort—in order to get them to stop, then I would do it. I hoped it would not come to that. The ladies already received far less money than they were entitled to. My husband was slightly more generous than his father, but he had not raised the allowances to where they should have been. At least Yizhu did not steal our clothes. He hadn't yet, anyway. I hoped the rebellion in the south would be brought to heel quickly before he felt the need to resort to such tactics.

To my surprise, a eunuch brought me a letter from my cousin Feiya.

My Dearest Zhen,
I am so pleased to tell you that I have safely delivered a son to
my husband. He is healthy and strong and so beautiful. I am
sorry I did not tell you beforehand of my condition, but since it
was my first pregnancy, I was terrified something would go
wrong. It is such a relief to know that I never needed to worry.
Hopefully, my son is only the first of many children to come.
I heard that the emperor's first consort selection was recently
held. Please write back and tell me everything. I am sure the
palace will soon be filled with so many children, you will have
more than you can handle.

I crumpled Feiya's letter up in my hands, intending to throw it into a brazier, but I stilled my frustration and jealousy and smoothed the letter out, placing it in a drawer in my writing desk along with all the others she had sent me since we were parted. She had made a habit of writing to me at least monthly. She must have had an educated servant on staff to be able to write so often.

I was surprised, and a little hurt, that she had kept her pregnancy from me for so long. But I suppose I was also grateful that she did so. I should have been happy for her, and I was, but it only reminded me of how empty my own womb was. Between Feiya and Ningxin both falling pregnant, they made the task seem so easy, so effortless. I was the empress, the daughter of Heaven, so why had I not been equally blessed?

Well, it mattered not. With the emperor's Inner Court full of healthy and beautiful young ladies, our family would surely be blessed soon. In truth, I would be just as pleased if a consort or concubine became pregnant instead of myself. Either way, I knew I would be a loving and doting mother.

I picked up a horsehair brush and laid out a piece of paper so that I could send Feiya a reply. As I ran the ink stick through the water on the inkstone, I tried to think of what I would write back to her. Congratulations, of course. I would send the new baby and his mother a selection of gifts—silver, tea, and warm clothes—but the words did not come.

Feiya seemed so happy in her new life. Her husband was apparently kind and generous to her. They often traveled to visit various tribes together, where she was greeted like a queen. She rode horses, went hunting with hawks, and had learned to love fermented yak milk. Every day was new and exciting for her, hundreds of li from the home where we had grown up. For me, life within the walls of the Forbidden City was not terribly different from the life I had lived back home. And as long as Empress Dowager Jing maintained her control, I did not see that changing anytime soon.

CHAPTER SIXTEEN

inally, the day for Lanhua's arrival had come! Actually, she had arrived the night before, but I could not see her then as she was taken straight to see Yizhu. But I would see her after morning audiences. I hardly heard a thing Empress Dowager Jing said, I was so excited. Several of the ladies tried to speak to me after the audience was completed, but I brushed them off, telling them I did not feel well. In truth, I felt wonderful. I could not remember the last time I had awoken with such joy in my heart.

When my litter bearers finally stopped outside Lanhua's palace, which was right next to my own palace, I nearly leaped out of the chair instead of waiting for a eunuch to help me alight. I had to pause for a moment and take a breath as a eunuch announced my arrival, just in case Lanhua was not as excited about seeing me as I was about seeing her. But I needn't have worried.

"Zhen!" Lanhua called as she ran out of the palace. We hugged as if we were old friends who had not seen each other in years.

"Oh, excuse me," Lanhua said as she pulled away from me, remembering to bow. "I mean, Empress Zhenxiu."

"Welcome to your new home, Concubine Lanhua," I replied.

"Ugh, I don't like my name," she said. "You are the empress. Can you change my name?"

"Orchid is a beautiful name," I said.

"It's so common," she whined, and I had to acknowledge that it was common for girls to be named after flowers. Still, I thought her name was beautiful.

"Well, it is not my privilege to be able to change your name," I said. "But the emperor could, if you pleased him enough that he raised your station."

"I am sure that will only be a matter of time," she said as she lowered her voice and looped her arm through mine, leading me inside her palace.

"So, last night went well?" I sat at a table, the chair wobbling a bit. Lanhua noticed and apologized.

"I have noticed that much of my furniture is well worn."

"I'm sorry," I said. "As a rank seven concubine and one of the last to move in, it would seem that you got the leftovers when it came to furnishings."

"I'm sure I can make do," Lanhua said, sitting next to me.

"No, it's unacceptable," I said. "You are a concubine to the emperor, not some commoner's wife. You should have the best. I'll speak to the Ministry of Household Affairs about it."

"You are too kind," she said.

"So, things went well with the emperor last night?"

"As well as could be expected, I suppose."

"You don't have any…concerns?"

"No…except…" Lanhua hesitated, and I held my breath. "Well, it is only that the emperor seemed to be in a hurry. As if there was somewhere he needed to be."

"Oh, well, I am sorry to hear that. Perhaps he had a lot on his mind."

"That was what I suspected," Lanhua said. "There is much chatter among the people regarding the Taiping rebels."

"Is there?"

Lanhua lowered her voice and leaned close to me. "Did you know that the rebels are cut out of paper?"

"Paper?" I was confused.

"Yes! If their numbers dwindle, their leader just cuts out more soldiers from paper, breathing life into them like God did to the first man made of dust."

"Because he is the son of God? The brother of Jesus?"

"That is what they say. In my old village, a woman was put to death for hiding a pair of scissors used to cut out the paper soldiers."

"But I thought you said their leader cut out the paper soldiers."

"I only know what I was told."

"But it is surely a lot of nonsense," I said. "You cannot believe there is any truth to what the people say."

"No, certainly not... But..."

"But what?"

"There must be a reason they are winning."

"They aren't winning," I said. "They just haven't been put down yet."

Lanhua stared at me, her large eyes blinking. "Do you not get news in the Inner Court about what is happening out there?"

"The emperor tells me what I need to know," I said.

"Yes, of course he does."

We sat quietly for a moment, the seconds stretching for hours. I was itching to know what Lanhua knew about the Taiping rebels that I did not know, and I could tell she was anxious to tell me.

"But he has been so busy lately with all his new consorts," I finally said. "Perhaps he has forgotten to fill me in on the latest information."

"I'm sure that's all it is," she said.

"So, if you wanted to tell me the latest news…"

"They are moving further north," she said. "They will soon take Jiangning."

"No!" I said. "That's impossible." Jiangning was a fortified city south of Peking. In earlier dynasties, it served as a capital city. Now, even though Jiangning was no longer the capital, it was one of the largest cities in the country and a major trading center. If Jiangning were to fall to the rebels, it could spell disaster for our country.

"It's true," Lanhua said firmly. "My father told me. He will soon take up a post in Anhui Province, so he has been following the rebellion closely."

"It cannot be as serious as all that," I said, but my emotions betrayed my words. I felt a headache building. Could we really be so close to ruin and no one told me? Why would Yizhu keep me in the dark about this?

"I am sorry if I have caused you distress, Your Majesty," Lanhua said, patting the back of my hand.

"It does no good to talk about such things," I said, shaking her hand off. "We are only women. What can we do? The emperor will keep us safe."

"I am sure he will," Lanhua said. "He was only so preoccupied last night. I wanted to let him know that he could talk with me if he needed someone to listen."

"Was he appreciative of the offer?"

"Not at all," she said with an awkward chuckle. "I think that might have made him leave me even more quickly."

"I am sure he has enough men to discuss such matters with during the day. At night, we are supposed to help the emperor relax and rest his weary head."

"Yes, my lady, of course. But…do you think you could put in

a good word for me with the emperor? He will surely listen to you."

I nodded. "Of course I will." In truth, I had not spent a night with the emperor since the consort selection. But I knew a full moon would be coming soon. I would have to take the opportunity to speak with him. Perhaps on a few matters.

"Do you have anything to add, Daughter?" Empress Dowager Jing asked me during a morning audience one day.

"Yes," I said.

"Oh, you do?" she replied, looking at me curiously.

She often asked me this, but it was mainly only a way for her to be polite. A way of showing deference to me as the empress without actually respecting my position. She never really expected me to say anything, and I rarely had before.

"I have been reviewing many of the ladies' account ledgers and found numerous errors, from characters being written incorrectly, to items costing too much, and arithmetic not being performed accurately. I am concerned that some of you are being taken advantage of by your eunuchs. They could be telling you that items cost much more than they do and are pocketing the difference. Or perhaps some of you are spending money you should not and are trying to hide it by inflating the costs of certain items."

Some of the ladies gasped in surprise while others looked away shamefully.

"The emperor is fighting a costly rebellion to keep us all safe. It is important to the emperor and, thus, all of us to be responsible regarding money.

"Therefore, I have selected Concubine Lanhua to help me oversee your accounts. You are to show her the same respect you show me in this matter. You are to hand over your ledger to her when she asks and dutifully institute any changes she requests of you. Does everyone understand?"

"Yes, Empress," the ladies all replied in unison.

"Is that all?" Empress Dowager Jing asked me, her tone flat, a tone she used to demonstrate her displeasure.

"Yes, Mother."

"Very well. All of you are excused."

The ladies all stood and took their leave. Empress Dowager Jing and I were always the last to leave in case any of the ladies wanted to speak with us further. I was talking with Lanhua when the empress dowager cleared her throat. I looked over and saw her staring at me.

"Excuse me, Mother. Did you wish to speak with me?"

"If there are problems with the girls, or if you wish to award special privileges to someone, you should speak to me first. Other ladies of the Inner Court would be far more suitable for the task you mentioned than Concubine Lanhua."

"I appreciate the advice, Mother. But Concubine Lanhua—"

"It is not merely advice," she said, interrupting me, her voice raised. "It is how things are done. I am the senior member of the Inner Court. Such things are to go through me, understand?"

I could feel my face burn with anger and embarrassment. Not only was Lanhua still present, but some of Empress Dowager Jing's favorites were as well, along with several eunuchs and maids. Word of Empress Dowager Jing dressing me down would soon spread throughout the entire Forbidden City, and probably beyond it, among the city's elite. My own parents might even hear of it. But I didn't know what to do. Empress Dowager Jing was wrong, but she was also my mother-in-law, and I was duty-bound to show her respect. Besides, how was I supposed to put her in her place? What authority did I really have?

"I'm sorry, Mother," I said.

"I thought the empress was the head of the Inner Court," Lanhua said.

"You dare to open your mouth to me without being asked?" Empress Dowager Jing nearly spat at Lanhua.

"In fact, it is the empress who is supposed to lead morning audiences as well, is it not?" Lanhua went on, her voice clear and confident.

"How dare you?" Empress Dowager Jing seethed.

"What are you doing?" I mouthed to her. I was so afraid, I could hardly utter a sound.

"Empress Zhenxiu, you manage the emperor's nightly calendar, do you not?" Lanhua said to me.

"Yes—" My voice cracked, so I cleared my throat. "Yes. Yes, I do."

"It would be a shame if all of Empress Dowager Jing's nieces suddenly were left off that calendar, right?"

At this point, it was unclear who exactly Lanhua was speaking to, me or Empress Dowager Jing, as her eyes flicked back and forth between the two of us. Though I supposed it didn't matter, as her words had the desired effect. I had been quite preoccupied with making sure the emperor's calendar was fair to as many girls as possible. Of course, I had given extra days to Lanhua and Lingrong, but not at the expense of the other girls. I had not considered wielding my authority over the calendar as a punishment or manipulation tool. The girls all had such little time with the emperor as it was, to take away time that was rightfully theirs seemed cruel. But, at this point, Empress Dowager Jing had been usurping my place and authority in the Inner Court for over a year. I had often lamented as much to Lanhua, but I had never expected her to do something about it.

I should have stopped her. I should have put Lanhua in her place. I should have even punished her for speaking in such a way to the empress dowager. But I didn't. I couldn't. Because I wanted what she was offering me. She had been bold enough to point out that I could leverage my authority and take control of the Inner Court. She had found a way to help me, and this would be my only opportunity to use it. If I didn't do it now, the opportunity would be lost forever, or at least until Empress Dowager Jing died, and who knew how long that would be.

"You would not dare sabotage the emperor's chances of having as many children as possible, would you?" Empress Dowager Jing asked me in challenge.

I looked at Lanhua, wondering if this was really the right thing to do. She gave me an almost imperceptible nod.

"I would never do anything to sabotage my husband," I said. "But I myself have not seen him in nearly a month. I think I should schedule some additional evenings for myself this week, like tonight."

"But it's my night!" one of the young ladies standing near Empress Dowager Jing said.

"Or tomorrow night," I said.

"Hey!" another young lady said. "Auntie, do something."

Express Dowager Jing raised her hand to silence the girls. "What do you want?" she asked me.

"Only what is mine by right," I said. "To be head of the Inner Court."

Empress Dowager Jing sighed. "Well, I knew it would come to this eventually. But I never thought it would come at the hands of a sly fox such as her." She stared pointedly at Lanhua, who only looked pleased with herself.

"Very well," Empress Dowager Jing said to me with an exaggerated bow. "Enjoy your place as empress—while it lasts."

After she and the rest of the ladies left, I let out a breath I didn't know I was holding. "I can't believe you did that," I said to Lanhua, the two of us holding hands as if for dear life.

"Are you pleased?" she asked me.

"Of course," I said. "But how did you know I would agree

with you? If I hadn't supported you, you could have been severely punished."

"We are friends, right? Friends watch out for one another."

"Yes," I said. "We are friends. More than that, we are sisters."

Her eyes teared up as she hugged me tightly. "I will always support you, Sister."

"And I you."

THE NEXT DAY, I held court at morning audience alone. Empress Dowager Jing did not even attend, which was fine with me. The ladies filled the room and listened to me as they would a loving mother. I smiled and gave them all a blessing for the day, on behalf of myself and the emperor. However, when I mentioned the emperor, one of the ladies began to cry. I noticed that it was one of the nieces of the empress dowager.

"What is wrong?" I asked her.

"Nothing, Your Majesty," she replied. I tried to ignore her, but for the rest of the audience, I could hear her sniffling and see her wiping her eyes. I finally called the meeting to an end and asked the young lady to stay behind. I feared that perhaps the emperor had been rough with her, and that was why she did not wish to speak up in front of everyone.

"Whatever has caused you distress, you may speak to me freely," I told her.

"Why did you do it?" she asked me. "Didn't you get what you wanted?"

I gaped for a moment. She was upset with me? "What do you mean? What have I done?"

"You kept the emperor for yourself," she said, stomping a foot. "I waited for hours last night, but he never sent for me."

"But I didn't see him," I said.

"You threatened to change the schedule," she said.

"But I didn't," I said.

"Then who did he see last night?" she asked.

I summoned my eunuch over. "Who did the emperor summon to his bed last night?"

"I will find out," he said before running off.

"The emperor has been very busy," I said. "He probably fell asleep at his desk." I had never known him to work so much that he neglected his evening companion, but I supposed anything was possible. A moment later, my eunuch returned.

"The emperor was with Consort Lingrong last night," he said.

"He was?" The news surprised me. "But he already had a night with her this month."

"He has had…six nights with her this month," the eunuch said.

"Six! Are you sure?"

"Yes, my lady."

"The emperor has fallen in love with Consort Lingrong!" the young lady exclaimed, bursting into sobs again.

"I'm sure it has not come to that," I said. "The emperor knows the dangers of such frivolity. Don't worry, I will speak to him."

"Thank you, Your Majesty."

I climbed into my litter and asked to be taken to see the emperor. He was in his study, and many men were with him, including Prince Yixin. Our eyes met, but I quickly looked away. We had not seen each other since he told me his wife was pregnant. I had been so busy since then with matters of the Inner Court, I had not had much time to think of him. But as soon as I saw him, I felt flutters in my stomach. How easy it was to lose focus when confronted with a handsome face. All the men stopped speaking and bowed to me before leaving the room.

"Did you hear the news?" the emperor asked me gleefully when we were alone.

"I'm not sure what you are referring to," I said, hoping it was good news regarding the rebellion in the south.

"My brother's wife delivered him a daughter. A worthless daughter!" He was practically crowing at his brother's misfortune.

"I had not heard," I said. "I will have to send his wife a gift."

"I don't suppose you have come to tell me that several of my ladies are pregnant?"

"No, my lord. I'm sorry, but I have not come to tell you that."

"It will happen soon, then, I'm sure. So, what is it you needed to see me about so urgently?"

"I'm sorry, my lord, but I have heard that you have taken Consort Lingrong to your bed many times this month."

"She pleases me."

"I am glad to hear that. It was always my intention to choose ladies who would bring you great joy."

"And you have. Is there anything else?"

"Forgive me, but you have taken Consort Lingrong to your bed at great excess, at the expense of your other ladies."

"Am I sensing a bit of jealousy in your voice?"

I tried not to laugh. "Not from me. But some of the other ladies have noted that they have been denied their scheduled time with you. You must know how much they look forward to seeing you."

"I am the emperor. I may take whichever woman to my bed that I wish."

"Yes, of course."

"It is your responsibility to teach the women of the Inner Court to control their jealousy."

"You are right, of course," I said. I had thought that by treating the women fairly, I could avoid feelings of jealousy brewing within the Inner Court. But it had not occurred to me that Yizhu would disregard my efforts and take whatever woman he wanted, thereby actively sowing jealousy among his ladies.

"I will speak to the ladies about this. But if you only kept to the schedule I have supplied you, the ladies would have no reason to be jealous."

Yizhu sighed in annoyance. "I cannot make love to a woman simply because I am ordered to."

This struck me as an odd thing to say. After all, I had been expected to make love with my husband even though I was ordered to marry him. And was it not his responsibility as emperor to spread his seed? The reason he had so many consorts and concubines in the first place was so that he could have as many children as possible. Why have so many women if he was going to limit himself to only one woman?

"I am enjoying Consort Lingrong," he said. "I will continue to take her until she no longer pleases me."

"Of course that is your right if you so choose, my lord," I said. "But, if I may, I would like to point out the many fine qualities of Concubine Lanhua."

He thought for a moment. "She has big eyes, right? One of the last ladies to move in?"

"Yes. She is quite striking, is she not? And she is very artistic. I think you would very much enjoy her company."

"She talks too much," he said.

"She is an excellent conversationalist."

"No, she talks too much about things she should be silent about."

"What do you mean?"

"She was going on and on about her father," he said. "She asked that he not be sent to Anhui, but to Mongolia."

"I believe her father was stationed there once, and the family was happy in the north."

"It doesn't matter," he said. "She should not be speaking to me of political appointments. They are not her business."

"I'm sure she was not thinking of it as a political matter," I said. "She was probably only thinking of her family's happiness."

"Well, speak to her about it. She should hold her tongue on such matters."

"Yes, my lord. Of course. The next time you summon her to your bed, I'm sure you be very pleased."

"We will see. I have no plans to send for her again."

I felt alarmed at this. He could not be serious. He could not let Lanhua, or any of the ladies, spend the remainder of their lives in the Forbidden City and never call her to his bed more than once. Lanhua could live another sixty years. Would he really doom her to a life of loneliness because she had misspoken once?

"The ladies have had nothing but flattering words to say about you," I tried.

"Oh?" It seemed I had piqued his interest.

"Yes, my lord. They are all quite pleased with you and very much look forward to joining you in bed again soon."

He chuckled and ran his hand over his slicked-back hair, stretching his arms. "The ladies? Or you?" He gave me that hungry look. The look that always made me wish I could run away, but kept me frozen in place at the same time. He limped toward me like a wounded animal, like something dangerous.

"I…I…" I tried to think of an excuse to leave, but then I thought of Feiya with her new healthy and beautiful son. And Ningxin, swaddling her new baby, even if it was only a girl. The only way I would ever have a child of my own if I submitted to my husband. So that was what I did.

When he finished, he patted me on the cheek like an obedient child. "There, now, no more petty jealousy, okay?"

Did he still really think that I was the one who was upset he was spending so much time with Lingrong? It took all my willpower to not curl my nose in disgust.

"Yes, Your Majesty," I said dutifully.

"Good. Tell the men to come back in when you leave."

"Yes, Your Majesty."

Out in the hall, the men all bowed respectfully, but as they passed me to go into the room, I could swear I heard them snickering at me. Did they know what the emperor and I had just done? My face bloomed in embarrassment and my eyes welled with tears. At least Yixin was not among them. But as I made my way back to my litter, I saw Yixin, leaning casually against a wall as he spoke to a palace maid. I then remembered how the prince had dared to kiss me—his brother's wife—at the Summer Palace. How he said he had been unable to bed his wife for love of me. He certainly seemed to overcome that little problem. I was about to turn and go another way when the prince—and the maid—saw me. The maid immediately dropped down, kneeling to me. But the prince ran up to me before giving me a bow.

"Are you finished with His Majesty?" he asked.

"Yes. He is waiting for you."

"Let me walk you to your litter."

"If you insist."

"Are you cross with me?"

"Why would I be? In fact, I meant to offer congratulations on the birth of your daughter."

The smile fled from his face. At least he had the decency to look ashamed. "Thank you," he finally said. "Most people have only been offering us condolences."

"Sons have value, but daughters serve a great purpose too. Who would our sons marry if no one had any daughters?"

The prince smirked. "Quite true. I plan to give her the same education as I would a son."

"Surely you jest."

"Not at all. The world is changing, and I want all my children to be prepared. Did you know that England is ruled by a woman? "

"You lie!"

"Not at all. Queen Victoria, she is called."

"So, you think your daughter will be empress one day? An empress without an emperor?"

He laughed. "No, of course not. But who knows where life will take her. At least she will be prepared for whatever comes her way."

"I am glad you have found happiness with your family."

"I am content, for the moment at least. Is that the same thing?"

"No, I do not think it is. But it is probably the most many of us can achieve in this life."

"And what of you, Empress Zhenxiu? Are you content?"

"Not at all," I said, surprised by my own candor. "Perhaps when children start arriving, I will feel differently. "

"Are any on the way?"

"No, not yet."

"I'm sorry to hear that."

"Heaven will shower down blessings in their time."

"I'm sure that's true."

We stood together awkwardly for a moment. I wanted to say more, but I had no idea what.

The prince scratched his chin and stepped closer to me, keeping his voice low. "I heard what happened between you and my mother yesterday."

"Oh, did you?"

"You should be careful about making unnecessary enemies at court."

I scoffed. "What can she do to me? I am the empress."

"You are the emperor's wife," he said. "Everything you do reflects on him."

"You know that he and your mother are not particularly close."

"But she comes from a large and powerful family," he explained to me. "Men my brother relies on for advice, support, money, allies. If they feel you have disrespected the dowager, they could hold back on support for the emperor—support he needs to fight the Taiping."

My head began to ache. I had no idea women could wield so much influence outside the Inner Court. Other than Feiya, I had very little contact with my family. My brothers had both received high-level positions in distant provinces. I had arranged advantageous marriages for my sisters and some of my cousins. But other than increasing everyone's income, I was unsure how—if at all—my family used my position to their advantage. My father was not very interested in politics, but only wanted to live peacefully. I suddenly wondered if this was Empress Dowager Jing's reason for selecting me—and Ayan, and Ningxin—all along. Was it because our fathers were not powerful men? Because none of us could actually challenge her in the Inner Court because of her connections on the outside?

"I...I had no idea," I stammered. "What have I done?"

"Nothing that can't be undone with a simple apology," he said, which only made me feel more ill. I couldn't believe that the first time I used my position as empress ended up being such a horrible blunder. I would now need to bend over my mother-in-law's roof and beg her forgiveness. Yixin must have seen the distress on my face. "Hey, everything is fine."

"Does the emperor know?" I asked. If he were truly angry with me, I suddenly feared for my safety.

"Not yet. The other men don't know yet either, only me. She said she was giving you time to come to your senses before she told anyone else."

I was pacing, chewing my thumb. My husband had already hurt me many times—and he wasn't even angry, only aroused. I truly feared what he might do to me if I made him lose the support he needed to battle the Taiping.

"Hey," the prince said, stepping in front of me and forcing me to stop. He tapped me on the nose. "Consider this your first lesson in politics."

"Are you the expert now?"

"I've learned a lot. Probably more than my brother."

"He's the emperor. What does he need with politics?"

"More than he'd like to admit. I swear, if he would just listen to me, we could defeat the Taiping and be done with them."

"How?"

He hesitated. "By joining forces with the foreigners."

Even I laughed at that. "You know Yizhu would never agree to that. You need to come up with another plan."

"Then you need to apologize to your mother-in-law. My brother will need all the help he can get."

"I will. Don't you worry. This isn't the first mistake I've made since becoming empress, and I'm sure it won't be the last."

"Don't be so hard on yourself. You had no way of knowing. You just need to be more careful about who you take advice from."

"You mean Concubine Lanhua?"

"Mother didn't bother learning her name, but is that the friend who goaded you into standing up to my mother?"

"She didn't *goad* me. She only thought she was helping me. And I thought she was helping me too. I agreed it was a good idea or I wouldn't have gone along with her. No, don't blame her. I'm the empress. It was my mistake. I own it."

"Still, you might be careful. Mother says the girl is quite outspoken."

"Are you quite done?" I asked, growing annoyed. "Or do you have more advice on being empress you need to import? How I should style my hair, or what I should have for lunch?"

He looked at my hair appraisingly. "Well, now that you mention it—"

I slapped his arm. "Don't you dare!"

"I'm only joking. You know I think you are beautiful."

The smile fled his face and my heart thudded hard in my chest. I knew he didn't mean anything by it. At least, it should not have meant more than any polite comment. He was my brother-in-law. A brother complimenting a sister, that's all it was—or all it should have been. But as we stared at each other, we both knew his words meant far more than that.

"Your highness!" a man called from the audience hall. "The emperor is waiting for you."

"Yes, I'm coming," he said. The man waited a moment and then went back inside, closing the door.

"Please excuse me, Empress," Prince Yixin said, bowing.

"Of course," I said. He walked toward the door, and I placed a hand on my stomach as I took a calming breath.

"I am always here for you," he said. I turned around to look at him. "You do know that, don't you?"

"I know," I said.

He pressed his lips, as if stopping himself from saying more. But then he nodded and went into the audience hall.

"That's the problem," I muttered to myself as I made my way back to my litter.

CHAPTER SEVENTEEN

"*W*hy did you apologize?" Lanhua asked me after we left morning audiences the next day. All the ladies had looked at me curiously when the empress dowager rejoined us and took her place at the front of the room, with me again relegated to the side. But Lanhua was the only woman brave enough to bring it to my attention after the meeting concluded.

"I am the empress and must consider the larger picture," I told her. "I must always consider what is best for the emperor."

"The emperor? He doesn't even like the old bat."

I stopped, nearly causing Lanhua to stumble into me. "You will not say such things about your mother-in-law. Do I make myself clear?"

Lanhua seemed surprised by my tone, but she did not press me further.

"Yes, Empress," she said. "I was only trying to help."

"I know," I said, resuming our walk. "And I appreciate it. But, from now on, please let me deal with the empress dowager how I will."

"Yes, my lady."

"Empress!"

I turned back and saw Lingrong trotting to catch up to me.

"Consort Lingrong, how are you?"

"I am very well, my lady," she said, nearly breathless. "I have news. My monthly visitor has not arrived. It is late."

I gripped her hands tightly. "How late?"

"Five days."

My hand flew to my mouth. Lanhua shrieked with glee.

"Quiet, quiet," I told them. I looked around to make sure no one could hear us. "We don't want rumors reaching the emperor before we know for sure. But how did you manage to keep this from me for five whole days?"

"It has not been easy," she said. "I swore my maid to secrecy under pain of death."

"Good," I said. "We must summon a physician at once. But we don't want to arouse suspicion. I will say I am ill and have him come to my palace."

So that was what we did. When the physician arrived, I explained the situation to him, that it was actually Lingrong who was having symptoms. Since he could not touch an imperial consort, he laid a thin handkerchief on her wrist before feeling her pulse. All of us held our breaths as he concentrated. Finally, a smile spread across his face and he looked up at me.

"Congratulations, Your Majesty," he said.

We could not contain ourselves and the three of us screamed in joy. All three of our eunuchs ran out of the palace, each hoping to be the first to tell the emperor that he was going to be a father. I kneeled down and hugged Lingrong around the shoulders.

"This is so wonderful! Congratulations."

"It's all thanks to you, Your Majesty. You were so kind to give me extra time with the emperor."

"You were the one to keep his attention. He seems quite enamored with you."

"He only likes that I have small feet," she said.

"What?"

"The emperor approaches!"

The emperor ran into the room before a eunuch could even finish announcing his presence. He must have run the whole way instead of taking a litter as he was out of breath. All of us stood and then bowed.

"Is it true?" he asked.

"It is," I said. "Consort Lingrong is with child."

The emperor went to her and pulled her up. "Do not bow any longer. You must not squish my son."

All of us laughed at how indulgent he was being.

"You will immediately start receiving double your usual ration of meat and milk," he said. "And whatever else the doctor says you need."

"I will share a list with her cook," the doctor said. "It will change month to month."

"Whatever she needs," he said, interrupting the doctor. "What do you need?" he asked Lingrong, leading her back to my bed as if she were ill. "Are you cold?"

"It is summer," she said, laughing.

"Well, what do I know of babies and pregnant women?" he said.

"There is nothing to be concerned about right now, my lord," I said. We only have a long time to wait at this point."

"Who knows how many more women will be pregnant by the time this baby comes," Lanhua said.

"Exactly," I agreed. "For now, my lord, simply rejoice in this happy news."

"Indeed," the emperor said. "Very well done, everyone. Doctor, follow me. I want reports on the health of her and my son daily, do you understand?"

As soon as he was out of earshot, Lingrong got to her feet. "Hopefully, I can now return to my own palace."

"It won't be your palace for long," I said. "You'll soon be moved to a larger palace, with more rooms to accommodate the baby and additional staff. You'll have nannies, wet nurses, more maids..."

"I feel like my whole life has changed in an instant," she said.

"Because it has." I hugged her, kissed her cheeks, and then sent her on her way.

"What a lucky woman," Lanhua said as we watched her go.

"It was likely to happen to her since she has been spending the most time with him."

"He will need someone to take her place in his bed," she said, clearly hinting that it should be her. I led her to my sitting room, where we sat across from one another.

"I would be more than happy to send you to his bed more often, but..."

"But what?"

"The last night you spent with him, he was...displeased."

"He certainly seemed satisfied when I left," she said, and I held back from chiding her for being vulgar.

"He said you talked too much."

She opened her mouth to respond, but I raised my eyebrow, and she stopped herself.

"See," I said. "That wasn't so hard."

"Does he really want me to be silent?"

"No, not at all. I think it was what you talked about. He said you tried to get him to change your father's appointment."

"It is a dangerous assignment. The Taiping are moving ever closer!"

I raised my hand to stop her. "The appointment was an honor. Isn't it the highest appointment your father has ever had? You should be grateful."

"Do you know what the Taiping do to the Manchu who are living in the cities they conquer?" she asked me, her voice grave.

"They kill them?" I said. It was a rebellion, after all.

"They burn them alive," she said. "After they rape the women. I heard that an entire village committed suicide when they heard the Taiping were approaching. They thought being murdered by the village elders would be less painful than dying at the hands of those monsters."

Her words made my skin break out in goose flesh. "How do you know all this?"

"Letters from my family. They keep me well informed. Doesn't your family?"

"Not particularly," I said. "They know such matters are not my concern."

"Not your concern? You are the empress. The mother of your people. Don't you care that they are dying?"

"Of course I do," I said. "But as you said, I am their mother, not their father. I cannot protect them. That's the job of the emperor."

"What is the point of being a consort, shut up here in the Forbidden City, if you cannot help the people you care about most?"

"If the emperor shuns you, if you end up in the cold palace, what good are you to anyone?"

She sighed, and I think she was finally resigned to my words. "Fine," she said. "What can I do?"

"Do you like opera?"

A smile spread across her face. "Yes."

"So does the emperor. Consort Lingrong said he spoke to her of opera often."

"That's easy," she said. "I have some of my favorite songs memorized."

"Good. Try that. Don't talk to him about politics or try to get favors from him. Not now. Not yet. Wait until you are pregnant. Wait until your position is secure."

"What about your position?"

"What do you mean?"

"Why don't you put yourself in his bed more often? Don't you want to get pregnant?"

"I do. But I had him all to myself for a year and nothing happened. I want him to have the best chance at having children—even if it isn't with me. And it worked. Consort Lingrong is pregnant."

"You are…" She sighed and shook her head. I waited for the compliment to come. I was used to them by now. People called me selfless. Kind. Benevolent. *Beautiful.* Prince Yixin's words echoed in my mind.

"…so very strange," Lanhua finally said.

"Excuse me?"

"I appreciate your willingness to help me. If I do fall pregnant, I will owe you my life. But…I don't know. I just can't quite figure you out."

"I can't quite figure myself out either," I said.

Due to her condition, Lingrong was unable to serve the emperor at night. Therefore, I completely removed her from his schedule, freeing up more opportunities for the other ladies, including Lanhua. I put her on his schedule several times in the following month so that if he passed her over for someone else once or twice, her name would still come up again and again. Eventually, my plan worked and Yizhu sent for Lanhua.

"So, how did it go?" I asked her the next day.

"I think it went very well," she said. "I took your advice and only spoke to him about opera."

"Excellent," I said.

"Well, not only opera," she said.

"Oh, dear."

"It's not as bad as you think," she said. "We talked about art. I told him about my embroidery skills, and he expressed his love of painting."

"Painting?"

She looked at me, confused for a moment. "Yes. Have you not seen his paintings?"

"Not since we were children. And I didn't think they were anything special."

Lanhua giggled. "Well, maybe not back then. But his skills have surely improved. He showed me several of his paintings. They are beautiful."

"Hmm. Well, that's wonderful."

"Yes. He said he would show me how to improve my own techniques if I am interested."

"So, he wants to spend time with you...outside the bedroom as well?"

"I suppose. But we will have to see. He is so busy, you know."

"Indeed, I do," I said.

I didn't know what it was, but her words left me feeling uneasy. It wasn't jealousy, not exactly. At least, not jealousy for time in his bed. But that he had shared something with her not related to the bedchamber that he had not shared with me, his wife. But I brushed my feelings aside. I had to serve as a model for all the ladies of the Inner Court, after all. It was clear that his growing fondness and attention for Concubine Lanhua grated on their nerves.

Over the following months, he summoned Lanhua to his bed more and more often, in the same way he had with Lingrong. But the fact that Lanhua was also my friend and companion seemed to make matters worse. That a young woman should be the favorite of the emperor *and* the empress was more than some women seemed to be able to handle. I tried to temper this by spreading out my attention as much as possible, inviting more women to walk or dine with me. But, in truth, many of them were quite dull, with few interests outside of being wives and future mothers.

In addition, I was busy helping Lingrong prepare for the birth of her child. I had to seek out and approve half a dozen wet nurses, several nannies, and four midwives. I had to select a new palace for her to ensure it was suitable for a new mother and child to live in.

Every day, I hoped another woman would fall pregnant to help spread the attention around, but it did not happen. Not even for Lanhua. I asked the midwives about things we could do to increase our chances of conceiving. The midwives spoke to each woman individually, examining them and asking about their chief concerns. For each woman, then, the midwives made individual suggestions. Some women needed more milk, others more eggs, other bone broth, and others fermented foods. They also prepared several herbal concoctions we were instructed to drink at various times of the day. All of us working together to improve our fertility gave us something to talk about and served as a healthy distraction while we waited for Lingrong's son to arrive and for more pregnancy announcements.

A few months after Lingrong fell pregnant, the emperor was so pleased with Lanhua that he promoted her from rank six to rank five. This was unsurprising, as I had often seen them talking about opera or art together during the day. They arranged for opera performances to be held in the Inner Court, and Lanhua would always sit by his side. This moved her into a new class of concubine that allowed her to have more servants, a larger allowance, and more time with the emperor. Lanhua was thrilled at her promotion and thanked me profusely. But only days after she was promoted, she received devastating news.

"My father is dead," she told me as tears streamed down her face.

"Oh, Lanhua, I am so sorry to hear that." I held her in my arms as she wept on my shoulder. "What happened?"

"The...the Taiping."

"He was murdered by the Taiping?"

"No. But he was fleeing from them. You know that Jiangning fell to them last month."

"Yes, I know." The news was so devastating, it had reached even me.

"Well, the Taiping have been working on consolidating their power in the surrounding countryside, including Anhui Province, where my father was stationed. My family fled, such was their fear. My mother said the journey proved too much for my father, and his heart gave out on him."

"I'm sorry," I said. "But perhaps he should have stood his ground. Or only gone to a nearby army garrison. My husband has sent thousands of troops south. Did he not try to find help locally?"

Lanhua stared at me for a moment, her face blank. "There is no help!" she finally yelled.

"Lower your voice," I said. I tried to be understanding when the women were emotional in my presence, but I could not abide being yelled at by women who were little more than servants. In truth, I should have punished her for her outburst, but I knew how distraught she was.

"There is no help," she said, her voice lowered, but her words slow and measured. "The emperor keeps sending more troops because the Taiping keep slaughtering the ones he sends. The only choice for people without weapons is to flee or kill themselves. Do you know what happened to the governor of Jiangning when he fled?"

I sighed. "He was beheaded."

"By the emperor!" she cried, doing her best not to raise her voice. "He did the best he could, but the emperor called him a traitor, a deserter."

"The emperor needs his men to stand firm," I said. "Of course the Taiping are going to win when he is only facing cowards who run away."

"My father was not a coward."

"Of course he wasn't," I said. "I didn't mean that."

"The emperor has to do something," she said.

"No," I said, my voice a warning. "You cannot question the emperor's decisions. You must not speak to him of this."

"I cannot speak to him about the death of my own father?"

"You can, but you must be careful. You cannot criticize the emperor's decision to send your father to Anhui. You cannot offer him suggestions on what he should or should not be doing regarding the Taiping. If you value your place here, your place at the emperor's side, you must stay silent."

"But there are people who can help us," she said.

"Who?" I asked.

"The foreigners. There are many in Wuhan, only a day's ride away. Not to mention the foreigner ships in Shanghai's port."

"Have you been speaking to Prince Yixin?" I asked her.

"No. Why would I?"

"He told me the same thing," I mumbled.

"If Prince Yixin knows, then the emperor surely knows this. Why has he not acted?"

"He doesn't trust the foreigners, and for good reasons."

"But—"

"No," I said, cutting her off. "You must stop this. Please. For your own sake."

LANHUA SPENT many weeks in mourning for her father. During that time, I noticed that Yizhu did not call other women to his bed either. I thought perhaps it was out of respect for Lanhua's father, who was, technically, his father-in-law. Though, that seemed a bit sentimental to me, considering he did not observe abstinence for his own father's death. I paid a visit to the Ministry of Household Affairs to see what they thought.

"According to my records," I told the chief eunuch, "the emperor has not summoned a lady to his bed for two weeks."

"That is correct," he said after consulting his own records.

"But doesn't that seem strange?" I said. "In all the years you have been keeping track of such things, has my husband ever gone so long without company?"

"Well, as men get older—"

"He is twenty-two years old," I said. The man pressed his lips, not wanting to speak further. "Is there something you are not telling me?"

"I am sure you have been apprised of any pertinent information you need, Your Majesty," he said.

I closed my record book and went back to my palace. It was clear that he was not going to tell me anything further. But I was certain my husband was not spending his nights alone. It had to be a maid. It was not uncommon for emperors to take concubines from among the palace maids. Because of this, women who applied to be maids underwent a selection process similar to imperial consorts. They were usually girls from poor families, girls who had either been passed over during a consort selection or who were not of the proper age to have attended the selection process in the first place. They had to be clean, well-mannered, not have any marks on their bodies, and be inspected for purity.

It was not an ideal way for a woman to become a concubine or consort, as the typical method of going through a selection process was in place for a reason. However, it was not scandalous for a maid to become a concubine. In fact, if Yizhu had found a maid who pleased him, it was his responsibility to tell me so that she could be officially recognized in case she fell pregnant. If Yizhu had taken a maid to his bed, why had he not told me?

There was a knock at my door, and a maid brought in Lanhua.

"How are you?" I asked her.

"Better," she said. "I am still sad, of course, but I do not want to stay away from the emperor for too long, lest he forget me."

"That would be impossible," I said. "You could never be forgettable."

"Are you all right?"

"Of course. Why do you ask?"

"You just seemed distracted when I came in, like something heavy was on your mind."

I tried my best to smile. "Nothing you need to worry yourself about. I will let the emperor know that you are eager to see him again."

THAT NIGHT, my mind was still uneasy with thoughts of Yizhu. I could hardly eat, sending almost my entire evening meal to be shared among my servants. Then, I could not sleep, tossing and turning for hours. I finally decided to get up and go for a walk. I was accompanied by a maid and a eunuch, who held a lantern in front of me to light my path. I knew Lanhua was with the emperor, but I still felt compelled to walk toward his palace. I was surprised and not a little alarmed when I heard yelling coming from inside his palace. I rushed over—which was easier than usual since I was wearing slippers and not pot-bottomed shoes—just as the door to the palace was flung open. I could see Yizhu standing in the doorway, a yellow robe wrapped around his person, and he was dragging Lanhua alongside him. He threw her out into the darkness just as I approached.

"Never speak to me of such things again!" he yelled.

Lanhua got down on her knees and kowtowed to the emperor. "Please, please do not be angry with me!"

"What is going on?" I asked, going to Lanhua's side. I thought my fears had finally come to pass and Yizhu's lusts had grown violent.

"Zhen." He seemed surprised to see me, but he quickly collected himself. "Zhen, I told you to speak to this girl about talking so much."

My heart sank. "I did, my lord," I said. "She knows that speaking to you on certain matters is not her place."

"Does she? She seems to have forgotten, then."

"I beg your forgiveness," Lanhua said, still kowtowing. "I only wish to help you."

"You are only an ignorant girl," he said, stomping toward us. I put my arms around Lanhua protectively. The emperor may have been angry, and rightly so, but I would not let him lay a hand on her if I could prevent it.

"You are right, my lord," I said. "Which is why you should not take her words seriously."

"I don't."

"Then there is no issue," I said. "Simply ignore her thoughtlessness."

"This is more than thoughtlessness," Yizhu said. "She has clearly thought about this a great deal."

"She...she..." I was frustrated at Lanhua for putting me in this position. I wanted to defend her, but what she had done could result in her being expelled from the Inner Court, sent to live with the other retired consorts where I would hardly ever see her again. "She is grieving the loss of her father. Surely you can sympathize with that."

Yizhu grunted, but he did seem to calm down. I stood and approached him so I could lower my voice. I was sure that the three of us yelling at each other was not helping the situation.

"My lord—"

"She should be punished," Yizhu said. "She should be whipped for her insolence."

"My lord! She is not a common fieldhand. She is an imperial concubine. It is below you to treat one of your women so meanly."

"She should be demoted then," he said. "I regret ever promoting her."

"Yizhu," I said, placing a hand on his arm. He seemed surprised at my use of his given name. Since we became emperor and empress, things had been far more formal between us. His face softened. "She loves you. All the ladies love you. She is only trying to help."

"Then she should not speak to me of those rebels. Or of the foreigners. I hear of it all day from my brother and his cronies."

The war had plagued my husband for the entirety of his reign, and now that the Taiping had taken Jiangning, I did not know if we would ever be rid of them.

"I promise she will not speak to you of such things again," I said. I did not know if I would be able to keep my promise. After all, I had warned her of this before. But perhaps now that she had truly faced Yizhu's temper, she would be more careful in the future.

"See that she doesn't," he said. He shrugged off my touch and stomped his way back into his palace, slamming the door behind him.

I went to Lanhua and helped her to her feet. Her face was dirty from having it on the ground, the dust mixing with her tears.

"I told you not to say anything," I said as I wiped her face with my sleeve and led her back toward her palace.

"I know, but I couldn't help it," she said. "I thought that if the emperor heard the suggestion from me, he might be more receptive. My father often listened to my suggestions when he had no one else to turn to."

"Your father sounds like he was an exceptional man. My father never asked for my opinion on anything. I can see why you miss him so much."

"I do," she said, sniffling. "I had dreamed of marrying a man like him. Someone who saw me as more than a vessel for bearing children."

"Well, you married the emperor, and he will never change. So, you must now be the wife he wants you to be if you wish to find any happiness here."

She let out a sigh. "I suppose you are right. We must bend to his will or be abandoned to the cold palace. Lost forever in obscurity."

"I can see why you love opera so much," I said. "It is so dramatic." We both laughed.

"I have thought about writing an opera of my own," she said. "Do you think the emperor would approve of that?"

"I think you would know better than I. He doesn't speak to me of such things."

"Perhaps I will bring it up to him, if he gives me another chance."

"I think he will," I said, stifling a yawn. I looked up at the sky and saw that the moon was full overhead. "It must be very late."

"Indeed. You should rest," she said. We kissed on the cheeks and I watched her go to her palace before retiring to my own. As I laid back down in bed, I fell asleep quickly, even as I thought I heard the shuffling of feet outside.

CHAPTER EIGHTEEN

*L*ingrong seemed to look even more beautiful than usual. Pregnancy suited her well. The emperor visited her as often as his schedule allowed, though he could not call her to his bed again until one hundred days after she delivered her child. The doctors and midwives agreed that Lingrong was healthy and would have an easy time giving birth. The emperor wanted Lingrong to take to her bed as early as her sixth month, but she only laughed. She took daily walks around her palace—her new, much larger palace—and she greeted guests herself, entertaining them with tea and conversation. Her guests were mainly the wives of important men around the country. Well, they claimed they were coming to pay respects to *me*, as the empress and future official mother of Lingrong's child, but that was merely a formality. Lingrong was doing the important work of bringing the emperor's son and presumed heir into the world. I often felt like a servant myself, tending to Lingrong's every need. Ensuring she would have all the staff she needed. Working with the doctors and midwives to see that her diet was suitable. Planning the festivities that would be held immediately following the child's birth. There would be fireworks. Announcements would be read in every major city throughout the empire. Everyone in China would be afforded five days of rest. Gifts of gold, silk, and food would be distributed. There would be a grand parade held with lion dancers and music. Monks would hold public prayers for the health of the boy, his father, and both of his mothers.

Of course, if the child were a girl, almost all of the festivities would be canceled.

But I could not think about that possibility, much less speak it out loud. To do so would be tantamount to cursing the child and the emperor.

In the meantime, I diligently maintained the emperor's evening calendar, which seemed to be a fruitless endeavor. My husband seemed to call his consorts to his bed less and less frequently. Of course, I knew he was very busy with much on his mind. The Taiping Rebellion still raged, and the foreigners still caused my husband trouble, though he barely spoke to me about any of these problems. He rarely spoke to me at all. He constantly held meetings with his councilors and Prince Yixin, with men coming to the palace from before dawn until long after dark. When finally, it became time for me to spend the night with the emperor, I almost missed him. I waited for hours for the emperor to send for me, but his eunuchs never appeared.

"Why has the emperor not sent for me?" I finally asked one of my servants.

"I do not know, my lady," a eunuch replied.

"Go to the emperor's rooms and ask," I said. "Perhaps he has merely lost track of the time."

I paced as I waited for an answer. Finally, my eunuch and one of the emperor's servants returned.

"Forgive His Majesty," the eunuch replied. "He will see you now."

It felt as though he was summoning me to a formal audience, not his wife to his bed. Still, I held my head up as I walked to the litter that would carry me to his palace, even though his palace was not terribly far from my own. When I arrived at his palace, I understood why his summons had felt so formal.

"What can I do for you?" he asked, hardly looking in my direction. He was still fully dressed and sitting at his desk with a horsehair brush in his hand, as though I had interrupted him writing in midsentence. He coughed and I noticed he looked rather pale, as though he had not been outside in many days.

I cleared my throat. "It is the full moon, our night together."

He finally looked at me, and I almost gasped at how wan his face looked.

"Forgive me," he said. "I have been preoccupied."

"I understand," I said. "But you have not been calling any women to your bed lately. Surely you desire to fill the Inner Court with children."

"Of course. I have merely been anxious for the arrival of Consort Lingrong's son."

"As are we all. But your ladies would love to give you more children to look forward to."

He sighed and ran his hand over his face. "Then let us get this over with." He grunted as he stood and limped over to his bed. I could not help but feel insulted. Of course I wanted to have a child of my own, but I was not a mere broodmare. I was his wife. His empress. Was I not entitled to a bit of affection? Or at least respect?

"Have you been taking a palace maid to your bed?" I asked.

"What? Why would you ask me that?"

"It is your right to do so," I said, trying to calm my irritation. "But since you have had no interest in your consorts, I can only imagine you have been giving your attention elsewhere."

"You are speaking nonsense."

"I do not think I am. I know what you are like. How much you enjoy nighttime activities. Please, if you have taken a maid as a lover, tell me so that I may welcome her into our family. If she were to fall pregnant before you acknowledged her, the other consorts could be gravely insulted."

"I have not taken a maid to bed," he said through gritted teeth. "I have a dozen Manchu consorts already. What could a maid offer me that is not already given to me freely?"

Something about his words worried me, sent a warning shiver down my spine. "What did you mean by that?"

"What are you talking about?"

"Why did you speak of the ladies being Manchu as though…" I sighed, trying to remember the way the word had poured from his mouth. "As though it were a defect?"

Yizhu ran his hand over his face, rubbing his eyes. "I don't know what you are talking about. I am tired and your voice is grating on my ears. Either do your duty or leave."

At that, I turned and rushed from his palace. I could not willingly submit to him this night, and I did not know when I would be able to again. I felt insulted, but I was not sure why. After all, we Manchu were the most cultured and civilized people on Earth. Our women were the most beautiful, with porcelain skin and hair like silk. Yet my husband, the Manchu emperor, spoke as though I were simple, ordinary. How could I give my body to a man who did not appreciate me?

Back in my own palace, I could not sleep, such was my irritation and anger. I sat up in my bed, in my nightclothes, with my arms crossed over my chest. Perhaps I should cease from sending women to my husband's bed altogether. Perhaps then he would gain an appreciation for us again.

"My lady," a maid asked me. "Should I run you a warm bath? Perhaps soothing waters would help you sleep."

"I do not think my mind can be soothed—" I stopped when I heard the shuffling of feet outside. "Did you hear that?"

The maid nodded. "It sounds like several eunuchs just walked by at once."

"Now?" I said. "At this time of night?"

Of course, there were always maids, eunuchs, and palace guards shuffling about the palace at all hours of day and night. But to hear so many people out at once was strange. I then realized it was not the first time I had heard such a ruckus.

I threw off the blanket and rushed to a window just in time to see several eunuchs turning the corner, carrying an enclosed sedan chair.

"What?" I asked, more of myself than anyone else. "Who would possibly be visiting the emperor this late at night?" I asked my maid.

"A councilor?" she offered.

"It is far too late for that," I said. I grabbed a robe and threw it around myself. I went outside and walked toward the emperor's palace. When I was just within sight of it, a eunuch stepped in my path.

"I'm sorry, Your Majesty," he said, "but the emperor is not to be disturbed."

"How dare you?" I said. "Get out of my way." I knew the servant was only following orders from the emperor, but a eunuch could never tell me, the empress, what to do, no matter where the orders came from. I could see sweat bead on his upper lip despite the chilly night air.

"I'm sorry, my lady," he said. "But I cannot disobey the emperor."

"Neither can you disobey me," I said. "I can also have you beaten." I could, of course, though I had never done so. But then again, I had never had a eunuch stand in my way before, either.

The eunuch dropped down into a kowtow, hitting his forehead on the ground. "Please, my lady, I beg of you."

"Tell me why I have been banned from seeing my husband."

"I do not know."

"Who was in that sedan chair?"

"I do not know."

I started to step past him.

"Please, my lady!" he cried out. "You will beat me. But he will execute me. Please, I beg of you!"

I heard the screams of the men who had been executed with the death by a thousand cuts in the back of my mind and felt a headache coming on. I also remembered how my husband raised his hand to my face. The way Ayan had come to me, limping and bleeding. I was well within my right to punish a eunuch who disobeyed my orders. But I knew my husband was far more willing to draw blood than I was. I did not want this pitiful eunuch to die on my behalf.

I turned on my heels and stomped back to my palace. There was nothing more I could do this night. But somehow, I had to find out who had been in that sedan chair.

"WE HAVE FOUND ten women who will be suitable nursemaids for the new prince," a eunuch from the Ministry of Household Affairs told me.

"Will that be enough?" I asked.

The eunuch chuckled. "Considering it usually only takes one woman to nurse a child, I think ten will be more than enough."

I frowned, and the eunuch quickly apologized.

"I *know* how many women it takes to nurse a typical child. But this is the emperor's son. We must anticipate all his possible needs. Have wet nurses been found for the children of the women you have enlisted?"

"We are still working on that, Your Majesty," he said.

"Be quick about it. Consort Lingrong is due in two months. The prince will be here before we know it."

"Yes, my lady. Do not worry. I was present for the birth of many of Emperor Daoguang's sons, including the current emperor."

My irritation toward him softened. I was anxious for everything to go perfectly since this was Yizhu's first child. But for many of the palace eunuchs, this was a familiar scenario, something they had been through many times before.

"Of course," I said. "I am sure you have everything well in hand. You may go."

The eunuch nodded to his own servants to get back to their work, but he lingered beside me.

"Did you need something else?" I asked him.

"Empress, might I inquire if something is bothering you?"

"What do you mean?"

"I heard that you have not been sleeping well. And that you and the emperor have been…not seeing eye to eye lately."

I nodded but said nothing. I did not know if I could speak freely with a eunuch. They often traded information with one another. A secret told to them was never secret for long. But if he knew that the emperor and I were in disagreement, then the whole palace probably already knew, and perhaps even people beyond the red walls.

"The emperor has not been tending to his nightly duties with his consorts," I said, something he surely already knew as someone who worked in the Ministry of Household Affairs.

"I believe he misses Consort Lingrong a great deal," he said. "And he is anxious over the arrival of his son."

I nodded. "But I don't think he is spending his nights alone. I believe he has taken a maid to his bed."

The eunuch rubbed his chin. "It is possible. Emperor Daoguang had several concubines who started as maids."

"I am aware. But then, why would the emperor keep this from me? Why has he not told me who the girl is so she can be promoted to concubine?"

The eunuch shook his head. "I don't know. I do not know of any maids he has taken to his bed. It has not been reported if it is true."

"I thought you would be the first person to be informed if it was a maid," I said. "Don't you keep your own records of the emperor's nightly activities?"

"I do," he said.

"So, you know who it is," I said. The eunuch said nothing. I let out an irritated sigh. "As your empress, I command you to tell me who it is."

The eunuch chuckled. "You know it does not work that way. I'm under orders from the emperor not to tell you. And running around threatening us will not get you what you want. If anything, it only makes you look jealous and bitter."

"I am only jealous for the wellbeing of my fellow consorts. I do not wish to see them neglected."

"I believe you," he said. "I know you have always been generous when it comes to allowing them to see the emperor instead of you."

"What am I to do, then?" I asked.

"I would advise you to not concern yourself. You are only causing yourself anxiety."

"What if I bribed you?"

He was quiet at this.

"I see. How much?"

He remained quiet.

"So, a rather large amount."

"I can tell you nothing," he said. "But perhaps someone else can."

"Who?"

"That is for you to discern." He bowed and took his leave.

I sighed and put my head in my hands. Of course, he was right. I could simply ignore this problem. And if the emperor had still been tending to the needs of his consorts, I would. But as things stood, it was impossible for the emperor to have more children if he did not spend time with his own women. If he was seeing a maid and she was to give birth without being a recognized consort, the child would never be recognized as a prince.

I knew the emperor was capable of making love several times a night. Why could he not see to a consort for the evening and then see his maid? But there was so much secrecy around her identity. Why? And who could I bribe to give me the answers I needed?

I realized that I was tapping my fingers along with a distant sound. It took me a moment to realize it was the clacking of a paiban. As I focused, I could also hear someone singing, though it was often interrupted. As I walked toward the sounds, I began to recognize it was some sort of opera song, though I did not know which one.

I found myself outside a small garden and watched as Lanhua was apparently being tutored in the art of opera by a eunuch. Their faces were painted in the traditional style, and the eunuch showed her how to dance, moving along with the percussion of the paiban. She made many mistakes, which often sent her into a fit of laughter. But as I watched, she gradually improved. Lanhua held a fan, and she slowly moved it in front of her face, peeking out from one side, and then the other. The eunuch showed her how to hold her head and free hand, where to place her fan. I noticed that several other palace ladies had also stopped to watch, such was the noise she was making. Eventually, after probably half an hour, the eunuch and Lanhua seemed to tire and called the class to an end. The ladies and I all clapped, and Lanhua took an exaggerated bow. She caught sight of me and trotted over. As she did so, I realized we were in a grassy area outside the emperor's audience hall. I could not see whether he also had been watching, but it would have been impossible for him not to hear her.

"You are clever, indeed," I told her after we hugged in greeting.

"Whatever do you mean?" Her voice was the pinnacle of innocence.

"Hmm." I took one last look at the emperor's audience hall and then turned to walk to my palace. "So, you have hired a tutor?"

"Well, I cannot have a real opera performer teach me. But that eunuch comes from an opera family. I was told he was the closest thing I could find to a proper opera tutor in the Forbidden City."

I nodded. An opera performer from outside the Forbidden City would have been an uncut man, and, thus, forbidden from entering the Inner Court and spending time with an imperial consort. And women were prohibited from performing opera in public, so there were no professional female opera performers. Which seemed a shame. Even women's roles were always played by men. How much more authentic would the women's roles appear if they were played by women? After watching Lanhua for only a few minutes, it was clear she had the talent for it. Perhaps, one day, it would become acceptable for women to perform opera.

"And you just happened to be practicing where the emperor could see you?" I said.

"It was a nice flat area to practice," she said.

"The entirety of the Forbidden City is a flat area."

"Is it?" Her eyes shined playfully.

"Has the emperor summoned you to his bed lately?"

"No," she admitted. "Though, I thought you knew that."

"I was hoping maybe you knew something I didn't."

"If you need information, I'm sure you can just buy it."

"So I've heard, but I'm afraid I'm not very good at that particular bit of court diplomacy. I tried it earlier today, but I must have asked the wrong person."

"Is it something I can help with?"

We had reached my palace, but I was not ready to go inside

just yet. I wanted to keep talking privately for a bit longer, so I led her into my private courtyard, where we sat on a bench.

"Do you have someone—a maid or eunuch—who you feel you can trust implicitly?"

"You can never have just one," she said. "Different people serve different needs. Have different connections. It depends on what you want to know."

I pressed my lips. Apparently, Lanhua had been doing a much better job than me of making connections within the Forbidden City. For the most part, as the empress, people simply did as I asked. I did not need to use subterfuge. Except when it came to my husband, it seemed.

"I want to know who it is that the emperor is spending his nights with," I said. "I think it is a maid. At least, I thought it was. But if it were, why would people be keeping her a secret from me? There is no shame in it. I only wish to be informed."

Lanhua nodded. "I have been wondering the same thing. The ladies of the court have not missed the fact that hardly any of us have been summoned since Lingrong fell pregnant. Life in the Inner Court, isolated as we are, is not easy. And being ignored by our husband has not helped matters."

"Believe me, I know," I said. "I have spoken to the emperor about this directly already. I am ashamed to say that I chastised him for it."

Lanhua clicked her tongue. "I am sure he did not respond well to that. You know how prideful he is."

"I know. I am worried I made matters worse. But I am only concerned for you, and all the ladies of the Inner Court. And the emperor himself. How many opportunities is he passing up to have even more children?"

"I know you only ever mean well. But you must find another way to deal with him. We cannot have him pulling even further away."

"So, do you have someone in mind?"

"I do," she said. "But it will take time. Even a eunuch cannot walk up to another eunuch and ask for information. He will have to make his own connections, his own trades. Listen. Then there is the cost…"

"Money is no object," I said. "Whatever it costs, we must find out who the emperor is spending his time with. I cannot confront him again without more information."

"I'll see what I can do," Lanhua said. "But we might need to prepare ourselves. We might not like the truth."

"What do you mean? It is surely a maid."

"I don't think it is. You said yourself, if it were a maid, you would be informed. But if the emperor—and others—are keeping her identity a secret, it must be a secret worth keeping."

"What do you think, then?"

Lanhua shook her head and thought for a moment. "A married woman?"

I almost barked out a laugh. "A married woman? You mean married to someone else?"

"Obviously."

"But who?"

"I don't know. But that would be quite scandalous."

"A secret worth keeping." I tried to think of married women my husband knew, but I had no way of knowing exactly who he knew or how well. For the most part, men and women lived very separate lives. We did not mingle together freely. The only women my husband would know at all who he was not related to by blood would be his sisters-in-law. But he only had one of those, Princess Ningxin. Princes Chun, Zhong, and Fu were not yet married. But I could not imagine Yizhu even looking at Princess Ningxin, much less spending so many nights with her that he forgot his own women.

"No, I don't think so," I said.

"Then, perhaps a prostitute."

"A what?"

"You don't know what a prostitute is?"

I shook my head. Lanhua chuckled a little.

"You are so innocent, even after all these years of marriage."

"It hasn't been too terribly long."

"Hasn't it been nearly five years?"

"No! Certainly…" I had not thought about it in some time, but I realized that she was right. I had been married to Yizhu for more than four years. I would soon be twenty years old. It, indeed, was strange that I had never fallen pregnant in that time. But more strange was that Yizhu still had no children. He at least had one on the way, but he needed to have many more as soon as possible.

"That is not important. What is a prostitute? Tell me?"

She lowered her voice to a whisper even though no one was around. "A woman who receives money to make love with a man."

"What? You mean…without marriage?"

"Of course."

"So…any man can pay this…prostitute to share his bed?"

"Exactly."

"But… No… Why?"

"I think it is cheaper than a concubine for some men," she said.

"But not the emperor. He has more concubines than most men. And if he wants more, he could just tell me. We don't have to wait ten years for another consort selection."

"Maybe he doesn't want to go to all the trouble of having a consort selection."

"But…I still don't understand. Why would the emperor want a woman who has been with other men? Does that not…hurt his pride?"

"I have no idea. Don't ask me to make sense of a man."

"No, it can't be that. I refuse to believe it."

"Maybe it's a man," she said.

"Now you are just trying to make a fool of me," I said, and we both started laughing.

"Or a eunuch!" she squealed.

"Please, stop!" I said. I was laughing so hard, I could hardly breathe.

"Empress!" A eunuch waved to me, and I motioned for him to approach. "The empress dowager is quite ill."

"Oh, I'm sorry to hear that. Does she wish to see me?"

"No," he said. "She only wanted you to be informed. I'm sure it is nothing more than a cold. But she said she would not attend audiences for the rest of the week, nor will she visit Consort Lingrong."

"That is prudent of her," I said. "We can't risk Consort Lingrong falling ill so near to her time. Tell the empress dowager that I wish her well. If she is in need of anything, let me know immediately."

"Yes, my lady." The eunuch bowed, then scurried off.

"Maybe you will be able to act like an empress before long after all," Lanhua said.

"Stop it," I said, playfully slapping her arm. "You are very naughty today."

"That's why you love me. I say the things you are too afraid to say."

"I'm not afraid. I'm smart. Your mouth is going to get you in trouble. In fact, I think it already has."

"That is true. I shouldn't have spoken to the emperor the way I did. But at least I had you there to save me."

"You need to be cautious. I might not always be able to shield you."

"But sometimes, don't you think you should be more bold?"

"I've tried that before. I usually end up with a bloody lip for the trouble."

"That doesn't mean you should give up."

"Am I not being bold now? I'm defying Yizhu by trying to find out who he is taking to bed."

"That's true. Maybe you are stronger than I give you credit for."

"I'm not sure if I should be flattered or insulted."

"Coming from me, it should always be taken as flattery."

"Empress!" another eunuch called out to me. I sighed and waved him over. The constant flow of people who needed my attention never seemed to end. "I need to update you on Consort Lingrong's condition."

"I should go," Lanhua said.

I nodded and watched her step carefully through the garden that surrounded my palace. The eunuch proceeded to tell me that Lingrong and the child were doing well, as I expected. In the many months I had been receiving daily reports, nothing ever changed. It was not until the final month that things would change daily, and I would need to be more mindful of those changes. Anything could happen at that point, no matter how careful we had been.

For now, my mind was not on Lingrong and the child, but on the emperor. I wished I could have just looked the other way. Not worried about it. But I had far more to think about than myself. If Yizhu had ignored me in the early years of our marriage in favor of another married woman, or even, Heaven forbid, a prostitute, I would have been glad of it. But he was not merely ignoring me, but his dozen other consorts. That was something I could not ignore or let stand.

Lanhua was right in that I was probably not going to like the truth, no matter what it was. But what else could I do? I had to know who my husband was sleeping with, no matter what.

CHAPTER NINETEEN

I nearly screamed in pain as Lingrong gripped my hand, but I knew that any pain I felt was a fraction of what she must have felt. I had been woken up in the middle of the night by a servant who said that Lingrong's labor had started. I was instantly alarmed as she was still only in her seventh month. It was much too early for the baby to come. Still, I wasted no time, tossing on my robe and practically running to her palace.

"Where is the doctor?" I asked as servants gathered uselessly around the room.

"They have been sent for, my lady," a maid said. "All of them."

I groaned in frustration. I had hired three midwives and three doctors, but none of them were present when we needed them!

Lingrong laid back on her pillow and sighed. "It…it seems to have passed for the moment."

"Contractions come and go," I told her. "Rest while you can before they start again." I had been present for the births of some of my younger siblings, so I knew some of what to expect.

I had even been present when one of my father's concubines went into labor early and gave birth to a stillborn child. What a nightmare that had been. The woman wailed long into the night and grieved for months. I saw the effect the loss had on my entire family. My mother—my father's first wife, not my birth mother—had been disappointed. It had been many years since my father had had a son. My father, too, had been despondent in his own way, closing himself away in his study for many weeks.

I did not want such sadness to descend upon the Forbidden City. Yizhu had been under so much stress from the constant threat of war, I did not know how he would be able to stand it should he lose his first son.

As for me, ever since Lanhua had pointed out that I had been childless for four years, the ache in my heart had been growing incessantly. I had already ordered clothes to be made for the child for the following year. I had helped Lingrong prepare the child's bedroom. I had also prepared a small room in my own palace should he stay with me on occasion. After all, if Lingrong proved capable of producing healthy sons, undoubtedly the emperor would want her to return to his bed as quickly as possible. I had even begun seeking a tutor for him even though he would not need one for many years.

Lingrong gasped and squeezed my hand again. "Oh, they are coming back."

I shook my head in dismay. If the contractions were indeed returning, then she probably was in labor. But it was much too early.

"Where are those useless doctors?" I asked.

But instead of a doctor, it was Lanhua who entered the room.

"Stand aside," she told a maid who had been rubbing Lingrong's feet.

"What— What is she doing?" Lingrong asked as Lanhua tossed Lingrong's blanket aside and propped her knees up.

"How long have you been feeling the pains, my lady?" Lanhua asked Lingrong.

"I…I don't know," she panted before falling back on her pillow again.

"Only about fifteen minutes, I think," I said.

Lanhua nodded and looked between Lingrong's legs. Then she pulled the blanket back over her. "It is good news. You are not in labor yet."

"What?" Lingrong and I both said at the same time.

"How is that possible? Look at the pain she is in," I added.

"It is very common," Lanhua said. "The pains should stop soon. It is simply your body changing as the child grows."

"How can you possibly know that, you stupid cow?" Lingrong yelled.

"There was a time when my family was too poor to hire a midwife for my mother," Lanhua said, undisturbed by Lingrong's outburst. "My mother taught me everything I needed to know so that I could help her myself. But your waters have not broken and your opening is not expanding. The child is not coming."

"How are you feeling?" I asked Lingrong.

"Like I'm ready to get this baby out of me," she whined, her eyes watering. "I'm already tired of being pregnant."

"It's only going to get worse," Lanhua said in a less-than-comforting tone. "You still have two months to go."

Lingrong let out another wail, and the emperor himself ran into the room. Those of us who could, bowed to him.

"What is wrong? Where is my son?"

"Right where he should be, my lord," I said, motioning to Lingrong.

"But he is coming, right?"

"I don't think so, my lord," Lanhua said, stepping forward

and looking straight at him. "She does not show any signs that she is in labor except the pain, which I think is temporary."

The emperor gaped at her, as if he did not know what to make of his concubine making a medical determination.

"What does the doctor have to say?" he asked.

I was about to tell him that the doctor had not arrived when an older woman made her way into the room.

"I suppose you can ask him when he arrives," she said as she walked past the emperor, hardly acknowledging him. "What's wrong with you, girl?" she asked, standing over Lingrong. All the midwives and doctors were familiar with Lingrong's condition and had examined her in their own way.

"I'm having a baby, can't you tell?" Lingrong asked.

"You are young and healthy. You are a long way from having a baby," the woman said. She then proceeded to examine Lingrong in much the same way Lanhua had, by looking between her legs.

"The pain was excruciating," Lingrong said.

"That was nothing compared to what's coming," the woman said. "Just wait until you really are in labor."

"What do you mean?"

"You aren't in labor yet. Your body is just getting ready for when it really is time," the woman said.

Lanhua bit her lower lip to keep from smiling in self-satisfaction, but I saw the emperor looking at her appreciatively.

"Thank you for coming," I told the midwife as I walked her to the door. "Can we do anything to ease the lady's discomfort?"

"A warm bath should be enough," she said. "Some calming tea as well."

"I'll make sure it is done," I said, giving her a small bag of coins for her trouble. I then instructed several servants to meet the other midwives and doctors as they arrived and tell them they were no longer needed. When I went back into the room, I saw the emperor sitting on Lingrong's bed, holding her hand and caressing her face.

"I want to make sure that a doctor or midwife is on duty at all times from now on," the emperor said.

"We have already made arrangements for that once Lingrong enters her eighth month, as is tradition," I said.

"We cannot wait until then," the emperor said. "She needed a doctor now and no one was here to help her. No one but Lady Lanhua."

"It was my pleasure to be of assistance," Lanhua said.

I bit my tongue and said nothing about the fact that I had rushed to Lingrong's side first. That I sent for the doctors and midwives immediately. That I had done all I could to calm and console her. But I had to admit I'd had no idea what was wrong with her. Lanhua had, indeed, been the first person to diagnose Lingrong's condition.

"Of course," I said. "I'll arrange for the doctors and midwives to move in immediately," I said.

"How are you feeling now?" the emperor asked Lingrong. She blushed.

"I suppose the midwife and Lanhua were right. I am feeling better, only tired."

"Of course," the emperor said. He kissed Lingrong on the forehead and then left the room, motioning for everyone except her maid to also take their leave.

I was the last to leave the room and pulled the door closed behind me.

"Until you are able to make arrangements for the doctors and midwives," the emperor said to me, "I think that Lady Lanhua should stay with her, just so she is not alone."

"I am sure that can be easily arranged," I said, even though Lingrong was hardly alone with half a dozen servants at her call at all hours and me only a few minutes' walk away. But the emperor was, rightly, nervous, so I would do whatever I could to help ease his worries.

"Good," he said. As he turned away, his gaze lingered on Lanhua for just a moment. He climbed into his litter to be carried back to his own palace for the night, and I wondered at how he had managed to be patient enough to be carried to Lingrong's palace in a litter in the first place.

I let out a sigh of relief, suddenly tired. "I am sure you may return to your own palace tonight," I told Lanhua. "Tomorrow, I'll have one of the rooms that was already prepared for a nursemaid outfitted as befitting your station. I doubt that Consort Lingrong will have any more issues tonight."

"She will probably keep any discomfort to herself for quite some time to avoid looking foolish in front of the emperor again," Lanhua said.

"There is no need for her to feel foolish," I said. "She is pregnant for the first time. How was she supposed to know what was happening?"

"I only hope that if anything goes wrong, she does not keep her concerns to herself. Better safe than sorry."

"Will you walk with me back to my palace?" I asked her. I had run over with one of Lingrong's servants and ordered all my servants to stay home. As such, I had no one to escort me back. Had it been daylight, I'd had no concerns. I often walked alone in the Forbidden City. But since it was night, it was quite dark. Red lanterns hung every few feet to illuminate the pathways, but this late, several of them would have already burned out. It was best to walk with someone to avoid tripping.

"Of course," she said. "I brought a eunuch who can carry a lantern for us. I wanted you to meet him."

I almost laughed at this. Why would I need to meet one of her eunuch servants? I hardly knew my own eunuchs' names. I was surprised, though, to see a boy of perhaps twelve waiting for Lanhua outside of Lingrong's palace.

"Empress, this is An Dehai. Or, as I like to call him, Little An," Lanhua said.

The boy kneeled down before me. "It is a pleasure to meet you, Empress," he said, and I could not help but smile. He was a beautiful boy with pale skin, a pert nose, and an eager smile. Had he not been castrated, I was sure he would have grown into quite a handsome man. I wondered just what tragedy had befallen his family that would force them to castrate a son with so much potential. Well, that was hardly my concern. And if being castrated and serving in the Forbidden City was the best option for him, then he did not deserve my pity, but congratulations.

"Hello, Little An," I said.

"Can you believe none of the other ladies wanted him as a servant?" Lanhua asked as Little An did his best to hold up the bamboo and silk lantern that probably weighed at least half of what he did. He was clearly struggling with this simple task, but he did not complain.

"He is quite young," I said. "They probably wanted a well-seasoned servant, not someone they had to train."

"But that is what makes him so wonderful. I can train him to serve me how I wish to be served. I don't have to undo bad habits or put up with a servant who thinks they know what I want better than I do."

I was not in the frame of mind to lecture Lanhua on the benefits of an experienced servant. That was something she could learn on her own in time. My mind started drifting and I wondered just how late—or early—it now was. I was sure I would fall asleep as soon as I lay down in my bed.

"Little An is very eager to help me," Lanhua was saying. "He will do anything I ask of him."

"That is why they are called servants," I said with a yawn.

"No," she said, shaking my arm. "He will do anything for me. *Anything.*"

It took me another moment to realize what she was saying. This was the servant that she thought could help us find out who the emperor had been sneaking into his bed. "Really? Are you sure you should trust a child?"

"My mother was married when she was his age," she said, and I thought about Princess Ayan. While girls were not often brought into the Forbidden City before the age of fourteen, it was not uncommon for girls to marry as young as twelve. Since I had not been married until I was nearly sixteen, I often forgot that people much younger than myself were often saddled with decidedly adult responsibilities.

"You think he is old enough to understand what we need? What the stakes are?" I asked.

"He's had a much more difficult life than either of us could imagine," she said. "He is more mature than he looks."

"And if he is caught?" I asked. "He could easily be intimidated, don't you think?"

"I would never betray you, Empress," he said. "Or Lady Lanhua. I would rather be put to death!"

I was surprised he spoke without being addressed, even if we were talking about him. I had a feeling that Lanhua was quite smitten with the pretty boy, as if he were an adorable, loyal, stupid dog. But even the most loyal of dogs can bite when frightened.

"Never speak to me out of turn," I said firmly. If Lanhua would not train her servant properly, I would.

"He is only eager to be of use," Lanhua said.

"Do not make excuses for him," I said. "You do not know what his future holds. He might not always serve you. If he were to act impudently with his next mistress, she could have him beaten—or worse."

"Yes, of course, you are right, my lady," Lanhua said. "But you cannot deny that he is what we need right now. Someone loyal and trustworthy. Someone who looks young and inexperienced. Someone who people will speak freely in front of without a second thought."

"Perhaps," I said. "I am more than willing to see if he can get the information we need. But he must be cautious. If any of us are caught looking into the emperor's private affairs, we could all be punished. Are you sure that you are willing to put your faith in him?"

"I am positive, my lady," she said.

I sighed and looked at the boy again. I noticed his eyes were downcast and he did not speak to either of us. He was, at least, a quick learner.

"And you, boy," I said to him. "Are you sure you are willing and capable of helping me with this task?"

"Yes, Empress," he said.

"Do you even know *what* we are going to ask of you?"

"No, Empress."

I raised an eyebrow at Lanhua.

"I trust him," she said. "And he trusts me."

"Fine," I said. "But if anything goes wrong, I'm blaming you."

"No, you won't." She said it playfully, but I knew she was right. After all, I was the empress. I was the head of the Inner Court—no matter what Empress Dowager Jing said. Anything that happened in the Inner Court was my responsibility, a responsibility I took seriously.

"Anything you hear, I want to know about it immediately," I told her.

"Of course," she said. "Come along, Little An. We have a lot to talk about."

It did not take long for them to be swallowed up by the darkness of the alleys between the palaces of the Inner Court in the dead of night. A slight breeze caused me to shiver. I only hoped I would not regret this.

CHAPTER TWENTY

I sat beside Empress Dowager Jing's bed and covered my face with my sleeve as she coughed. I did not think she had a disease that was catching, but I still did not want to breathe in any foul air. Empress Dowager Jing's condition over the last several weeks had not improved. Instead, she had worsened significantly. She was receiving constant care from several doctors who were feeding her all sorts of concoctions of medicinal herbs, but nothing seemed to help. I had not been present for most of her illness as I did not think she would appreciate my company. But she had summoned me to her bedside.

"Leave us," the empress dowager told everyone in the room but me. The consorts I knew were related to the empress dowager wept silently and eyed me wearily as they left the room.

"I'm sorry you are unwell, Mother," I said when we were alone.

"You will probably rejoice once I am gone," she said. "You are just chomping at the bit to rule the Inner Court by yourself."

"That is not true," I said. "I thought we would work together when I became empress. I did not expect you to dismiss me and treat me like a child. I thought you liked me."

"I do like you, Zhen," she said. "It was selfish of me to choose you as a consort for Yixin. I thought… Well, I suppose it doesn't matter what I thought."

My eyes watered at that. "It is not your fault that things turned out the way they did."

"Well, you are empress now. And soon, you will be the only empress."

"I'm sure you will recover. The doctors said—"

"The doctors lie. Being a doctor for the Forbidden City is a curse. It is the highest honor—and highest pay—they could ever achieve. But they are also often punished for delivering bad news to the emperor. So, they lie to make things seem not as bad as they are. I'm dying, Zhen. That is the truth of it."

"You must not give up," I said. "You will be a grandmother soon."

"I'm already a grandmother," she said. Her words struck me hard in the chest. I had almost forgotten that Princess Ningxin had given birth to a daughter.

"A grandmother to a prince," I said. "Another Qing emperor! You surely want to meet him, don't you?"

She shook her head. "Not my grandson. Not really."

"Don't speak like that."

"It is true," she said. "I never loved Yizhu the way I love Yixin and my daughters. It is unnatural to love a child that is not your own."

"I don't believe you," I said. "I already love Consort Lingrong's son. I will love all my husband's children."

"No, you won't," she said. "Because he will never love you the way he will the woman who gives him a son." She broke into another coughing fit.

"That doesn't matter to me," I said after she drank some

warm water to calm her coughing. "I don't care if Yizhu loves me. I only want his respect."

She smiled, revealing teeth that had started to decay. "Then it must be so hard for you, considering who Yizhu has in his bed every night."

My heart thumped hard in my chest and I felt my cheeks bloom. "You...you know?" I managed to choke out even though my mouth had gone completely dry.

"Of course I know," she said. "I know everything that goes on in the Forbidden City."

If she had been kinder to me, more helpful in my time here, I would have asked for her advice. Asked her to teach me to be the empress she was. A woman who knew everything. A woman who knew how to leverage her position. But it seemed to me that Empress Dowager Jing never had any intention of helping me succeed her as empress. I remembered how I had told Ayan to go to the empress dowager if she needed any help. I wondered now if she ever had. If the empress dowager had rebuffed her, or simply ignored her. If Empress Dowager Jing had been a kinder woman, a more helpful woman, maybe Ayan would not have felt so alone. Maybe she never would have killed herself. Maybe...maybe I would have been married to Prince Yixin after all. I grew angry as I realized that everything bad that had happened in the Forbidden City in the last several years had all been Empress Dowager Jing's fault. Suddenly, I was glad she had not taught me. Had not taken me under her wing. I had no desire to be an empress like her.

"Why did you summon me?" I asked her, getting to the point. Even if she did know who Yizhu was spending his nights with, I didn't want to hear it from her.

"I have heard that Yizhu has been spending time with Concubine Lanhua again," she said. At least I had also heard that much. He was not summoning her nightly, but the fact that he had summoned her at all was a good thing as far as I was concerned.

"I know," I said proudly.

"You will not be empress for long if you let that continue," she said.

I scoffed. "That is ridiculous. Lanhua and I are friends."

"She's not like you. You didn't care about being empress, did you? You wanted to be happy, whether that meant being the empress or not. She cares about being empress. She cares deeply."

"The only way she could be empress is if I were dead or deposed, and I don't think either of those things will happen."

"Really? You don't think she could whisper against you in the emperor's ear?"

"Of course she could," I said. "Any of them could. I can't control what anyone tells the emperor when I'm not around. But I believe she won't. Lanhua and I are friends. I trust her."

"And you don't think she would poison your tea if it got her one step closer to the throne?"

I stood up. "I will not listen to this. Good day, Mother. I hope your health improves."

"You will regret the day you met her, I promise you," she yelled as I left the room, not waiting to be dismissed. She fell into another fit of coughing and her servants and doctors rushed back to her side as I left the room.

I could not believe that the empress dowager had summoned me to her sickbed to say such a thing to me. I could not understand her motivation for doing so. After all, she had never helped me before. Why would she be trying to help me now? And did she think that driving a wedge between me and Lanhua was helpful? I would sooner believe she was only trying to make my life more difficult. Lanhua was my closest friend in the Forbidden City. Without her, I would have been so lonely, so despondent. I shook my head to dismiss her words from my mind. I would not consider them again.

When I arrived back at my palace, Lanhua and Little An were there waiting for me.

"We have news," Lanhua told me as we took a seat in my sitting room. I made sure to dismiss all my servants, and we told Little An to guard the door to prevent anyone from eavesdropping on us.

"Already?" I asked her. She had only introduced Little An to me about a week before.

"I told you that no one would take notice of him," she said. "He was raking leaves near the emperor's palace and overheard some of the emperor's eunuchs talking."

I glanced out the window. "It is summer. There are no leaves to rake."

"That is just how inconspicuous he is," she said with a laugh. I shook my head and wondered just how many times I had spoken without taking note of the servants around me, so far below my notice they were.

"Go on, then," I said.

"Only if you are sure you want to know," she said. "Believe me, the news is rather dire."

"Well, now you must tell me, for I'll never be able to stop wondering."

She nodded and leaned forward to whisper even though we were completely alone. "He is seeing prostitutes."

"Prostitutes?" I could barely get the word out. "As in...more than one?"

"The only good news is that he doesn't seem to have a favorite," she said, her voice closer to normal. "He has an arrangement with a brothel in the city. When he summons a girl, they send whoever is available."

"But I don't understand," I said. "Why? He has the most

beautiful girls in all of China at his beck and call right here. Thirteen of them! Why would he need more girls?"

"Because it gets worse," she said. "They are Han prostitutes...with bound feet."

I nearly vomited. That the Han people bound the feet of their daughters was one of the cruelest, most barbaric, and uncivilized things about them. For many years after the founding of the Qing Dynasty, when the Manchu first rose to power, the emperors tried to outlaw the practice. But that seemed to make the Han people only hold on more dearly to it. There were few things I hated more than catching sight of a Han girl limping along, hardly able to walk due to her tiny, broken feet. Not only were girls with bound feet crippled, but the feet were often diseased and stank of rot, or so I'd heard. I'd never been close enough to a Han girl to know for myself. But for all her life, the girl had to keep her feet wrapped tightly in silk. This would cause the feet to bleed and weep. For girls who were too poor to afford soap, they could not clean the wrappings properly, leading to bad smells and even infections. Many girls died from the process. And all for what? The hope of making a better marriage? But what sort of man would want a crippled wife? One who could not cook or clean or take care of children? I did not know how the women bore it, to be so useless for all of their lives.

"W...what?" I finally managed to ask. "Why?"

"I knew you would ask me that, so I had to ask around. I did not know either. I mean, I knew prostitutes existed, but I had never thought that a man would *prefer* a bound-foot whore. What could the appeal be? Anyway, some Manchu men seem to think that women with bound feet are...more sexually satisfying."

I shook my head. "I don't understand."

"Have you ever seen a bound-foot woman walk?"

"Hobble is a more accurate description."

She nodded. "You know how they sort of sway? Since their feet are broken, they use their hips more, their knees sort of locked together."

I closed my eyes and groaned. I didn't want to think about it. It was horrible. How could any parent do that to their child? Much less a mother to her daughter?

"Some men believe that this makes the woman's pelvis smaller. That it will make, you know—" She sort of motioned toward my own hips. "—your *cave* smaller."

"That is ridiculous," I said. "Why does it need to be smaller? Is it not painful enough as it is?"

Lanhua stared at me for a moment. "What do you mean? Making love is painful for you?"

"Isn't it for you?" I asked back.

"It was at first," she said. "But not anymore. It's quite pleasurable."

"For him, you mean."

"No, for me too. And it should be for you as well."

I was rendered speechless at her words. I had no idea that I was supposed to enjoy making love with my husband. I thought it was simply something to be endured. That the joy of making love came from giving pleasure to my husband. Or later, the joy of motherhood.

But then I remembered the way I had felt around Yixin. The feel of his lips on mine. The quivering I felt in my belly. The desire. Indeed, I had wanted to make love to him. I could imagine such an act with a man like that being truly pleasurable.

"Still," I said, ignoring my thoughts about a man who was not my husband. "Yizhu always achieves his pleasure when he is with me. And I suppose he does with you as well. And we know he did with Consort Lingrong, since she is with child. Why would he need a woman to be...smaller?"

Lanhua shook her head and made a swiping motion with

her hand. "Who knows? I think men are impossible to understand. I'm more worried about what sort of horrible disease he might contract from such a woman."

"What do you mean?"

Lanhua rolled her eyes. "I forget that I have to explain every aspect of this to you. Remember how I said that such women would make love to any man with enough coin?" I nodded. "There are certain illnesses, like rashes, that can be shared between lovers. Because prostitutes have so many lovers, they often have these illnesses, which they share among their lovers."

I groaned, feeling sick again. How could I ever make love to my husband again, knowing this?

"I will have to speak to him," I said. "I cannot let him put us at risk."

"I don't think you should," she said. "He will be angry with you."

"I have faced his wrath many times before, but it is my duty to protect you, all of the women of the Inner Court. I would feel terrible if any of them contracted some prostitute disease."

"If you feel you must speak to him about this, please be careful. Do not alienate yourself from him further. There may come a time when you need him."

"That sounds like advice I would give you," I said.

"Perhaps I'm learning."

THAT NIGHT, before the emperor could summon anyone to his bed, I went to see him myself. Even though it was long after all his councilors had gone home, he was still working, so he seemed surprised to see me.

"I didn't send for you," he said.

"I know. But I need to speak with you."

"About what?"

I gulped even though my mouth was dry. My heart was racing in my chest. I needed to speak plainly, but I was terrified. I had no way of knowing how he was going to react.

"About the fact that you have been summoning Han prostitutes to your bed," I said. He looked up at me, his face blank. My voice had been so small, I was afraid that he had not heard me.

"Did…did you hear what I said?" I asked.

"I heard what you said. I am only shocked you dared to say such a thing to me."

"It is true, then?"

"Did you doubt it? Did you think it was mere rumor?"

"No. No, I did not doubt it. I knew you were summoning women to your bed whom you should not. I suppose I only expected you to try and deny it."

"Why should I deny it?" he asked, standing up and coming around his desk toward me. I took a step back. "I am the emperor. I may bed any woman I wish."

"That is not true," I said. "You cannot bed a married woman. You cannot bed a widowed woman. You are not supposed to bed any woman who is not your own." I felt my strength, or perhaps my anger, growing. "And you are certainly not supposed to bed a Han woman. It is against the law for a Manchu man to take a Han woman to wife."

"I am not taking any Han woman to wife," he said.

"Taking her to bed is the same thing," I said. "It is something that should only be between a husband and wife. It is something that should result in children. You cannot have a Han child."

"You are clearly upset," he said. "You are being irrational. I am the emperor and can do whatever I want."

"*I* am being irrational? How can you say that? What is rational about sharing a Han whore with countless other men? Where is your pride? Where is your honor? Your dignity?"

"How dare you question my honor? I am the emperor!"

"Stop saying that!" I knew I was growing emotional, but I didn't want to stop. He had to know how his actions were impacting his women. "Believe me, I *know* that you are the emperor. No one knows that better than me. But being the emperor does not mean you are free to do what you will. No one in the empire has more responsibilities than the emperor."

"You think I don't know that?" he yelled back, stepping close to me, but I did not back down this time. I was not doing this for me, but for all the women of the Inner Court. "Day and night, I work for this cursed, ungrateful country. Rebellion after rebellion. Sanction after sanction. The people, the foreigners, everyone wants something from me every minute of every day. Can I not have at least a few moments to myself in the middle of the night that are just for me?"

"No," I said without hesitation, shaking my head in disbelief. "You are not a mere man, but the Son of Heaven. Heaven chose you to be emperor. It is your responsibility to give all of yourself for your country. And that means preserving your seed for your consorts. For the women who can actually give you sons to follow after you and daughters to strengthen your ties with allies."

"I have no need of worthless daughters," he said. "And soon, I will have a son to follow after me. Consort Lingrong has promised me."

I said nothing to this. While I hoped she did, indeed, give birth to a son, I knew nothing was guaranteed. I only hoped that Lingrong would not regret her promise.

"That is not enough," I said. "You were your father's fourth son, were you not?"

He could not reply because everyone knew it was true. The Daoguang Emperor's first two sons died young. His third son, he adopted out to his brother to replace his dead son. He had done so before his first two had died, though, so he thought he had sons to spare. The Daoguang Emperor went from having three sons to none within a year. Many considered it a miracle that he went on to have as many sons as he did—five in total, not including the one who had been adopted away.

"You never know what might happen. You must have as many sons as possible. You should know this better than anyone."

The emperor turned and walked away from me. He knew I spoke the truth. Perhaps it was hard for him to hear. After all, things could have turned out very differently had his brothers not died. Or had his father not adopted out the other brother. Or if his father had selected Yixin as his heir. It seemed that mere chance had led Yizhu to the Dragon Throne. Or was that how Heaven worked? Small, seemingly insignificant maneuvers that changed the course of a person's—or a country's—destiny?

"Besides," I said, softening my tone, "your consorts love you. They miss you. They want nothing more than to please you and give you sons. They sacrificed everything to be here for you. Most of them will never see their families again. You are all they have until they have children. You must do your best to give them that."

He sighed and rubbed his eyes. I thought, for a moment, that I was getting through to him. Instead, he turned on me. Stepping close to me, his eyes were full of anger.

"How dare you presume to tell me how to be a husband? An emperor?"

"I presume nothing," I tried to say.

"Yet you dare to criticize me?"

"When you need to be criticized? Yes!" I said, finally having enough. I leaned back because I knew that a slap would follow my words. When my husband's hand missed its mark, his eyes opened wide in shock. But then he lunged forward, and I was too afraid to run away. I was afraid his punishment would go beyond a slap to a beating, so I let him grab me. He threw me to the floor. But he seemed surprised that I did not fight back, so some of the anger flew out of him.

"Get out," he ordered me. "I'll not see your face again."

I then remembered Empress Dowager Jing's warning that Lanhua would try to take my place. I had said that such a thing could only happen if I were dead or deposed, neither of which I thought would happen. But when the emperor said he would not see me again, I was struck with the fear that he very well could depose me. Send me home to my parents in disgrace, where I would never again be allowed to marry or have children.

"Please, my lord," I said, kowtowing before him with my forehead all the way to the floor. "Forgive me. I only want what is best for you."

"You and everyone else," he says. "All day, I hear nothing but men quacking like ducks in my ear. *Do this, do that.* Am I to hear such clucking from my women as well?"

"I know some of what you feel, only on a much smaller scale. As empress, I am responsible not only for your happiness and mine, but all the women of the Inner Court, from your mother down to the lowliest maid. It has not been easy. And I cannot imagine that your life has been easy either."

He held a hand out to me and helped me to stand. "Our lives did not turn out how we expected, did they?"

"Did you not expect to be emperor?"

"I had always hoped it would be so, but I did not realize just how difficult of a job it was. My father seemed to have kept many of his struggles to himself."

"I think your father knew that the path ahead would not be easy. He believed that you would be able to withstand the storm."

"I think you are the only person living who believes in me," he said.

Perhaps I was the only person who did not have the heart to

tell him the truth. I did not believe he was the best choice for emperor. I believed that many of the rebellions he faced were of his own making or had not ended because of his decisions. I still, even now, so many years after the death of the Daoguang Emperor, believed that Yixin should have been named heir.

But what good would it do to say such things out loud? Yizhu was emperor. His decisions set the course for the whole nation. All I could do was encourage him to make the best choices—for all of us.

I was trying to think of the right thing to say, but before I had the chance, Yizhu stepped close to me, took my face in his hands, and kissed me. He pulled back and looked down at me, running his thumb over my lower lip. I felt he was looking at me with something akin to love. With desire. It was similar to the way Yixin had looked at me when he kissed me in the garden. But Yizhu did not stir feelings of love in me the way Yixin had.

"I need you," Yizhu said.

"I am yours," I said, which was nothing more than the truth. As his wife, I belonged to him. Yet, my words seemed to arouse him further.

In only a few moments, we were tangled together on the floor, both of us only half-dressed. I wished I could have enjoyed it. I longed to feel the pleasure Lanhua had spoken of. But I could not. As he penetrated me, I could only imagine his member covered in some prostitute's diseases. Indeed, the love-making could not be over quickly enough for me. When we finished, Yizhu held me in his arms, but I only wished to run back to my palace where I could bathe.

"Once my son is born, everything will be better," Yizhu said.

"In what ways?" I asked.

"I believe some people still think I should not have been named heir," he said. "They doubt my legitimacy. But once I have a son, no one will be able to doubt that I have the Mandate of Heaven."

"We only have to wait a couple more weeks," I said. "Consort Lingrong's pregnancy is still developing normally. I am sure you will have a healthy son before you know it. And then many more will follow."

"We will see," he said. His words concerned me. I noticed he still had said nothing about not seeing the prostitutes anymore. Or that he would give more attention to his consorts. But before I could ask him anything, he stood and dressed. "I still have much work to attend to, Zhen."

With that, I was dismissed. I dressed quickly and practically ran back to my palace, where I ordered the maids to pour me a bath, ensuring the water was as hot as possible. I scrubbed every inch of my body, from my scalp to between my toes, until my whole body was bright pink. Still, I could not erase the feeling of bugs crawling over me as I tried to sleep.

CHAPTER TWENTY-ONE

inally, Lingrong's real labor pains had begun. She was about two weeks earlier than the doctors had projected, but they said it was not unusual for children to come a little early or a little late. Her labors had started not long after sunrise, and it was now midafternoon on a bright early summer day. The room was stifling, so I had three maids fanning us and all the windows open. I held Lingrong's hand as Lanhua mopped her brow with a damp towel.

"Why isn't he here?" Lingrong moaned.

"He is coming soon, my lady," one of the doctors said. "Not much longer."

Lingrong groaned and laid back on the pillow, looking up at me. "It is a prince, isn't it? Tell me it's a prince."

"Of course it's a prince," I told her. "In only a moment, you will see him for yourself."

I glanced through an open window and saw Yizhu outside, pacing. He would not come into the room. Men were never present when their wives gave birth. But he wanted to know the moment his son was born. He could not bear to even wait in his own palace for a messenger. He had not eaten or seen any of his councilors. From the moment Lingrong's labors had begun, he had been outside pacing, waiting.

"I think it is time," the doctor said. He motioned one of the midwives over to confirm.

The midwife nodded and grabbed a silk blanket trimmed in yellow and embroidered with five-toed dragons. "Now, my lady, sit up and push as hard as you can," the midwife said.

Lanhua and I helped prop Lingrong up as she grunted and bore down as hard as she could.

"Almost!" the midwife said, smiling. "He's coming!"

Lingrong let out one more scream and then sighed in relief as she fell back on her pillow.

"He is here!" the midwife said.

I released Lingrong and went to the midwife's side as she held the baby, wiping blood from its face.

"What is it?" Lanhua asked.

"Let me see him," Lingrong said, panting.

I could not see the child's sex right away, as the midwife fumbled with the umbilical cord. I reached out, my fingers aching the hold the baby. The midwife tied off the cord and then handed the baby to me, wrapped in the blanket.

"Your...daughter, Your Majesty," she whispered.

For the briefest second, my heart ached and my eyes welled with tears. I knew that Yizhu would be disappointed. But the moment I looked down into her little face and heard her cry, oh, how I loved that baby girl!

"My son!" Lingrong said, reaching toward me. "Give me my son."

I sat by her side and offered her the little bundle. "It is a daughter, Sister. A beautiful little girl."

She pulled her hands away as though I had burned her. "What? No!"

I opened the baby's swaddling cloth just so I could check for myself. Indeed, the baby was clearly a girl. A perfect girl with ten fingers and ten toes, a tiny nose, and a large mouth with a healthy pink tongue.

"We have a daughter," I told Lingrong, my eyes watering, but this time from joy. I offered her the baby again. But again, Lingrong refused to take her.

"No! Where is my son? I was supposed to have a son." She burst into wailing sobs. You would think that her child had been stillborn by the way she was carrying on.

"Sister," I said, more firmly, "Heaven has blessed you with a wonderful daughter—"

"Get that thing away from me!" she yelled. Then, she cried out in pain. "Is there another child? Is my son still coming?"

"No, my lady," the midwife said. "It is only the afterbirth."

While Lingrong struggled with her birthing pains, I stepped away to the window. Outside, I could see Yizhu speaking with a eunuch. I held the baby up, hoping he would look to see his new daughter. Instead, he punched the eunuch in the face, sending the man sprawling to the ground. Without even looking toward the palace, Yizhu stormed away, limping heavily.

The baby—my daughter, our daughter, China's daughter—began to cry. Could she tell that both of her birth parents had rejected her? I knew that her situation was not uncommon. Sons were often preferred to daughters, at least among peasants. When it came to upper-class families, daughters were often celebrated, especially if there was only one or two. But no family, no matter how much money they had, could endure having too many daughters before a son came along. It seemed that both the emperor and Lingrong had put far too much faith in the hope that this child would be a boy. Hopefully, after the shock and disappointment wore off, Lingrong could find joy in the birth of her daughter. Yizhu, however, whether he came to love his daughter or not, would now have to do his duty by his wives and work toward having a son—and soon.

"My lady?" a woman who had approached me said. "Would you like me to nurse the baby?"

I realized that she was one of the wet nurses I had hired. Naturally, I wanted to say yes. The child had to be hungry. But at the same time, I didn't want to let the baby go. I wanted to hold her forever. I wanted to nurse her from my own breasts. But of course, that would be impossible. I finally forced myself to hand over the child.

"Give her back to me as soon as you are done," I said, my arms feeling empty without her.

"We will wash her first," one of the nannies said. "Then we will wrap her up and bring her back to you."

"Oh, of course," I said, suddenly feeling stupid. Of course the child needed to be washed. I had several younger brothers and sisters, but what did I know about raising a child? She was only a few minutes old and already I was forgetting to feed and wash her. Here I was, the empress of China, and even I felt as though this little creature deserved better.

"Consort Lingrong is resting," Lanhua said quietly as she came up next to me. I looked over and saw that she was indeed sleeping, but she did not appear to be resting peacefully. There were tearstains down her cheeks and her jaw was tight.

"Of course, we all wanted the child to be a boy, but surely everyone—even Consort Lingrong—knew there was always the chance it would be a girl, right?" I said.

"Some people seem to think they can simply speak their will into existence. But the world isn't like that."

"Do you think she will accept the girl eventually?"

Lanhua smirked at me. "Do you want her to?"

"What does that mean?"

"I saw the way you were looking at that baby. You want her for yourself."

"I don't know what you mean," I said. "The baby would simply have two doting mothers."

"I don't know. She was more distraught than I would have expected. Sadness, yes, that makes sense. But she seemed almost angry that the child was a girl. I'm not sure she will be able to forgive her."

"Forgive her? You mean, forgive the baby?" Lanhua nodded. I scoffed. "She can hardly blame the baby for being a girl. It wasn't her choice."

"Perhaps that is easier than blaming herself. For missing her chance."

"Missing what chance?"

"Her chance at having the emperor's first son."

"She still could."

"Do you think the emperor will give her another chance? Don't you think it is more likely that he will look elsewhere?"

"She is at least fertile and capable of giving birth to a healthy child. Surly the emperor will try again."

"Not before he tries with someone else first, I think."

"If he does at all," I said. "After what Little An found out…" I sighed and shook my head. "I don't know what is going to happen. What could Yizhu possibly be thinking? Surely he realizes that he is putting the whole dynasty at risk."

"Does he care?" she asked. "He seems rather selfish to me. That he would rather pursue his own pleasures than do his duty."

I wasn't sure what to say to that. We shouldn't say such things out loud, of course. If the emperor ever found out she had said such a thing, and that I had listened without punishing her, he could depose us both. But I had a feeling she was right. On the one hand, Yizhu was obsessed with preserving his father's legacy. With maintaining the empire that his forefathers had built. But on the other, he was selfish. He wanted things done his way and only his way.

"What are you going to call her?" Lanhua asked when the nursemaid brought the baby back to me. The baby was sleeping soundly, making little wheezing sounds through her nose. I brought her up to my face and inhaled her scent, rubbing her head with my own. Her cheeks were soft as rose petals and she smelled so sweet.

"How about Lifen?" I asked.

"A flower name?" Lanhua asked, wrinkling her nose. "So common!"

"Not a flower," I said, "but sweet like a flower. And clever."

"Flowers are not clever," Lanhua protested.

"I don't know," I said. "They do tend to pop up in the strangest of places."

"You are thinking of weeds. You can't name her after a weed."

"You say they are weeds; I say they are flowers," I said. "Just like some people might not be happy that this baby is a girl, but I could not be more overjoyed. Yes, I think Lifen is a perfect name."

"I suppose it will do," Lanhua said, leaning over and looking down at the baby for herself. "She is a pretty thing."

"She looks like Consort Lingrong, I think," I said. "Maybe when she wakes up, she will feel differently about her precious daughter."

BUT LINGRONG DID NOT FEEL DIFFERENTLY. She refused to hold the child at all. Once when the child cried and Lingrong's breasts started to leak milk, she refused to even have the child in the room with her anymore. She was worried that if her milk did not dry up, she would not be able to get pregnant again. The midwives told her she should not rush to get pregnant again too quickly, but she did not want to listen. She took medicinal herbs to stop her milk and to bring her monthly visitor back.

At first, I would spend all day at Lingrong's palace, helping the wet nurses and nannies take care of the baby. I would then spend the night in my own palace, but I did not sleep very much. I worried the whole night through about the baby. What if the nannies fell asleep? What if the baby got tangled in a blanket? What if someone tried to kidnap her? Most of my concerns were ridiculous, of course, but I couldn't stop my mind from running wild when we were separated.

One morning, when I returned to Lingrong's palace after yet another fitful night, Lingrong was incensed. Lifen was crying, and the nanny could not stop her. As soon as I took the baby into my arms, she quieted down, cooing as I bounced her up and down.

"The baby cried all night," Lingrong said.

I looked to the nannies. "Is this true?"

The women did not seem concerned. "That is what babies do. They cry."

"All night?" Lingrong asked.

"Sometimes," a wet nurse said.

"Was she hungry?" I asked.

"Not at all, my lady," the wet nurse said. "She was clean. She was fed. She was held. She was put in her bed. Nothing was wrong with her. She just wanted to cry."

"Or she wanted her m— me." I had almost said "her mother," but I had meant me. I didn't want to upset Lingrong further, though, so I had caught myself at the last moment. "She is used to me holding her."

"You spoil her," Lingrong spat.

I laughed. "You can't spoil an infant. Not yet, anyway. Isn't that right?" I asked Lifen, tickling her chin. The baby smiled, and I thought she laughed, but then I heard her release wind. "Are you dirty already?"

"I'll change her, my lady," one of the nannies offered. I

handed the baby over and went to stand next to Lingrong, who was looking out a window at her garden.

"He hasn't come to see me, you know," she said. "Not once."

"I haven't seen him either. He hasn't come to see the child."

"He sent gifts," she said. "My mother said he sent them some gold and silks. A eunuch made a big proclamation in the street. A few people clapped, I guess. But it was all just a formality. He is not happy with me. With her."

"We all knew there was a possibility the child would be a girl," I said. "That's just how it is."

Lingrong ran her hands over her face. "I didn't believe it. As long as I prayed hard enough and believed it completely, I thought a son would come."

"If it were that easy, China would have no daughters and we would have all died out long ago," I said.

Lingrong snorted a laugh. "If only men saw it that clearly. Saw that we do have some value."

"Some men do," I said. "But not emperors."

"Will you speak to him?" she asked. "Speak to him on my behalf?"

"Of course," I said. "I want nothing more than for you—for all of the consorts—to have as many children as possible. But I want you to be careful. Be gentle with yourself. This is a natural process. If you rush to change things, you could hurt yourself."

"Nothing will hurt me as badly as not having a son," she said. "The only way I can have value in my husband's eyes is to have a son. The only way I will…be remembered."

"I'll remember you," I said.

Lingrong scoffed. "When we die, no one will know who we were. Well, some people might remember your name because you were an empress. But it's not like that for the rest of us. The only way my name will get preserved in the family tablet hall is if I give birth to a son. A prince. An emperor."

"I didn't know you felt this way. That you worried about being forgotten."

"Because I thought I was going to have a son. I thought that my job was done and my future was secure. But now...now, I'm right back where I started. Just one concubine among many."

I wasn't sure how to reply to that. What else was there for women? We weren't meant to be remembered. People remembered emperors. Great battle heroes. The only women people remembered were often bad women. Cruel women. Women like Wu Zetian, the woman who dared to name herself emperor. She even killed her own sons so she could rule unopposed—or so I'd been told. She'd lived a thousand years ago. How could anyone know what really happened back then?

"I'll speak to him," I said.

"Can you do one more thing for me?" she asked.

"Anything."

"Can you take the baby to live with you?"

My mouth gaped at this. I knew she was disappointed that Lifen was a girl, but I thought that by having the baby remain living with her, she would eventually get over her disappointment and grow to love the baby as I did. But it seemed that she could never love Lifen.

"I don't want to replace you as her mother," I said. "She deserves both of us in her life."

"No," Lingrong said. "I can't."

"How can you not love your own daughter?"

She looked at me, her eyes red with tears. "I love her more than you will ever know."

"Then...why are you sending her away?"

"Because I am afraid that she will be enough for me. That if I keep her close, I won't need to have another child."

"But I don't understand," I said. "Plenty of women have lots of children."

"Plenty of children with husbands they have more time

with," she said. "The emperor will replace me soon enough, either with another concubine he already has or a younger woman later on. I need to be ready to have another child as soon as he will take me back to his bed. I can't risk my future on a girl child now."

I both understood and yet could never understand what she was saying. As the empress, as someone whose position did not rely on having a child, as someone who didn't want the physical affections of her husband, as someone who—as Lingrong had put it—would already be remembered, I couldn't understand the lengths she would go to to have a son with her husband.

"I will do as you ask," I said, placing my hand on hers. "But, I beg of you, don't forget her. I promise that she will not forget you."

She put her hand on mine. "You are a good woman, Zhen. Don't ever change."

When Lifen started crying again, I went to her. I then ordered the wet nurses and nannies to start packing to move to my palace. I then carried my daughter to her new home.

"SHE IS BEAUTIFUL," Prince Yixin said when I showed him Princess Lifen. The prince had been waiting outside the emperor's study when I arrived to finally force Yizhu to recognize his daughter.

"Thank you," I said. "She looks like her mother."

"And I take it the mother is healthy and happy?"

"Quite," I said. "And already eager to have many more children."

"That is how you know a woman is a good mother," the prince said. "Did you hear? Princess Ningxin is with child again. She should deliver in the autumn."

My jaw clenched of its own accord, but I quickly corrected

myself. "How wonderful. Soon we will be celebrating the arrival of your son."

"We hope so," he said. He reached out and ran a hand over Lifen's head. "But daughters, they are rare pearls indeed. Nothing brings me greater joy than seeing the smile on my daughter's face at the end of the day."

I felt the prince lightly place his hand on my shoulder. I leaned into him and thought I heard him sniff my hair. Standing next to him with a baby in my arms, I had a glimpse of the life I should have had. But it was nothing more than an illusion. A baby that was not mine and a husband who belonged to someone else. I straightened up just before the door to my husband's study opened, and Prince Yixin quickly dropped his hand.

"What is it?" Yizhu asked me brusquely, without any etiquette at all. I did not answer but walked straight into his study.

"How dare you speak to me like that in front of others," I said. "I am not a maid. I am the empress."

"You are right," he said. "I apologize. I just didn't realize you were bringing...*that* with you."

"*She* is your daughter," I said. "A daughter of the Dragon. A princess of the first rank who deserves your attention."

"Did you give birth without telling me?"

I only scowled at him.

"Then she is not a first-rank princess, is she? She's a second-rank princess. My father had half a dozen of those by the end. Hardly worth nothing."

"He also had half a dozen sons," I said.

Yizhu slammed his hand on the table so hard, even Lifen shuddered in my arms. "You dare to complain about how I speak to you when you fail to show me the respect an emperor deserves?"

"You have no son," I said.

Yizhu ran his hand over his head as he regained control of his temper. "I know. I know…"

"Please, I beg of you, return to your women, your lawful concubines and consorts. I ask, not for myself, but for them—and for you. Please, do your duty by them."

Yizhu sat back in his seat and exhaled. "I know. I will. I promise." For the first time, I noticed how tired he looked.

"Thank you, Your Majesty," I said formally, a way to apologize for my earlier behavior.

"Bring her here," he said.

I walked over and showed him his daughter for the first time. He couldn't help but smile, like everyone who looked at her.

"She looks like Consort Lingrong," he said.

"I know. She is so beautiful."

"We should name her Butterfly, like my mother."

"Oh," I said, not a little disappointed.

"You don't like the name?"

"No," I said. The emperor frowned at me. "I mean, no, it's not that I don't like it. But I have been calling her Lifen."

"Oh. Well, I suppose that is a fine name as well. We can call our next daughter Butterfly."

"I can certainly agree to that," I said.

"But only after I have a son."

"I will do my best," I said.

"I was thinking of summoning Lanhua back to my bed," he said. "I have seen her practicing opera in the garden. She is quite talented, don't you think?"

"She is," I agreed, and I marveled at how clever Lanhua was. "She has told me many times how much she enjoys opera."

"I will summon her tonight."

"Very well, Your Majesty," I said. I was about to leave the room when a eunuch entered, breathless.

"What is wrong now?" the emperor asked.

"The empress dowager!" the eunuch said. "She is dead!"

That was when I heard Prince Yixin let out the most pained yell I'd ever heard from a man.

"She's dead?" Yizhu asked, confused. "I thought she was merely ill. Zhen, did you know she was that sick?"

"I had no idea," I said. "But... Forgive me, I have been very distracted by the new baby."

"That is understandable," he said. He rubbed his head. "I don't have time for this right now."

While I thought it was a rather callous thing of him to say, I supposed I understood the sentiment. He had been so busy with the various wars he was fighting, his concerns with money, his disappointment in not having a son. And the death of an empress dowager was usually treated with much pomp. Not as much as the death of an emperor or empress, but very nearly.

"Zhen, can you take care of this?"

"I'll arrange what I can," I said. "But I'm rather busy with the baby. Do you mind if I ask for help among the ladies?"

"No, of course not. Why don't you ask Lanhua to help you? She always seems eager to be of use."

"That is a wise idea, my lord," I said. I was surprised he didn't suggest Lingrong, but he probably thought she was still recuperating from the birth. She should have been, but I had already seen her taking walks around her palace.

"Thank you," Yizhu said.

"For what?" I asked.

"For bringing my daughter to me. I am sure she will be a source of joy to me in the future—once my son is born."

"I am sure she will be too."

"And for taking care of her. I have heard that Consort Lingrong has had a difficult time bonding with her."

"She is as anxious to give you a son as you are to have one," I said.

"Yes, well..."

I waited, but the emperor did not continue. I bowed and made my way out of the room. I returned to my palace and left Lifen with her nannies. Then I went to Empress Dowager Jing's palace to pay my respects and get started on the funeral preparations. A large crowd of people was already gathered at her palace, ladies and servants, and I noticed that one of her daughters had already arrived. I realized many extended family members would be arriving soon, not to mention the empress dowager's friends and anyone hoping to make a good impression on the emperor. The Forbidden City would soon become a circus. How I wished I wouldn't have to be here. That I could take Lifen away to the Summer Palace, where it would be quiet and the air cooler. But that would be impossible. I would have to be here to pay my own respects to the empress dowager and lead everyone else. The mere thought made me feel exhausted. But at least I would have Lanhua to help me.

Everyone parted to make room for me as I entered the palace. I saw Prince Yixin kneeling before his mother, wailing in pain. I knelt next to him and wrapped my arms around his shoulders.

"I'm sorry for your loss," I told him.

"She told me she was going to hang on until she met her grandson," Prince Yixin said, tears streaming down his cheeks. "I thought she meant my next child. I didn't think she meant Consort Lingrong's child. I didn't think that having another granddaughter would kill her."

I bit my tongue to keep from telling him how ridiculous that was. In truth, I wanted to slap him for saying something so hurtful. I did not want evil rumors to spread around Lifen. For her to grow up thinking she was cursed.

"She was ill for quite some time," I said, remembering that the last time she and I spoke had been months ago. "I'm sure she was only being brave for you, but it was simply her time."

"Yes, of course," the prince said. "I just did not expect it. She seemed to always be such a powerful force in my life. I never imagined her dying. I thought she would hold on forever."

I had to suppress a laugh. Yes, I could see her as the sort of woman who would live forever if she wanted to. But, in the end, death comes for us all.

"Though, I had not expected my father to die so suddenly either. I never seem to be prepared when someone close to me dies."

"I don't think any of us are ever ready to lose someone we love."

"I wish I could give her a full mourning," he said, wiping his cheeks. "But my brother needs me."

"I'm sure he will give you all the time you need to grieve."

"The foreigners are amassing off our shores," he said, his voice low.

"What?"

"Their warships have been seen from Canton to the Dagu Fort."

"The Dagu Fort?" This alarmed me. The Dagu Fort was the nearest port to Peking, only a half day's ride away. If we were ever invaded from the sea, that was where the enemy would land. "What do they want?"

"What they always want. More trade ports open. More money. More foreign missionaries allowed in. To import more opium. Always more."

"Will they use force?"

"No. No, I don't think so. China is a massive country. Far larger than the foreign countries combined. They cannot possibly have the men needed to invade."

I hoped he was right. I remembered seeing England on a map and noticing it was a mere island. But England had a history of invading and conquering. They had conquered India. They had once colonized America. Not to mention the fact that we were still fending off the Taiping rebels in the south. Since we were in a weakened state, now would be the perfect time to attack. From behind the walls of the Inner Court, I had no idea how things were on the outside. How many men had we lost already? I had no way of knowing.

"Do I need to worry? We are so close to the sea here."

"No, of course not," Yixin said, giving me a half-smile. "I will always keep you safe. I promise."

His words were reassuring, but his eyes lacked surety. I suspected things were much worse than he wanted me to know. But what could I do about it? Nothing.

"I must go," I said, standing. "I have many things to prepare for your mother's funeral."

"Thank you for taking care of her," he said. I nodded and squeezed his shoulder.

In truth, not even a small part of me was sad she was dead. Initially, I had thought that she would be a good and helpful mother-in-law, someone I could lean on for help and work with as I found my place as empress. Instead, I had found her to be a shrewish and selfish woman. A woman who had refused to step aside when it was her time. A woman who would not let go of the past and look toward the future.

A woman who lived in *my* rightful palace.

I went to find Lanhua. We would need to start arranging the funeral immediately before the empress dowager's body began to stink.

CHAPTER TWENTY-TWO

*T*hankfully, the emperor only ordered three days of mourning for Empress Dowager Jing. However, he allowed Prince Yixin and his family to continue mourning for another week in his home. I was glad for it. I was ready to take my rightful place in the empress's palace and was afraid that Prince Yixin might have been upset or even felt slighted if he saw me moving his mother's things out so soon after her death.

I could not move soon enough. My previous palace, though generous in size, had not been arranged with a child in mind. So, when Lifen moved in with me—along with all of her staff—we found ourselves in cramped quarters rather quickly. Instead of rearranging my entire palace, it was much easier to move to a new home.

I sent all Empress Dowager Jing's servants back to the Ministry of Household Affairs for reassignment. Many of them were dismayed at this. I think many of them assumed that I would accept them into my household since I would need a larger staff, but I could never trust someone who had served the former empress.

Many of the empress dowager's personal items were bequeathed to her daughters and granddaughter, Prince Yixin's daughter. I noticed she left nothing to Lifen, but I didn't care. As my daughter, she would want for nothing. After the empress dowager's will was taken care of, she still had a whole household of items to disperse. Most of her jewels were now mine as they belonged to whoever held the position of empress and she should have handed them over to me years ago. Still, she left behind fabulous gowns in the finest silk, rooms upon rooms of intricately carved furniture, beautiful embroidery pieces, stunning paintings, elegant shoes, ivory chopsticks, and delicate porcelain tea sets. I kept some of these things for myself, but other items I distributed among the consorts as gifts. I had all the windows thrown open and the rooms fanned out by maids. I summoned several Buddhist priests to come to bless the home. When everything was finally ready for me to move in, it was not like stepping into a renovated space, but a brand-new palace. Not a trace of the empress dowager was left. I was standing at a window, overseeing servants who were tearing out some old and dried-out plants from my new garden to be replaced by lush flowering bushes, when Lanhua came to see me.

"I had no idea how beautiful this palace was," she said as she looked around. "It always seemed so dark before."

"Yes, well, the empress dowager had a way of making everything dark," I mumbled as I turned to check on Lifen, who was fussing in her cradle. I summoned a nanny over. "I think she needs to be cleaned. Go ahead and give her a full bath while the sun is still out."

"Yes, my lady," the woman said as she took Lifen away.

"You are such a hands-on mother," Lanhua said. "I think most ladies who can afford nannies simply hand their children off until they are old enough to behave themselves."

"I enjoy caring for her, ensuring her needs are met. Seeing her smile. Watching her grow and change every day. I know the day of her marriage will come much too soon. I don't want to miss a moment with her. I don't know how Consort Lingrong can stand not having Lifen by her side."

"She misses her," Lanhua said. "It is very clear. But she is holding on to the idea that the sacrifice will be worth it."

"Because she thinks she will have a son? The emperor hasn't even sent for her since the baby was born."

"He has sent for me."

"I know. And was he...able to perform?"

"Adequately," she said. "Quickly."

"Better than not at all, I suppose."

"Well, I won't have to worry about that anymore. Not for a while anyway."

"What do you mean?"

When Lanhua didn't respond, I turned to look at her and saw she was smiling. I gasped.

"You don't mean...?"

"Yes, my lady," she said. "I'm pregnant!"

"Oh. Oh!" I could hardly string words together, I was so excited. Lanhua and I hugged each other, bouncing from one foot to the other.

"This is wonderful, wonderful news," I said, squeezing her hands. "How do you know? How far along are you? Have you spoken to a doctor?"

"I asked one of the doctors to check me when he came to see how Consort Lingrong was faring. My monthly visitor was nearly a week late."

"Why didn't you tell me?"

"You have had enough to deal with lately, with a new baby of your own, the empress dowager's death, moving to a new palace. I didn't want to bother you if it wasn't a sure thing."

"Oh, Lanhua, this is the best news. I am so happy for you. So happy for all of us. We must tell His Majesty."

I left Lifen with her nannies as Lanhua and I were carried to the emperor's study in our litters. My new palace was not much further from the emperor's palace than my previous palace had been, but I didn't want Lanhua walking very far in the sun and heat. It was August, and we had not sojourned to the Summer Palace this year, so we had to suffer in the sweltering heat of Peking.

"Must you bother me about every little thing when I am working?" the emperor asked when the three of us were alone.

"Only if you think the possible birth of your son is a little thing," I said, beaming, my arms around Lanhua.

"You are with child?" he asked me, his tone flat.

"No," I said. "Lanhua is."

He was quiet for a moment. "Are you sure?" he finally asked.

"A doctor confirmed it. Her monthly visitor is a week late. I think we can safely say that, yes, a son is on the way."

"A child," he said. "Not necessarily a son."

I clicked my tongue and was about to chide him when Lanhua spoke up.

"Please do not let your disappointment in the birth of Consort Lingrong's child sour you on the birth of this one. We have to believe it is a son. To think otherwise would tempt fate."

I did not want to go down this road again. While there was no harm in hoping for a son, to believe with one hundred percent certainty that the child would be a son was delusional.

"Surely the birth of any child is a blessing and comes with many benefits," I said. "Just think of the marriage alliances you could make, my lord."

"Maybe we could marry Lifen to Hong Xiuquan and end this fucking rebellion," he muttered.

"Don't ever say that," I said firmly. "Do not speak that man's name in my presence, especially not in connection with my—our—your daughter."

"Do you have any idea how much territory that man controls now?" the emperor asked me. *Of course I didn't.* "Almost all Southeast China, more than a quarter of my empire! If I had to throw Lifen off a mountaintop to appease Heaven and end this war, I would do it!"

The emperor was shaking with rage, sweat dripping down his forehead. His eyes were wild. I didn't know what was wrong with him, but he didn't seem to be in his right mind.

"I have clearly come to see you at a bad time," I said. "Lady Lanhua and I will not bother you again except to tell you when your son is born."

"I guess I won't be seeing either one of you ever again, then!" he yelled after us as we left the room.

The men in the hall bowed to us. I looked around for Prince Yixin, but did not see him. I wanted to ask him if he thought the emperor was behaving irrationally. I approached one of Yizhu's cousins, Prince Zaiyuan, and asked him if he knew where Prince Yixin was.

"The prince is not here, my lady," he said.

"Where is he? Is he ill?"

"No, my lady. The emperor banished him."

"What?" I nearly screeched. "How? Why?"

"The prince was greatly distraught over the death of his mother."

"Naturally."

"Well, the emperor thought he was too distraught."

"How can one be *too* distraught over the death of a beloved parent?"

Prince Zaiyuan sighed. "Too much for the emperor's liking, apparently. He was moping around here for days."

"So, the emperor banished him for that?"

"I think it was just a ruse. An excuse. Good riddance if you ask me."

I raised an eyebrow, prodding him to continue.

"The prince always wants the emperor to capitulate. To give into the foreigners, give into the Taiping. Make alliances and friendships at the cost of money and land that is rightfully ours. We need to fight! Fight to the very last man!"

"Then why are you here and not down there in Jiangning fighting?" Lanhua asked.

"I will if it comes to that."

"I'm going to hold you to that," Lanhua mumbled.

"That's enough, Sister," I said. "It is not for us to have an opinion on such matters. Though, I am disappointed that the emperor would dismiss his own brother. It was the will of their father that they work together."

"I think the late emperor only said that so Yixin wouldn't feel slighted for being passed over as heir. In truth, Emperor Daoguang knew Yixin didn't have the strength to be emperor. He wouldn't have the will to hold the empire together the way Yizhu does."

"Well, let us hope that the fighting ends soon, for all our sakes," I said. "Good day, Cousin."

"Good day to you, my lady."

"Can you believe that Yizhu dismissed Yixin?" Lanhua asked me when we were alone again.

"No, I really can't. I mean, I know they haven't been seeing eye to eye on many things. But to dismiss him altogether, it seems rather extreme. The emperor didn't look well to me. What do you think?"

"He did look a bit feverish," she said. "Do you think he is ill?"

"It's a possibility," I said. "Or it could just be this heat. We need to get out of the city, all of us."

"We could have a doctor recommend it," she said. "We can

summon one to check on me and then ask him to call on the emperor."

"That is a good idea," I said. "And then we can announce your pregnancy publicly. But first, we better tell Consort Lingrong. I want to be there when she hears the news to ensure she doesn't do something stupid like hurt herself."

"You don't really think she would do that, do you?"

I didn't want to think it. But after what happened to Ayan, I couldn't underestimate the sorrow of a desperate consort.

CHAPTER TWENTY-THREE

"*I*mperial Concubine Lanhua has given joyous birth to a prince!"

The pronouncement rang throughout the empire the moment the midwife placed Lanhua's son into my arms. Just like his sister, he was perfect and beautiful.

"Give him to me," Lanhua said, her arms outstretched. Even though she had just given birth, she appeared rested and serene. Her labor had gone much more quickly than Lingrong's, and the baby came easily.

"Your son, Sister," I said as I sat on the bed next to her and handed her the pink baby boy.

"You did it, my daughter," Lanhua's mother said, hovering over her daughter's shoulder. For the last month, Lanhua's mother had been allowed to come into the palace and live with her daughter, attending to her every need. Lanhua had obviously been overjoyed at having her mother by her side, but it meant that I had not gotten to spend as much time with Lanhua as I would have liked. Not that I had as much time to spend with her as I did with Lingrong.

Lifen was growing quickly and healthily, but at almost ten

months old, she seemed needier now than when she had been an infant. She wanted my attention constantly and often cried when I did not hold her. If I had work to do and handed her off to a nanny, they would have to take her out of my palace so that her crying would not disturb me. The nannies assured me that this was normal. That all children of her age had a strong attachment to their mothers, but I could not help but feel that I was doing something wrong. Even now, as I rejoiced with Lanhua and the birth of a boy, in the back of my head, I was anxious to return to Lifen, knowing that she was crying for me even in the wee hours of morning.

The emperor entered the room, panting. Unlike with the birth of Lifen, Yizhu did not wait outside the palace for the child to be born. He seemed convinced that his second child would also be a girl. He had refused to plan for the birth of a boy. "Wait and see" was all he told me when I asked for help in preparing the celebrations. I had done all I could, but the truth was that we were woefully unprepared for the birth of a prince. Announcements had been sent out, but that was about it.

Everyone stood and bowed to the emperor, clearing a path to Lanhua's bedside. Yizhu fell to his knees next to her and marveled at the sight of the baby in her arms.

"A son. I have a son." He seemed to be in a daze, in complete awe at the boy who was still only minutes old.

"What is the child's name?" Little An asked. The boy had been standing just outside the room since Lanhua went into labor. Indeed, it seemed that wherever Lanhua was, Little An was not far behind.

"Zaichun," Yizhu said.

Union and order. I thought this was rather wishful thinking on the emperor's part. He claimed he wanted nothing more than peace and prosperity throughout the empire, but he had done little to bring that to fruition. He seemed to think he could simply force people to follow his will without giving anything in return. I did my best to avoid any talk of the troubles facing the empire. They only caused me fear and anxiety. But it was impossible for talk of war and famine and poverty to not leak into my home through the letters the many consorts and concubines received from their families. Their relatives were scattered throughout the empire, and it seemed as though all of their lives had been touched by tragedy in one way or another. Thanks to the Taiping, some of the concubines' families had been left homeless, destitute, or were even wiped out.

"An excellent name, my lord," Little An said.

Everyone agreed, but I thought it was rather a lot of pressure to put on a child who, only moments ago, the emperor did not even think was going to be born. I wished that the emperor had returned to his nightly duties as he had promised me. He had kept to his word for only a few weeks. But after it had been announced that Lanhua was pregnant, he had once again stopped summoning his women to his bed. He and I fought about it constantly. He did not believe that Lanhua was going to give birth to a son, yet he refused to leave his prostitutes and do his duty by his consorts. It was clear that my husband was able to sire children, so he should have had an Inner Court full of them. But he simply refused to do what was required of him. Of course, that was partly my fault. I refused to sleep with him as well. I couldn't bear the thought of contracting some vile illness from the brothels he frequented. But there was nothing I could do to protect the few ladies of the Inner Court he did occasionally call to his bed, such as Lingrong. I could never tell them what Yizhu was actually doing on the nights that he did not call a woman to his bed. They would have been devastated, horrified, disgusted. Worse, they might have told their maids or families about it as well. I couldn't let it become common knowledge that the emperor preferred bound-foot whores to his own refined and elegant ladies. The empire was struggling enough as it was.

"What would you ask of me?" the emperor asked Lanhua. "Anything you want is yours."

I was surprised when Lanhua looked to her mother and not to me for advice. Not that I knew what she should ask for. But it seemed that she and her mother had discussed this possibility at length.

"My sister, Wanzhen," Lanhua said, motioning to a girl of about thirteen by her mother's side. I had taken little notice of the girl since she had been here. She was quiet and timid and had said nothing to me aside from "yes, Empress" and "no, Empress" in the month she had been here.

"Make my sister a princess," Lanhua said. "Give her to Prince Chun."

One of Yizhu's younger half-brothers, Prince Chun, was now sixteen years old. I remembered how Empress Dowager Jing had used her position to elevate her own family, a lesson I never seemed to fully grasp. But Lanhua knew exactly how to help her family. And I had to admit, I was a bit impressed that she was elevating her sister and not one of her brothers. After all, Yizhu still had unmarried sisters as well. Perhaps she thought that her brothers could help themselves. For women, the only way they could better their lives was through marriage. And a girl could hardly make a better marriage than with a prince.

"It will be done," the emperor said without a pause. "And you will be elevated for giving me this great gift. You will now be known as Consort Lanhua."

"Thank you, my lord," Lanhua said, but she was clearly displeased with this gift of being elevated only a single rank. Still, she at least was no longer a concubine, but a consort, which would be accompanied by many new gifts and privileges.

"I must prepare a grand celebration," Yizhu said, standing. "Everyone will want to come and pay homage to my son."

We all bowed as he left. "Oh, great rejoicing to our master of ten thousand years," we said, as was tradition.

"Congratulations, Little Sister," I said to Lanhua.

"Thank you, Your Majesty," she said in a small voice, her eyes never rising from the floor.

"Well done," Lanhua's mother said to her. "You could not have done better."

"He could have elevated me higher," Lanhua grumbled.

I had to admit that she was right. As the mother of the emperor's first and only son, he easily could have elevated her to Imperial Noble Consort, officially making her the second-highest ranking woman in the Inner Court next to me. As it was, no one held that position, and there were three ladies currently at a level higher than Lanhua, including Lingrong, who had only given birth to a daughter. It was a bit strange, as women who gave birth to sons often outranked those who gave birth to daughters. As it was, the emperor was sending a clear message that he preferred Lingrong to Lanhua, and he seemed to still be holding out hope that Lingrong would eventually give birth to a son of her own. If she did, I wondered if Yizhu would choose her son as his heir instead of Lanhua's son simply out of his love for her.

Of course, it was terrible to already be imagining a future conflict about a child who did not even exist. But I could see Lanhua's mind turning, and I knew she was thinking about the same thing, and probably many other things as well.

I WAS IN A GARDEN, playing with Lifen and Zaichun, when war finally came to Peking.

It was a typical early summer day. The skies were clear and I could hear the peaceful sounds of birds singing and ladies laughing. Lanhua was nearby, sitting in the shade, watching us.

Lanhua loved her son very much. She doted on him and gave him every comfort, but she also had no issues with letting me care for him. She often seemed eager for a break from the child to focus on her own pleasures—napping, listening to opera performances, and courting the favor of the emperor. As the only other woman in the Inner Court who knew about his proclivity for prostitutes, I would have thought that she would have avoided him as I did. But she did not. She returned to his bed as soon as she was given permission from her doctors. As such, I often had two babies sleeping in my palace, which meant that I hardly got any sleep anymore. Still, I would rather not sleep at all than sleep with a man who enjoyed prostitutes.

Suddenly, a door slammed and I could see several men practically running out of the emperor's study, including Prince Yixin. Over the past several months, the emperor and the prince had patched up their differences and had been seen working together more often again. The prince was talking to several men as I approached, a baby on each hip.

"What is going on?" I asked.

"The British have declared war on China."

"What? Why?"

"There was an incident with a British ship. They claimed they were merely a merchant vessel, but one of the emperor's advisors, Sushun, was certain it was a military vessel. Before I could find out the truth, Sushun had the vessel destroyed. Britain said it was an act of war. I think they were just waiting for their chance to attack us, to force my brother to give in to their demands."

My heart was racing in my chest as I tried to follow what the prince was telling me. How could we be at war with the foreigners? What would this mean for us? What about the Taiping rebels?

"What does this mean? What must we do?"

"I am going to try and meet with the British emissaries.

Hopefully, I can do something to stop this from getting worse. I have to believe the British don't really want a fight."

"What should I do?"

The children began to fuss, and they were growing heavy. I called for a nanny to take Zaichun back to Lanhua, but Lifen stayed with me.

"Can you try and keep the emperor calm?" Yixin asked, gripping my upper arm. "Or distract him? I need him to not do anything to provoke the British further while I try and calm the situation."

"Me? How can I—"

"He has men at his side—Sushun, Zaiyuan, Jingshou, others —who say we should attack before more British ships arrive. That we can defeat the British now, but I don't think we can. We can perhaps defend ourselves, repel them for a while, but we cannot defeat them. I need time to reach out to my contacts, to find out if we can come to peace terms before things get worse. Help me, please."

"I...I..." I was completely lost for words. I had no idea how I could possibly help in this situation. Yizhu hardly listened to me regarding matters of the Inner Court. He certainly wouldn't listen to me regarding matters of the throne. But someone attracted the prince's attention and he ran off without another word to me. I saw that the door to the emperor's study was open, so I went inside. The room was a mess, with letters, maps, and papers strewn about, as if all the men had left in a hurry. The emperor was at the far side of the room, looking out the window at the garden where I had been playing with Lifen. There were a few men with him, and they were all talking in low voices.

"Your Majesty?" I said to get the emperor's attention. He turned to me, and the other men bowed.

"Zhen. What is it? What do you need?" Yizhu asked me.

"Is it true? Are we at war with the British?"

"I am afraid it's true," the emperor said with a weary sigh. "It was only a matter of time, though."

"Do not be afraid," one of the men said. "Be glad! As you said, it was only a matter of time. The foreigners have been trying to push their way into our country for too long. Finally, you can do what your father failed to do—you can show them who the true Dragon Emperor is and crush them under your boot!"

"Prince Yixin just went to try and broker peace with the British," I said. "We should wait and see what he comes back with." Lifen started to fuss, so I tried to shush her as I bounced her on my hip.

The man who had spoken before sneered at me. "Perhaps the empress should focus on taking care of babies and not worry her feeble mind with matters of war."

"Excuse me?" I said. "I was addressing my husband, the emperor. How dare you speak to me without being invited?"

The man lowered his head. "Of course, Empress. My apologies."

"I don't even know who you are," I said.

"Zhen, this is Sushun, one of my advisors. This is his brother Duanhua. And this other man is Muyin."

"I know who you are, Empress," Duanhua said. "My daughter-in-law is your cousin, Feiya. She speaks well of you."

I couldn't help but smile at the mention of Feiya. "I miss her dearly."

"I am sure you do," Duanhua said. "She is much loved by her husband and the rest of our family."

I wanted to speak to him further about Feiya and her life up north. But now was not the time.

"All of you, leave," the emperor said. "I would speak the empress alone."

"Do you really want war with the foreigners?" I asked Yizhu as soon as the door closed.

"I want the foreigners to stop trying to force their way into *my* country. I want them to stop smuggling opium through Canton. I want their gods to stop muddling the minds of the peasants."

"Those are all fair concerns, my lord," I said. "But with the Taiping Rebellion, are we not already stretched too thin? How can you defeat the British when we are already in a battle that has raged for half a decade?"

"I do have a source of soldiers as yet untapped," he said. "The Mongols."

"What about the Mongols?"

"They are our neighbors, and we have created strong bonds with them over the years through marriages. Hardly a Mongol noble exists without a Manchu wife."

I thought about Feiya and knew that to be true.

"So far, they have been protected from the foreigners because they are landlocked. The foreigners would have to go through China to get to Mongolia. The Mongols have a vested interest in ensuring we succeed against the foreign aggressors. Sushun and Duanhua are Mongol lords and they have assured me of Mongol support."

"Are you sure?"

"They are already on their way."

For once, I wondered if Prince Yixin was wrong. I knew the foreigners had been causing problems in China since I was a child. We had gone to war with them before over opium and lost. We had lost land and wealth, and because they were importing and smuggling in opium, our country was being eaten away from the inside. I did not want war with the foreigners, but like my husband, I wanted the foreigners repelled. Maybe Yixin did not know that the Mongols were willing and able to help us. If he knew that, surely he would support his brother in fighting back. In defending our own borders.

"Is there anything I can do to help you?" I asked. I did not expect him to say yes, but I at least wanted to make the offer.

"There is. Take the women to the Summer Palace."

"Without you?"

"Things around here will surely be very busy. I do not want them to see the men coming and going and fret."

"I see." I was not excited about the idea of leaving the Forbidden City and going to the Summer Palace without the emperor, but I understood his reasoning.

"Also, I need you to censor their letters."

I stayed quiet. I did not like that idea at all.

"Their families will undoubtedly write to them about what is going on. They will only frighten the ladies or ask for aid that cannot be sent. It would be best if the ladies knew as little as possible."

"Very well," I said. "I will speak to the Ministry of Household Affairs about it. I'll need the department's assistance since the letters are received through there."

"Very good," the emperor said. "You should leave as soon as possible. I am sure that news about the war will spread quickly."

"Very well," I said, bowing as well as I could while holding a baby. "I will make preparations as soon as possible." I started to back away.

"Zhen," the emperor said. I glanced up and our eyes met. His gaze was so gentle, so appreciative. He looked at me in a way in which he had not in a very long time. "Thank you."

"Of course, Your Majesty," I said. As I left the room, I wondered if there was still hope for us to have a happy life together. From the day Yizhu became emperor, he had been plagued with troubles. He had inherited troubles from his father. If he could, in fact, defeat this foreign threat and repel them with the aid of the Mongols, could Yizhu find some peace? Could he focus on being a husband and father instead of an emperor for just a little while?

But then I remembered the short while that we were married before he had been emperor. Even then, he had not been a good husband to me. He had been rough and demanding. He had been cruel. But according to Lanhua, it seemed as though he had only been that way with me. Well, and Ayan as well. None of the other ladies had complained about him causing them pain. I did not know why the emperor had treated me with such disdain. He had clearly wanted to marry me. He had wanted to choose me at the selection ceremony. After Ayan died, it was Yizhu who suggested me to his father as a replacement. I didn't know why he wanted to marry me so badly just to treat me so poorly.

Well, I supposed none of that mattered now. Whatever happened next, I was the empress, and I would be until the end.

CHAPTER TWENTY-FOUR

"*F*eiya!" I yelled as I ran toward my cousin.

"Zhen!" She kicked off her pot-bottom shoes so she could run to me more quickly. As we hugged, the years we had been apart seemed to melt away, as if we had seen each other only yesterday.

Apparently, when the Mongol men announced that they were going to help defend Peking, the women demanded that they be brought along. Most of the women had not seen their families for years, and they did not want to miss this opportunity, especially during a war. Since the men were all fighting or counseling the emperor, it fell on me to entertain the women. We were still living at the Summer Palace, so I was more than pleased to welcome the visitors to stay with me in a much more beautiful and relaxed environment.

Following behind Feiya were nannies with three children, two boys and a girl.

"Children, say hello to the empress," Feiya told her boys.

"Hello, Empress," the older boy said. The other one hid his face behind his mother's gown.

"They are adorable," I said. I motioned for Lifen's nanny and

Lanhua to come forward. "This is my daughter, Lifen. And this is my dear friend Lanhua, and her son, Zaichun."

"Oh, Zhen, she is beautiful," Feiya said. "And Zaichun is so handsome already." She then took a baby from one of the nannies. "This is my daughter, Hailan."

Even though Hailan was a mere babe, only a couple of months older than Zaichun, it was clear that she was beautiful, and probably would be for the rest of her life. She had a small nose, large, dark eyes, and perfectly formed lips. Before I saw Hailan, I had thought it impossible for a baby to be more beautiful than Lifen, but the proof was there before me.

"Oh, Feiya, I had no idea you would have such beautiful children," I said. "The emperor should have married you instead."

"If he had married me, his children would have come out looking like frogs," she said. "I am afraid my children get their good looks from their father."

"Your husband is handsome?" Lanhua asked as the three of us took the children to play in a green space near Kunming Lake, where the refreshing breezes would keep them cool. The older boys were able to run and toddle through the grass. Lifen crawled and walked a few steps with help from the boys or her nanny. Zaichun and Hailan were too small to do much more than sleep in their mother's arms.

"Well, not as handsome as the emperor, I'm sure," Feiya said humbly. "But he has the thickest black hair and such kind eyes. You can't really see his mouth for his beard, but his lips are so soft. I have to admit, I was terrified of becoming a wife, but my husband is so gentle and kind, I could not have asked for a better man."

"I am so happy for you, Feiya," I said. I wished I could have told her that I was jealous. Growing up, we thought I would have the most charmed life. My family was wealthier, my father better connected. We knew I would at least marry a prince, if not an emperor. Feiya was jealous of me when we were little.

But looking at her now, with the glow of love on her face and three children of her own, jealousy threatened to eat me up inside. Of course, I loved Lifen. But I was only her mother because the woman who had birthed her wanted a boy. I would always be grateful to Lingrong for allowing me to be a mother, and always pity her for not being able to be the mother she should have been.

"He can be strict, though," Feiya said. "He is a Confucian scholar."

"Is he?"

"He is the only Mongol to have ever passed the Imperial Examinations," she said.

"I remember hearing about that when I was younger," Lanhua said. "It caused quite a stir at the time, did it not?"

"Apparently, though I don't remember it," Feiya explained. "But it is not typical for Mongol men to study the classical philosophers the way Manchu and Han men do. So, he was also self-taught."

"I am surprised he does not serve the emperor in Peking," I said. "Surely a man of such talents would be more useful here than in the wilds of the north."

"He serves the emperor well from home. As a Confucian, he is utterly devoted to the emperor. Not all Mongols feel that way. Many feel that we should remain a separate people."

I found it interesting that Feiya seemed to speak of herself more as a Mongol than a Manchu. But I supposed it should not have been surprising after hearing how she praised her husband. She was clearly in love with him.

"So, my husband ensures that the Mongol high officials also remain loyal to the emperor and fulfill their obligations. If it wasn't for my husband, I am not sure the Mongol armies would have come to help defend the forts."

"Is that what they are doing here?" I asked. While I was glad to be out of Peking in the peace and quiet of the Summer

Palace, I also had no idea what was going on with the war against the foreigners.

Feiya nodded. "You had not heard? The foreign alliance attacked the Dagu Forts."

"What alliance?" I asked.

Feiya paused, as if waiting to see if I were making a joke. "All the foreign powers who have joined forces against us."

"The French joined the British first," Lanhua said. "Then the United States and Russia."

"How do you know that?" I asked her.

"I have ways of getting information."

"How?" I asked. "You aren't supposed to be getting any information like that from the outside. I've been censoring all the letters."

"You've been censoring letters?" Feiya asked. "As in the ladies' letters from home? Why would you do that?"

"You've been censoring *my* letters?" Lanhua asked. "I knew there was something nefarious going on! I had been blaming eunuchs for my missing letters."

"The emperor ordered me to," I said. "He didn't want the ladies to be upset by information about the war."

"But the war affects all of you," Feiya said. "Especially you, as empress. You shouldn't be kept ignorant about such matters."

"You said your husband is a strict Confucian," I said back. "But I heard that it was the Mongol women who ordered the men to bring them here."

"Well, I didn't order him. I only asked nicely. But Mongol women are far more outspoken than Manchu women. Did you know that the Great Kahn even allowed his wives and daughters to counsel him on matters of the throne?"

"Does that mean your daughter won't learn to read or write?" Lanhua asked Feiya. "Confucius said, 'An educated woman is a worthless woman.'"

"I'm sure she won't have much use for reading or writing,"

Feiya said. "If she has a husband as kind as mine, being a submissive wife and mother will be easy for her."

"Then call me a Confucian wife," I said. "I was only doing what he told me to do with the letters."

"He shouldn't have asked that of you," Feiya mumbled.

"What did you say?" I asked. "Did you speak against the emperor?"

"Of course not. I'm sure he knows best... Only..."

"Only what?"

"An uneducated woman and an ignorant woman are not the same thing," she said. "My husband discusses all matters of import with me. After all, he is not home all day. He doesn't know the children and the household the way I do. We are a team. He makes final decisions, of course, but not without at least asking my opinion."

I waved a fly away from buzzing around Zaichun's face. "We should go inside. It's getting much too hot for the children out here."

"Yes," Feiya said. "The boys need a nap." The boys began to whine and complain, throwing themselves on the ground. But the nannies were quick to scoop them up and take them inside.

"I'll see you at dinner," I told Feiya as I turned to take Lifen inside.

"Zhen," Feiya said before I could go. "I hope I haven't upset you. Of course you should do what your husband tells you to do. It is the only right thing for you to do."

"Even if you know that what your husband is telling you is the *wrong* thing to do?" Lanhua asked.

"That is the man's responsibility," Feiya said. "Not yours. He will be held accountable when he meets the ancestors in Heaven."

"Meanwhile, it will be the wives and children who pay the cost of those wrong decisions while they are still living," Lanhua said.

"I do not believe that the emperor has made any wrong decisions," I said. "He is doing what he believes is best for all of us. And as emperor, who are we to question him?"

Lanhua and Feiya both looked away, shamefaced.

"That's what I thought," I said. "I think the heat is making all of us short-tempered. Let us retire for a rest and come back together for the evening meal, refreshed and ready to enjoy one another's company."

"Yes, Empress," Lanhua and Feiya both said before returning to their own quarters with their children for the rest of the afternoon. I summoned a eunuch to me from the Ministry of Household Affairs and asked that Lanhua's letters be delivered to her, all of them.

"And what of the letters to the other ladies?" the eunuch asked me.

"Hold on to them for now," I said. "As soon as this war is over, I intend to return all of them."

"Yes, my lady," he said.

I exhaled and lay on my bed while a wet nurse fed Lifen, but I could not rest. I could not believe that Feiya, a woman who obeyed her husband in all things, questioned my husband's decisions. Well, perhaps she was free to do so since the emperor was not her husband. But since her husband was following the emperor into battle, he surely believed the emperor was acting rightly. Of course, I wished the emperor would consult me more, but that was not my place. My place was in the Inner Court. The emperor had asked me to keep the peace here—for him—and I would do that. But now that Lanhua knew her letters were missing, there would be no peace until she received them. It mattered not. No matter what her family told her, she could take no action. There was nothing we could do about the war. We could only sit and wait and hope that peace would come soon.

CHAPTER TWENTY-FIVE

*I*t was a time of celebration. The Chinese and Mongol troops had managed to defeat the foreigners, who were now limping away from China, back to their home countries. The emperor summoned all of us back to Peking, where we were to hold many days of feasting and celebrating before the Mongols all returned back to their homeland.

The emperor was in rare form as he laughed and drank with the Mongol generals and nobles who had helped him defeat the foreigners. He invited several Peking Opera troupes into the Forbidden City to perform for him and his guests for many days straight. It was clear that the performers were exhausted, but they would not pass up an opportunity to perform for the emperor, who paid them generously.

Of course, I was glad that the emperor had been successful. I was proud that he had been vindicated. Never before in all the years that he had sat upon the Dragon Throne had his rulership been more secure. There were none in the world who could doubt that the Daoguang Emperor had done the right thing when he chose Yizhu to succeed him as emperor.

No one, perhaps, except Prince Yixin.

Prince Yixin, along with his wife, had been part of the celebrations, but it was clear that his mind was worried. He did not smile or dance or laugh at the comedic opera performances. His face was a perpetual scowl, his arms crossed over his chest.

"He fears that the foreigners will return in even greater numbers," Princess Ningxin said to me one evening when I asked her if Prince Yixin was ill.

"Is it likely, though?" I asked her. "I heard that they suffered rather significant casualties. Perhaps they now realize that China is a stronger force than they realized. They will think twice before attacking us again."

"They might think twice," Princess Ningxin said. "But that doesn't mean they won't learn from their mistakes and return."

Even Princess Ningxin, who I remembered as a rather loud and silly girl, seemed subdued. She only spoke if spoken to, and even then, her responses were curt. I preferred this version of the princess—at least, I would have if it had been her true nature. But since I knew it was not, her sullen attitude concerned me. It was clearly a reflection of her husband. While I hoped that it was my husband who had been proven right, it was Prince Yixin who knew the foreigners better. As far as I knew, my husband had never even seen the foreign envoys. He only ever sent his emissaries to speak to them. And I knew that the emperor had never seen the foreigners in battle. He was given daily updates from generals at the front lines, but he had never been in war himself. Prince Yixin also had not fought the foreigners, but he had, at least, been to the forts and had seen the foreign navy for himself. He had also been to areas of fighting in the west and the south, where the Taiping still raged from their capital in Jiangning. No one would dare say it to the emperor, but it seemed as if China had been divided into two countries, the war with the Taiping had raged for so long. But that appeared to be a problem for the emperor for another day.

For now, one would think he had succeeded on every front from how he celebrated.

On the last night of feasting before the Mongols, and my dear Feiya, were to return home, my husband finally grew tired of Prince Yixin's sulking. He sat on a raised dais with several important Mongols, Lingrong, and Lanhua. I was seated in the middle of a long table down one side of the room, with Princess Ningxin, Feiya, and other high-ranking ladies. Across from me, on the other side of the room, were all the other important men, including Prince Yixin.

"I daresay that my brother wishes we had lost the battle," the emperor called out from his elevated seat in the grand dining hall.

Prince Yixin stood from his seat across from me. "That is not true. I am glad of your success, brother. I only fear that it is temporary. I have no desire to turn my back to an injured foe before the head has been cut off."

"I have a hundred men here who disagree with you," the emperor said, motioning to the crowd of Mongol leaders among us. There were not a hundred men present; there were maybe half that. But the emperor was making his point that more men agreed with him than with Prince Yixin.

"I hope you get their assurance that they will return should you have urgent need of their services again," Prince Yixin said.

The emperor's nostrils flared. "Their services will not be needed again!"

"That is not true," Prince Yixin said. "China has many things that the foreigners want, not least of all the money they can earn by smuggling opium through our borders. Even if they have little chance of success, the foreigners will return—again and again they will return. They cannot resist such a large and beautiful target. Now is not the time to relax. We should be preparing for the next battle—for it will come sooner rather than later."

"You want me to fail!" Yizhu yelled, jumping up from his seat.

"I only want the opposite," Yixin said, remaining calm. "I want you to be prepared for the next attack so that you are successful."

"You question my decisions? My wisdom?"

The room had gone completely silent. No one dared speak. Even the musicians had gone quiet. From where I was sitting, I could see that it was taking all of Yixin's strength not to roll his eyes and sigh in frustration. Somehow, he managed to remain the pinnacle of respect and decorum.

"No, Your Majesty," the prince said, keeping his tone even. "But our father wanted me to advise you. I would be derelict in my duties if I did not do just that."

"There is wisdom in celebrating every victory," Lanhua said. Princess Ningxin sucked in a breath. I think she expected the emperor to strike Lanhua, there in front of everyone. But he did not. He allowed her to continue. "Celebrations warm the heart and give encouragement to the soul. Can we not celebrate today and prepare for the next battle tomorrow?" she asked.

The emperor looked down at her in her seat. She did not flinch or back down, but held her head straight as she stared ahead at Prince Yixin. While I did not think the emperor would strike her in front of so many people, I did fear that he would have her dismissed the next day. But to the surprise of all, the emperor began to laugh. Many of the men in the room followed suit, though I doubted they knew what they were laughing about.

"To hear a woman speak of wisdom is humorous, is it not?" the emperor said.

"Something can be humorous and true at the same time," Feiya's husband, Chongqi, who was sitting on the dais, said. I had a feeling he had grown tired of the posturing between the emperor and his brother. "I thought we were here for a celebration. Tomorrow, my people and I have a long ride ahead of us. We should drink and rest well."

"Of course," the emperor said, raising his cup. "To the eternal union between our people and the end of foreign encroachment on our country."

"May the emperor live ten thousand years!" Chongqi said. Everyone in the room echoed the words three times.

The emperor smiled as everyone cheered for him, his eyes glowing. It seemed as if he thought everyone really wanted him to live for a thousand years and that it wasn't just a respectful sentiment.

As we all sat down, a maid tapped Feiya on her shoulder. Feiya listened to what she had to say and then turned to me.

"I'm sorry, Empress," she said. "But my children need me. I don't think I will be back tonight."

"I'll walk with you," I said. She nodded, and we left the banquet hall together. "What is wrong with the boys?"

"They are fussy and refuse to sleep," she said. "Normally, I would not worry, but with the start of a long trip tomorrow, they need to rest."

"Of course," I said. "And how will little Hailan fair on the journey, do you think?"

"She did well on the trip down, sleeping most of the way. Hopefully, the return trip will be much the same way."

"I have enjoyed your visit. I shall miss you greatly when you are gone."

Feiya turned and gave me a hug. "And I you. But I am certain we shall see each other again."

"What would you think if Hailan were to marry Zaichun?"

"Really?" Her cheeks were like those of a squirrel, full of joy. "That would be wonderful. Do you think the emperor would allow it?"

"He is pleased with the Mongol support," I said. "And, as you said, it is largely due to your husband's loyalty. He has said nothing of it to me yet, but when the time comes, I will be sure to remind him that he owes this success to your family. I think it would be a good match. Plus, it would give you a permanent excuse to visit Peking often, if not move back permanently."

"I do miss Peking," she said wistfully, her eyes looking up at the night sky.

"Really? Judging by your letters, I thought you were so happy in Mongolia that you'd never want to return here."

"Hmm." She was quiet for a moment, and I thought she wouldn't continue, but then she spoke again. "You know I cannot write very well. I have to have someone else write my letters for me."

"I thought you must have had a scribe in your household since you were able to send me letters so often."

"I could not always dictate what I was thinking. Everything I say or do is reported back to my husband."

"Oh," I said. "So, things were not as happy as you made it seem?"

"For the most part, what I said was true. My husband does treat me well. We have a good life there. But adjusting was not easy. It is very cold there, and I don't speak Mongolian. But most of the ladies who have married Mongolians don't, so we have a small community of our own. All women married off to men we didn't know in a culture that is quite foreign to our own."

"Are Mongols so very different from us?"

"They are and they aren't. My husband's loyalty seems to be an anomaly. In truth, most Mongols yearn for a return of the Yuan Dynasty.

"It seems everyone wants to rule China. The Mongols. The Han. The Taiping. The Foreigners. Us Manchu."

"There was a time when you trusted Prince Yixin," she said. "Do you still?"

"I do."

"Does the emperor?"

"Probably not as much as he should."

"If the foreigners attack again, I do not think we will come back."

"Are you sure?" I asked.

"As I said, my husband discusses all matters of import with me. He told me that he agrees with Prince Yixin's assessment, that the foreigners will come back—and soon. But he has exhausted his authority with the Mongolian High Council for now. If the worst happens, we will not be able to rescue the emperor again."

"Why are you telling me this?"

"Because, Cousin, I fear you are in grave danger. The foreigners are attacking from the sea. The Taiping from the south and west. You are being hemmed in from all sides."

"It has been that way nearly from the day my husband became emperor. We have always succeeded before. I am sure we will again."

"Perhaps. After all, the emperor has a son and heir now. That does make a difference."

"And all the more reason why Zaichun should wed Hailan. If we form a marriage alliance with the Mongols, they would have to support us against an invasion."

"Any marriage alliance would probably be too far off to be of any use."

"I will speak to the emperor about it as soon as possible. Even if the children cannot marry until they are older, they could be betrothed now."

We stopped in front of the palace where Feiya was staying with her family. I could hear a boy inside crying.

"Sounds like you are needed. I fear I shall not see you again for a long time."

"Oh, Cousin." We hugged each other for a long moment. "If

you must flee, come north. My home will always be open to you."

My eyes watered at the thought. If I had to flee for my life, things would have to get very dire indeed. Though, it had happened before. After all, the Ming had built the Forbidden City when the Han had last ruled their own country. But the Manchu had overthrown them in a moment of weakness. Were we not in a moment of weakness now? Perhaps everyone outside the Forbidden City could see what those of us inside could not—that we were in clear danger. Still, what could I do about it? I had to obey my husband.

"I will remember that," I said. Feiya and I broke apart. She started to go inside, but then she turned back to me.

"Oh, one more thing. Watch out for Lanhua."

"What do you mean? I thought you liked her." In the several weeks we had all stayed in the Summer Palace together, I thought Lanhua and Feiya had gotten along rather well.

"I do," she said. "But she is clearly outspoken. The way she spoke tonight…" She shook her head. "I fear she is going to get the two of you in a lot of trouble."

"I've heard that before. But I appreciate Lanhua. She has always looked out for me, and I promised I would do the same for her."

"Just…be careful," she said, squeezing my hand.

"Of course. I will," I said.

She gave me a tight smile, then let my hand slip from her fingers as she went inside her palace to her children.

As I walked back toward the dining hall, I felt frustrated. I didn't know what I was supposed to do. I could not counsel my husband. I could do nothing but what I was told to do. Part of me believed that Prince Yixin was right, that the foreigners would return stronger than ever. But he also thought the foreigners would defeat us the last time they attacked, and he was wrong. My husband had been right, and China had been victorious. Perhaps he would be right again.

He had only won with the support of the Mongols, though. If Feiya was right and the Mongols would not come to our aid again, we could be in trouble. But I thought that my plan to betroth the emperor's son to Feiya's daughter was a good one. Perhaps this was how I would be of service to my husband and my country, through proposing this marriage alliance.

Just before I reached the dining hall, I was startled by someone outside. He stumbled toward me, clearly drunk, a wine cup in his hand.

"Yixin!" I called out as he almost fell over on me. I did my best to help him stay upright, but I was not very strong, and we nearly tumbled over. Thankfully, there was a bench nearby, so we collapsed onto that.

"Zhen?" he said, sounding confused.

"What's wrong?" I asked. "You were fine when I left here a few minutes ago."

"How long ago was that?" he asked. He started counting on his fingers. "Oh well. A long time."

Perhaps my walk with Feiya had taken longer than I thought. "You shouldn't be drunk. You never know when the emperor might need you." I took the cup from him and emptied it out onto the ground.

Yixin laughed. "I think the only people who know the emperor needs me are me and you. Shhh! It's a secret."

"What's a secret?" I asked, worried someone was going to find us alone in a garden together.

"The emperor needs me," he whispered.

"Yes, well, he doesn't need you drunk," I said. I tried to stand, but he grabbed my arm, pulling me back down to sit beside me. He leaned his head on my shoulder. I should have pushed him away. My husband and Yixin's wife were inside the next building. And there were many more people around than usual due to the festivities. Anyone could come upon us at any moment. But having him next to me was oddly comforting. It was the most contact I'd had with a man in months. It took me a moment to realize that Feiya's words had rattled me. I wanted Yixin to tell me that she was wrong. That the foreigners weren't going to come back. That the Mongols would be there to help us. That we would always be able to defend ourselves if we needed to. But in his current state, I didn't think he could tell me anything of the sort. So, I just let him lay his head on my shoulder and I laid my head on his.

"What are we going to do?" I asked, even though I thought he was probably asleep. He didn't respond, but I noticed that his breathing was calm. I patted the back of his hand. "I'm sure you will know what to do when the time comes. You always seem to know what to do."

I heard laughter and cheering from the dining hall, but it was so muffled, it seemed rather far away. If Feiya was right, the Mongols knew they were abandoning us and wouldn't be back. Some allies they were. Did I really want to marry my son to such feckless people? Well, at least if I did, it might keep them from trying to overthrow us. We were already being attacked from the south, west, and across the ocean. We would never be able to survive an attack from the north. I wondered why the Mongols didn't take their chance and do away with us. Perhaps they did not feel they were strong enough to take on the foreigners or the Taiping on their own. Besides, the Han barely supported us as it was. If the Mongols tried to move back in and take over, they would throw all their weight behind the Taiping and be done with us northerners.

I heard Prince Yixin mumble something. I had almost forgotten he was there.

"What?" I asked.

"Survive," he said. "We survive. It's what we do."

"Oh, so you did hear me."

Yixin sat up and rubbed his head. "What happened? How did I end up out here?"

"I don't know. I came back from walking Feiya to her palace and found you out here so drunk you couldn't stand up."

"Ugh, that rancid yak milk."

"You finally tried some?"

"It was forced upon me by diplomacy."

"I think I'm glad I don't have to play politics if it involves fermented yak milk," I said.

"At least it wears off quickly."

"You cannot be sober already," I said.

"Not completely," he said. "But at least I can sit up again."

"What were you drinking to?"

"I tried to get Chongqi to agree to come back if we needed him. He challenged me to a drinking contest. I think I failed."

"According to Feiya, the Mongols won't be back, so don't blame yourself."

"They already decided that, did they?" He let out a long exhale.

"Don't worry," I said, bumping my shoulder against his. "I have a plan."

"Do you?"

"A marriage plan. Zaichun to Chongqi's daughter."

The prince shook his head, which proved to be a mistake. He put his hands to his head as if to stop it from spinning. "Won't work," he finally said.

"Why not?"

"Here is a little politics lesson, Empress. Never try to make a marriage pact in a time of war. The Mongols will never agree as long as the Taiping are in power and the foreigners are floating off our shores. If they agreed now, then they would be agreeing to fight a war they aren't sure they can win. No, your only chance of a marriage pact is for China to be at peace. Then make a marriage pact so you are better protected in the future."

"Are you sure? Don't you think I should at least mention it to Yizhu?"

"I don't think you should. Mainly because it is a good plan, but it will fail, which will only make Yizhu even more angry with the Mongols."

"He's angry with them?"

"Why do you think we are throwing this huge party?"

"To celebrate the foreigners turning back?"

He shook his head while he gathered his thoughts. "He knows the foreigners will come back. He is trying to convince the Mongols that we are rich and powerful and confident enough to spend days feasting and drinking while the enemy regroups. He wants the Mongols to stay. But it's impossible."

"What should we do?"

"All we can do is wait. We don't have a navy of our own that can chase them down. We can't attack them on their own soil. No, all we can do is wait for them to come back and see what they do."

"Well, shouldn't we—"

The prince interrupted me with a kiss. But his mouth tasted like spoiled yak milk, so I pushed him away before I vomited. Either I pushed him harder than I thought I could or he was still weak and disoriented from being drunk because he practically fell head over heels off the bench and into a shrub. I slapped a hand over my mouth to keep from laughing. It was so dark, I couldn't see where he landed.

"Prince Yixin?" I called out after a moment. I strained my hearing and eventually heard the even, nasal breathing of someone asleep. I assumed he was fine and went back to the dining hall, where it appeared that everyone was dispersing for the night.

"Good night, Empress," Chongqi said as he left with a bow. "It was wonderful to get to meet you. I know it brought my wife great joy to visit you."

"I have missed her so much over the years. I do hope you will allow her to come and visit me again soon."

"I know she would like that very much," he said. "Perhaps when there is not a threat of war on the horizon, I will consider it."

"Thank you," I said. I had a feeling he would not be considering it for a very long time.

"It will be nice to be rid of all these obnoxious guests," the emperor muttered to me when almost everyone was gone.

"You did not have to invite them to stay for so long," I said.

"Of course I did. I had to remind them that they were only helping us. That we were the superior power. They might have had an untapped fighting force, but we have money. We have resources. We have everything we need to defeat the enemy, given enough time. I only summoned them because I wanted the foreign threat put down quickly."

"Of course, my lord," I said. "Do you think we could use them against the Taiping? We would have so many more of our own men at our disposal if we could defeat the Taiping once and for all."

"The Taiping will burn themselves out soon enough," he said. "They took Jiangning and then stopped advancing."

I had no way of knowing if that were true. But the emperor's confidence helped put my mind at ease on the issue, at least for the moment.

"I hope you are right," I said. "We have been at war for so long, I hardly remember peace."

"You will know it soon enough," he said. "We repelled the foreigners. We have a son. Everything is as it should be. I promise you."

"It does seem as if we are overdue for a bit of peace."

"Don't let people like my brother worry you. Why do you think I demoted him? He doesn't have the same view of the future that I do. We will succeed. And we will be stronger for it."

Despite everything Feiya and Yixin had said, I wanted to believe my husband. He had worked hard for this victory and deserved to relish in it. We all deserved this moment of peace.

"I had an idea," I said, suddenly anxious to tell him my plan to wed Zaichun and Hailan.

The emperor laughed as though I had told a great joke and put a finger to my lips. "The last thing I need is a woman trying to help. What? Will the rats offer suggestions next?"

My stomach sank and I laughed along with him to stop myself from crying. Prince Yixin had said it was a good idea. But he also had told me to keep my idea to myself. Perhaps it wasn't a good idea after all. Maybe the prince was only being kind to me. I supposed it was best for me to keep quiet instead of embarrassing myself.

"Of course," I said. "I'm sorry. I should retire. I will need to rise early to see our guests off."

"Very well. Good night, Empress," he said.

"Good night, my lord." I bowed and he walked away. For a moment, I was surprised he did not ask me to stay the night with him. But I supposed he wanted to sleep by himself since he also had to wake up early. But I knew it was probably more likely that he already had plans for an evening companion. I hoped it would be Lingrong, but I knew it was more likely one of his bound-foot prostitutes again. At least he had a son. After our guests were gone, there would be time to pressure him about having more children. At least, for this moment, I could rest easy.

CHAPTER TWENTY-SIX

*B*efore the Mongols had been gone long enough to settle back home, the foreigners had returned. They attacked the Dagu Fort so quickly and with such force, the emperor barely had time to react. And just as Feiya had warned, the Mongols refused to come back to our aid. The emperor had moved the entirety of his household, including himself, to the Summer Palace. He said it was a more strategic location since it was outside of Peking, but everyone thought it was because he was afraid that the foreigners were going to sack Peking—and the Forbidden City.

Even from inside the Summer Palace, we could hear the endless stomping of feet and hooves on the nearest road as people vacated Peking. Many high-ranking Peking families, including my own, headed north, toward Rehe Palace, located near the Muran Hunting Grounds and the Mongolian border. Rehe Palace was an old hunting lodge that had been used by emperors of the past, but it had not been used in decades. I had hoped that we would not have to go there. It would certainly be run down, cold, and without stores of provisions.

I had been doing my best to keep the women calm, but it

seemed to be a losing battle. They were all terrified—for themselves and their families. I had caught many of them trying to smuggle food and provisions out of the Summer Palace to their families as they passed along the road. I was supposed to punish them, according to Yizhu, but I could not do it. They were afraid, and I could not blame them.

I went to call on Lingrong when I heard that she was ill, but she explained away her illness in a way I did not expect.

"I'm pregnant," she said, kneeling over a porcelain bowl.

"Are you sure?" I asked her.

"As sure as I can be," she said. "I have been unable to summon a doctor, but the symptoms are the same as before."

"I don't recall you being sick like this before," I told her.

"The midwife was able to give me medicine to calm my stomach," she said. "But I have not been able to reach her either."

"They probably fled the city along with their families," I said. "Don't worry. Just try to stay calm and rest as much as possible. Hopefully, this news will cheer the emperor—at least as much as he can be cheered. In the meantime, try to drink some ginger tea. It should calm your stomach."

"Thank you, my lady," she said as a maid helped settle her into her bed.

I made my way to Yizhu's study just as the doors flew open and I saw the emperor and Prince Yixin fall to the ground outside. They had come to blows, and the men around them seemed to be doing nothing to stop it. I thought I even saw a couple of the men placing bets on who would win.

"Stop this!" I said, but no one could hear me. I elbowed my way through the crowd and realized that the prince was letting the emperor hit him. The emperor was not doing much damage, and I thought the prince could defend himself easily. Over the years, the prince had increased in physical strength, while the emperor, who rarely left his rooms, had grown thinner. But if the prince were to strike the emperor, even in self-defense, he could be charged with treason. Perhaps that was what the emperor wanted. I knew things had been tense between the brothers ever since the foreigners had returned, even more tense than usual, but I could not have imagined it would come to this. They had not fought like this since they were children. They were both men now and should have been in better control of their emotions.

I looked around and saw that still, no one was interfering. The emperor might not have been as strong as Prince Yixin, but if Yixin did not defend himself, the emperor could end up killing him. I finally did the only thing I could think of to stop the fight. I pushed one of the men next to me into the fray. He fell on top of Prince Yixin, taking a few punches from the emperor in the back. It took a moment for the emperor to realize what was happening, but when he did, he took a step back to collect himself.

"Get up!" he yelled to his brother.

The man I had pushed shuffled away as Prince Yixin kneeled, his hair falling out of his usually smooth queue and his clothes covered in dust and shoeprints.

"I will not fight you, Your Majesty," Prince Yixin said.

"But you will tell me how to be emperor?" Yizhu shouted. "You think you have the right to tell me what to do?"

"What is a council except a bunch of men who tell you what to do?" Yixin asked.

"*Council*," Yizhu stressed. "Give suggestions. Not orders. You don't tell me what to do!"

"And I never have! But I can warn you of the consequences. If you do this, the foreigners will sack Peking, I promise you."

I gasped, my hand going to my mouth. What had the emperor threatened to do?

"Let them!" the emperor said. "But I will not let those bastards into my sight. I will murder every single emissary they send me before I let them stand before the Dragon Throne."

"You can send them away without killing them," Yixin said. "Without torturing them."

"Then they will only send more," Sushun said, standing next to the emperor. "We have sent them many warnings. They refuse to listen. Maybe they will listen now."

"I agree," said Prince Zaiyuan. "They kidnapped Viceroy Ye and then killed him in a foreign country."

"He died," Prince Yixin said. "That doesn't mean they killed him. We don't know what happened."

I tried to remember to Viceroy Ye was. I remembered that he was someone the emperor had appointed to his council early in his reign, but I could not recall why or what his role actually was.

"Still," Prince Zaiyuan said. "Blood for blood."

Many of the men around us cheered in agreement.

Yixin pointed at the men. "If you go through with this, the foreigners will make sure every single one of you pays for it."

"And when we are victorious," the emperor said to Yixin, "it is you who will beg my forgiveness. Be gone from my sight."

The prince gave his brother an exaggerated bow. "As you wish. I'll be waiting for your summons when you have no one else to turn to." The men all watched as Yixin left the area.

"What is going on?" I asked again, sure that everyone could hear me this time.

The men all turned to me as though surprised I was there. I supposed they had been so focused on the fight, they never noticed me.

"The foreigners sent emissaries to come to terms," the emperor said as I followed him into his study. We were trailed by many of the men who had been watching the fight.

"That is a good thing, is it not?" I asked.

"They wanted to deliver the terms to me in person," he said.

"But they said they had to be excused from performing the kowtow."

I pressed my lips and breathed through my nose. I agreed that the foreigners were being unreasonable. The emperor deserved respect. He was appointed by Heaven just as they believed their queen had been. But I still did not see why the disagreement had become so violent.

"Prince Yixin believes the foreigners will destroy Peking if you make them kowtow?" I asked.

"No. He thinks they will attack the city after all their emissaries are dead from the kao-niu."

I blinked and had to think for a moment, sure I had misheard him. "No," I said.

"No?" the emperor asked me, his voice nearly a hiss, as if he was daring me to speak again.

"Forgive me," I said. "I only thought I misheard you. You said kao-niu?"

"I did," he said. "It is already being carried out."

"It is a mercy," another man, I thought his name was General Jiao, said. "It should be the death by a thousand cuts."

Considering that the death by a thousand cuts usually killed a person in about fifteen minutes, it seemed that such a punishment would be more merciful than the kao-niu, which usually took days to kill a man. Kao-niu was a way of binding a captive, with the hands and feet tied behind the back. Water was often poured on the bindings to make them pull tighter as they dried. The hands and feet often died from a lack of blood flow, falling off the dying man. It was a brutal way to murder someone, especially an emissary sent under a mission of peace.

"Is not kao-niu often reserved for prisoners of war?" I asked. "But you said this man was an emissary."

"We are at war," the emperor said. "They are all prisoners of war."

I felt dizzy, sick at the idea of what was happening. I heard a man chuckle. I turned around and saw Sushun laughing at me.

"See, Your Majesty. This is why women should be locked in their quarters and not allowed to wander freely. You never know when they might hear something that will make them swoon."

"Kao-niu does not make me swoon," I shot back. And indeed, the mention of the practice did not. But the idea that it might be used on an innocent man made me shudder. I suddenly understood why Yixin had been so upset. When the foreign military leaders found out what happened to their emissaries, they were sure to be furious. If they came after us, if they caught us, what would they do in return?

Still, the men continued to laugh at me.

"What will you do when the foreigners retaliate?" I asked.

"They will not retaliate," the emperor said. "I am sending more troops to the front line as we speak. According to my advisors, Parkes is their lead military strategist. With him in my custody, the morale of the foreigners will collapse. We will easily defeat them."

"Victory will be ours!" Sushun announced, raising his fist.

"People have been fleeing Peking for days," I said. "Should we follow suit?"

"We are perfectly safe here," the emperor said. "Stop questioning my judgment."

I looked around for a friendly face, a face of reason, but there was none. If Prince Yixin had been helpless in dissuading the emperor from this course, what could I do?

"Very well," I said. I gave a bow and began to back out of the room. There was nothing I could do or say to change things.

"Why did you come?" the emperor asked as I reached the door.

"What?"

"Why did you come here in the first place? I didn't summon you."

"Oh." I had to think for a moment, as I had forgotten myself. "Consort Lingrong is pregnant, my lord. But she has been unable to summon a doctor or midwife in all the commotion."

The emperor's smile faltered for a moment. "Well, she is young and strong. She delivered a healthy child once before. This should be easy for her."

"Yes, my lord. Of course," I said, not taking my eyes off him. I was worried about Lingrong. The stress of the situation alone could cause a miscarriage. Not being able to find a doctor or midwife made things much worse. Should Lingrong have complications, there would be no one to help her. And what if we had to flee? I did not want her to have to make an arduous journey in her condition. I hoped my concerns were plain on my face. I hoped the emperor saw them.

Some of the men muttered some version of congratulations, but no one cheered in joy or excitement.

"If there is nothing else…" I said.

"No," the emperor replied. "You may go."

I nodded and walked out of the room. My hand was to my stomach as I retched the garden. My head was aching so badly, I felt nauseous. Everything was going from bad to worse, and I did not know what to do about Lingrong. I felt a strong hand on my arm pull me off the main path. He put his other hand over my mouth.

"Don't say a thing," Yixin said. I nodded and he lowered his hand. "I need your help."

I shook my head. "You know I can't help you. The emperor doesn't listen to me."

"Fuck the emperor," he said, spitting. "This is about more than him. This is about saving all of us."

"What do you mean?"

"We have to rescue Harry Parkes and his men."

"Who?"

Yixin grunted. "The men the emperor sentenced to kao-niu. We cannot let them die. I need your help."

"Me? Why?"

"I have an idea. But I need a woman."

"What about your wife?" I asked.

He shook his head. "I have already sent her to Rehe Palace, along with our children and her family."

"That was probably wise," I said. "I would go there myself if I could."

"You should prepare for it," he said. "It is only a matter of time before the foreigners come here."

"I'll add it to my list of things to do. Right under finding a midwife for Consort Lingrong."

"Consort Lingrong is with child?" he asked. I nodded. "And the emperor knows?"

"He does. But he seems completely unconcerned."

"Of course he does. If he suddenly wanted to send her to Rehe Palace, he'd have to admit he made a mistake. And we both know that isn't going to happen."

"So, what can we do?"

"I need you to come with me back to Peking to help the prisoners. They are being held in the Ministry of Punishments."

"You want me to go with you? Back to Peking? In the middle of the day? To rescue prisoners from the Ministry of Punishments? Are you mad?"

"Not right now," he said. "But we can leave tonight. If we go by horse, we can be back by sunrise."

I stepped closer to him, but only so I could point my finger in his chest. "You're insane." I started to walk past him again, but he grabbed my arm and turned me to face him.

"Zhen," he said so softly it was almost a whisper. "Zhen. Zhen. Zhen." He rubbed my shoulders and put his forehead to mine. "I need you."

My eyes filled with tears. How I'd longed to hear those words from him. How I had dreamed of them at night. I could not respond with words lest I burst into tears. I placed my hand on his chest and felt his shallow breaths. I wanted to say yes. I wanted to go with him. I wanted to run away from him to the ends of the earth.

But I couldn't. I was not merely a woman, but an empress. A mother. A wife. A friend. If the emperor ever found out that I had helped Prince Yixin save the foreigners, he would not only depose of me, he would kill me. I could not do that to the women and children who depended on me.

"No," I finally whispered.

"What?" he asked, nearly to tears himself. He didn't believe I could resist him.

"No," I said more clearly as I pulled away. "I can't help you."

He held my hands as long as he could as I walked away. I left him there in the garden. I had no idea what he would do, but I turned my back on him and returned to my place among the women.

CHAPTER TWENTY-SEVEN

*I*t was my husband's birthday. The Xianfeng Emperor was thirty years old. But the only person who seemed to be in a festive mood was the emperor himself.

It had been a couple of weeks since Sushun and his followers had captured Harry Parkes and his men and bound them in kao-niu. I did not know how long the men could survive, but I feared that every day would be the day they died and the foreigners would seek their revenge. The emperor still attempted to keep me ignorant of what was happening, but I needed to know the truth. I needed to be prepared. I was responsible for all the members of the Inner Court and did not want to be caught unawares.

I had stopped censoring the women's letters. I read all of them myself before sending them to their intended party. I also sent my eunuchs out into the surrounding areas to gather information to bring back to me.

I learned that the emperor had kept much from me regarding China's relations with the foreigners. About a year before, there had been another skirmish at the Dagu Fort. One we had lost. As a result, the foreigners had demanded that my husband sign a series of treaties—which he did. But when it came time to ratify the treaties, he had refused. That was why they had attacked the fort again. My husband had been prepared for that attack, though, by summoning the Mongols to his side. However, the Mongols had learned of the emperor going back on his word to the foreigners and about his brutal ways of dealing with them. The Mongol leaders, including Feiya's husband, had begged the emperor to change tack. When the emperor refused, leaning on the advice of men such as Sushun, the Mongols decided to retreat. They would be far safer north of the Great Wall in their land-locked country. I learned that we were severely outnumbered. It was only a matter of time before the foreigners took Peking. When that happened, we could either flee or allow ourselves to be captured.

I knew what happened to women who were captured in warfare. Lanhua had been quite vocal about what the Taiping had done to the women and children in the towns they had sacked. They were raped and murdered. I would die before I allowed myself to be raped. Suicide was preferable to dishonor. But what about my children? I had heard that many people in the path of the Taiping had killed their own children to save them from being tortured to death. But I could never do that.

I had heard that white foreigners, barbarians though they were, often took imperial children as their own. They were sometimes set up as puppet rulers, or they were taken to England to be raised as pets of nobles. I did not want either of those fates to befall my children. Lifen needed me. Zaichun needed me and Lanhua. Children need their mothers. So, I decided we needed to flee should the foreigners come for us. The emperor, however, disagreed with me. Prince Yixin was by my side when we tried to convince him that we needed to leave the Summer Palace. Lanhua was present as well, sitting in her chair next to the emperor's, her son, Zaichun, on her lap. It was a rare occasion when Sushun and his cronies were gone from the Summer Palace. I did not know where they had gone, nor did I care.

"I would rather die than be chased from my own home by a bunch of rabid dogs," the emperor said.

"But if we leave, we could prepare for your return," I said. "Running is better than forfeiting your throne."

"I will never forfeit my birthright," he said.

"But that is exactly what you will do if you stay here," Yixin said. "If the foreigners capture you, they will either kill you or make you their puppet."

"I would kill myself first," he said.

"Then, if you stay here, you will die," I said. "Either the foreigners will kill you, or you will kill yourself. Is that what you are telling me?"

"I suppose so," he said.

"You have fought for your throne for this long, you cannot give up now."

"But if I flee, the people will think I am a coward."

"The people are fleeing! Thousands of people have marched past the gate of the Summer Palace already. They will understand."

Yizhu shook his head. "They will never understand. No one will ever understand."

"You must go," Yixin said. "If you go north to Rehe Palace, you will be safe there. The road is dangerous, and winter is coming. The palace is well fortified. The foreigners will not pursue you there. You can regroup for a response in the spring."

The emperor seemed to give this some thought. I held my breath, waiting for his response.

"I will consider it," he said, followed by a small cough. I noticed he looked rather thin, but I supposed we all did. I wasn't eating, and I was hardly sleeping. I didn't see how anyone could feel relaxed in this atmosphere of fear and uncertainty.

The emperor turned away after giving us his non-answer. He did not seem to limp, but more dragged his lame leg behind him, as though he did not have the strength to pick it up.

"Now," he said as he slumped into his chair. "As for the real reason I summoned you both. What are the preparations for my birthday celebration?"

Prince Yixin and I exchanged a glance.

"There are no preparations," Yixin said. "I have been focused on preserving our empire."

"*You* have been focused on being a running dog for the foreigners!" the emperor yelled. Zaichun fussed in his mother's lap. Lanhua bounced him up and down, shushing him. The emperor reached over, patting his son on the head. How I wished he would show such tenderness to Lifen! But he had never even visited her. He only saw her when I took her to see him, but such instances had become quite rare as of late.

"I am sorry that my duties with the Inner Court have prevented me from making any birthday arrangements, my lord," I said.

The emperor nodded. "The women have been even more fussy than this baby."

I pressed my lips to keep from responding. The women were terrified, for themselves and their families. Many of them wanted to run away on their own, to be allowed to return to their families as they fled the city. I could not allow it, though. If they left the Summer Palace, I had no way of knowing what might happen to them. One of the women had even been caught trying to escape from the Summer Palace dressed as her maid. Thankfully, she had been caught before she even made it out the gate. She was now under house arrest in her palace.

"We should invite an opera troupe to perform, my lord," Lanhua suggested. "I know how you enjoy the performances."

"Sister," I said, "that is not appropriate. People are fleeing for their lives. We are at war. The emperor should not be seen celebrating—"

"I think it is a grand idea," Yizhu said. He took Lanhua's hand, kissing the back of it. Lanhua preened like a cat at his attention. "It is my birthday. It is my right to celebrate. Everyone—no matter their circumstances—should want me to be happy on this one day."

I was flabbergasted. I looked at Yixin, who appeared nauseated. But it was clear that the emperor was not going to listen to reason. I was tired of wasting my time speaking to someone who had already resigned himself to death. I gave a bow.

"Very well, my lord. I am sure Lanhua can make the arrangements. I will return to my duties." I turned to leave and left Yixin to argue with his brother alone. If Yixin wanted to keep banging his head against a brick wall, I would leave him to it.

Outside, I summoned my chief eunuch. "We need to start preparing to leave."

"Leave?" he asked, confused.

"The foreigners are steadily approaching Peking. It is only a matter of time before they take the city. They will certainly come looking for us."

His face went white, and I feared he was going to faint. I grabbed his arm and shook him.

"I need you to be strong. I need your help."

"Yes... Yes, of course, Your Majesty."

"I need you to start packing. Start with the things that are the most valuable. Cash, gold, jewels. After that, consider only necessary items. Clothes, food, blankets." It was October, and winter would be close on our heels. "Send me the chief of the Ministry of Household Affairs. I need the same done for all the ladies, the prince, and the princess. And I need special care taken of Consort Lingrong—"

"Zhen!"

I saw Prince Yixin coming toward me. I nodded to the eunuch. He knew his tasks. He bowed and scurried away. Once everyone found out I was preparing to flee, the entire Summer Palace would be in a frenzy.

"Brother," I said. "I am preparing the court for the journey to Rehe Palace."

"Good," he said. "If my brother really chooses to stay here, I want you to leave."

"If it comes to that, I am not sure I will be able to," I said. "I can only hope that Lanhua and I can convince him to leave as well."

"What do you mean you won't be able to go without him?"

"I am his wife. It is my duty to be by his side."

"To die by his side?" he asked. "Or worse?"

I wrung my hands, unsure how to answer. As empress, my duty was to the emperor. As a wife, my duty was to my husband. But as a woman, I feared that I was a coward. That I would run if I knew my life was truly in danger.

"I don't know," I said, ashamed.

"Listen," he said, taking my arm and leading me away, where we could talk privately. "You must get Lanhua on your side."

"Lanhua?"

"She keeps Zaichun at her side at all times. I doubt you will be able to get him away from her. But if Yizhu decides to stay here, you must leave and take Zaichun with you."

"Take the boy from his father?"

"He is no mere boy, and his father is the emperor. Whoever controls the heir controls China. If Yizhu does something rash, like take his own life, Zaichun will be the next emperor. You must keep him out of the foreigners' hands. It just might save Yizhu's life."

"What do you mean?"

"If the foreigners capture Yizhu and Zaichun, they could kill Yizhu and put Zaichun on the throne under their control. But if they do not control Zaichun, killing Yizhu does them no good."

I nodded, starting to understand what he was saying. "Do you think the emperor is a lost cause?"

"I think he is despondent," he said. "He believes that he failed our father. Father hated the foreigners. Yizhu thought that by driving them out of China, he would please the ancestors. Unfortunately, he has discovered that driving them out is not as easy as he thought. He now understands why our father could never do so himself."

"Why are you not so despondent? You haven't given up. Do you think we can still be victorious?"

"Victorious? No. But we can survive. I understand the foreigners in ways that Yizhu does not. I speak their language; I've studied the ways they have dealt with other nations. They use money to get what they want. Then, they take control of younger rulers as the old ones die off. We can always earn more money. But we cannot create more heirs. Keep Zaichun away from the foreigners and we will survive this."

"Does the emperor know this?"

"He won't listen to me. You saw that for yourself."

"What about his other advisors? Sushun? Prince Zaiyun? Do they still think that we can win?"

Yixin scoffed. "They claim they are doing their best to hold the foreign troops back, but I know many of them are with their families, cleaning out their houses. They are trying to cart as many of their possessions as possible to Chengde, near Rehe Palace."

I had to shake my head in disgust. If we somehow all survived this, surely my husband would punish them for their bad advice and cowardice.

"When should we leave? Today?"

"Not just yet. I think I might still be able to reason with the foreigners. I might be able to come to terms with them."

"How?"

"I am going to release Parkes and his men."

"They are still alive?"

The prince hesitated. "Some of them."

"Some?"

"...Fewer than half of them."

My hand flew to my mouth. They had been suffering for weeks. I had thought they must all be dead by now. If they were still alive, they would surely be dead soon. If any of them had survived, they would have been scarred for life.

"I know," he said. "That is why I must go. I must try and save them."

"How...how did they survive this long?"

"I had help."

I then remembered that he had asked me for help, and I had refused him. He must have found someone else.

"Who helped you?"

"It's not important," he said, stepping away. "Just continue as you were, preparing to leave. Wait until I come back before you do so, though. You cannot travel unescorted. I fear the people will turn on you if they find out you are on the road. If I am able to get the foreigners to come to terms but then you flee, they might think I was negotiating in bad faith. But make sure Lanhua and Consort Lingrong are with you. Whatever happens, you must get Zaichun and Consort Lingrong's unborn son as far away from here as possible."

"Very well," I said. "I will do as you ask."

Yixin stepped to me again, our chests practically touching as he looked down at me. His hand brushed my cheek. "You are the only person I can fully trust."

He looked down into my eyes and had the same smoldering look as he did once before, right before he kissed me the night his father died. The night his brother became emperor. He licked his lips, and I took a deep breath. I did not know if I could allow him to kiss me or not. I wanted him to—oh, how I wanted it! But I was a different woman than I had been a decade ago.

Thankfully, the choice was taken from me. We heard the door to the emperor's audience hall open, so we stepped away from each other quickly. It was Lanhua, Prince Zaichun on her hip. Lanhua looked at Prince Yixin, and then at me. I felt my face blush, but I did not look away from her. If I looked away, it would be proof that the prince and I had done something inappropriate. But we hadn't. Nothing had happened.

Prince Yixin ran his hand over his mouth. "Remember what I said," he told me. I nodded and he left without a word to Lanhua.

"What did I just walk in on?" Lanhua asked me with a sly smile as soon as the prince was out of earshot.

"We need to prepare to leave," I told her.

"The emperor seems intent on staying," she said. "I am to summon an opera troupe to perform for him as soon as possible."

Zaichun wiggled in his mother's arms. She put him down so that he could toddle around the garden.

"I am aware," I said. "But we must still try to convince him to leave. We must keep him away from the foreigners."

"Yizhu will not allow himself to be taken captive by the foreigners," she said. "You know him better than that."

"I know," I said. "But if that is the case, we must protect Zaichun."

"You don't think that Yizhu would…hurt his own son, do you?"

"I don't want to imagine it," I said. "But do you think he would let the foreigners take his only son?"

Lanhua did not respond. I imagined she was thinking about the families who had committed suicide together rather than allowing themselves to be killed by the Taiping. If Yizhu killed himself, would he take his consorts with him? His empress? His son?

"I know you are loyal to the emperor," I said. "But I also know how much a mother loves her children. I would never let anyone hurt my daughter. I know you feel the same way about your son."

"Do you think we can truly defy the emperor?" she asked.

"I hope it will not come to that," I said. "We must do our best to convince him to flee with us. We can't give up. We can't leave him behind if there is still a chance we could all leave here together—alive."

"Very well," she said. "What do you want me to do?"

"Have your eunuchs prepare for your departure, for you and Zaichun, but do not tell the emperor. Instead, try to bolster his mood. If he is happy, maybe he won't want to give up. Maybe he won't want to die. That way, when Prince Yixin tells us that it is time to leave, we will be ready, and hopefully we can convince the emperor to join us."

Lanhua giggled. "I had no idea you were so brave. So devious. So cunning."

"I am not cunning," I said. "I am only trying to protect my family."

"Of course," she said. "Well, excuse me while I try to find an opera troupe among the people fleeing Peking willing to perform for the emperor while the foreigners are marching toward us."

"You make it sound so easy," I said, and we laughed together.

How we found the courage to laugh against such odds was strange. But that was Lanhua. She was able to find humor in any situation, and she had the strength to remain optimistic no matter what.

CHAPTER TWENTY-EIGHT

*T*he opera troupe performed for four days and four nights. Apparently, Lanhua was able to find a large enough troupe that they could perform in shifts. Still, I doubt any of them got much sleep, if any at all, with such racket playing. I enjoyed the occasional opera performance, but after a few hours, the high-pitched voices and repetitive clapping of the paiban become too much to bear, making my head ache. But Yizhu seemed unable to get enough. He sat on a balcony, overlooking a wide and flat lawn. The troupe performed there day and night, with the emperor looking down on them. I noticed that the troupe seemed to stick to operas that were on the more humorous side, such as *The Drunken Concubine*, or those that told the story of military prowess, such as *Lady Mu Guiying Takes Command*.

For the most part, Lanhua sat by his side. When Zaichun grew fussy or bored, Lanhua would send him off with me to care for him. I had no idea if Lanhua was able to speak to the emperor during those days. If she did, I don't know how he would have been able to hear her. My palace was quite a distance away from the opera performance, but I could still hear the singers and musicians clearly.

Though, even if the Summer Palace had been completely silent, I do not think I could have slept. I did not know when Prince Yixin would return, if he ever would. Perhaps he would come to some agreement with the foreigners, and we would be able to return to the Forbidden City in peace. Or they would come to no agreement and Prince Yixin would arrive suddenly to tell me it was time to flee.

The worst thought that kept coming to my mind was that the foreigners would execute Prince Yixin in retaliation for what had happened to Parkes and his men. I tried to banish this thought as soon as it came to my mind, but it returned, time and time again. Every time it did, a wave of nausea would wash over me and I would have to sit down for a few minutes until it passed.

"Are you okay, Mama?" Lifen asked one day when she saw me with my head in my hands. Covering my eyes from the light seemed to help settle my stomach.

"Of course, Darling," I told her, hugging her close and kissing her on the top of her head. I did not want to frighten her, but I was sure she could sense that something was wrong. "We are just preparing to go for a little trip."

"To the hunting lodge," she said. "Is Baba going to go hunting? Will he allow me to go with him?"

"Perhaps," I said as I stood and checked our luggage once again, as I had more than a dozen times before. "When your father was younger, he quite enjoyed hunting. But he hasn't done so in a long time."

"It's how he hurt his leg," she said.

"That's right. Who told you that?"

"One of the nannies. I can't remember which one."

"Have you finished packing? Did you make sure to take only

your favorite toy with you? The others should all be packed away."

"I don't know. Nanny Bai says that we shouldn't be going. She says winter is coming and we could get trapped in the snow."

"Is that so?" I made a mental note to dismiss Nanny Bai as soon as it was prudent. I could not employ people who would second guess my decisions and speak ill of me behind my back to my own child.

Not that the nanny's concerns weren't valid. The cool weather of autumn had already descended on Peking, with the nights growing chilly enough to light the braziers. Rehe Place was so far north, we would go past some sections of the Great Wall. It was located in a mountainous area, just south of the Mongolian steppes. It would take us at least a week to get there. By the time we arrived, winter would already be rearing its ugly head. We would not be able to return to Peking until the spring, if we were able to return at all.

"It will be fun to see that much snow, don't you think?" I said. "You can sled down the hills, and we can go skating on the ponds."

"Really?" she asked, jumping up and down. "I have to go tell Zaichun!"

As she ran to the door, she almost bumped into Lingrong.

"Watch out, little one," Lingrong said, putting her arm protectively around her barely showing pregnant belly.

"Excuse me, Mother," she said with a quick bow before squeezing around her and running on her way. Even though Lifen had called her "mother," it was a formal version, one she used with all of her father's consorts. I had tried to explain to her before that Lingrong was the woman who had given birth to her, but she seemed to be too young to fully understand what I was telling her.

Lingrong watched as Lifen ran out the door, her gaze

lingering long after the child was gone. She and I never spoke about the fact that she had given birth to Lifen. We both pretended that I was Lifen's natural mother. It seemed easier on her that way. So how she really felt about having abandoned Lifen, I didn't know. I didn't want to know.

"How are you feeling?" I asked Lingrong.

"I'm not sure," she said. "The morning sickness has not abated. My lower back hurts. I am not sure if this pregnancy is different because I am carrying a boy this time, or if it is different because of the anxiety with the war."

"I am sorry that you are feeling anxious. I told your servants to do everything. That you should not have to lift a finger."

"That might have made things worse," she said as she took a seat. "I have nothing to occupy my mind but worry."

I knew she meant her words to sound lighthearted, but they fell flat.

"Well, the only thing you should be concerned with is growing a healthy son for the emperor."

"I know," she said. "I am only thankful that I am not further along. I can't imagine taking such a long journey if I were closer to the birth."

"Thank Heaven for small blessings," I said. "You are sure you will make the journey with me—even if the emperor refuses to go?" I had spoken with her not long after Prince Yixin had left us. I needed her to be prepared to leave, and for her to understand how important it was for the emperor's heirs not to fall into enemy hands.

"I will go," she said. "I promise. I am not looking forward to the journey, but I know it is the right thing to do. I have to protect my son—whatever the cost."

"Good," I said with a nod. I looked through the window and saw how dark it was. I wasn't sure of the time since I hadn't been sleeping, but it had to be late. "You should do your best to rest."

She scoffed a laugh. "With that noise? My palace is even closer to the performance than yours is."

"Sorry about that," I said. "We could ask one of the other ladies to switch with you."

She waved me off. "That would be more hassle than it is worth, I'm sure."

"Well, if we don't leave anytime soon—"

I was cut off when Prince Yixin pushed the door open and stepped into the room. "It is time."

Lingrong let out a gasp and looked at me.

"What has happened?" I asked.

"Parkes was returned to them alive, but he is in poor shape," he said. "But so many men died, and so many others are…" He stopped and shook his head. I could tell he did not want to go into graphic detail. I did not press him on the matter, especially in front of Lingrong.

"So, they are out for revenge," I said.

"I was able to stop them from destroying the Forbidden City," the prince said. "But they are coming here. I can only imagine they will do their worst when they arrive."

I thought about the hundreds of opulent palaces, some dating back to the years of Qianlong the Magnificent. The precious artifacts. The beautiful gardens. Surely, they would not destroy this magical place. Steal whatever they could? Naturally. There were countless items of pure gold throughout the palaces that were worth a fortune. But hopefully, they would not do any damage that could not be repaired or replaced.

"It doesn't matter," I said. "What matters is leaving here with our lives intact. You know what to do."

Prince Yixin and Lingrong both bowed to me and then got to work. I summoned my chief eunuch and gave him his orders. Like busy ants preparing for a rainstorm, orders drifted from one person to the next in quick succession. I had spent the last four days preparing not only myself, but every person in the Forbidden City for this moment.

First, I went to Prince Zaichun's room and took him from his worried nannies. From now until we reached the hunting lodge, the prince would not leave my arms. I would not leave him here under any circumstances, even with Lanhua, should she change her mind.

Then, I went to confront the emperor. I opened the door to his palace without waiting to be announced. I walked onto the balcony and yelled down at the opera troupe, "Go! Now!" At first, they seemed confused, but several palace eunuchs ran onto the makeshift stage to explain that it was time to leave. They immediately stopped what they were doing and left—without even asking the emperor if they could be dismissed.

"What is going on?" Yizhu asked me, his head lolling to one side as he looked up at me.

"What is wrong with him?" I asked Lanhua.

"He is drunk." She called down to the eunuchs in the court-yard to come up and carry the emperor to his waiting donkey cart.

"He doesn't look drunk," I said as I touched his cheek. It was then that I smelled the sickly-sweet odor of opium. I looked down and saw that a pipe was smoldering next to the emperor's chair. "Oh, Lanhua. You didn't…"

The emperor abhorred opium. He, like his father before him, believed that the drug was a cancer that was devouring China from the inside out. As far as I knew, he had never used the drug before. He did not think he could be a good ruler if he allowed the smoke to addle his brain.

"I told him that if he was going to die, he might as well enjoy it," she said.

I shook my head, but I could not disagree with her method. At least in this state, we could get the emperor out of the

Summer Palace without argument. He might be angry with us later, but at least we would be safe.

Outside the gate of the Summer Palace, our donkey carts were waiting. The emperor would ride in the first cart. I would ride in the second cart with Prince Zaichun and Princess Lifen. Following me would be Lanhua and Lingrong. After that would be all of the other consorts.

Yixin was waiting by the emperor's cart when we got outside. "What is wrong with him?" he asked.

"Opium," I said.

Yixin cursed to himself and slapped his brother's cheeks to wake him up. "Brother," he said. "My emperor. The foreigners are coming."

The emperor squinted to try and see his brother better. "Prince Gong. Prince of the Blood. The Iron Cap Prince. The Sixth Devil." Yizhu laughed after saying that last one. Some people, mainly Han Chinese, who didn't think we Manchu should rule China, called the emperor's sons "Devils." It was a derogatory term, but I supposed the emperor found it humorous in his inebriated state.

"Yes, Brother," Yixin said. "It's me. Do you want me to go with you? Or should I stay here? The foreign barbarians are coming. What should I do?"

"Only a devil can stop devils," the emperor said.

"You want me to try and negotiate with them?"

"Do what you will," the emperor said, slumping to one side. "That's all you ever do."

Prince Yixin shook his head and let the emperor pass out in his seat.

"Come with us," I told Yixin, but he shook his head.

"I will stay. They won't hurt me. I have to try and stop them."

"There is no shame in running away if that is what you must do," I told him. "The emperor needs you. Your nephew needs you."

I need you.

I wanted to say it, but I couldn't. But I think Yixin must have been thinking the same thing. Even though we were surrounded by people, even though we were running for our lives, for a moment, it seemed as if we were the only two people in the world.

"I will see you at Rehe Palace," he finally said. He took me by the hand and led me to my donkey cart. He helped me into my seat and held my hand as we drove away.

Ahead of the emperor walked a contingent of eunuch guards. They worked to clear the narrow road ahead of us as we made our way to Rehe Palace. Fewer people were along the road than usual since it was the middle of the night, but many people had dropped what they could no longer carry. The sides of the road were littered with furniture, clothing, bags of food, and hobbled animals, both living and dead. There were people, too. People who had been sick or injured had been left on the side of the road to die or fend for themselves. Elderly folk and women with bound feet had been dropped like sacks of rice. There were also children. Children whose parents had been killed by bandits or whose families thought they were burdens no longer worth carrying. I had two children, a boy and a girl, placed in the back of my cart. If nothing else, they could be trained for service. I had other children picked up as well and put in the following donkey carts.

"This is foolish, Your Majesty," my eunuch told me after we picked up a fifth child. "These piglets aren't worth the clothes they wear."

"I'll turn these sows' ears into silk purses," I said. "You'll see."

I was not sure how long we had been traveling, or how far. Since our carts were being led by eunuchs, we were only going as fast as the men could walk. It might have been toward the end of the first full day, or perhaps the early morning of the second. I only remember that the sun was either rising or setting as we made our way up a tall hill. It was cold, and the tall grass was brown as it swayed in the breeze.

I looked over Zaichun's head and saw something rustling in the grass. I saw a flash of red slipping between the patches of grass, and I thought it must have been a fox. I was surprised to see it so near a busy road, but before I could see it clearly, someone in the long line of carts yelled, "Fire!"

I looked back, expecting to see that one of the carts had somehow caught fire. With the grass so dry and brittle, a fire could quickly spread. But off in the distance, I only saw smoke.

"Stop!" I ordered my cart driver. I stood up on my seat to get a better look. Down the hill, on the edge of Kunming Lake, the Summer Palace was burning. My heart ached as I thought about the hundreds of years of Manchu history, Manchu greatness, Manchu accomplishment being devoured by the flames.

Ahead of me, I could hear the emperor groaning in pain. I jumped down from my cart and ran to him. The emperor leaned over the side of his cart and vomited onto the road, barely missing my shoes as I jumped away. The emperor had regained consciousness and could see what was happening. He climbed out of the cart and limped toward the burning buildings, though they were many li behind us.

"No!" he cried as he tore at his robe and pounded his fists on the ground. "I'll see every one of you in hell, you foreign devil bastards!" he shrieked.

"Your Majesty!" I said, tugging him to try and get him to stand. "You must control yourself! Everyone is watching."

"Let them watch!" he said. "Let me die! You should have left me there."

"Never," I said. "I would never abandon you."

"You!" he said, pointing behind me. I looked over my shoulder and saw that he was pointing at Lanhua, who had gone to my cart to check on Zaichun.

"Me, my lord?" she asked.

"You conniving woman," he growled. "You fucking sly fox. You did this. This was your idea."

"I don't know what you mean," she said innocently.

"You drugged me," he said, making his way toward her. "You planned all this to make it look like I was running like a coward."

I put myself in front of him. He had barely eaten in days and was still groggy from the opium and alcohol, so he could not even push me aside, weak woman that I was.

"Lanhua was only trying to help," I said. "I asked for her help."

"But you never would have done this," he said, staggering away from me. "You never would have taken the choice away from me. You would never have *forced* me to do your will."

"Because she is stronger than me," I said. "She had the courage to do what I could not."

"Courage?" Yizhu said. "You call it courage. I call it devious. She is a cunning woman. A scheming woman. A woman who does whatever it takes to get her way."

"A woman who loves you," Lanhua said to Yizhu.

Yizhu seemed taken aback by her words. He shook his head and rubbed his eyes with the palms of his hands. The hillside was so quiet, I could hear the crackling of the fire many li away.

"Snow!" Zaichun said. He held out his tongue as a small flake fell from the sky.

I did not think it had been cold enough to snow, but everyone looked up, mesmerized, as flakes fell and danced around us. I held out my hand and caught a few flakes on my fingers. But when I rubbed my fingers together, they were not wet with melted snowflakes, but streaked black with ash. I realized the wind had carried the burning embers from the Summer Palace up the hill toward us. I looked around at the dry grass and realized that a single spark could start a fire from which we would have no escape.

"We must go," I said. "Everyone to their carts."

Two eunuchs helped the emperor into his cart, and I could see his shoulders shake as he cried silently.

As we slowly climbed hills and then mountains to reach Rehe Palace, the fire raged below us. By the time we staggered through the gate of the hunting lodge, I knew there would be nothing left of my beloved Summer Palace.

CHAPTER TWENTY-NINE

*A*s soon as we arrived at Rehe Palace, the emperor took to his bed and did not leave it again. Even when Lingrong went into labor, he did not go to her. When she gave birth, he did not ask to see the child. And when the infant died two hours later, he did not weep.

"My boy! My boy! My beautiful boy!" Lingrong screamed when she was told that the child had died. I had Princess Lifen and Prince Zaichun sequestered in my room as she mourned. They never knew that they had a little brother, or that he had died. I did my best to safeguard their innocence as long as I could.

It was November, and the emperor was weak and ill. The chill from the time on the road settled into his lungs and never seemed to leave. We summoned every doctor we could find in the cold and desolate area around the hunting lodge, but there were no major towns nearby. Since the lodge's purpose was to hunt wild animals, it was strategically built away from any large cities. As such, it made getting doctors or midwives difficult. It was also hard to procure food. The servants had to travel for days to the nearest town of Chengde, facing cold temperatures, treacherous roads, and bandits, and return with whatever food-stuff they could find in the middle of winter.

The few doctors we could find could not seem to agree on what was wrong with the emperor or how to treat him. Some said his lungs were too dry, others too wet. Still others said his lungs needed to be cleared of impurities. Some said he needed to clear his spleen or nourish his heart. All of them prescribed different herbal concoctions, some of which helped only a little, while others seemed to make him much worse.

Despite his illness, though, the emperor continued to work. Everyone at least agreed that the emperor needed to rest, but he refused. Edicts began pouring into the hunting lodge, all of them needing the emperor's immediate attention. From morning until night, the emperor continued meeting with his advisors—who were all already in Chengde, waiting for him—in order to devise the best way to govern the country from afar and with foreigners in the capital.

It seemed that the emperor finally conceded that it was Prince Yixin who knew best how to deal with the foreigners, not his many other advisors. He gave the prince his full authority to come to peaceful terms.

The terms that Prince Yixin returned with were shocking. China had to pay eight million taels to England and France. Hundreds of thousands of square acres of land were ceded to the Russians. More treaty ports were opened. More foreign legations were opened in Peking. Foreign preachers were given full civil liberties, including the right to own land outside the legations. Foreign ships were allowed to take indentured Chinese slaves to the Americas. And, perhaps worst of all, the opium trade was legalized.

I expected the emperor to balk at the terms. Even if he was no longer in a position to fight back, he could at least try and negotiate. Though, perhaps he knew that Prince Yixin had already done all the negotiating he could. If this was the best

Yixin could do, the emperor knew he could do no better. The emperor signed and stamped the edict and then handed it back to his brother. The two men clasped forearms.

"You did well, Brother," the emperor told Yixin.

"Thank you, Brother," Yixin replied, and I thought I saw tears in his eyes. This is what Emperor Daoguang had wanted all along, to see his two sons working together for the betterment of China. I did not know how we were going to pay the indemnities, but as Prince Yixin had told me, the country could always earn more money. Somehow, we would get through this.

But as soon as the prince left the room, the prince threw his copy of the treaty to the floor.

"Fucking running dog," the emperor spat.

"Who does Prince Yixin work for?" Sushun asked. "The foreigners, or you?"

"He will pay for this," the emperor said. "I will make sure he pays for this." He devolved into another fit of coughing, this time with blood on his handkerchief.

"Once the foreigners let their guard down, we should disregard the treaty," Sushun said. "We should attack them while they sleep."

This horrified me. Were we not in this position because Yizhu had gone back on his word to sign a treaty in the first place?

"My lord," I said when Yizhu's coughing subsided, "I am sure the prince did the best he could. We will find a way to repay the money."

"Why are you even here?" the emperor asked as he lay back on his pillow.

"You…you summoned me," I said.

"I did?"

"You said that I should see how peace was made so that I could tell our son when he is older."

"Oh, that's right. Come, sit by me," he said, patting his bed. "All you men, get out."

The men grumbled as they left the room but did as they were told.

"I'm dying," Yizhu said as soon as we were alone.

"Don't say such things," I said.

"It's true," he said. "I know it. I can feel it. I feel the ancestors calling me."

"You are young," I said. "You cannot be dying yet." I had never loved Yizhu. How could I when he had treated me so badly? And yet, I did not want him to die. Not yet. I had always harbored a hope that things would get better. That he would learn to treat me kindly. That we would eventually have a child together of our own. But it seemed that Yizhu had given up. Indeed, he had given up back when we were in the Summer Palace. The only reason he was even still alive now was because I had refused to leave him behind.

"Stop talking," he said. "I'm trying to tell you something important."

I cleared my throat and sat silently. The emperor reached under his pillow and handed me a piece of parchment.

"What is it?" I asked as I skimmed the document.

"It is an order for Lanhua's death."

"What? No!" I said, rolling the paper back up and handing it to him.

"It is not for right now," he said. "When I am gone, Zaichun will be too young to rule. I will appoint a regent to help him, but he is still a little boy. I know he will look to his mother for guidance."

"Lanhua," I said.

The emperor nodded. "But he should be looking to *you*. *You* are my empress, not her. *You* are his mother, not her. You will be the empress dowager when I am gone. It is you who should guide my son."

"Then why are you giving me this?" I said, shaking the parchment.

"Because Lanhua is a cunning woman," he said. "She will try to take your place. She will try to rule our son herself."

"That's ridiculous," I said. "Lanhua is my friend. And she is Zaichun's birth mother. We can raise and guide Zaichun together, as we have been."

"You are an idiot if you believe that," Yizhu said. "She will push you aside the first chance she gets. Worse, I feel she will try to exert power over the Dragon Throne itself. But if you have this order, you can use it to get rid of her. It is already signed and sealed."

"I think you are worrying needlessly," I said. "You aren't going to die, not yet. And if you do, Lanhua loves your son. *Our* son. She would only ever do what is best for him."

The emperor went quiet, looking at me, his eyes heavy. "Do you know why I wanted to marry you?"

"Hmm." I picked up a rag and used it to mop the emperor's face. "I don't know. I always assumed it was because of how beautiful I was."

Yizhu chuckled, his breath coming out a bit ragged. "You were an ugly rat next to Ayan."

"I would agree with you there," I said. "She was so…dainty."

"Do you remember my mother?"

I shook my head. "I was too young when she died."

"I was five years old when she died, but I remember her so clearly. She looked like you. She had the same eyes and gentle manners. I remember swimming in a pond in the Forbidden City. She would take off her shoes and dip her feet in the water. Her feet were so small, I think they were the same size as mine."

I had to laugh at that. "Well, that would be impossible."

"That's how I remember it."

"Then you must have had very big feet as a child."

We laughed together, and I think it was the only time during our whole marriage we did so. Why did it have to be on his deathbed? If he married me because I reminded him of his mother, why was he so cruel to me?

He spread his arm out and beckoned me to lay beside him.

"Don't die," I said.

Please, don't die.

THE XIANFENG EMPEROR, my husband, died on the twenty-second of August, 1861. He was not yet thirty-one years old. My son, Zaichun, was four years old. I knew that emperors of the past had also taken the throne at a young age, but looking at my son, so innocent, so gentle, I did not see how he could possibly be the ruler of one of the largest empires on earth.

But that was what a regent was for.

Yizhu's will was opened almost as soon as he took his last breath. Everyone expected Prince Yixin to be appointed as regent. After all, even the emperor had told me he would appoint a regent for his son. And after the disastrous war with the foreigners, it was Prince Yixin who put everything back together again. At first, the emperor had been angry about the terms, but what else could Yixin have done? The foreigners had set up camp within the Forbidden City. Rumors said the foreign leader, Lord Elgin, even slept in the emperor's bed. Prince Yixin had no option but to agree to their terms. And for the next several months after the treaties had been signed, Yizhu and Yixin seemed to have buried the hatchet. Yixin often traveled up to the hunting lodge, which was a much faster and easier journey on a horse and without the road being crowded with people. The brothers would sit and eat and drink together and talk about good times, those of the past and those yet to come. The emperor never lost his love of opera and often watched it for days on end, his brother and Lanhua at his side.

So, when the emperor's will was opened and we all learned that Yizhu had not named one regent, but eight, and that Prince Yixin was not among them, the fear, anger, and confusion in the room were palpable. Except among the regents, who laughed and congratulated one another.

Some of the men I knew, but a few I didn't. They were Sushun, his brother Duanhua, who was the father-in-law of Feiya, Prince Zaiyuan, Jingshou, Muyin, Kuangyuan, Du Han, and Jiao Youying. All of them were men who had encouraged the emperor to fight the foreigners at every step. To reject the earlier treaties. To capture and torture Harry Parkes. They were the men who had led my husband—and all of China—to disaster.

I could not let them do the same thing to my son.

But what could I do? I was now only the empress dowager, the mother of the next emperor. I could advise my son when he grew older. But for now, I could do nothing. In effect, those power-hungry, war-mongering men were the eight-headed emperor of China.

If Yixin had been made regent, I knew I would have no reason to worry. I could trust him to do what was best for the country and my son. But now, I feared for Yixin's life. What if the eight regents decided that he was a traitor? They could sentence him to death and no one could stop them. I had to do something, and quickly. The regents could not harm Yixin for now. It was against the law for blood to be shed for one hundred days after an emperor's death. Even animals could not be butchered. But how could I make Prince Yixin regent?

I went to Lanhua for help.

"You should be regent," she told me.

"Me?"

"Yes, you. Empress dowagers have been regents in the past."

"I don't think Wu Zetian is a name I should be conjuring up right now," I said. "Men hate her."

"Because she proved them all wrong," Lanhua said. "She was able to rule China on her own without the aid of a man. She proved that women are just as smart and capable as any man."

"Still, even if I am the empress dowager, how can I be regent now? Zaichun has eight regents already. Adding me to the list isn't going to make much difference."

"We will have to kill them," she said a bit too easily.

"What? We can't commit murder," I hissed.

"No, nothing so inelegant as that," she said. "We could accuse them of treason."

I opened my mouth to argue with her, but then I stopped. After all, I was sure the men were going to accuse Yixin of treason and have him executed. I would just have to do it first.

"It...might work," I said. "But then would I automatically become the regent? What about Prince Yixin?"

"Forget about Prince Yixin," Lanhua said. "You can be the regent. You don't need Prince Yixin."

"I do," I said. "I don't know anything about ruling."

"*I* can help you," she said.

"You?" I laughed, but then I realized that she was serious. "What do you know about ruling a country?"

"What does a five-year-old know? Anything Zaichun can learn, I can learn. And, fine, we can make Prince Yixin an advisor, just like he was Yizhu. Only this time, we will actually listen to him."

"Wait," I said. "*We* can make him an advisor? It's *we* now? I thought you said I could be regent."

"Maybe we can both be regents," she said. "Yizhu appointed eight, so there's no reason there can't be two. And it would be easier on you if I was also a regent."

"But I'm the empress dowager," I said.

"Maybe we can both be empress dowagers."

"What? That can't be done."

"Why not?" she asked. "I don't think a child emperor has ever had eight regents before, either."

"So, we are all just making the rules up as we go?"

"Why not?" she said.

So that was what we set out to do. We didn't have all the steps to our plan yet, but Lanhua suggested that by starting small, the regents would not have any idea what we were really up to.

We went to the regents and asked to both be titled empress dowagers. At first, Sushun rejected the idea. But Little An, clever little creature that he was, found that there was, indeed, precedence for having two empress dowagers. When the Kangxi Emperor succeeded to the throne in 1662, almost exactly two hundred years previously, his mother had also been a concubine, but she, along with his father's empress, was named an empress dowager. When Sushun demanded to know why this was so important to me, I told him it was so that Lanhua could stand beside her son during the mourning rituals for Yizhu. That seemed to placate him.

Together, Lanhua and I helped prepare the emperor's body to return to Peking, and then to the Western Mausoleum, southwest of Peking, to rest for all eternity next to his ancestors, all the way back to Emperor Shunzhi.

I led Princess Lifen in the mourning rituals, and Lanhua led Zaichun. Lifen did everything exactly as she was told, even wailing in sadness when we kneeled before his coffin. At first, I thought the poor child was greatly distraught by the death of her father, but then I noticed that she shed no tears. And why should she? She hardly knew her father.

Out of all of Yizhu's consorts, it was Lingrong who mourned him the most, crying by his coffin day and night, with genuine tears flowing down her cheeks. But I felt like she had also lost the most. Far more than a husband. She had given up her daughter in order to give her husband a son. Now, she had no husband, no daughter, and no son—and she would never have a chance to have those things ever again.

When the time came to travel back to the Forbidden City, Lanhua was starting to fret about our plan.

"How are we going to accuse them of treason?" she asked me. "What have they done that they cannot defend themselves against? The emperor approved everything they did."

I had no idea, but I hoped we would think of something. We had plenty of time. Much like how we had traveled to the hunting lodge, we would slowly amble our way back to Peking by donkey carts. In fact, we would travel back even slower since we would stop at every town along the road so villagers could properly mourn their emperor. At least this time, we were better prepared for the journey. We had plenty of food, and we took large tents that would be erected for us each night and torn down each morning.

One night, on the journey back, I couldn't sleep. I was worrying about what would happen when we arrived in Peking and those men were able to take control of my son and the throne. More than anything, the war had shown that we were utterly alone in the world. The British, French, Americans, and Russians had all joined forces against us. They had a seemingly endless supply of troops and warships. We had no one. The Mongols had abandoned us, and the southern half of the country was in turmoil as the Taiping still had control of most of the region. If the regents wanted to continue fighting the foreigners, we would lose. We had to find a way to peacefully coexist with them.

I finally got up and decided to go for a walk. I wrapped my robe around me and went to stand near a bonfire. Several bonfires had been lit throughout the camp for light and protection. I was startled when a tent flap opened and a man and a woman stumbled out, laughing. It was Sushun and a woman I didn't recognize. But they were so enchanted with each other, they didn't even notice me.

"Will I see you again?" the woman asked him.

"Only if you want to walk twenty li down the road to where we camp next," he said. They kissed again. When the woman pulled away, she held out her hand. Sushun made a show of dropping several large coins into her outstretched palm. It was then I realized this was one of those prostitutes that Lanhua had told me about. She did not look how I expected. Since prostitutes sold their bodies and were often riddled with disease, I had expected her to be thin, filthy, and pockmarked. But this woman was beautiful. Her hair was long and glossy, her skin smooth, and her clothes were expensive. I didn't understand it. But what surprised me the most was that the woman did not have bound feet, which must have meant that she was a Manchu prostitute.

The woman sauntered away until she ran into another man. They talked for a moment, and then he led her into another tent. I was so disgusted I wanted to spit. Sushun wandered away from his tent toward the darkness. When he stopped, I wondered what he was doing, but then I heard the splashing of water and realized he was urinating. Everything about this man, even the most basic of bodily functions, repulsed me.

As he made his way back to his tent, he finally saw me. "Sorry, little lady. Try me again tomorrow night if you can get here before your friend."

"Excuse me?" I said, horrified.

He paused and squinted to get a better look at me. "Empress?" He laughed. "Sorry, I didn't recognize you with your hair down. You almost look attractive this way."

"Hold your peasant tongue!" I said. "I should have you whipped for such impertinence."

Sushun walked toward me until he was practically standing over me, so I couldn't help but feel intimidated, which I assumed was his intent. Still, I was the empress, so I did not move. Sushun reached out and took a lock of my hair between his fingers, twirling it.

"Would you be doing the whipping?" he asked, his voice low. I didn't know exactly what he meant, but judging by his tone, I had a feeling he was referencing something sexual in nature.

My heart was racing. I knew I needed to say something, but I also didn't want to give him the satisfaction of getting a rise out of me.

"You should know your place," I said as evenly as possible, though I could feel my voice shaking.

"Oh, yeah," he said with a chuckle. "I like it when a woman gives the orders. I think you and I are going to be very, *very* good friends."

This time, I did not respond. Nor did I move. I would not let him goad me into running away. I had no idea how long we stood there, but I would have stayed frozen to that spot all night if I had to. Eventually, I think he realized that I wasn't going to play whatever sick game he thought we had started, and he retreated back to his tent. Only then did I turn and head back to my own tent, nearly collapsing onto my cot. But then, an idea struck me. I had to see Lanhua immediately. Thankfully, her tent was right next to my own.

"Lanhua!" I whispered loudly as I entered her tent. She was sleeping soundly. Zaichun was lying next to her, and they were both dead to the world. I had to shake Lanhua to get her to respond.

"Zhen?" she said, rubbing her eyes. "Is it time to pack up already?"

"No. But I needed to talk to you."

"Now?" She pulled her blanket up and laid back down.

"Yes," I said, pulling her blanket away.

"Hey," she said. "Don't wake the baby." She was a bit more

awake now. She tucked her blanket around Zaichun and sat up to look at me. "What's going on?"

"I just saw Sushun with—" I lowered my voice even though we were alone. "—a prostitute."

"Ugh, you woke me up for that?"

"You knew?"

"No," she said. "But it doesn't surprise me. He's horrible. I feel sorry for his wife, whoever she is." She turned as if she was going to lie back down.

"But, Lanhua, don't you see? This is it. It's treason to engage in sexual activities while mourning the emperor."

For the first time, Lanhua's eyes shot open, wide awake. "You're right. I had forgotten about that."

"Most people do, I think," I said, remembering how Yizhu had forced me to make love to him while we were mourning his father.

Lanhua was rubbing her lower lip with her finger, thinking. "But we would have to catch him in the act. Do you think he will do it again?"

"He told the woman he would see her again tomorrow night."

"Still, it might be hard to catch him, you know, literally doing it. And by the time we summoned witnesses, he would stop. And the woman certainly wouldn't testify as to what they were doing. No, we need to set him up with someone we can trust. Someone who would speak against him."

We were both quiet for a minute.

"You could do it," Lanhua said.

"Me?" I said. "Why me?"

"I've seen the way he looks at you," she said.

"What do you mean?" After my conversation with Sushun earlier, I believed he was attracted to me, but I had never thought so before. What had Lanhua observed that I had missed?

"But I'm the empress dowager—"

"*We* are empress dowagers."

"Yes, fine. Anyway, if I got caught with him, it would be double treason. Treason for betraying my husband's memory and the emperor's period of mourning."

"So, it can't be either of us," Lanhua said. "What about the prostitute? Is she still out there?"

"She went into a tent with a different man," I said.

"Who?"

"I don't know."

"Would you recognize her if you saw her tomorrow night?"

I thought back and tried to recall the woman's face, but I could only see Sushun. He was who I was focused on. The only thing I remembered about the woman was that her feet were not bound.

"I…I don't think so."

Lanhua blew out her cheeks. "I suppose it doesn't matter. She would never testify as to her actions."

"What woman would?" I asked.

"What about one of the other consorts?"

"We'd run into the same problems. She would be betraying the emperor."

"But when we become regents, we could pardon her. We just need someone who would be willing to testify that she and Sushun made love during the emperor's mourning procession."

"That's…true," I said. "But it is awfully dangerous. I can't think of anyone who would take such a risk."

"You aren't close to any of the other consorts?"

The only woman I could think of who I was close friends with was Lingrong, but things had been strained between us ever since I had adopted Lifen, even though it was at her request. But she had only asked me to adopt the girl so that she could possibly have a son. And it had worked, but now that son was dead. And with Yizhu dead, Lingrong would never have another child. It was highly improper for an imperial consort to remarry.

But there was perhaps one offer I could make her.

"You want me to become a nun?" Lingrong asked, confused.

"It is not that I want you to become a nun," I explained. "But it is the only alternative I can think of to a life of solitude in the Forbidden City."

"A life of solitude in a nunnery?"

"Nuns are not nearly as isolated as consorts," Lanhua pointed out. "People visit temples with nunneries all the time for blessings and such. And your family could visit you."

"Nuns are also educated," I said. I remembered how she once told me her father was a literary scholar, so I thought that would appeal to her. "You will be taught to read the scriptures and to write your own prayers and musings. You could even teach other women to read and write as well."

Lingrong considered this for a long time. "Will I be able to see my daughter again?"

My heart seized as she referred to Lifen as *her* daughter. I had always believed that women who shared a single husband should love all the children born to him as their own. But I was beginning to understand how that wasn't always—if ever —the case. I would be devastated if Lifen were ever taken from me, even just to be closer to her birth mother. In my heart, I truly believed that I was Lifen's real—and only— mother. And as much as I loved Zaichun, it was clear that I did not love him as much as Lifen. Though, I would never tell him that. I would never admit it to anyone. I would continue to believe and tell other women that they should love all of their husband's children as their own, as that was the ideal. Still, as much as I loved Lifen, how much more the woman who birthed her must have loved her. I could not fathom a love for Lifen deeper than my own, but it surely must have existed.

"Of course," I said. "After all, she is a princess, not a consort. She will be allowed to leave the Inner Court when she marries."

"But I will not be able to see her grow up?" Lingrong asked.

Lanhua looked at me, giving me a nod. If we wanted our plan to succeed, I would have to give Lingrong whatever she wanted.

"I will send her to visit you whenever possible," I said.

"I also want my consort allowance," she said.

"Nuns are supposed to live a frugal life, free of material—"

"I will not live in poverty," Lingrong said. "For the second time in my life, I will be leaving my home, my family. I am not asking for a life of extravagance, merely comfort."

"Very well," I said. "Consider it a donation to the temple. But you may disperse the money how you wish."

Lingrong tried to suppress a smile, but I could see she was pleased with this agreement. Indeed, I hoped she would find some measure of happiness in her new life. It would come at a great cost.

"So, what do you want me to do?"

Lanhua and I looked at each other. We had not yet told Lingrong what we wanted her to do, only that we needed her help to remove the eight regents from power. She had agreed that the regents were a large reason why China had fallen into such disaster, sending our husband to an early grave, and was eager to help us.

"We need you to seduce Sushun," Lanhua said.

"Seduce him?" Lingrong asked, horrified. "You mean…"

"Make love with him," I said.

"Oh, no," Lingrong said. "No, no, no, no, no. Are the two of you insane?"

"We know what we are asking," I said. "But as empress

dowagers, we cannot do it ourselves. We would be sentenced to death as well."

"So would I!"

"But we can pardon you," I said. "We can claim that we are both punishing you and showing you mercy by expelling you to a nunnery. No one would ever need to know of the other terms we've agreed to. They would only be between us."

"But I would be shamed," she said.

"So are many women who are sent to nunneries," Lanhua said. "Many girls who have acted wickedly are sent to nunneries."

"I am sure people would quickly forget why you were sent away," I said.

"Why not just hire some desperate woman to do this? A prostitute?"

"There is no one else we can trust," I said. "We need someone willing to make a public testimony about what happened."

"But how can I trust you?" Lingrong asked, looking pointedly at Lanhua. "You are asking me to risk my life."

"You dare question the integrity of the empress?" Lanhua asked.

"Never," Lingrong said to Lanhua. "Empress Zhenxiu is an honest and loyal woman. You, on the other hand..." She let her words hang in the air.

"I trust Lanhua," I said. "I always have, and I always will."

Lingrong shook her head. "You may come to regret that. If your plan fails, all of our heads could roll."

"That is why we have to stick together," Lanhua said. "The plan will work—but only if we are a team."

"Please," I said. "This is our only chance, and we are running out of time. Every day we draw closer to the Forbidden City, the stronger the regents' power grows."

Lingrong let out a resigned sigh. "Fine, I'll do it. But does it have to be Sushun? He's so...big and sweaty and gross. Can't it be Prince Zaiyuan instead?"

I couldn't help but let out a little snort of a laugh. It was true that Prince Zaiyuan was more handsome than Sushun, but I never would have admitted such out loud.

"Sushun is clearly the leader of the regents," Lanhua said. "Whatever he says, the other men fall in line."

"I believe he was also the man who most influenced Yizhu," I said. "If I had to choose one man who led our husband down that terrible path, it would be Sushun."

"What about the others?" Lingrong asked. "Even without Sushun, there are still seven other regents."

"We will need Prince Yixin's help for that part, I think," Lanhua said.

"Should we speak to him before or after we catch Sushun with Consort Lingrong?" I asked.

"After," Lanhua said. "We need to show the prince what we are capable of."

"Very well," I said. "So, we are all in agreement?"

The three of us looked at each other in turn, and then nodded.

"Agreed."

CHAPTER THIRTY

"$\mathcal{H}$ow late are we going to wait?" I asked Lanhua as I paced in my tent. We had decided to share a tent for the night to make it easier to coordinate our actions.

"Lingrong said she was going to try and catch his attention outside his tent after the hour of the rat."

The night watchman would announce each hour through the night. He had announced the hour of the boar quite a while ago. Or it at least seemed to have happened a long time ago. Every minute we waited seemed to stretch for hours.

"What are you waiting for, Mama?" Lifen asked as she lay in my bed, sucking her thumb.

"Why are you still awake?" I asked, kissing her forehead.

"I hate sleeping in a tent," she said. "I miss my bed. It's too noisy, and I'm so hot!"

I nodded and brushed her hair away from her face. "I know, my dear. But we will be back home to the Forbidden City soon. Roll over and face the wall. You sleep better on your side."

"Fine," she said with a sigh as she did so. Only a few minutes later, she was breathing steadily, and I could hear the little honking sound she made with her nose. Zaichun had fallen asleep hours ago in Lanhua's bed. He never seemed to have trouble falling or staying asleep.

"Hour of the rat!" a voice called out. I wanted to shush him to keep from waking the children, but he quickly moved on, his voice much quieter the next time he announced the time.

"Now what?" I asked.

"How long do you think it will take Lingrong to seduce Sushun?"

"I don't know, but he seemed rather eager to bed me last night, and that was after he had already been with the prostitute." I then had a terrible thought. "What if Sushun gives Lingrong one of those diseases you told me about?"

"Maybe we will time things just right and Sushun won't have had a chance to infect her."

"But we have to catch them in the act!" I said, and I could feel myself beginning to panic. I had started pacing again without realizing it. "There are so many things that could go wrong. Can we go now? I think I might be ill if I have to wait any longer."

Lanhua made sure both of the children were comfortable. "Fine, let's go. But we should be very quiet. We don't want to interrupt if they are only talking."

We stepped outside, where the air was considerably cooler than inside the tent. We had arranged things so that our tent, Sushun's tent, and Lingrong's tent were not far from each other. We tiptoed in our silk slippers toward the large bonfire that had been set outside of Sushun's tent, but we made sure that we were still in the shadows. I didn't see anyone at the bonfire.

"Do you see anything?" I whispered to Lanhua.

"No. Maybe they are already inside his tent."

"Or he could be in there with someone else."

"If he were in there with someone else, Lingrong would be out here, but she isn't. They have to be together."

I let out a breath. "Okay. Let's go. I can't keep waiting."

We crept toward the tent, each of us standing to one side of the opening, the edges of the flaps in our fingers. Then we counted silently. *One...two...*

We opened the flaps at once, only to find the tent empty.

"Where are they?" I practically screeched.

"Shh!" Lanhua said. She dropped her flap and then practically pushed me back to the shadows.

"Where is Lingrong? We have to find her!" All sorts of scenarios ran through my head. Sushun had discovered our plan and taken Lingrong as prisoner. Or maybe he had been so angry, he had killed her. Or maybe someone else had seen Lingrong outside alone late at night and kidnapped her. She could have been raped or murdered or both!

"Come on," Lanhua said, taking my hand.

"Where are we going?"

"Lingrong's tent," she said. "Maybe she just fell asleep."

I breathed a little easier at that perfectly reasonable thought. Maybe nothing at all had happened.

Lanhua didn't bother counting when she arrived at Lingrong's tent. She opened the flap before I even reached the other side of the opening.

"What the hell?" a man's voice rang out.

Lanhua screamed. Lingrong screamed. I looked inside the tent just as Sushun stumbled from Lingrong's bedding on the ground. At the sight of him naked, I screamed.

"What is going on here?" I demanded. Sushun grabbed one of Lingrong's blankets to cover himself, but she held on for dear life.

"Guards! Guards!" Lanhua screamed.

Sushun managed to find his robe and wrap it around himself. "What are you doing here?" he asked, stomping toward me.

"What are *you* doing in an imperial consort's tent?" I asked back.

"What? But she's not—" He looked back to Lingrong. "Who are you?"

Lingrong burst into tears. I couldn't understand her words through her blubbering. Several guards converged on us at once, along with several other members of camp.

"Guards, arrest them both," I said. "They have dishonored the late Emperor Xianfeng."

"What?" Sushun roared. But then he paused and thought for a moment. Then he started to laugh. "I see what happened here. You set me up," he said to me.

"I have no idea what you are talking about," I said. "I couldn't sleep and was coming to visit with my friend when I came upon a most distressing scene."

Lanhua and I stepped aside as the guards moved in to arrest Sushun and Lingrong, but they paused when they realized they had nowhere to put them while we were on the road.

"Where should we keep them?" one of the guards asked me.

"At night, keep them under guard in their own tents. During the day, they can walk with their hands in chains."

"What?" Lingrong squeaked. I realized we hadn't discussed this, and I knew I could not allow her to be thrown into prison when we arrived back in Peking. Who knew what the guards would do to her if she were not under my direct protection and supervision. But, for now, I had to uphold the impression that she was well and truly under arrest for her egregious actions.

"You heard me!" I said, turning and walking away from the scene, Lanhua right behind me.

"You'll pay for this!" I heard Sushun yell at me, but I did my best to not smile.

I saw some of the other regents, Duanhua and Zaiyuan specifically. They bowed deeply before me, as if they did not want me to see their faces. I was sure that word would spread to the other regents about what had happened within a matter of minutes. Lanhua and I had to find out what our next step was, and quickly.

LANHUA and I were unable to sleep, and Prince Yixin arrived at the camp before dawn.

"What have you two done?" he asked as soon as we were dressed enough to admit him.

"What had to be done," Lanhua said. "We could not allow those men to rule in our son's name. They would have only ensured the complete destruction of our great country."

"I agree with you," Prince Yixin said. "But why did you not discuss this with me? How did you ever convince a fellow consort to give her life in name of such an insane and pointless plan?"

"She isn't going to give her life," I said. "We will pardon her."

"If Sushun dies for this," Prince Yixin said, "the regents will make damn sure that Consort Lingrong does too, if not the both of you as well."

"But they won't *be* regents anymore," Lanhua said. "We will be. I mean, the three of us will be."

"How?" he asked.

Lanhua and I looked at each other.

"Well, we were hoping you might have an idea," Lanhua said sheepishly.

"What?" the prince cried out. "Oh, by Heaven! You two really have gone insane, haven't you?"

At that, Zaichun began crying. I hadn't even realized that he had been listening to us. I thought he was still asleep. Lanhua ran to his side and cuddled him. I was glad I had asked one of the nannies to take Lifen for the morning.

"Oh, darling! What is wrong?"

"Uncle Yixin yelled at mamas!"

"I'm sorry, nephew," Prince Yixin said. "I did not mean to frighten you. I am just…" He sighed and paced, running his hand over his hair. "I can't believe you did this. What are we going to do now?"

"Somehow, we need to be appointed as regents," Lanhua said. "We need you to make the petition."

"You?" Prince Yixin asked. "But you are women. Why not me?"

"Well, you can't nominate yourself," Lanhua said. "And we can't nominate you because, as you said, we are women. We don't have any authority. You might not be a regent, but you are still a high-ranking member of the court. You can put forth suggestions and edicts before the emperor and the regents. But after Zhen and I are made the *sole* regents, we can also have you made a regent."

"As well?" Prince Yixin asked dubiously. "You want me to rule alongside two women? The rest of the court would never agree to that."

"We can worry about that later," I said. "What can we do right now?"

"I can write an edict nominating you as regents," Prince Yixin said. "But the other regents will never agree to it without some sort of leverage against them."

"Do you have anything you can blackmail them with?" Lanhua asked.

"If I had known this was going to happen, I might have been able to collect some," he said to Lanhua through gritted teeth. "But since I had no idea this was coming, no, I don't have any. And you can be sure that anything I might have been able to dig up will be buried so deep now I'll never find it. The other regents will make sure their reputations are spotless."

"Just kill them, then," Lanhua suggested.

"I'm not going to commit murder!"

"Be quiet before someone hears you!" I hissed at both of them.

Zaichun cried again, and he was beyond consolation this time.

"Look what you've done!" Lanhua said to Prince Yixin. "Oh, he soiled himself."

Lanhua went to summon a nanny to take care of Zaichun.

"I'm sorry, my lord," Prince Yixin said, kneeling before his nephew. "I didn't mean to scare you."

"I pottied," the little boy said, rubbing his eyes.

Prince Yixin laughed. "You don't need to be embarrassed. It happens to the best of us."

"You...frightened the emperor," I said, more to myself than anyone else.

"I didn't mean to," Prince Yixin said, standing as Lanhua returned with a nanny to take the boy away.

"No, I mean..." I started pacing again. "You hurt the emperor's feelings, made him cry, frightened him so badly that he wet himself. That must be a punishable offense."

"Hey!" Prince Yixin said, holding up his hands in defense. "We are on the same side here."

"I know, I know," I said. "But if it happened once, don't you think it could happen again?"

"You mean the with regents?" Lanhua asked. "Have them offend the emperor?"

"Exactly," I said. "The emperor can have them charged with offending the throne. That's treason."

"We would just need to provoke them into yelling at us, which will frighten Zaichun," Lanhua said.

"It will be difficult," I said. "He might not react the way we want him to."

"Don't worry," Lanhua said. "I know my son. He will do it."

"Very well," the prince said. "If anything, it will at least get some of the regents off the board."

"No," Lanhua said. "We need to get all of them. If even one of them remains, that one could rally support against us."

"After the funeral procession reaches Peking, call a meeting of the regents on behalf of the emperor," Yixin said. "I'll present the edict, stamped by the little emperor himself. That should be enough to provoke an argument with the regents. It will be your responsibility to stir them up into enough of a frenzy to frighten Zaichun. Though, I can't help but feel sorry for the boy."

"As long as we all do our parts, there is no way we can fail," Lanhua said.

"I should go," the prince said. "We don't want the regents to suspect anything."

The three of us nodded to each other, and the prince left the tent.

"If the prince gets caught with that edict before Zaichun stamps it, he could end up being the one charged with treason," I said.

"We have to be careful," Lanhua agreed. "The regents will be keeping their noses clean. We need to be doing the same. Anything we do wrong could be held against us."

"Then we better not make Zaichun cry anymore," I said. "He can't lose his regents and his mothers."

CHAPTER THIRTY-ONE

*A*s soon as Yizhu was interred in his tomb, everyone returned to Peking. Zaichun took his seat on the Dragon Throne and was given his father's seal. He was given a stack of edicts to stamp, things that had already been given approval by the regents that only needed to be stamped to make it official. Hidden in my robe was the edict Prince Yixin had written appointing Lanhua and me as regents as well. I slipped it among the others. The edicts were then given to Prince Yixin to carry out. For the moment, none of us said anything about Lanhua and me being appointed to the board. We had to wait for our moment.

The trial of Sushun and Lingrong was held not long afterward. Since Sushun was a general and a regent, and Lingrong was an imperial consort, they could only be tried by the emperor himself. Or, in this case, his regents. Lanhua made her opposition to the proceedings clear as soon as they began.

Zaichun was seated on the Dragon Throne. As empress dowagers and his mothers, Lanhua and I were allowed to stand on the level below him. The regents and other important men of the court, including Prince Yixin, stood at ground level, looking up at the three of us.

Sushun and Lingrong kneeled directly in front of the throne, both of them in chains. Consort Li had been allowed to stay in her palace under house arrest. She had bathed and was wearing clean clothes, but her skin was dark from being forced to walk in the sun all the way back to Peking. I had not been to see her, but I had heard that her feet were severely blistered and she had fallen ill from dehydration. I only hoped that I would be able to make amends with her after everything was over.

Sushun, however, looked like the prisoner he was. He had been held in the Ministry of Punishments and not allowed to bathe or change his clothes. He was filthy, his queue had come undone, and his clothes had been reduced to mere rags. If Lanhua and I failed to have him executed, I was sure he would seek revenge on us quickly.

"The seven remaining regents should be recused," Lanhua said. "As one of their own is on trial, they cannot be trusted to give a fair ruling."

"How dare you call my honor into question!" Prince Zaiyuan called out.

I noticed he did not say "our" honor. "Are you speaking for yourself or for the regents as a whole?" I asked the prince.

The prince hesitated before answering. I supposed he was weighing the pros and cons of either answer.

"Well?" Lanhua said. "The emperor requires your answer."

"The whole board," the prince replied. This led to a chorus of murmuring throughout the court.

"Except for Sushun," another regent, Muyin, said. "Sushun should be removed as a regent immediately."

"But Sushun was, and still is, a regent," Lanhua said. "Do you speak for him now, Prince Zaiyuan?"

"We should make a motion to remove Sushun as a regent, effective immediately," the prince said.

"So, you believe that the will of the late emperor, Xianfeng, can be amended?" Prince Yixin asked.

"The will of the late emperor has already been carried out," Prince Zaiyuan said. "The regency was created. The fact that Sushun offended the throne demonstrated that he is no longer fit to carry the title or responsibility of regent."

"Is it the will of the majority that Sushun should be removed as a regent immediately?" I asked. All of the regents agreed. A court scribe worked on writing the declaration up right then so that Zaichun could stamp it.

"The next order of business," Prince Yixin said, "is the punishment of Sushun and Consort Lingrong for their offenses to the late Emperor Xianfeng."

"I am not guilty of the crime for which I am accused," Sushun said.

"How can you say that?" Lanhua asked. "Empress Dowager Zhenxiu and I both saw you."

"It is true that I had…lustful intentions toward this woman," Sushun said. "But you came into the tent before I was able to act upon those urges. I thank you for you saving me from *truly* offending my dead lord."

"Consort Lingrong," Prince Yixin said. "Is this true? Did you not…copulate with Sushun?"

Even from my raised position on the dais, I could tell that Lingrong was breathing hard. Her jaw was clenched tight. When she looked up at me, I did not see fear in her eyes, as I expected, but anger. Our entire plan hinged on her word, and I was sure she knew this. I gave her what I hoped was a pleading look. She had to know that no matter what happened here, I would never let her be executed for her supposed crime.

"Sushun is lying," Lingrong finally said. "We did, indeed, copulate, as you say."

The men in the room burst into fits of anger or jubilation, depending on whether they were a supporter of Sushun or not.

"You lying whore!" Sushun spit at Lingrong. But Lingrong held her head up. She knew that Sushun could not hurt her.

Prince Yixin held up his hand to quiet the proceedings. "I would like to make a motion that Sushun be taken from this place immediately and put to death as soon as possible. His head should be stricken from his body."

"I agree with that motion," Prince Zaiyuan said. "And I make the motion that Consort Lingrong be given the same punishment."

The men all shouted their agreement. I looked over to Lanhua, expecting her to say something, but my jaw nearly dropped when I saw her nodding in agreement.

"What are you doing?" I asked her through clenched teeth.

"We cannot let them know that we conspired with Consort Lingrong to get to this point," she replied, not moving her lips. "If they suspect us, we could be on the chopping block next."

I looked down at Lingrong, who seemed to be laughing. She had always suspected that she could not trust us. Could not trust Lanhua. But I would never go back on my word to her.

"My lords," I said, raising my voice and my hand. "Never has an imperial consort been executed publicly. Doing so would only bring further dishonor to my late husband. As head of the Inner Court, it is my responsibility to see that any necessary punishments are meted out. Consort Lingrong will be taken back to her palace to await the arrival of a white handkerchief sent by myself."

My heart raced in my chest as the men of the court debated this among themselves. Finally, the men voiced their agreement with this decision.

"Mama," Zaichun whined to Lanhua, "I'm tired."

"I know, my darling," she said. "We will leave soon."

The little emperor whined and slumped sideways on the throne.

"The last issue up for discussion," Prince Yixin said,

removing the stamped edict from a pocket in his sleeve, "are the appointments of Empress Dowager Zhenxiu and Empress Dowager Lanhua as regents until Zaichun comes of age."

This caused all the men of the court to shout out various questions and not a few curses.

"Ridiculous," Prince Zaiyuan said.

"That's impossible," Du Han said.

Prince Yixin held up the edict for all to see. "This edict, appointing both empress dowagers as regents, was stamped this morning by Zaichun himself."

"Let me see that!" Prince Zaiyuan said, grabbing the edict. "This… I never approved this!"

"It matters not," Prince Yixin said. "It is stamped. That makes it the will of the young emperor."

"He can't even read!" Regent Kuangyuan yelled.

I heard Zaichun whimper. I couldn't help but give a small smile to Lanhua. The plan was working.

"Women cannot take part in rulership. 'Women taking part in governing is the root of chaos,'" Prince Zaiyuan said, quoting an ancient book of wisdom.

"Hens cannot announce the dawn," Sushun's brother, Duanhua, said, misquoting another proverb. The room erupted in laughter.

"We would never attempt to rule," Lanhua said. "But our son is simply that—our son. And it is only natural for a boy to occasionally seek advice from his mothers."

"Mama! Mama! Mama!" Zaichun said, reaching for Lanhua. She eagerly took him from the throne to cuddle in her arms, sending a pointed look down at the regents.

"An empress might be a dowager," Prince Zaiyuan said. "But she cannot be a regent."

"There are ample examples of empress dowagers serving as regents while their sons were small," Prince Yixin said. He took a paper handed to him by Little An. Little An had proven himself to be a fast reader and an excellent researcher. "All the way back to the Han Dynasty, women have been regents. The Han Dynasty, the Jin Dynasty, the Northern Wei Dynasty, the Tang Dynasty, the Song Dynasty—"

"Shut up!" Zaiyuan said. "Chinese. All weak Chinese rulers. We are Manchu!"

This sent many tongues wagging around the room. Of course, we Manchu knew we were better than the Han Chinese people we ruled over, but we had to be very careful about saying such things in their presence. As it was, many advisors, lords, and important men around the country were Han. The Han people outnumbered us a hundred to one. They allowed us to stay in power by maintaining the illusion that over the last two hundred years we had, in many ways, become Chinese. But there were some who refused to believe this. The Taiping Rebellion's main contention was that the Manchu were foreigners. That the Han Chinese should be allowed to rule themselves.

As if on cue, Zaichun let out a yelp and began to cry. I noticed that Lanhua did not try to console him.

"The emperor is the emperor of *China*. Manchu, Han, Mongol, Zhuang, Miao, Hui, Yi—all of them," Prince Yixin said, listing some of the many ethnic groups that made up this vast country of ours.

"It doesn't matter," Zaiyuan said, tearing the edict in half. "Women cannot rule. I reject this edict!"

Zaichun yelped again and cried some more, but Zaiyuan was so incensed, he didn't hear him.

"You tore up an edict from the emperor!" Muyin said, grabbing Zaiyuan's arm.

"That did not come from the emperor," Zaiyuan said, ripping his arm from Muyin's grasp. I thought the two men might come to blows. Zaiyuan pointed up at us. "They must have forged it!"

Zaichun squealed again, squirming in Lanhua's arms. He was crying so much, I thought he was starting to panic. It hurt me to allow him to cry, but I knew that what we were doing was for the best—for him!

"You idiots!" Sushun finally yelled. "How could you approve something without reading it?"

"I didn't sign anything!" Zaiyuan yelled back.

"Death by a thousand cuts!" Regent Jingshou yelled at Sushun.

"That's my brother you're talking about!" Duanhua yelled back.

At this point, all the regents were yelling at each other, so I could no longer track what they were saying. Zaichun was still crying and squirming. I didn't know how Lanhua was still holding onto him, and I wasn't sure how much longer we could allow this to go on.

Finally, Lanhua cried out. "Oh, the emperor has soiled himself!"

"How dare you men raise your voices and frighten the emperor?" I said. "You have behaved disrespectfully, causing the emperor to soil himself before his subjects. You have bullied him by destroying a decree that he himself had stamped."

"For such wickedness, every one of you should be sentenced to death!" Lanhua said. She nodded, and Little An ran forward. He had already written out a copy of the decree to sentence the regents to death since this had been our plan. He also had the decree from earlier, sentencing Sushun and Consort Lingrong to death. Finally, he had a second copy of the decree appointing Lanhua and myself as regents. We knew it was possible that someone might try to destroy the original decree.

Before the regents even knew what was happening, Lanhua and I helped a squirming and screaming Zaichun to stamp the edicts, making them law before more than a hundred witnesses. Tears were streaming down the little emperor's face as we forced his hands to touch the seal as we stamped the edicts. Guards rushed into the room, placing all the regents under arrest.

"How should they be put to death, regents?" Prince Yixin asked us.

"Quickly," Lanhua said, meaning they should also be decapitated.

"Wait," I said, grabbing her arm. We had not discussed beforehand how the men should be put to death. I spoke to her in a whisper. "We should show mercy."

"Mercy?" she asked. "If they live, they will surely seek revenge."

"No, I know they have to die," I said. "But we can allow them to say goodbye to their families. We can send them white scarves."

"It's too risky," Lanhua said. "I would rather it be over and done with."

"I know," I said. "But we can show people how we mean to lead Zaichun. To be an emperor who is just and merciful."

Lanhua sighed. "Fine. Do as you will." At that, she took Zaichun down the dais and out of the audience hall. The little emperor had played his part perfectly. He deserved to rest.

"The seven guilty regents will be put under house arrest and sent white scarves," I said.

The men continued to yell and voice their objections. Now that I was left alone on the dais, I was unsure what to say. The gravity of what we had just done was suddenly beginning to weigh on me. I looked for Prince Yixin, but he was lost in the crowd.

"Attention," I said, my voice feeble. No one heard me or even took notice of me. "Attention!" I tried a little louder. Instead, it seemed as though the din of the crowd escalated. I saw one man push another. The second man turned around and shoved a different man. Before I could stop it, a brawl had broken out.

I clapped my hands. "Stop this!" I said. Still, no one paid attention to me! How was I going to do this? How could I help my son rule a country when I could not even get a room of China's highest-ranking men to stop fighting with one another?

A low rumbling sound seemed to shake me to my core. At first, I thought perhaps it was an earthquake. That Heaven was letting its displeasure be known. I lifted my eyes to the great golden pearl sitting precariously in the dragon's mouth, afraid it was about to fall and crush me for defying the will of my dead husband.

But as the sound grew louder, I realized it was coming from somewhere in the room. The men must have heard it as well, because they began to calm down and look around in confusion. I finally realized that it was laughter. Sushun was laughing at me. His laughter grew from a low chuckle to such a raucous that he was crying.

"What is so funny?" I asked him when the room quieted enough for my voice to be heard.

"You," he said, glaring at me. "I underestimated you, empress dowager. But you underestimated that concubine. Today, my head will roll, but it is only a matter of time before you meet the ancestors as well."

"How dare you threaten the empress dowager!" Prince Yixin said, stepping out of the crowd and grabbing Sushun by the hair, bending his head back to expose his neck.

"What are you going to do to me? I'm already condemned to death. And it is no threat, only a promise. Only a fool would trust that woman—even another woman."

"Kill him!" someone yelled.

"Death by a thousand cuts!" someone else yelled out.

Before the room erupted into another fight, I held up my hand to silence everyone. "Guards, take Sushun away and carry out his sentence. Take the other former regents out to serve as witnesses. Then, take them to their homes where they may prepare for their own deaths."

There were a few cheers as the former regents were dragged away. At least I had the support of some.

"Take Consort Lingrong back to her palace," I said. "I will visit her soon to deliver the white handkerchief myself."

This led to more cheers of support. The men seemed pleased that I accepted this responsibility. I hoped they would not find out—or would not care—that I spared her life. It was something I wanted to keep quiet.

"Tomorrow," I said, "audiences before the emperor will resume as normal."

"May the emperor live ten thousand years!" someone yelled.

"May the empress dowagers live for ten thousand years!" someone else called out. Then, everyone still in the room kowtowed before me, repeating the phrase three times. My heart swelled with joy and relief. Of those who were left, it seemed that Lanhua and I had their support.

I descended the dais and started to leave the room, but I was quickly swamped by men, all of whom seemed to have urgent business. They asked me about the foreigners. About the Taiping. About the land the regents owned. About marriage for a princess. My head began to ache, and I had no idea where to begin.

"Prince Yixin," was all I could think to say. The prince, as if by magic, appeared at my side. "Walk with me."

The prince bowed and we quickly left the audience hall, closing the door behind us. I let out a breath I didn't realize I was holding and felt dizzy. My hand went to my head as I leaned on the door.

"Zhen? Are you all right?" the prince asked.

"I'm fine," I said. "A little lightheaded is all. That was…terrifying. But it worked. I can't believe it, but it worked."

"We did it," he said. "You did it."

I let out a relieved sigh and almost laughed. He was right. We had done it. I could hardly believe it. We had just managed to overthrow eight regents and take control of the country. I was no longer merely an empress. The head of the Inner Court. I was a regent for a four-year-old child. I was the ruler of China. Not alone, of course. Lanhua and I together were regents. And while there was precedent, such a thing had not been done in hundreds of years. Indeed, what was I to do next?

"What do we do now?" I asked.

"Just what we planned," he said. "We uphold the treaties. We look for new sources of revenue for the throne. We find a way to defeat the Taiping. We bring peace and prosperity to our country, something that has not been seen since before my father was emperor."

"Do you really think we can do it?"

"I would not have agreed to this crazy plan if I didn't think so."

"So, next, we need to work on making you a regent as well," I said.

"As soon as it is prudent," he said. "We do not want to make another change too quickly. We don't want the regency to appear unstable."

"You should have been emperor," I said without thinking.

Prince Yixin put his hand over my mouth. "Shh," he whispered, standing so close, only his hand seemed to separate our lips. "Never say such a thing. I have to believe that Heaven put my brother—and now my nephew—on the throne for a reason." He lowered his hand, his eyes searching my face.

"Did Heaven give me to Yizhu for a reason?" I asked, my voice barely above a whisper.

He sighed and then looked away for a moment. "I believe we are all right where we are meant to be at this moment."

I closed my eyes to keep from crying. Perhaps he was right. If I had married Yixin, if Yixin had been emperor, I liked to think that everything would have been different. We would have been happy. China would have been at peace. But there was no way to know that. Things might have turned out much worse. I had to learn to accept things the way they were and not wish for a life that was impossible.

"I do not know how to rule," I said.

"I will help you," he said. "Tomorrow, Zaichun will oversee a whole new court, with you and Lanhua behind him."

"Tomorrow, then," I said.

He stepped back, putting more space between us. "Tomorrow, my lady." He bowed and then left, returning to the throne room.

I stood tall and ran my hands down the front of my robe. I still had work to do.

I made my way to Lingrong's palace. I was surprised to see so many guards outside, about half a dozen.

"You are all dismissed," I told the chief guard.

"Your Majesty?" he said, confused.

"You may go," I said. "Consort Lingrong is no longer under arrest."

The guards all looked from one to another, unsure of what to do.

"Was I unclear?" I asked.

"No, Your Majesty," the chief guard said.

"Then go," I said. The guards all bowed and then filed away from the palace. I walked up to the front door, surprised when it didn't open ahead of me. I realized that all of Lingrong's servants had been dismissed as well, so I had to open the door myself.

When I entered the palace, Lingrong was waiting for me, sitting on a chair, straight as a board. Her eyes filled with tears when she saw me and her jaw quivered. I rushed to her, taking her in my arms.

"I thought…I thought I was going to die," she said.

I rocked her and shushed her. "No! Never! Why would you think that? I promised that you would be safe."

"Lanhua would have let me be executed," she said. "She showed no pity for me. If you had not been there, I would have died!"

I held her tighter. I did not want to frighten her, so I did not acknowledge that she was right. But maybe that was why Heaven had seen fit to make Lanhua and I co-regents. She had the strength to do what was necessary, but I was able to stay her hand when mercy was needed.

"It's alright," I said. "Sushun is no more. Tomorrow, your new life will begin."

I had already arranged for some Buddhist priests who served at the Forbidden City to escort Lingrong to a nunnery outside of the city.

"I am afraid for you," Lingrong said.

"I'll be fine," I said. "Now, why don't you finish packing and have a good rest."

She nodded. "I will never forget what you have done for me," she said. "After the loss of my son and the death of Yizhu, I thought my life was over. I had no children, no husband, and could never remarry or return to the home of my family. I felt lost and trapped. I have spoken to the priests about life as a devotee, and I have to admit that I am looking forward to it. It will be a very different life, but one full of possibilities."

"I am so glad," I said. "I only want you to be happy."

"If you ever find yourself in need again, I will always be there for you."

"Thank you, Sister."

We hugged, and I left her palace, satisfied that I had done right by her.

When I reached Lanhua's palace, I was surprised to hear Zaichun still crying. I could not believe that the fight among the regents had upset him that terribly. I entered the palace and saw

Lanhua working with her maid to prepare her outfit for the next day.

"We need to look like the empresses we still are," she said.

I wasn't sure it mattered all that much, but I nodded as I went into Zaichun's room. I dismissed his nanny and went to hold the boy, but Lanhua took him instead.

"He's just so sensitive," she said. I nodded. He was a gentle boy. I sat nearby as Lanhua coddled him, getting him to calm down.

"Prince Yixin said that we don't need to rush to make him a regent," I said. "We need to project an image of stability. But I think we should still do it as soon as possible. We will need his help."

"Oh, I don't know," Lanhua said, fussing with Zaichun. "Maybe we don't need to appoint him as a regent after all."

"What do you mean? We need him."

"As an advisor, of course. As an ally. But he doesn't need to be regent."

"Lanhua," I said, my tone a warning. "We don't want to make an enemy of Yixin."

"Of course not! But let's just wait and see how things go for a while. Like the prince said, we should only make another change when the time is right."

I nodded but was disquieted that Lanhua was already thinking of going back on her word to Yixin. Had that been her plan all along, for only the two of us to be regents?

"We will have to keep audiences shorter than usual," Lanhua said. "Zaichun cannot be expected to sit and listen to men prattle on for four hours straight."

"He will have to do it one day," I said.

"When he comes of age. He's still only a baby. Besides, his presence will only be a formality. He cannot make decisions. He needs to be educated first. We need to find him a tutor." Lanhua smirked, and I realized what she had just said. Lanhua and I had not been educated to rule either, yet we would be the people making decisions until Zaichun came of age.

"What have we done?" I asked, rubbing my temple.

"What had to be done," she said, adjusting Zaichun on her lap. He winced but did not start crying again. "Think of it this way. If those men had been allowed to be regents, we would certainly be heading to war again, right?"

I nodded.

"So, as long as we don't end up in a war, we will at least be doing better than them."

"Avoiding war seems easy enough," I said. "But there must be more to ruling than that."

"I'm sure there will be, but we will learn as we go. After all, Yizhu was raised to rule and look what happened. Everyone has the capacity for success or failure."

"How do we make sure we will be successful?"

"Unfortunately, I don't think we will know for sure until we see the results."

"That's not reassuring." I sighed and looked away from her, wondering if we'd made a mistake. But no. Allowing the regents to continue their path of destruction would have been the mistake. We had done the right thing in removing them. But how would we know the right thing to do next?

"Hey." Lanhua tapped my leg so that I would look at her. "We will figure it out, okay? Together."

"Together," I said. As I reached for her hand, I heard a rustling in the pocket of my sleeve. I reached into it and pulled the paper out.

"What is that?" Lanhua asked me.

I looked down at the order to have her executed. I was going to burn it privately. I didn't think she needed to know that Yizhu did not trust her. It would probably ruin her memories of him. But he was gone. I needed her to know that *I* did trust her.

I handed her the order so that she could read it. I watched her face change as she did. She looked up at me, her eyes wide.

"Yizhu wrote this?"

I nodded.

"Where did you get it? Did Sushun have it?"

"No." I took the paper back and rolled it up. "Yizhu gave it to me before he died."

"To you? Why?"

I shook my head. "It doesn't matter. He thought you would try to take control of Zaichun and push me aside."

"Zhen, I would never—"

I held up my hand to stop her. "I know. I believe you. I trust you. I'm showing you this because I'm going to destroy it." I tore the edict in half and then walked over to a brazier. I put the papers into the fire one at a time, watching them burn completely. I went and sat back down next to her. "I was going to destroy it in private. I wasn't going to tell you about it. I didn't want to ruin any memories you had of Yizhu."

"What made you change your mind?"

"I don't know. Everything. All of it. We've been through so much." I took her hand. "We are sisters, truly. I don't want any secrets between us. And I want you to know that I trust you completely."

She squeezed my hand and smiled. "I trust you too. No matter what, we will always know that we can rely on each other."

"My lady," a maid said, getting Lanhua's attention. "Are these the ornaments you wanted to wear tomorrow?"

"No!" Lanhua said. Zaichun had fallen asleep. She put him into his bed and followed the maid out. "I'll show you…"

Zaichun whimpered. I moved to her chair and reached down to rub his back since he was sleeping on his stomach. When I noticed a red spot on his clothes, I lifted his shirt and saw that his back was bandaged. I gasped at the sight of half a dozen pinpricks deep in his skin beneath the gauze. Several of the marks were still bleeding. I then remembered how Zaichun wailed during the audience with the regents—*as if on cue.*

I couldn't believe it. Lanhua had picked up Zaichun during the meeting, and then the child cried as the men started fighting. Lanhua had purposely hurt her child to get the response she needed.

"My poor darling," I whispered to the little boy.

At first, I was angry. He didn't deserve to be treated like that. But then I realized that if he had not cried and soiled himself the way we had needed him to, we might not have been able to depose the regents.

She had done what was necessary.

I replaced the bandage and pulled his shirt down over it. I was upset that she hadn't told me what she was going to do. After all, Zaichun was my son too. But I knew I never would have agreed to cause harm to our child. Lanhua had to know that too. She knew me as well as I knew her. I looked at the brazier where I had burned the edict. I knew I had done the right thing. I would never have used it against her, and now she knew how much I trusted her. But I wished she had told me what she had done to Zaichun. I knew why she hadn't told me before she did it, but she should have told me after.

We had promised we wouldn't keep any secrets from each other. But I wasn't sure I could trust that she would always be completely honest with me. I knew she would never hurt me. She would never betray me. I could trust her with my life. I also believed that Lanhua would always keep secrets from me.

"Are you alright?"

I looked up and realized that Lanhua was looking at me. I had been so deep in my thoughts, I hadn't heard her come back.

"I'm fine," I said. I chuckled to myself. I was already lying to Lanhua as well. After all, I knew what she had done, but I wasn't going to confront her about it. I stood up to leave. "I'm tired. We should all be well-rested for tomorrow."

"Tomorrow, everything changes," Lanhua said, looking down at Zaichun.

"Hopefully not everything," I said. "Not between us."

"No," she said. "Never between us."

"Goodnight, Sister."

"Goodnight."

CHAPTER THIRTY-TWO

*W*e held a grand ceremony to enthrone Zaichun as emperor. Lanhua and I decided his reign would be known as Tongzhi—order and prosperity—since that was all we wanted for our country and our son. At that time, Lanhua and I were also allowed to take new names since we also had a significant change in status—both from imperial consorts to dowagers and then to regents. We decided that since we were co-regents and considered ourselves to be sisters, we would take names that complimented each other. I took the name Cian—which meant kindly and serene—while Lanhua took the name Cixi—which meant kindly and joyous. While Cian became my official name on all documents and I would be addressed as such formally, in private and among those who knew me well, I continued to be called Zhen. Lanhua, on the other hand, made it clear that she preferred to be called Cixi by everyone, even me. It took some getting used to, but after a while, calling her Cixi came naturally. She clearly loved her new name, as she couldn't help but smile when it was used. I knew she had never been fond of the name Lanhua, but I didn't realize how much of a difference it made to call her by the name she preferred. Merely using her new name was enough to brighten her mood on a dark day.

We did not normally hold morning audiences in the grand hall with the Dragon Throne. Most emperors only used that room for formal occasions. We met in the smaller audience hall behind it, the Hall of Imperial Peace. There was still a raised dais for a small throne for Zaichun, but in order to reinforce that Zaichun was the emperor and that Cixi and I were only issuing orders and decrees on his behalf, we sat behind two yellow screens beside him. The silk used in the screens was quite thin, so we had little issue seeing through them to the men in the hall, but it was harder for the men to see us.

Harder still was it for us to hold audiences with Zaichun at all. All of us had to rise at the hour of the rabbit. We had to bathe, eat, dress, and have our hair styled before convening in the audience hall at the hour of the dragon. Emperors would then usually hold audiences for four hours straight, listening to petitioners who had come from all over China. Zaichun, though, would start to fuss after a mere half an hour. I had hoped that he would be able to sit for two-hour audiences, but it was not possible. He would whine and talk and play so loudly, it was impossible to hear what the petitioners had to say. We then limited the audience to one hour. And while the little emperor was better behaved knowing he had only one hour to sit through, this proved to be insufficient time to hear petitions. After a week, the petitions ended up backlogged for a month. I suggested that the councilors schedule fewer petitioners each day, but it would take a long time for the new schedule to take effect. And many people had traveled for days—if not weeks— to appear before the emperor. Zaichun had been emperor for a few weeks when it was decided that he was too young to sit for audiences.

Zaichun's education became my primary focus. I went to work getting recommendations for and then interviewing tutors. I appointed a man named Weng Tonghe as Zaichun's primary tutor. Tutor Weng was the son of the man who had tutored all of Emperor Daoguang's sons, so he came highly recommended by Prince Yixin. It was Tutor Weng's responsibility to give Zaichun a classical education like his father, his grandfather, and most of his ancestors had received, and he also needed to teach the boy how to be a good emperor. Since Zaichun was already the emperor, there was no question as to whether he would sit on the Dragon Throne when he was old enough. Tutor Weng's job, then, was to ensure that Zaichun would have all the tools he needed to govern the country when it was time. Traditionally, a child emperor ascended to the throne when he was sixteen years of age. It seemed almost impossible to imagine that this little boy, who was still running around in split pants and throwing grasshoppers at his sister, would be ready to rule in only eleven years. It was a daunting task, to be sure, but one all of us had to take part in.

When Zaichun stopped attending audiences, I did as well, for the most part. I wanted to be present for Zaichun's lessons, both to make sure he was learning and to educate myself. To help Cixi, since she was dealing with audiences alone, I read the daily reports from the councilors and gave recommendations. I would either tell the councilor to do as he proposed, ask for more information, or give suggestions for improvement. When the edicts from the morning audiences arrived for the emperor to stamp, I helped him do so.

One thing that Cixi and I did together as soon as we could was make Prince Yixin the head of the Grand Council, or head of advisors. We had all the regents who had been executed replaced with advisors whom Prince Yixin suggested, all men who were open-minded and forward-thinking. Prince Yixin also established a Foreign Office so that he could more easily and directly liaison with foreign envoys. Whenever Yixin asked us about making him a regent, Cixi always had a ready excuse to demure and postpone. After a while, the court began functioning rather like clockwork, so there seemed to be no reason to make Yixin a regent. It was clear that he was unhappy about this, but without Cixi's support, there was nothing he could do about it, so we let the matter drop.

Things came together so quickly and easily, I had almost forgotten the deadly coup we had arranged only months before. That was, until a letter arrived from Feiya.

> Cousin,
> the death of my father-in-law, who was a kind and generous man, has caused great pain in my family. However, it has come to our attention that my husband's family lands and property outside of Mongolia have been confiscated by the throne, including his family home in Peking. As such, it will be impossible for me to visit you again. While my father's family escaped the persecution following the governmental reorganization by the new Empress Dowager Cixi, they would be unable to house my extensive family.
> I understand why my father-in-law and others like him were deposed. They were led astray by his brother, Sushun, and followed bad counsel. Emperor Tongzhi will always have the loyal support of my husband and our family.
> I wish you well.

I showed the letter to Prince Yixin and asked his opinion of it. Since he was head of the Grand Council and I was a regent, we now had reason to see each other on regular occasions.

The prince rubbed his chin. "Did she write this with her own hand?"

"No, she cannot write. A scribe servant writes for her. But what is this about lands being confiscated?"

"It is protocol to confiscate the property of a man who is convicted of treason," he said, handing the letter back to me. I rubbed my head; I could feel another headache coming on.

"But not the property in Mongolia?"

"No, we don't have any authority over that. The Mongolian Council of Elders would decide what to do in that case. It sounds like at least Duanhua's lands went to his eldest son, Chongqi. I don't know about Sushun's lands, though. I can inquire, if you care to know."

"No," I said. "It doesn't matter. I was only concerned about my cousin."

"You were quite close," Yixin said. "You seemed happy to spend time with her."

"It was good to see her. I had hoped that our children might even be married one day. But if her family is now in bad standing with the throne, I fear it will not happen."

"It still could," he said. "Marriage for Zaichun is still many years away."

"Well, what does she mean here about Dowager Empress Cixi's governmental reorganization? Does she not know that Cixi and I took the regency together?"

Prince Yixin looked away from me. "I wouldn't worry about that."

"Worry about what?"

He hesitated. "Most people seem to be giving Cixi credit for removing the regents."

"What do you mean most people? What people? Who?"

"No one," he said. "Just peasants. The common people. Their opinion doesn't matter."

"Oh. Why?"

"I think because she was the one who sentenced them to death."

I snorted. "We both did that."

"She was the one who actually said the words, though."

"And how would the common people know that?"

"I don't know. There were eunuchs and maids present. Or they overheard the story from their masters. Gossip spreads among rats like diseases, you know."

"So I have discovered." I paced the room, watching as Lifen and Zaichun played in the garden. "I only wish—" The room began to spin and the color red seemed to tint my vision. I held my arms out to catch my balance, but it was impossible on my pot-bottom shoes. I tripped, twisting my ankle.

"Zhen!" Prince Yixin sounded like he was very far away, though he had been by my side only a moment ago. I felt weak and tried to call out, but I couldn't make a sound. I began to fall, but I felt Prince Yixin catch me. I could feel him shaking me, but I couldn't respond. Everything turned black.

I COULD ONLY open one of my eyes. I tried to talk, but it felt as though my mouth was stuffed with silk.

"Wha...wha..." I could only utter the most basic of sounds, and even that sounded distorted in my ears.

"Sister!" Cixi said, sitting next to me.

"Mama!" Lifen and Zaichun fought to sit on my other side. I was trying to ask what was going on, what had happened to me, but I couldn't form the words. Cixi moved aside as a doctor took her place.

"Empress, can you hear me?" he asked.

"Ye...ye..." I grew frustrated that I couldn't say the simplest of words!

"Nod your head," the doctor said.

I did so, but even that took great strength.

"I believe you have had a palsy," the doctor said.

A palsy! I had heard of that, but didn't it usually happen to elderly people? I was only twenty-five years old!

"Are you sure, Doctor?" Cixi asked.

"I am afraid so. It is often brought on by great emotional distress, which the empress dowager has certainly been under lately."

"So have I," Cixi said.

"Well, stress does not impact everyone the same way. But don't worry. There are many treatments available. We simply need to get the qi flowing again…"

His voice melted away as I began to cry, but I could not even wipe my tears away and felt them flood into my ears. Why was this happening to me? What had I done wrong? Was Heaven punishing me? Sushun had said that we would all be meeting the ancestors, but I did not think it would happen to me so soon. I could not leave Zaichun and Lifen. I still had so much to do…

It took me a month to be able to speak simple words again, and many months more to be able to walk on my own. I did not know what caused the palsy, but the doctor said that since I had suffered from headaches for many years, it had probably been coming for a long time. I had to undergo many painful treatments, including acupuncture and cupping. I forced myself to endure cup after cup of foul-tasting medicinal herbs. I could not abandon my children or Cixi to govern the country alone. It was far too large of a job for one woman.

And yet, I was unable to help her for so long. When I finally felt strong enough to return to my duties tending to the daily reports and helping Zaichun stamp edicts, I was shocked at what all she had accomplished.

The Taiping Rebellion was over.

"How did you do it?" I asked her.

"I had Prince Yixin ask the foreigners for help," she told me as we walked through the garden. I still did not have enough balance to wear my pot-bottom shoes, so she did not wear hers either. She held my hand tightly as we strolled together.

"Are you sure that was the best course of action?" I asked her. I was a little disappointed that she did so without waiting to ask my opinion on the matter. I wasn't sure what I would have said, but it was such a significant issue, I felt that it was something we should have discussed.

"The foreigners were as frustrated with the Taiping as we were," she said. "The foreigners desire peace and order. War is not profitable. At least, that was what Prince Yixin told me."

I thought about Prince Yixin and Cixi working together closely for all the months I had been incapacitated and felt a little jealous. He had visited me many times, but for a very long time, I could not speak to him. It was so painful to see him looking at me with pity in his eyes. I was sure he was grateful that we had never married. How awful it would have been for him to be saddled with an invalid for a wife. I reached up and wiped a tear from my eye.

"Yizhu was always afraid that the foreigners would take advantage of the situation," I said.

"I know," she said. "I thought about it for a long time. I had no way of knowing if I was making the right decision. But slowly, things are returning to normal in the south. I have appointed dozens of new governors to the southern provinces. They are sending back reports about rebuilding projects and sowing the land for the next harvest."

"I have seen some of them," I said. "That is good. The reports are optimistic. But how will we afford the rebuilding projects that are needed?"

"Through trade and taxes," she said.

"The people will not want to be taxed after just surviving a war."

"No, taxes on the foreigners," she said. "Everything they want to bring into China, they have to pay a tax on, including opium."

"And they pay it?" I asked.

"According to Prince Yixin, it is a normal cost of doing business. All countries do this. So, if the foreigners want to import opium so badly, they can pay for the privilege to do so."

I was a bit dumbfounded by all this, and it wasn't the palsy. I supposed it was good that we were making money off the import of opium, but didn't that mean our people were using it?

"But we shouldn't be encouraging the opium trade," I said.

"We don't have a choice. It was part of the treaty that Prince Yixin wrote to end the war. We had to legalize the import of opium. At least the money we earn from it can be used to rebuild our country. We can worry about getting rid of opium later."

"You know I support Prince Yixin," I said. "Working with the foreigners is something we have to do."

"I agree—"

"But," I interrupted, "Yizhu was not wrong in his distrust of them. They are not paying taxes because it is in China's best interest. They are doing it because selling opium here makes them a lot of money. It also weakens our people. They nearly defeated us in battle. They took over the Forbidden City and burned down the Summer Palace. If our military becomes overrun with opium eaters, the foreigners could attack us again."

"Prince Yixin believes that they will follow their agreements," Cixi said. "As long as we adhere to the treaties, the foreigners will have no reason to attack us again."

I wanted to believe that she was right. That the foreigners would behave honorably, but I had my doubts. "I hope you are right. But just be careful of dealing too closely with them. China needs to become self-sufficient again."

"And we will, Sister," she said, nuzzling her head against mine. "We have done what we set out to do. And your health is on the mend. Must you worry so? Be happy for a moment."

CHAPTER THIRTY-THREE

Ten Years Later...

"I hate this!" Zaichun groaned and threw his horsehair brush across the room, splattering ink over his desk and on the floor. A maid rushed over to wipe up the ink before anyone stepped on it. A eunuch picked up the brush and put it back on the table. Lifen giggled and Tutor Weng sighed in frustration. I looked up from my pile of reports.

"What's wrong?" I asked though I knew the answer. Zaichun did not enjoy his lessons with Tutor Weng. He was not a natural student like his father had been, or like his sister. With no husband to tell me otherwise, I had allowed Lifen to receive the same education as her brother. Lifen loved reading, and her calligraphy was like the finest and most elegant artwork. Zaichun, however, found the classical texts boring, and he did not apply himself to writing.

"I've been here long enough for today," Zaichun said. "Guoming should be here any minute. We are going riding."

"You've barely been here an hour," I said. "Guoming knows not to come until after the midday meal. Now, get back to your lessons." Guoming was Prince Yixin's eldest son. The prince and the emperor were close in age and had many of the same interests, so they had become fast friends.

Zaichun grunted again and fidgeted in his seat. "This chair is too hard!"

I looked at a eunuch. "Fetch the emperor a cushion for his seat." The eunuch blinked in surprise, his eyes flicking to the emperor's chair, which already had two cushions. "Now," I said.

"Yes, my lady," the eunuch said as he ran off.

"You have such a delicate butt," Lifen said.

"Shut up," Zaichun said, tossing one of his pillows at her.

Lifen ducked and then screeched. "Hey! You smeared my poem! Mama!"

"Mama!" Zaichun mocked.

"Zaichun! Apologize to your sister," I said.

"Why do I have to be here!" he yelled, throwing himself on the floor.

I rubbed my head, looking down at the same report I had looked at four times already. Tutor Weng and I locked eyes. Some of China's past emperors had ruled the empire at a younger age than Zaichun. But at fourteen, my son was throwing a fit on the floor like a toddler. I stood up and walked over to the boy, looking down at him with as stern a face as I could muster.

"You are here to learn to be a good emperor," I said.

"Then let me rule," he said. "Reciting these stupid verses all day have nothing to do with being emperor."

"Fine," I said. "Tomorrow, you will rise before dawn and go with your other mother to hear audiences and deliver your verdicts."

"Really?" he asked, jumping up, his face beaming.

"It will be a good test to see how far you have come and how far you still have to go."

"Yes!" He ran around the room, hooting and hollering. Lifen

watched him, a frown on her face as she plopped back down in her seat and tried to fix the characters her brother had smeared.

"Zaichun, sit down," Tutor Weng said. "There is still much you need to learn by tomorrow."

"For my first order, I will sack Tutor Weng!" Zaichun said, followed by a cackling laugh. He picked up a scroll and attacked a eunuch with it, waving it around like a sword. The eunuch playfully dodged the attacks.

"Well, that will be your first mistake," I said as I went behind Lifen and ran my fingers through her hair. "We are never too old to learn."

Lifen growled and crumpled up her paper, tossing it to the floor. A maid ran over and picked it up almost before it hit the ground.

"Why did you do that?" I asked her. "I was reading it."

"It was ruined! I'll have to start over."

I kissed the top of her head. "My little perfectionist."

Tutor Weng shook his head and began packing up his things.

"Are you done for the day already?" I asked.

"It seems *he* is done for the day, so what is there left for me to do?"

"You still have another pupil," I said, motioning toward Lifen.

"A girl of fifteen should be preoccupied with other matters," the teacher said.

I pressed my lips and breathed out my nose. I was well aware that many girls Lifen's age were already married, but I could not bring myself to make an arrangement for her. I loved her and enjoyed her company too much.

"Do you think Zaichun is ready to start attending audiences with Cixi?" I asked the tutor.

"I think you know my answer to that question," he said, handing me one of Zaichun's recent exam papers. The writing was nearly illegible, and the answers were simplistic, not showing much depth of understanding.

"He is an intelligent boy," I said. "He simply does not apply himself."

"That is an understatement."

Zaichun had chased the eunuch out into the garden. Tutor Weng and I wandered over to a window to watch him play. He ran and rolled around on the grass.

"Were Emperor Daoguang's sons like this?" I asked. Tutor Weng's father had been the chief tutor for Yizhu and all his brothers, and I knew that all of those young men grew up to be quite scholarly on their own. Tutor Weng was the same age as Yixin, and he had attended many of the boys' lessons, learning from his own father alongside them, so he knew all the princes intimately.

"No," he said. "But those boys were in competition with one another. They did not know which one of them would be selected as heir, so they all worked hard to prove themselves to their father. Zaichun has no need for that. He is already emperor. What more could he accomplish?"

"Then what are we to do?" I asked. "How can we motivate him?"

"Perhaps letting him attend an audience with Cixi is a good idea. If he fails in front of his mother, maybe he will see the need to apply himself in his studies."

"Cixi will not be pleased. She might fire you."

Tutor Weng chuckled. "I know I will have the more kindly empress to protect me."

"You are quite spoiled as well."

"I don't think we need to worry too much about the young emperor," he said. "All young men settle down in time. And you and Cixi will be there to help guide his hand. All will be well, I assure you."

"We will see what tomorrow brings. Good day, Tutor Weng."

Tutor Weng bowed and then took his leave. I looked back out at Zaichun, who seemed to have run out of energy. He lay in the sun, snoozing. I heard laughter and saw Cixi walking with Little An, who was now her chief eunuch. Their heads were together as they talked in low voices, as they usually did. Though, it seemed awfully early in the day for Cixi to already be done with audiences.

"I'll be right back," I said to Lifen, who was still working diligently, though I don't think she even heard me.

I walked quickly to catch up with Cixi, which was still a bit slow. Ever since my palsy many years ago, the left side of my body was weaker than my right, so I had to walk carefully in my pot-bottom shoes. I had taken many tumbles over the years in them, and I wished I did not have to wear them at all.

"Sister!" I called out. Cixi and Little An stopped and let me catch up to them. Little An stepped behind Cixi and bowed his head, not looking directly at me.

"Sister," Cixi said, walking over to give me a hug. "What are you doing out here? Are not the children still in their lessons?"

"Why are you not at audiences?" I asked, trying not to pant.

"Oh, the day was simply too nice to be kept indoors, don't you think?" She lifted her face to the sky and took a deep breath. "We so rarely get beautiful days like this here in the city. It must be heavenly out at Kunming Lake."

Even though we had not been to the Summer Palace since the foreigners destroyed it, Cixi often spoke about it. We'd had the area cleared, much of the rubble taken away, but rebuilding would be impossible. The cost would be astronomical, and the buildings would never be the same.

"I need to speak to you about Zaichun," I said. There was a long pause as I waited for Little An to excuse himself, but he did not.

"Go ahead," Cixi said. I cleared my throat while looking at

Little An, and he finally realized that he had overstayed. He bowed and took his leave.

"He seems to be forgetting his place," I said when he was out of earshot.

Cixi only giggled. "I need him by my side so often, he just forgets that sometimes we need to talk alone." She took my hand in her arm to help steady me as she led me through the garden. "So, what did you want to tell me?"

"Zaichun wants to attend audiences with you tomorrow."

"No!" she said with more opposition than I expected. "I mean, he couldn't possibly. He hasn't assumed power yet."

"I know. But he has grown quite obstinate in his studies. Today, he simply refused to do anything, throwing himself on the floor in a fit."

"Can't you punish him?"

"How? He is fourteen and, technically, the emperor. He could assume power today if he wanted to and banish us to the Inner Court."

"Let's hope it does not come to that," she said. "But what is the point of him attending audiences tomorrow?"

"I am hoping he will see that it is much more difficult than he realizes and will understand the need for him to apply himself more in his studies."

"You want him to fail?"

"No…but also yes."

"Don't worry. I'll make sure he sees the error of his ways."

"Thank you. But also, we do need to start thinking about his marriage and wedding. He is fourteen. Everyone is expecting him to assume the throne when he is sixteen."

"It is hard to imagine him married, a husband."

"I know."

We had arrived back at the room we used for the children's schooling, which was where I also did most of my work. Lifen saw us and ran over to show us her poem.

"What do you think?" she asked.

It was a lovely poem that, on the surface, was about the changing of the seasons. Its true meaning, though, was more subtle.

With spring flowers, autumn moon,
The winter snow, and breezy summer air
If in your heart there's not a single care,
Any season will be the finest hour.

"Oh, Lifen, it is beautiful. Look how the stanzas are perfectly balanced, and the characters are in such harmony."

"Most poems are only about flowers or springtime," Lifen said. "But I wanted to show that every season is lovely in its way."

"It's exquisite," I said. "It is like a painting with words. What do you think, Cixi?" I noticed that Cixi was not smiling, but almost scowling at the poem. She blinked and shook her head.

"Oh, it's fine, I suppose."

"Fine? It's wonderful. Just wait until you show Tutor Weng tomorrow."

"I don't think he will like it," Lifen said, rolling the parchment up.

"What makes you think that?" I asked.

"Can I go play now?" Lifen asked. "Zaichun left a long time ago."

"Of course," I said.

She bowed to both of us and then ran off to find her brother.

"Tutor Weng does not appreciate how smart she is," I said. "I was thinking I might need to find a new tutor for her."

"You need to find her a husband."

I was alarmed that Cixi was the second person to tell me the same thing that day. "No, not yet."

"You don't want her to be too old to have children, do you?"

"Of course not," I said. "There is still plenty of time left for that."

"We can't wait too much longer."

"We need to talk about finding a wife for Zaichun," I said. "If he is to be married at sixteen, we should have already ordered the wedding silks from Suzhou." All imperial silk came from Suzhou, a city near Shanghai along the Grand Canal, a manmade waterway that ran all the way from Peking to several major cities in southern China. When I had helped oversee the consort selection for Yizhu many years ago, I had helped design the wedding clothes and had sent a trusted senior seamstress from the Forbidden City to oversee production. The late Empress Jing had told me that was how things were usually done.

"I have already been thinking about that," Cixi said.

"Oh, good. You have some designs in mind?"

"No, but I was thinking about who we should send to oversee production."

"I'm sure one of the court seamstresses will—"

"I want to send Little An!" she said, pure excitement on her face.

"What?" I did not think I'd heard her correctly.

"Little An, we should send him."

"Umm... Why?"

"He would enjoy it!"

"So?" Never in my life had I considered whether something would bring a eunuch joy. All eunuchs held privileged positions for their sacrifice and should be grateful.

"He has a birthday coming up. It would make a fine present for him, don't you think?"

I was very confused by the mere substance of the conversation. "Cixi, eunuchs cannot leave Peking. It is against the law for them to do so." The only exception to the rule was when the emperor was traveling, such as to the Summer Palace or Rehe Palace, neither of which Zaichun had ever done.

Almost all eunuchs served in the Forbidden City. While some were allowed to live in Peking, either with other high-ranking families or with their own, none were allowed to leave Peking. Eunuchs, no matter who they were allowed to serve, were the exclusive property of the emperor.

"Come now," Cixi said. "We have bent the rules before. After all, we shouldn't even be regents, but here we are! You don't really think people will care very much if we let one eunuch take a well-deserved birthday trip along the canal, do you?"

"Yes. I think they will care very much. You know how people feel about eunuchs."

While eunuchs served an important function in the Forbidden City and were known to most people of Peking, they were generally looked down upon by society, and they were practically nonexistent outside the city. Most people did not trust them and did not see them as real men.

"Well, this can serve as an example to the people that they are wrong," Cixi said. "Eunuchs are human beings. They should be treated with dignity and respect."

"They are servants," I said. "They forfeited any kind of normal life in exchange for a lifetime of service in the Forbidden City. I know you are fond of Little An, and that he has served us well. But you should not even consider sending him outside Peking. His life could be in danger if you were to do that."

Cixi waved me off. "You exaggerate. We can send guards with him if you are worried."

"No! No, no. We will not be sending guards because we won't be sending Little An. Do you understand?"

Cixi pouted and dropped the subject, at least for the moment.

"Now, we should start considering who would be a suitable empress for Zaichun."

"Empress?" Cixi asked. "Don't you mean consort?"

"No. Since Zaichun will be assuming the throne as emperor, not merely heir apparent, his first wife will be an empress, not a consort. When she enters the Forbidden City on her wedding day, it will be as an empress! She will be able to use the south Meridian Gate! The first woman to do so in two hundred years!"

Well, that is quite thrilling," Cixi said. "We must get started right away."

"I'm surprised you hadn't already been thinking about it. It's been on my mind for years."

"Yes, well, the children are your responsibility. I've been far more busy with running the country."

"We are *both* supposed to be running the country," I said, remembering the stack of reports on my desk I'd barely looked at.

"You know what I mean," she said. "It's a lot, running the country and raising children. I can't believe it takes two empresses to do the job of one emperor."

I rolled my eyes and walked back to my desk. "Emperors don't raise children; empresses do. We are both doing the jobs of two people. But it doesn't matter. It will all be over soon."

"What do you mean?"

"When Zaichun becomes emperor, he will take over the duties of running the country, and he will have an empress of his own to take care of the Inner Court and raise children. In less than two years, our jobs will be done."

Cixi sat in a chair across from me. "Well, that's very tragic. What will we do with ourselves?"

"I hadn't really thought about it. I suppose whatever it is the other retired ladies do."

Cixi and I both went quiet, and I imagined she was trying to picture what it was that the other retired court ladies did with their time. In truth, I avoided them as much as possible. Many of them were near to me in age, in their early thirties, but they were all widowed and childless, and their situation would never change. It was considered dishonorable for a widow to remarry, and it was the responsibility of the emperor's family to set the example for the nation. For the most part, the ladies were free to fill their time how they wished—as long as they did not leave the Inner Court. They could learn to read or write, play music, do embroidery work, watch opera performances, invite their female friends and relatives to visit for tea and chitchat, and... Well, that was about it, I supposed.

"How very dreadful," Cixi finally said.

"It's not dreadful. It's the way things are. I am sure you will find something to keep you busy."

"Are you sure we couldn't keep things the way they are for just a bit longer? Maybe until Zaichun is eighteen?"

"Shh," I said. "Don't say such a thing. We promised the Grand Council that we would only hold power until Zaichun came of age. If they thought that we wanted to stay in power longer, they could accuse us of trying to steal power from our son. It would not go over well, you know that."

"Yes, of course. Well, we will see how Zaichun does tomorrow at audiences."

"Indeed. I am looking forward to that."

APPARENTLY, word had spread that Zaichun would be attending the audiences that day, so the room was even more crowded than usual. Zaichun took his seat on the throne, and Cixi and I took our places behind the yellow screen. At the hour of the dragon, the first speaker was summoned. It was Prince Chun, Prince Yixin's younger brother, who was married to Cixi's sister. I thought that perhaps Cixi had arranged for Prince Chun to present first to give the emperor an easy entrance into ruling. But I quickly saw that I was mistaken.

"Wise emperor, kind empress dowagers, men of the Grand Council," the prince began. "I am here today to speak to you about the growing menace in our country—that of the foreign barbarians."

Cixi sighed and rolled her eyes. It appeared this was not the first time Prince Chun and Cixi had discussed this topic. Indeed, I had seen Prince Chun's reports regarding the actions of foreigners in the capital and around the country. For the most part, I ignored his suggestions as they were untenable. I, too, was leery of the foreigners and their intentions in China. But I could not deny that the money we had earned taxing their imports had helped dig us out of the financial hole my husband and father-in-law had put us in. The last decade had been relatively peaceful, and prosperity around the country had grown, in spite of the ever-increasing reports of opium addiction among the lower classes. Prince Chun, however, seemed to want to return to the policies of his father and elder brother by expelling the foreigners completely. Had Cixi or I been overseeing the audiences that day, we surely would have shown Prince Chun the door. As it was, we had to wait and see what Zaichun would choose to do.

"I would like to remind you of the terrible destruction the foreigners—the British, the Americans, the French, and others —have wreaked upon our country. After destroying our beloved Summer Palace, they stole many of our priceless treasures, which they now display in museums for their own pleasure and amusement. Anything that was not nailed down, they stole. And I do not mean simply golden figures or ancient porcelain. Why, I heard that one man even stole a little dog from a retired consort who died of fright! This little dog was a breed never before seen in the West. The dog now sits on the lap of the British Queen instead of on the laps of our own beloved empress dowagers."

"Must have been a very long-lived dog," someone in the crowd piped up, causing the whole room to burst into laughter. I expected Zaichun to at least chuckle, but he was sitting completely straight, gripping the arms of his throne. I thought I even saw a bead of sweat dripping down the side of his head. It was not even a hot morning.

"Yes, yes. You might laugh at this," Prince Chun continued. "But let us not forget that the destruction and ransacking of the palace literally broke the heart of Emperor Xianfeng, my dear brother. About the foreigners, he declared that he would not live under the same sky!" He raised his voice, speaking powerfully. "He died hundreds of li from his own home, in the cold and barren north, such was his hate for the foreigners."

"We are very aware, perhaps even more than you, who was a mere child when the emperor died, what Xianfeng's feelings about the foreigners were," Cixi said, unable to stay quiet any longer. "What is it that you propose to our current emperor?"

"Emperor, nephew," Prince Chun said, "it is your responsibility to fulfill your father's dying wish and exterminate the foreigners in our lands."

There were many murmurs of disagreement throughout the room at this.

"You must issue a decree to all provincial governors that they should encourage the people, both landed gentry and peasant, to burn foreign churches, loot foreign goods, kill foreign merchants, and sink foreign ships. All of this should take place at once so that not a single foreigner may escape.

"Emperor, nephew, you must not let a day go by without thinking about revenge for your late father, my beloved brother, and never forget it for a minute. Thank you."

Prince Chun bowed, indicating that he was finished, and several men in the audience clapped. My heart was racing in my chest. Zaichun could not show favor for such an extreme proposal. To entertain it at all could send the message that violence against the foreigners would be tolerated or even supported by the throne. But I remembered how violence against foreigners nearly destroyed the empire only a decade ago. How could Prince Chun forget?

I looked at Cixi, who was breathing hotly through her nose. She sat on the edge of her chair, as if she wanted to jump up at any moment. She was as anxious for Zaichun's reply as I was.

"Thank you, Uncle," Zaichun said. "Umm... Your words... Appreciate... My father's love..."

I looked at the crowd and saw that people were leaning forward, squinting, trying to make out what Zaichun was saying. I was sitting right behind him and could barely make out a sentence. I looked toward a side door, where Tutor Weng was standing. He was shaking his head, rubbing his face with his hands.

"Speak up, my son," Cixi said, kicking the back of his throne.

"Umm...I..." Zaichun wiped his brow and looked down, fidgeting his fingers.

"Do you agree with my proposal?" Prince Chun asked.

"I.. Umm..."

"*No!*" Cixi hissed to Zaichun.

"No... Umm... I..."

"*Louder!*" Cixi said.

"No!" Zaichun shouted. Several men in the room began to chuckle and murmur from behind their hands and fans. Cixi looked sharply at the crowd. Even though she was behind a screen, the men seemed to sense her anger as all of them fell silent. Zaichun finally looked at me, his eyes pleading. "Mama," he whispered. I nodded to him.

"The emperor would like to thank you, Prince Chun, for sharing your thoughts with the throne. I know how deeply you hold your beliefs to your heart." I nodded to Cixi to continue.

"Even if we do not forget the grievances for even a day," Cixi said, "grievances are not addressed by killing people and burning houses. Also, taking such a violent stance against the foreigners would only lead to a war we could not win. Therefore, your proposal is rejected."

Prince Chun was clearly disappointed at this ruling, but he could not have really hoped for another answer. For the first time in many years, China was at peace and growing in prosperity. Why would he want that to change?

Cixi stood up, and she motioned for Zaichun to do the same. I followed suit.

"Forgive us, but the emperor needs a break. We will reconvene in fifteen minutes."

Zaichun practically ran down the stairs and toward the door where Tutor Weng was waiting. I had to descend the stairs carefully with the help of a maid. By the time I caught up with Zaichun, Cixi, and Tutor Weng, the three were already arguing.

"What kind of a teacher are you?" Cixi was saying.

"Why did you embarrass me like that?" Zaichun asked Cixi.

"If you had been more diligent in your studies..." Tutor Weng was saying. I looked out into the audience hall and saw that everyone was watching us.

"That's enough, all of you," I said, motioning for everyone to go outside.

Once we were outside, I closed the door behind us. I looked from Zaichun to Cixi to Tutor Weng, unsure of where to begin. It was clear that Zaichun was not ready to rule on his own. But he had not even been able to speak at a level anyone could hear. He had not asked questions or thanked his uncle for being present. Would Zaichun be ready even two years from now? Zaichun's eyes were red, as though he were about to cry. I could not put the child on the spot. I turned, instead, to Tutor Weng.

"What is your suggestion?" I asked. "After what you saw today, how do you intend to prepare the emperor to rule?"

Tutor Weng looked at me, his face blank. If we had been alone, I think he would have told me there was nothing that could be done. But since Zaichun himself was present, as was Cixi, the teacher knew he had to come up with something.

"It is possible that he will be ready," he said. "Today was perhaps a bit much for the boy to take in. But most of the time, such presentations will not be pressing matters. The reports will not be as had to read as the classics, and the edits will be drafted by people of varying academic abilities."

"He must at least be able to ask simple questions and give brief directions," Cixi said. "I did little more than that at first. I admit that it takes a little time to get used to listening to men speak and knowing the right thing to say in the moment. But you could at least say please and thank you more clearly."

Zaichun seemed frustrated by her words, his own nose flaring.

Tutor Weng nodded. "We can focus our lessons on how to ask questions. After all, that is an important skill. No one knows everything. We must be comfortable asking for clarification when it is needed."

I nodded, relieved that everyone had come to an agreement on how to help Zaichun improve. "Perhaps it would also be beneficial for Zaichun to start attending audiences again, merely to observe."

"I think that would also be a wise decision," Tutor Weng said. "Perhaps what was the last hour of tutoring should now be spent in quiet observation. What do you think, young emperor?" Tutor Weng patted Zaichun on the back.

Zaichun nodded. "Yes."

"Good," I said, kissing the top of his head. "Why don't you go back to the classroom and see what your sister is working on? Tutor Weng shall go with you."

He nodded and walked toward the study room, dragging his feet. Tutor Weng hesitated. It was clear he wanted to speak to me further, but I was not in the mood. I needed a moment to think before we spoke again.

"That was a disaster," Cixi said as soon as we were alone, as I knew she would.

"I know," I said. "I knew it would not go well. I wanted it to go badly so that Zaichun would see the need to spend more time on his studies. But that went even worse than I anticipated. He is not ready for this at all."

"Are you sure we should be planning on him taking over in only two years?"

"I think that should still be the plan. But... Well, maybe we should not be surprised if Zaichun asks us to help him rule for a bit longer."

"And if he is unable to swallow his pride and ask for help?"

"We will just have to hope he is ready."

Cixi was clearly unhappy with my answer, but there was no point in continuing to argue about it right then. Zaichun was the emperor and quickly becoming a young man. The little time we had left to guide him was running out.

CHAPTER THRTY-FOUR

"Oh, this pattern is exquisite. Don't you think, Sister?" I asked Cixi. We were in my palace sitting room, looking at silk samples that had been delivered to us from Suzhou. The head seamstress from the clothing department was sitting with us, reviewing the various items of clothing needed for the emperor's wedding. Robes and gowns would be needed for the emperor, the empress, the emperor's two mothers, the emperor's sister, all the emperor's uncles, aunts, and cousins, and the empress's family as well. I was holding up a sample silk cloth in bright yellow that had been embroidered with phoenix birds and the symbol for double happiness.

"That is beautiful," Cixi said, though with much less enthusiasm than I had shown. "Will there be a matching silk for the emperor, but with the five-toed dragon?"

"That can be arranged," the seamstress said, making a note. "I'll need to get the emperor's measurements so that the robes can all be made to his size in Suzhou."

"Little An has them," Cixi said. "He only took them last week."

"Very well," the seamstress said. "I'll be sure to get those from him."

"There is no rush on that," I said. "Wait and take them just before you go. He might grow between now and then. He seems to be a little taller every day."

"That is a good idea, Your Majesty," the seamstress said. "And we will need to know who the lucky bride is soon so that her clothes can be made as well."

"Yes, Empress Dowager Cixi and I will have to discuss that in earnest," I said, giving Cixi a smile. Cixi smiled back, but with more reticence.

"I think that is all for today," the seamstress said. "I will have to take all these samples to the princes' wives as well and see what they think."

"I didn't see anything suitable for the princess," I said.

The seamstress nodded. "I am thinking of making her gown myself. She is such a precious thing. I love working with her. I have some ideas, but I want to see what she thinks first. I know she is excited to look her best for her brother's wedding."

"Hopefully she will catch the eye of a husband of her own before she starts sprouting gray hairs," Cixi said.

"Thank you," I said to the seamstress as I saw her out. "Why are you being so surly?" I asked Cixi as soon as we were alone. "Aren't you excited about our son's wedding?"

"Of course," she said. "But it is still ages away. And he's still just a little boy. I don't want to think about him being a man already."

"It does seem impossible that he is grown up already. But what can we do? We can't forbid him from getting older."

"I have no idea who we should choose as his bride. All the young ladies I know are so…headstrong."

I had to laugh at that. "What do you mean?"

"Honestly, they are like Lifen, and not in a good way."

My mouth gaped. "What can you possibly mean?"

"It's all Prince Yixin's fault. He started the trend of educating daughters like sons. And then he started that university for western sciences. Did you know some families have even started sending their daughters abroad to be educated?"

"I had heard. But we wouldn't choose a Western-educated girl for Zaichun. I think all girls should at least know how to read and write so that they can help their husbands and sons. Look at us. Where would Zaichun be if he didn't have mothers who were at least literate? Zaichun needs a wife who will be there for him should the worst happen."

"Don't even say such things," Cixi said. "Surely Zaichun will not need a wife to step in for him the way Yizhu needed us."

"No, of course not," I said. "I just mean, in general, all men should have useful wives. Whoever we choose, she will be the new head of the Inner Court. She will need to be able to keep the emperor's evening calendar, manage the household budget, and so on."

"Who do you suggest?" Cixi asked.

"What do you mean?" I replied innocently.

"Come now, you clearly have someone in mind."

I hesitated, putting my writing brush down carefully. "I was thinking of Hailan, the daughter of Chongqi and Feiya."

Cixi went quiet, staring at me for a long moment. "Chongqi? The Mongol?"

"Exactly," I said. "You must admit that we have not had very close relations with the Mongols since they abandoned Yizhu at the end of the war with the foreigners. They are our vassals and nearest neighbors. I think it would be good to resume familial ties with them."

"Oh, please," Cixi said, getting up and walking over to me, leaning on my desk. "This has nothing to do with good relations with the Mongols and you know it!"

"Of course it does," I insisted.

"No, it doesn't. This is about Feiya."

I went quiet, looking at my hands.

"Admit it!" Cixi said.

"So what if it does!" I jumped up from my seat and walked around my desk toward her. "You've helped your family. You made your sister a princess. Why can't I do the same thing for my family?"

"That is not the same thing," Cixi said. "We didn't have to put my sister's father-in-law to death. Chongqi cannot be trusted. He must harbor ill will toward us. We killed his father. His uncle!"

"Chongqi is a Confucian scholar. He completely supported Yizhu in everything—"

"Until he didn't—"

"That wasn't his fault—"

"You don't know that—"

"I made a promise!"

Cixi held her hands up in frustration, letting out a long groan as she took a calming breath. "What do you mean?"

"When Feiya last visited us, during the war, we talked about marrying Zaichun and Hailan. I told her that I thought it would be a beneficial match. I gave her my word that I would try to unite our families when the time came."

"You said you would try. Congratulations. You tried."

"Lanhua!" I cried, stomping my foot. "I haven't seen her in over a decade."

"Then invite her to visit."

"I've tried," I said, my eyes watering. "She always has some excuse not to come. She rarely writes to me anymore, and when she does, the letters are short and cold. The only way I could tempt her to come back is with an offer of marriage for her daughter."

"We can't marry our son to a traitor," Cixi said.

"I'm sure they are not traitors," I said. "Chongqi could have turned the Mongols against us when his father was ordered to death, but he didn't. He always makes sure that the taxes are paid on time. He sends us troops whenever we need them. If we hadn't executed Sushun and Duanhua, you have to admit that Hailan would be an excellent match for Zaichun."

"Maybe," she said. "But I think it is a terrible risk to take. She could turn Zaichun against us."

"But she's *my* niece. Feiya is my cousin. And consider her traditional upbringing. If we want a young lady who will be a subservient daughter-in-law, I don't think we could choose anyone better."

Cixi sighed and considered my words. "We can invite the family down so we can meet the girl. I mean, for all we know, she could be ugly and wild as a horse. She was raised by Mongols, after all."

"That's all I ask," I said, running over and hugging her. I was already composing the letter in my mind. I was sure Feiya would be as excited about making amends as I was. "I'll write to them right away. We could even return Duanhua's Peking house to them so they have somewhere to stay—"

"I want something in return," Cixi said.

"Oh. Well—"

She smiled demurely. "I want Little An to go to Suzhou to procure the wedding garments."

I immediately felt that my plans to see Zaichun and Hailan wed were ruined. I couldn't believe she was asking such a thing of me.

"Cixi, Sister..."

"Please!" She actually fell on her knees in front of me.

"He could be in danger!"

"The law says that a eunuch may leave Peking with explicit permission from the throne," she said.

"That may be so, but in practice, it has never been done before. Men hate eunuchs. He could be killed by some random passerby—"

"We can send guards with him for protection."

I sighed, completely at a loss for how to talk her out of what was clearly a bad idea.

"Why are you doing this?" I asked.

"I told you. He would enjoy it so much—"

"No," I said. "Why are *you* doing this? You can't go with him. There are other ways to reward faithful service."

"What else could I give him?" she asked. "I've given him money, gifts, a house. He even has a wife!"

I shook my head. I knew that Cixi had given Little An a maid as a wife. It was not an uncommon practice to reward faithful eunuchs with wives and even children so that their family name could be carried on. Little An was not even the only eunuch presently serving to have a family. But he was the youngest eunuch to ever be given such gifts. I was unsure of his exact age, but I knew he was at least ten years younger than Cixi and me. The gift of a wife to a eunuch would typically come after many, many long years of service. But as the chief eunuch to a regent empress dowager, Little An could certainly climb no higher.

"Are you in love with him?" I finally asked.

"What?" Cixi stammered and sputtered, feigning shock that I would ask such a question. Rumors about Cixi's relationship with Little An had been circulating for years. Whenever I heard them, I would quickly punish the gossiper. But I had no idea how far outside the Forbidden City the rumors had spread.

"He is a eunuch," I said, my voice firm. "A servant. A slave. He could never, will never, be your equal."

"I know," she said. "But he loves me anyway."

"Or he is simply using you to get all the presents you shower on him."

"No," she said, shaking her head. "I know him. You don't understand because you've never been in love."

Her words hurt my heart. Not because she was right—but

because she was wrong. But I had ignored my feelings for Prince Yixin, pushed them so far down into my soul even I barely knew they were there. To do otherwise would have been to betray my husband, my emperor, and my country. I could not imagine the consequences if I had done otherwise.

"If I let you do this," I said, "you will have to live with the repercussions."

"There won't be any repercussions," she said. "Everything will be perfectly aboveboard. I promise you."

I felt a sickness in my stomach. I knew this would come back to hurt her—if not all of us. But I was selfish. I wanted Feiya to come back. I wanted to see my cousin again. I wanted this marriage for our son. I wanted to finally be able to do something to help my family.

So, I agreed.

"If everyone is in agreement that Zaichun should marry Hailan, then I will agree to let Little An go to Suzhou."

Cixi squealed in delight. She hugged me and kissed me on both cheeks. "Thank you, Sister! Thank you so much. Little An will be so excited!"

Cixi ran off to find Little An and give him the good news. I sat down at my desk, my hand over my mouth. I felt nauseous and could feel a headache building. I had to remain calm to prevent another palsy from coming on. But whatever happened, the responsibility would fall on Little An and Cixi. They would have to live with the consequences. I sat at my desk and began writing a letter to Feiya before I could change my mind or Cixi saw reason.

CHAPTER THIRTY-FIVE

"*F*eiya!" I held my arms open as I walked toward my cousin. She seemed a bit more hesitant to approach me than the last time I had seen her. She was older, but she also had three more children in tow. I held her in my arms and felt her stiff frame relax. When I pulled away, she held my hands tightly.

"I wasn't sure how this meeting would go," she admitted.

"It will be just like old times," I said.

She nodded in agreement. Chongqi and all of his children bowed to me. When he presented Hailan, she had to pull back a fur-lined hood from her face. Her beauty nearly left me speechless. She had been a beautiful baby, so I had no doubt she would be a lovely young woman. Still, I had to blink to make sure that she was real and not a classical painting. She had pale skin, eyes shaped like crescent moons, a long, narrow nose, and perfectly formed lips.

"It is a joy to see you again, Hailan," I said to the girl.

"I am humbled to be invited to court, my lady," she said, never raising her eyes to me. For being raised so far from court, she certainly had been taught her manners.

"Come," I said, taking her arm in mine.

I led them into a large room where Zaichun, Cixi, and Yixin were waiting. It looked as though they were arguing, but they quieted down by the time we got within hearing distance. Since Yixin was the head of the Grand Council, he was often present to discuss matters of import with the young emperor. I knew Zaichun would be interested in his uncle's opinion on his possible future wife. When we were close enough, Chongqi, Feiya, and all their children kowtowed to the young emperor.

"Hello," Zaichun said when I finished introducing everyone. His eyes did not linger on Hailan the way I would have expected them to. In fact, he seemed to take no notice of Hailan at all.

"Son, what do you think of Lady Hailan? Would she please you as a wife?"

"I guess," he said. "Can I go now? Guoming and I have plans."

I chuckled to hide my embarrassment. "Don't you want to get to know Hailan a little bit? Do you have any questions for her?"

"I don't know," he said with an annoyed sigh. "What do you like to do?"

"I enjoy reading poetry and can recite many from memory," Hailan said.

"Anything else?" he asked.

"I am familiar with all the classical texts and can discuss them with you."

"My daughter is being modest," Chongqi piped up. "I taught her all the classical texts myself. I knew my daughter would one day marry a learned man who would be educated the same way. Though, I did not expect her to be presented to the emperor himself."

I nodded but felt a little nervous at this. Zaichun had been given a classical education, but he had not taken to it very well. As I looked at Hailan, standing demurely, I had a feeling she was more learned than Zaichun. I hoped that this would not cause problems for them. Though, I supposed it could be a boon. If Zaichun would not listen to his teacher, maybe he would listen to this enticing young woman. At least, she should have been enticing to any young man. But Zaichun did not seem interested in her at all.

I nodded to Zaichun to acknowledge his future father-in-law.

"Thanks," he said. He then looked at Hailan again. "So, you believe a wife should obey her husband, right?"

"According to *Analects for Women*, 'Women should listen carefully to and obey whatever your husband tells you.'"

Zaichun finally gave a half-smile at that. "Fine." He then turned to Cixi. "She will do, I guess. Can I go now?"

"Yes, you may go," Cixi said. I opened my mouth to argue. I thought that Zaichun was being rude to our guests, but before I could say anything, he was already out the door. I gave Feiya and Chongqi a smile to hide my embarrassment.

"Young boys are so full of energy. You must understand that with so many of your own," I said. I doubted my words, though, as I watched Feiya's boys, four of them of varying ages, all standing quietly and politely.

"I am sure all the children are ready for a break," Feiya said, handing her youngest child to Hailan. "Why don't all of you go explore the gardens?"

Prince Yixin held out his hand to Chongqi. "My lord, please walk with me. I'm sure we have much to discuss."

Chongqi nodded and went with Prince Yixin outside, leaving Feiya with me and Cixi.

"We are truly honored," Feiya said. "My husband could not tell you so himself, but he is greatly relieved that our families are finally reconciling."

"It was my pleasure," I said. "And Cixi also sees the wisdom in the union."

"Yes," Cixi said as the three of us took a seat and I ordered tea and sweets be brought to us. "You have been much missed at court over the years."

"I have to thank you for returning our property," Feiya said.

"Are you planning to stay long?" Cixi asked.

"I'm not sure," Feiya said. "The engagement would be quite long, correct?"

"At least a year," I said. "It will depend on when all the arrangements for the wedding can be completed. We will also have to hold a consort selection so that we may find additional consorts and concubines for Zaichun."

"My husband's appointment is back in Mongolia," Feiya said. "He is the head of the Council of Elders now."

"Would it please you to know that Prince Yixin is discussing a new appointment for your husband?" I asked. "One here in Peking."

"Is that so? I would be thrilled if that were true."

"I thought you liked Mongolia," Cixi said.

"I do," Feiya replied. "But I miss home. I miss my mother. And I miss my cousin." She gave me a wink and I nearly choked on my tea as I laughed.

And just like that, it was like old times. My cousin, my dear friend, had returned.

SEVERAL MONTHS LATER, Cixi and I were waving Little An off as he, six other eunuchs, several bodyguards, and Little An's mother and sister rode in donkey carts that would take them to the Grand Canal, where a pleasure barge was waiting to take them to Suzhou. I had tried several more times to talk her out of it, as had others, including Prince Yixin and Prince Chun. But Cixi had refused to listen to any of them.

"My only regret is that I cannot go with him," Cixi had told me at one point. "We have not even left the Forbidden City since we became regents."

"I am aware," I said.

"Yizhu took plenty of respite holidays to the Summer Palace," she grumbled.

"Well, we don't have a Summer Palace to go to anymore," I replied.

"Still, we should be able to take some time outside of Peking for ourselves. Don't we work ourselves to exhaustion for the sake of our son?"

"Patience, Sister. We will be able to step down soon. After the wedding."

"Will Zaichun be ready?"

"Tutor Weng is working him for long hours every day. Zaichun doesn't complain about the lessons as much anymore. I think he knows he has a lot of work to do to be ready."

"He seems to pay attention during morning audiences. I only hope he is absorbing what he needs to and isn't sleeping with his eyes open."

"You should start giving him more opportunities to speak," I suggested.

"Yes, perhaps I should."

I took comfort in the fact that Little An's trip was not secret. Many members of the Grand Council were aware of Little An's excursion, and he had permission from both empress dowagers. The emperor had stamped his letter of assignment to procure the garments from Suzhou. All we could do now was wait.

Not that I had a lot of time to sit around and wait for news about Little An's trip. The wedding was only months away. Chongqi's city home had fallen into disrepair during the years it had sat abandoned. It needed to be completely refurbished. I had to approve the repairs and upgrades to ensure it looked like a future empress's family home. I had also been putting together crates of gifts for Hailan and her family. I had to arrange the procession, which would consist of sedan chair bearers, singers, musicians, and holy men. The main road heading toward the Meridian Gate of the Forbidden City had not been used for such a procession in two hundred years. Over the centuries, the road had become considerably more narrow as more buildings had been erected. Many of those buildings had to be torn down so that the road could be widened. The people who owned those buildings had to be compensated and relocated. A consort selection had already been held, but in the end, only four concubines had been selected. I could not understand why Zaichun simply did not seem interested in selecting women for his Inner Court.

"Don't pressure him," Cixi had said. "He's just a boy. He will grow more interested later, I'm sure."

I was less sure. When Yizhu had been Zaichun's age— younger, actually—he had shown ample interest in women.

"He is going to be an emperor soon," I said. "And he will need to have a child of his own as soon as possible."

"You mean make us into grandmothers?" Cixi asked.

I couldn't help but shudder at the thought. "Maybe we can have his children call us something else."

"Grand dowagers?" she suggested.

"That might be acceptable," I said as we laughed together.

My days were busier than ever as I handled my regular daily duties in addition to planning for Zaichun's wedding. I slept soundly at night, and had nearly forgotten that Little An had taken his trip until one night, when there was a frantic banging on the front door of my palace.

"What? Who is it?" I asked my servants. They rushed to see who it was as I stumbled from my bed and pulled a robe around my shoulders. I knew something terrible had happened when Cixi stumbled into my room, barefoot, her face streaked with tears.

"He's been arrested! They arrested him!"

"What? Who?" I was so groggy, I had no idea what she was talking about.

"Little An! Dehai! He's been arrested!"

I was suddenly jarred awake. "Who?"

"An Dehai!" she screamed, shaking me. I pushed her away.

"No! Who arrested him?"

"The governor of Shandong Province."

I racked my brain, trying to remember who the governor of Shandong currently was. His name finally came to me. Ding Baozhen. He had once been the governor of Sichuan and had proven a loyal and effective ruler. He had been appointed to Shandong to move him closer to Peking, where he could be of more use to the throne. He was a good man, but was known for being a stickler for the rules. It should not have surprised me that he was offended by a eunuch passing through his capital city.

"Who told you this?" I asked.

"Prince Chun," she said. "He just arrived with the letter from Shandong. Zhen, they want to kill him."

"What? Why?" I took the letter from Cixi's hands and tried to read it by the light of a lantern, but my eyes were not cooperating. I had more lanterns lit as Cixi paced the room, chewing on her nails.

"Why is this happening? Little An is innocent. He has never hurt anyone."

"I don't know," I said as my eyes finally focused enough for me to read the letter. According to the complaint, Little An's retinue was behaving lewdly, with loud music that disturbed the peace. Large quantities of alcohol were delivered to the barge, along with prostitutes, both male and female. The party was cited for making a mockery of the throne and causing great embarrassment to the emperor. The punishment for a eunuch in such a situation was death.

"Do you know if any of this is true?" I asked.

"How could it be?" she replied. "Have you ever known Little An to behave in such a manner?"

"Not here," I said. "But who knows how he might have acted when he was finally outside the city walls."

"Prostitutes? You really think that Little An would cavort with prostitutes?"

"He's not the only person on that boat," I said. "There are six other eunuchs, not to mention the guards and his family members. Maybe he was unable to stop them."

Cixi cried out, gripping her head in both hands. "We have to help him!"

"I warned you—"

"No!" she screamed. "Don't say that to me, not now. What if this was someone you cared about? Someone you loved? Wouldn't you do everything in your power to protect him?"

I tried to put myself in her position. What would I do if Prince Yixin's life were in danger? Wouldn't I help him? Of course. But I never would have put him in such a precarious situation in the first place. I would never allow rumors about a love affair to seep through the city like an infectious disease. I would have kept Yixin safe at home, not allowed him to leave and flaunt his position for all to see. But if there was anything I could do to help Little An, I would do it. He was a loyal servant to Cixi, and to me. He had been the one to discover that Yizhu had been seeing Han prostitutes. He had done much of the research needed when Cixi and I wanted to remove the former regents. I did not have a complaint against him.

"I will try," I said, even though I had warned her that I wouldn't. But I could not abandon my friend, even if she had acted foolishly.

"Thank you, Zhen. Thank you!" she cried as she kissed the backs of my hands.

I got dressed and went to the audience hall where Prince Chun and Prince Yixin were waiting to speak to me.

"What is going on?" I asked them.

"You saw the letter," Prince Chun replied flippantly.

"Obviously," I said, holding it up. "And you know that Eunuch An is on official court business. He has papers stamped by the emperor himself."

"The letter only permitted him to go," Prince Chun said. "It did not permit him to flaunt the law and act foolish. He has brought shame to this court and needs to be punished. He should serve as an example for anyone who might think that they are above the law."

I crossed my arms. "What is this really about? Is this about Cixi refusing to support your measures to have the foreigners banished?"

Prince Chun did not reply.

I looked at Prince Yixin. "And you? What is your grievance with Cixi?"

He was quiet for a minute.

"I know you don't agree with Prince Chun regarding the foreigners," I pressed. "So, what could have made you join forces with your brother in this?"

"I supported the two of you to oust the former regents because *I* was supposed to be made regent."

"What? Are you serious?"

His face went stony.

"That...that was more than a decade ago! How can you still be angry about that?"

"Cixi is not to be trusted," Prince Yixin said. "She went back on her word. She needs to be reminded that she is nothing more than the mother of the emperor. She is not a queen."

"Cixi and I are merely regents, empress dowagers," I said. "As soon as Zaichun is married, he will sit on the Dragon Throne alone, and Cixi and I will retire. She knows this. Why are you fighting with her now."

"Many members of the council are afraid that Cixi will not

step back when she is supposed to," Prince Chun said. "An Dehai's death is just to remind her of her place when the time comes."

I could hardly believe what I was hearing. It was such an extreme measure to take for fears that were not even valid. Cixi had never indicated to me that she was going to try and stay longer on the throne. Well, I supposed that was not completely true. She had said that she did not think Zaichun was ready to rule on his own. But she wasn't wrong about that.

"Zaichun will need help," I admitted.

"That is what the Grand Council is for," Prince Chun said. "Not dowagers."

I finally understood what Prince Chun really wanted. He wanted to make sure that Cixi and I were out of the way so that he could influence the young emperor himself.

"And you?" I said to Yixin. "You agree with what your bother is doing? Isn't this why we got rid of the former regents in the first place? To keep people like Prince Chun from influencing the throne?"

"Prince Chun is not nearly as extreme as Sushun and his ilk," Yixin said. "But I have seen the way Cixi has ruled over the years. How she has pushed you to the side and not helped train Zaichun to take over. I think she does need to be reminded that her place is in the Inner Court—with you."

"But this is cruel," I said, fighting back tears. "An Dehai has never hurt anyone. He has been a good and loyal servant. Even Zaichun will be heartbroken when he learns of this!"

"Then Zaichun will learn an important lesson," Prince Chun said.

"He will," I said. "But probably not the one you think."

Prince Chun gave me a mere nod, not even a bow, as he turned and left the darkened audience hall. Prince Yixin stood still, waiting for me to dismiss him. But I would not do it. He could stand there until he passed out for all I cared. I couldn't believe he was doing this to Cixi, to all of us, because he had been slighted all those years ago.

I turned to storm out of the room, but Yixin grabbed my wrist, turning me back to him.

"I'm sorry," he said. "I never expected you to get so upset over a eunuch."

"I am upset for her," I said. "She is my sister and I love her. This is going to break her heart. You might be able to ignore that, but I am the one who will have to see her cry. I am the one who will have to hold her in my arms when she is too weak to stand."

"But would she do the same for you?" he asked me. "If your heart was broken, would she cry for you?"

"My heart broke a long time ago," I said.

"For me?" he asked. "Or for him?"

"You know that I never loved him."

Prince Yixin stepped closer, running his thumb over my cheek. The audience hall was vast. Only two lanterns had been lit in the middle of the room, giving us a little light to see each other by. But in the shadowed corners of the room, anyone could be lurking. A person was never truly alone in the Forbidden City.

"We can't," I said, my voice barely a breath.

"Your heart didn't need to break," he said. "You never lost me."

I reached up, just barely tugging on his robe. We couldn't kiss. Couldn't stand any closer than this. And yet, this was the most exposed I'd ever felt to anyone. Without saying the words, he knew I loved him. We loved each other. Was that how Cixi felt about Little An? It had seemed foolish to me that she would love a man she could never be with. But was I any different? Prince Yixin might as well have been a eunuch since we could never touch, never kiss, never make love.

"Zhen?"

I ran my hands over my face and stepped back, looking at Cixi.

"What is happening?" she asked.

I looked back at Yixin, but he was already leaving the room. I wiped my eyes as I turned to face Cixi.

"You spoke to the princes? Are they going to do something?"

I shook my head. "No. There is nothing they can do. I'm sorry."

"How can you say that?" she screamed. "Don't you care about me at all? They are going to kill him! We have to do something!"

"From the first day you stepped foot into the Forbidden City, I have been there for you. I made sure you were selected. I protected you when you spoke out of turn to Yizhu. I protected you from the edict he stamped for your execution. I protected you from the regents. But I can do no more."

Cixi began to shake, stomping her foot. "But we must! We must!"

"I can't help you anymore!" I screamed back.

I heard a loud snapping sound, like a twig in my ear. I looked to one side and saw a red flash, like a fox running through the shadows of the audience hall. I spun around in a circle, following the flash of red. I then felt dizzy, as if the world around me was falling away.

"Zhen?" Cixi said. But I couldn't respond. I fell into darkness once again.

CHAPTER THIRTY-SIX

"*H*ow could you do that?" I finally managed to ask Cixi. I had once again been struck with the palsy and had been bedridden for months. I had been unable to do anything but work on regaining my strength. While I did so, Cixi had complete control over the court and the country.

"It was time!" Cixi said. "She was sixteen years old!"

Tears streamed down my face at the knowledge that I had missed my daughter's wedding. I'd had no say in the selection of her husband. I had to admit that the marriage was an advantageous one. His name was Fuzhen, and he was a member of my late husband's family. He was a first-class duke. It would have been nearly impossible for her to marry any higher.

But I had no idea if he was kind to her or cruel. If he allowed her to continue her education or had relegated her to a traditional womanly role. Was she happy?

"I want...want to...see her," I said clumsily out of the right side of my mouth. A maid helped wipe the drool from my chin. I started to cry again. How could this have happened to me? I ate only what the doctors approved, when I ate at all. I drank bitter herbs every day. I did not exert myself. I had grown so delicate, I'd overheard maids calling me "the fragile phoenix." I remembered how many people, including myself, had referred to Yizhu as the limping dragon and was struck with guilt.

"Don't worry, Mama," Zaichun said as he sat by my side. "Lifen likes Fuzhen." He had been such a sweet and dutiful son since I'd fallen ill. He had visited me daily. He would read to me and tell me gossip from the court. He would sing opera songs and even perform some of the dances for me. I had been so focused on his education, I had forgotten that he was also a caring and sensitive boy.

But even he had not told me of Lifen's marriage until after it had happened. He knew the news would devastate me and I was powerless to stop it. I looked at Cixi, who was not at all remorseful for sending my daughter out of the Inner Court. I wondered if this was her way of getting some sort of petty revenge on me for not stopping Little An's death.

In truth, I was glad I had not been present when news came that his death had been carried out. Cixi would have turned to me for comfort, but I would have been unable to feel much compassion for her. His death was her fault. Not because she loved him, but because she allowed him to leave Peking.

Perhaps it was because she loved him. She loved him so much, she spoiled him, which led to his death. Though, perhaps his death would have come no matter what. Prince Chun had been growing increasingly frustrated with Cixi's refusal to do anything about the growing number of foreigners in the country. But Cixi was not the only person to blame for that. Prince Yixin, while he was not a regent, was a powerful force at court and a trusted advisor to Cixi and me. Having cordial relationships with the foreign powers was something that could not be avoided. It was the only way to prevent open war with them. And their money was making China rich. I did not understand Prince Chun's fierce position. Something would have to be done about him.

For now, all I could do was focus on my health. I was still young, not yet forty years of age. I had many years of happy and peaceful retirement ahead of me. My daughter was married, and Zaichun would soon be married to the lovely Hailan. I would soon be a happy and doting grandmother, I was sure.

I WAS NEARLY BACK to my full strength by the time of Zaichun and Hailan's wedding. The ceremony took place on the sixteenth of October, 1872. Early in the morning, while it was still dark, under a full moon, Hailan was collected from her home in Peking and placed in an exquisite sedan chair carried by twenty men. Guards stood every couple of feet along the route to the palace, keeping the roads clear of people and dogs. Musicians and singers marched ahead of her, while holy men followed behind.

Cixi and I stood outside the front of the Hall of Supreme Harmony and watched as for the first time in over two hundred years, the Meridian Gate was thrown open and an empress was carried through it into the Forbidden City. My heart swelled with excitement, so thankful that I was present to witness this remarkable occasion.

Zaichun and Hailan kneeled before Cixi and me to perform the tea ceremony. I thought for a moment that, were Yizhu still alive, the young couple would have bowed to only my husband and myself, as Zaichun's official parents and the reigning emperor and empress. Even though she was Zaichun's birth mother, Cixi would have had to stand aside, along with the other guests and family members. Traditionally, most emperors who married after the death of their fathers bowed only to one empress dowager. But I had agreed to share the duties of empress dowager with Cixi, and I would not waver in that agreement now. Indeed, I had to be grateful to have her at my side. What would have happened if I had been stricken with the palsy and she had not been here? Zaichun could not have ruled on his own. Of course I was grateful for all that Cixi had done for me. We were like sisters. And yet...

When I had first married Yizhu, I had been forced to stand aside by Empress Dowager Jing. As long as she was alive, I was not allowed to fully take my place as empress. She died a couple of years before Yizhu, but for most of that time, we were in exile, living in Rehe Palace. We did not return to the Forbidden City until Yizhu was dead. And by then, I had agreed to take over as regent for Zaichun along with Cixi. I had been empress for more than twenty years, but in all that time, I had never stood on my own. Now, a new woman, Hailan, would be Empress Xiaozheyi, and I would go into retirement in the Inner Court, with Cixi by my side as my fellow empress dowager.

I supposed I was simply feeling sorry for myself. I missed my daughter greatly. I no longer had reports to read, meetings to attend, or even morning audiences to oversee. Zaichun was now the emperor, and Hailan was now the head of the Inner Court.

Cixi shared my frustration. We were so bored!

"So, tell me," I said to Hailan and Lifen as we had tea in my palace one morning. "How are the two of you enjoying marriage?" Lifen did not live in the Inner Court, but since she and Hailan were near in age, the two had become good friends, so she visited often.

"Better than I expected," Lifen told me, which made my heart glad.

"I met your husband at Zaichun's wedding," I said. "He is delightfully handsome."

Lifen blushed. "Yes, he is. When Mother Cixi first told me

that I was to be married, I was terrified that she was going to pick an old man."

"Did she ever tell you why she rushed your marriage? Why could it not wait until I was able to have some input?"

"Not really," she said, chewing thoughtfully on a sweet cake. "She said something about Fuzhen's family looking for a bride, so she had to act quickly. But when I asked him about it later, he said that his mother hadn't been thinking about marriage for him yet, so she was surprised when Cixi approached her."

"Hmm," was all I could say to that. I knew that Fuzhen had been a good choice for Lifen, so if his family had been looking for a bride, it would have made sense that Cixi needed to act quickly. But if that had not been the case, why had she done it? I sighed and tried to push my concerns from my mind. It did no good to dwell on it. The matter was closed, and Lifen was happy. That was all that mattered.

"And things between you are going…well?" I asked, trying to hint to my daughter that she could talk to me about her private relations with her husband if she needed to. I hoped that Fuzhen was as kind and respectful to Lifen in the marriage bed as he was in all other matters of life. It would have broken my heart to know she had been married to someone who was brutish to her the way Yizhu had once been to me.

Lifen blushed. "Mama!" Then she snorted a laugh.

"So, is that a yes?" I asked her. "Will I get a grandson soon?"

"I suppose it could happen any time," Lifen said. "But I am in no rush. Fuzhen is a scholarly man. He often invites many forward-thinking men to our home to discuss various topics. And he lets me listen as well."

"Does he allow you to speak?" Hailan asked. She had been quiet for most of the discussion, but that was normal for her. She was generally a quiet and timid girl.

"I do not have much to say most of the time," Lifen said. "But if I want to speak, Fuzhen allows it. In fact, he says I should speak up more. He admires you, Mama, and Mother Cixi. He thinks you both did good things for the country when you were regents. He is a lot like Uncle Yixin in thinking women should be educated and given more rights. He thinks Uncle Yixin should open a school for girls at Tongwen Guan."

Not long after Prince Yixin created the Foreign Office, he established Tongwen Guan, a school for training interpreters. But soon, the school expanded to teach many more subjects, such as geography, mathematics, and astronomy.

"Your husband sounds like a radical," I said. "I don't see why girls should go to a school. Can't they just learn at home?"

"Perhaps if they have the right tutor," Lifen said.

"You didn't like Tutor Weng?"

"He only taught me because you ordered him to. He didn't really care if I learned anything or not. I felt like I was teaching myself most of the time."

"I'm sorry about that, darling." I reached over and squeezed her arm. "I had no idea you felt that way."

"It's fine. You didn't know any better. It wasn't like we had a lot of options. But when it comes time to educate my own daughters, I will be very picky about who their tutor is."

"That sounds wonderful, dear. I hope it happens soon."

Lifen rolled her eyes and sighed. She may not have been in a hurry to have children, but there was little she could do to stop any from coming if she and her husband were performing their bedroom duties diligently.

"So, Hailan," I said, turning to the young empress. "You have been quiet. How are things between you and Zaichun? You have been married for a month now."

"Everything is well, Mother," she said, not looking up from her tea.

"Are you sure?" I asked. "You seem...less enthusiastic than Lifen."

Hailan blew on her tea, which seemed to have gone cold

some time ago.

"Hailan?" I pressed. She did not reply, but I thought I saw her hand shake a little. I grew anxious, afraid that Zaichun had inherited some unfavorable tendencies from his father. I placed my hand on her knee. "Daughter, you can talk to me."

"I don't know what you want me to say."

I cleared my throat. "Do you know…how to become pregnant?"

"Not really," she muttered into her cup.

This alarmed me for completely different reasons. "What do you mean?" The young empress remained quiet. "When you go to the emperor's quarters, what do you do?"

"He has not summoned me since our wedding night," she said.

"What?" I nearly shrieked, causing both girls to jump. Hailan's tea spilled from her cup onto her gown. "I'm sorry," I said as I used a napkin to help her clean up.

"My brother has four concubines," Lifen said. "Perhaps he has summoned them."

"Indeed," I said. "I will have to look into it. But, Hailan, what did you and Zaichun do on your wedding night?"

"I…I recited poetry to him," she said.

"And then?" I asked.

"He fell asleep."

I sat back in my seat, my mouth hanging open. I couldn't believe what I was hearing. If Hailan was to be believed, she was still a virgin. How did Zaichun expect children to come if he did not do his duty by his wife?

"I'm sorry to hear that," I finally said to Hailan. "I will speak to him about this matter at once, I promise."

I quickly ushered the girls away since I could concentrate on nothing else. I went to the Ministry of Household Affairs and spoke to the chief eunuch.

"Has the emperor summoned any of his women to his bed

since his wedding night?" I asked.

"He has summoned each of them once, but no more than that," he said. I then visited each concubine, in turn, to find out if any of them had performed conjugal duties with the emperor. It took a bit of work with each one to get them to open up to me. They were all still virgins and all reluctant to speak about their time with Zaichun. But, in the end, I heard the same story over and over again. Zaichun asked the girls to read to him or tell him a story, nothing more.

"What are we going to do?" I asked Cixi the next day. I paced in front of her desk, worrying my hands.

"Someone will have to speak to him," she said. "And that is not the only problem."

"What do you mean?"

"Look at this." She handed me a letter from the governor of Shanxi Province, congratulating the emperor on his marriage and finally taking the throne. At the bottom, it had been stamped by the emperor, along with the order to "do as you propose."

"But...there is no proposal," I said.

"Exactly," Cixi said, handing me a whole stack of papers, all with the same order: *Do as you propose.* Some of the reports were proposals, but most were not. Zaichun had been simply writing the same thing on each report, apparently without reading them.

"What does this mean?" I asked.

"He has been sleeping in later and later in the morning," Cixi said, "and doing the bare minimum of work each day. He is being lazy."

I sighed and then told a eunuch to let the emperor know that his mothers wished to see him.

"I have no idea what to say to him," I said as I resumed my pacing. "I can't believe we have to tell our son to bed his wives!"

"If he has not bedded his wives, then he is still a virgin, too,"

Cixi said. "Maybe he is just nervous."

"Maybe we shouldn't talk to him about this," I said. "Maybe a man should do it, like Prince Yixin."

"That's a good idea," Cixi said. "But we have to talk to him about his work—"

"Good day, Mothers," Zaichun said when he entered the room. He gave each of us a bow. He seemed in high spirits. Now, at sixteen years old, Zaichun had gained height and more confidence. He was a handsome young man as well. I had to think that the young empress and consorts who had been chosen for him were pleased to have him as a husband. How could he not want to do his duty by them?

"Explain this," Cixi said, handing her son the letter from the governor of Shanxi Province. Zaichun looked it over and then handed it back to his mother.

"What about it?"

"You told him to do as he proposed."

"So?"

"He didn't propose anything!" Cixi nearly yelled.

"He didn't? Let me see that." He took the paper from her and looked at it again. "My mistake. I meant to send a thank you response. I am sorry for my error. I'll be more diligent in the future."

"And all these?" Cixi asked, throwing the other papers on the floor in front of him. "They all say the same thing."

Zaichun sighed, realizing he had been caught. "What do you want, Mother?"

"You promised me, and Tutor Weng, and your other mother, that you were going to work hard and apply yourself to being emperor. It's been barely a month and you are already slacking."

"Okay, I'm sorry," he said. "I'll do better."

"I'm going to have to start following up on your correspondence myself—" Cixi started to say as she went back to her desk.

"I've been thinking, Mothers," Zaichun said, walking around us. "You can't possibly be happy living here in the Forbidden City."

"What do you mean?" I asked. "We are content."

"Mother," he said, walking to Cixi, "you have told me so many stories about the old Summer Palace. How beautiful it was. How much you and Father enjoyed it. Indeed, my only happy memories of Father were at the Summer Palace."

"I'm sure that is true," Cixi said.

"And when I think about how the foreigners destroyed it, I get so angry."

I was afraid that Prince Chun's calls for revenge had started to sway Zaichun's way of thinking. "It was a long time ago—" I started to say.

"Exactly," Zaichun said. "It was a long time ago. Far too much time has passed for the Summer Palace not to have been rebuilt."

"Rebuilt?" Cixi and I both asked at the same time.

"I was thinking that I should have at least parts of it repaired and rebuilt so that I can give it to the two of you as a gift for all the years of service you put in as regents."

Cixi let out a little gasp of joy. "Really? Do you mean it?"

"Yes, Mother. I think it would be a perfect retirement home for you. Get you out of this hot and dusty city."

"Oh! My son!" She hugged Zaichun, practically jumping up and down with excitement.

"Wait," I said. "Can we even afford it? I know the country is doing much better financially than when the palace was destroyed. But if we have that much money lying around, I am sure there are better uses for it. A navy, perhaps."

"You are not the regent anymore," Zaichun said, his voice still friendly, but I couldn't help but feel a sense of warning behind it. "You don't need to worry about money. I've already spoken to the Grand Council about it, and they agreed that this is a worthwhile cause."

"When will the construction start?" Cixi asked.

"Right away!" Zaichun said.

"Wait just a moment," I said. "We should discuss this further—"

"Sorry, Mothers," Zaichun said. "I have an important meeting to attend. Good day to you both." He gave us quick, cursory bows and then fled the room.

"Can you believe it?" Cixi said, her earlier concerns about Zaichun completely forgotten. "The Summer Palace rebuilt, and just for us!"

"Come now," I said. "He only said that so you would stop hounding him about work."

"Do you think so?" she said.

"You dropped the issue awfully quickly when he brought it up," I said.

Cixi thought for a moment. "Perhaps I did. But can you imagine it, Zhen? The Summer Palace! The shady trees. The lush gardens. The breeze off Kunming Lake. Wouldn't you rather be living there than here?"

"Of course," I admitted. "But he can't be serious. The cost would be enormous! We can't possibly have stockpiled that much money in so little time. We were completely broke by the time Yizhu died."

"But don't we deserve it?" Cixi said. "Most emperors have such places to go to once in a while to recover from the daily stresses of running an empire. We ruled for twelve years without a single day off. Well, except when you were bedridden."

"That was hardly my choice."

"Exactly! Didn't the doctors say that the palsy was brought on by great emotional strain? You almost worked yourself to death!"

"Sister, I know you loved the Summer Palace," I said. "But this cannot be a wise use of funds."

"We should speak to Prince Yixin about it. We need to talk to him about the emperor's bedroom activity anyway."

"I can agree to that."

"MOTHER! MOTHER!" Lifen came to my palace in a panic.

"What is wrong?"

"It's Uncle Yixin! Brother just sentenced him to death!"

"What?" I stood up quickly, tipping over a tea tray, sending the porcelain tea things crashing to the floor. "How did you hear this?"

"Hailan and I were walking near the audience hall and heard a great commotion! We went inside to see what was wrong, and Uncle was on his knees, begging the emperor for forgiveness. I could hardly believe my ears when I heard Brother say that he would not rescind his order, and that Uncle should be dragged away to the execution grounds immediately!"

"Has your brother lost his mind?" I asked as I stomped toward the audience hall. "Go and fetch Mother Cixi."

"Hailan went to alert her."

Indeed, Cixi was already walking through the door to the audience hall when I arrived.

"What is the meaning of this?" Cixi demanded when she walked into the room. Everyone but the emperor kowtowed to her. I was nearly out of breath when I arrived right behind her.

"This doesn't concern you, Mothers," Zaichun said, his arms crossed, his nostrils flaring. "I am the emperor!"

"You are the emperor," Cixi said. "But that is your elder cowering before you, the uncle who has been like a father to you."

Yixin said nothing, his forehead practically plastered to the floor, his hands folded tightly over them. He seemed to be shaking. He truly thought the emperor was about to execute him.

"You should have heard the way he spoke to me!" Zaichun yelled, his voice cracking.

"What did he say?" I asked. I had never known Prince Yixin to speak down to his nephew, even when he was a baby.

"He forbade me to rebuild the Summer Palace," Zaichun said. "Me! The emperor! No one forbids me, do you hear me, Uncle!" Zaichun ran toward Prince Yixin as if he would kick him. I grabbed his arm and was able to hold him back.

"My son!" I said, doing my best to keep my voice low. Zaichun was already infuriated and probably embarrassed by whatever Prince Yixin had said earlier. I did not want to add fire to this little flame. "Please, you must remain dignified."

Zaichun ripped his arm out of my grip and smoothed down the front of his robe. "Let Prince Yixin's death serve as an example. No one is above the emperor. No one!"

"Stop this!" Cixi said to Zaichun. "You cannot act this way."

"You are not the empress!" Zaichun yelled at her, growing angry again. "You obey me! I'll kill him!"

I dropped to my knees in front of Prince Yixin. "Please, Emperor! My son!" I cried. I waved to Lifen, Hailan, and Cixi to follow suit. Lifen and Hailan did so without hesitation. Cixi, however, remained standing, as shocked by my actions as the emperor himself.

"Emperor Tongzhi," I said with the utmost respect. "I apologize for the thoughtless words of my brother-in-law. I asked him to speak with you on my behalf. If you are angry at anyone, be angry with me."

"What, Mama?" Zaichun said, his voice softening. "Why would you have Yixin speak to me about this? The Summer Palace is my gift to you and Mother."

"I only wanted him to make sure the project was financially responsible. I do not wish to cause you trouble with such an expense. I want nothing more than for your reign to be more prosperous than any reign before it."

"Mama, stand up," Zaichun said with a chuckle, offering me his hand. "You are acting ridiculous."

I took his hand and stood but kept my eyes downcast.

"Mama, I feel that it is my filial duty to give this palace to you and Mother," he said. "There is no need to worry about money. Money will continue flowing into the empire as it has done for all these past years."

"Of course," I said. "I am sure you are right. Forgive me for questioning your wisdom on this matter."

"It has been very hard watching our son grow into the man he is today," Cixi said, rubbing Zaichun's shoulder. He shrugged her touch away.

"I understand," Zaichun said. "But you do not need to worry yourselves about such matters anymore. You should both resign yourselves to matters of the Inner Court from now on."

"Yes, of course," I said. "And your uncle?"

Zaichun smiled as he remembered Yixin. "Stand up, Uncle. All is forgiven."

Yixin stood up, but he, too, kept his gaze down. "Are you sure, Emperor? I humbly apologize again for the tone I took with you."

"Everything is fine," Zaichun said. "But in the future, perhaps you will think twice before speaking on behalf of these two busybodies."

Everyone laughed, but there was little humor in it.

"I'm finished for the day," Zaichun said. "You are all dismissed." He left all of us without another word, even walking past his wife without a second glance.

Prince Yixin let out a long exhale and seemed a little uneasy.

"Are you alright?" I asked him.

He shook his head. "I need a moment. I really thought that he was going to kill me."

"Well, you shouldn't have forbidden him from rebuilding the Summer Palace," Cixi said. "You have to be more tactful than that."

"I didn't forbid him from anything!" Yixin said. "He was just mad that—" He looked around at everyone, then shook his head again. "It was nothing."

"Wait, why was he mad?" I asked. Yixin's eyes flicked to Hailan, then back to me. "Well, I supposed it doesn't matter now," I said, getting the hint. I turned to Hailan. "Why don't you girls head on back?"

"Yes, Mama," Lifen said, leading the young empress away.

"Come on," Yixin said to me and Cixi when the girls were gone. He led us to Zaichun's old schoolroom, which wasn't used for much of anything anymore. The room was dark, and everything was covered with a thick layer of dust. I sneezed as soon as we entered the room.

"What is it you couldn't tell us in front of Hailan?" Cixi asked.

"Zaichun was still angry with me after a discussion we had privately last night," he said. "I confronted him about not doing his duty by Hailan."

"I am guessing it didn't go well," Cixi said.

"No, it did not."

"I thought he liked Hailan," I said. "They met before they were betrothed. He said that she would do."

Yixin shook his head. "He admitted to me last night that he chose her because she was compliant. She would do as she was told and wouldn't complain."

"Well, he was right about that," I said. "I had to drag it out of her that they weren't actually making love."

"But why isn't he?" Cixi asked. "Don't tell me he has a thing for bound-foot whores like his father."

"Bound-foot, no," Yixin said. "Whores, yes."

"Are you serious?" I asked, about sick to my stomach. I

simply didn't understand it! Why would any man prefer a woman who was shared with other men to women of his very own?

"He isn't bringing them to the palace," Cixi said. "I would know if he were."

"He's been sneaking out, apparently," Yixin said. He turned away, looking a little embarrassed. "I learned he and Guoming have been going to brothels together for years."

"Guoming?" I said. "Your son?"

"The boys are fast friends," Yixin said.

"How could you let this happen?" Cixi demanded.

"I didn't know!" Yixin said. "But I put an end to it. Guoming is locked in his room for now, literally. And I said he could not see Zaichun again."

"Ever?" I asked. "That's a bit harsh."

"Well, I said until Hailan fell pregnant."

Cixi and I looked at each other.

"That seems a bit fair," Cixi said.

I wasn't quite sure about that. "I'm assuming that Zaichun was not happy."

"No, he was not. But I knew I had to be firm with him. With both of them. I thought he would have cooled off overnight, but I guess I was wrong. As soon as I questioned his decision to rebuild the Summer Palace, he sentenced me to death. I think he would have done it if you hadn't interfered."

"I'm sure he would have come to his senses," I said.

"I don't know. I've never seen him like that before."

"Well, let's not worry anymore for now," I said. "The boys have been punished, and Zaichun knows what is expected of him. We should give him a bit of time and space to see how things go. He is the emperor, after all, and growing older every day. We cannot impose our will on him forever. We have to hope for the best."

CHAPTER THIRTY-SEVEN

$\mathcal{T}$he ride from the Summer Palace back to Peking seemed to take forever.

Over the last two years, several small buildings at the Summer Palace had been repaired, enough that Cixi and I stayed there much of the time. This had been both to give Zaichun space and so that Cixi could oversee the repairs herself. I did not enjoy my time outside the city as much as I had hoped. I missed Lifen, and I still was not a grandmother. I was lonely and wasn't sure how I would be able to face another twenty to thirty years living in such a way.

But tonight, Cixi and I had received devastating news.

The emperor was ill.

He had contracted a fever a few days before and it had not abated. The doctors told us not to worry, that we would be alerted as soon as there was any change, but we wanted to be with our son. No one could care for him the way we could.

As soon as we arrived, it was clear that Zaichun was very ill. He was weak and vomited often. His sister was there already, as she lived in the city. Since we didn't know what he had, we sent her away. We did not want her to contract whatever it was.

"But, Mama," Lifen said. "You could fall ill too."

"Don't worry about me," I said. "Your mother is stronger than you think."

The doctors did all they could to treat Zaichun. He was administered all sorts of bitter herbs to drink. He was stuck all over with needles, and cups were used to draw the infection out.

But nothing seemed to work.

Finally, on the ninth day of his illness, the cause was discovered.

Cixi had been wiping his brow and neck with a damp cloth to keep him cool. I was mixing yet another bowl of herbs for him to drink when I heard her gasp.

"Zhen!"

I looked over her shoulder and saw the thing that we dreaded most.

"Smallpox!" I exclaimed. The spots were flat and red for now, but it would only be a matter of time before they became inflamed and pus-filled.

The Grand Councilors told us that we should leave Zaichun immediately, lest we fall ill as well. Smallpox was a terrible disease with no known cure. There were many treatments, but they treated the symptoms more than the disease, with many people considering it a death sentence. Still, we would not leave our son's side. Cixi and I caught only an hour of sleep here or there for days on end. One day when I returned to the emperor's room after a quick nap, I saw Cixi next to him, helping him sign a paper.

"What are you doing?" I asked her.

"Something that has to be done," she said, rolling the paper up.

"Give it to me," I said. She did not fight me but handed the paper over willingly. I unrolled it but did not have to read past the first line to know what it was.

"You are asking the Grand Council to make us regents again?" I asked.

"Only if the worst happens," she said.

"I can't believe you are even thinking of this right now!" I said. "Our son is fighting for his life!"

"It is only a precautionary measure," Cixi said. "I'm sure that Zaichun would approve...if he could speak."

"There is no precedent for this!" I said. "If he dies, we aren't the dowagers anymore—Hailan is."

Cixi scoffed. "That woman can't even decide what to wear in the morning. Do you really expect her to be able to helm this country?"

"It doesn't matter," I said. "That is how things are."

"Zaichun doesn't have a son!" Cixi said, jumping from her chair and facing me. "Lifen doesn't have a son. If Zaichun dies, who is going to be the next emperor?"

"I...I don't know," I said. "I can't think about that right now. I have to hope that he will still live."

"Well, one of us has to think about it, because I assure you that the Grand Council is thinking about it. Do you want to end up with a bunch of selfish, short-sighted regents again? Will I have to kill another eight men to keep this country running smoothly?"

"I will always do what is best for this country," I said. "As I always have. You are not the only person who risked her life to overthrow the regents. You are not the only empress dowager around here. You have never even been an empress!"

"I was twice the empress you ever were! You never had a son!"

"There is more to being a mother than giving birth," I said. I turned away and went back to sit at Zaichun's side.

"Zhen," CIxi said. "I'm sorry. I didn't mean that."

"Go on," I said, waving her away. "Go do whatever you were going to do."

I heard Cixi walk away. I took Zaichun's hand in mine. He had not been awake for a couple of days. His blisters had broken open, and he looked to be in terrible pain. I knew he would not survive, but I still prayed that he would.

I did not know how China could survive without an emperor.

EMPEROR TONGZHI DIED on the twelfth of January, 1875. He was only eighteen years old. He did not have an heir or a will. There had not been any construction work started on his tomb. All of China mourned his death, but the court was in a panic. Who was going to rule?

To my surprise, Cixi did not present the edict that she'd had Zaichun sign on his deathbed. I had no idea what she had done with it. But it appeared that she did not need it. Only days after Zaichun's death, Cixi and I appeared before the Grand Council. Cixi plainly asked them if they would like for her and me to take over once again as regents.

"Yes," Prince Yixin said without hesitation, and before anyone could object.

Cixi nodded. "The two of us have made our decision and we are in complete agreement."

In truth, Cixi and I had not spoken about it at all. We had not spoken about anything since our fight as Zaichun lay dying. I supposed we were both rather embarrassed to have fought over such a thing while our son was fighting for his very life. Still, I was a bit confused. The Grand Council had made us regents, but regents of whom? Who would the heir be?

I went to Hailan to ask her if there was even the slightest chance that she could be pregnant. I had not paid the slightest attention to her while the emperor had been ill, but I was shocked by her appearance. She was thin, painfully thin.

"Daughter!" I said. "Have you not been eating?"

"No," she said.

"Please," I said, leading her to a chair and offering her some fruit from a bowl on a table. "Eat something. You must."

"No," she said, slapping the apple from my hand pitifully. She had hardly any strength in her.

"My dear, I know you are distressed, but you must be strong! You are the dowager now."

"No," she said, shaking her head. "I must…I must follow my husband." Her eyes were heavy, as if she could pass out any moment.

I thought she must have lost her senses. "Hailan," I said, sitting across from her, Zaichun has died, but you are still alive."

She looked at me, blinking languidly. "My father sent me a gift." She pointed to a traditional bridal box, often used by young ladies to carry their personal items to the home of their new husbands. This style of box was specifically used to carry foodstuffs. Hailan had not used such boxes when she came to the Forbidden City, since all her possessions were sent to the Forbidden City in crates before her arrival. So, this box must have been sent to her recently. But when I opened the box, it was empty.

"Did you already eat everything that was in the box?" I asked her.

"No," she said. "It arrived that way. I must obey my father and follow my husband to the afterlife."

I slumped down into a chair, my confusion making my head ache. There was a time when women often did as Hailan was suggesting. Even the wives and concubines of emperors were sometimes entombed with their dead lord, left to starve to death in pitch-black darkness. I supposed it was possible that some people still carried on this tradition in more rural areas, but I had never heard of it happening in my lifetime. I went to my knees before Hailan, clasping her hands in mine.

"No, I will not let you be a yellow bird," I said, referencing a classic poem that extolled the virtues of accompanying one's lord into death. "I have lost a son; I'll not lose a daughter too."

"It's alright, Mother," Hailan said, running her hand down my face. "I have already spoken to Mother Cixi. She will take care of everything."

"Cixi?" I repeated. Hailan nodded. I did not want to think that Cixi had encouraged Hailan to kill herself, but I could not ignore the way my skin prickled at the thought.

"Daughter," I said, "is there any chance you could be pregnant? If so, you must live, for your child's sake if not your own."

She looked at me, her sunken eyes already nearly lifeless. "Zaichun could never had made a woman a mother."

I stood and went to find Cixi, who was kneeling before Zaichun's casket, which had already been sealed. She was weeping, her shoulders shaking. I walked up next to her, placing my hand on the back of her head.

"So young," she said between gasping breaths. "He was so young."

"I know," I said. "But there was nothing we could have done."

"Have you heard the rumors?" she said, wiping away her tears.

I shook my head. "You know I don't pay attention to such things."

"Some people, servants included, say that Zaichun died of the big pox, not smallpox."

"Whoever is saying such things should be punished," I said. Big pox was one of the diseases often carried by prostitutes, so I'd learned over the years.

"I have already had two servants whipped for saying such things," Cixi said as she stood. "But, apparently, ever since we moved to the Summer Palace, the emperor did not bother hiding his preference for prostitutes, even bringing them into the Forbidden City most nights."

I shook my head. "Well, my understanding is that it takes many years to die of big pox. Zaichun was taken from us in a matter of weeks. Some of his servants and eunuchs fell sick with the disease as well. They have all been sequestered. Their bodies will be burned when they expire to keep the disease from spreading."

Cixi nodded, and we were quiet for a moment as we looked at our son's casket. I had almost forgotten why I had been looking for Cixi in the first place.

"Did you know that Hailan is refusing to eat?"

"Her father seems to be even more traditional than I ever could have imagined," she said.

"Did he really send her that empty food box?" I asked.

She looked at me, her face pained. "What do you mean? Of course it came from her father."

"Her family is in Mongolia right now," I said. "I heard from Feiya. She sent a letter of condolence as soon as she heard about Zaichun's death. She told me to look out for Hailan, to take good care of her. She said they would be returning to Peking as soon as possible, but the trip takes several weeks."

"It would not surprise me if Feiya didn't know what Chongqi was up to. I know that she is a submissive wife, but would she support her husband telling her daughter to commit suicide?"

I let out a sigh as I thought about it. I tried to reconcile the loving mother I knew Feiya to be with the dutiful wife she also was. She had told me that Chongqi was a very traditional man, but that he also consulted his wife in all things. This would be a terrible break in trust between the two of them if he contributed to his daughter's death without telling her.

"Hailan said that she spoke with you," I said. "She said you told her you would take care of everything. You cannot encourage her to do this."

"I didn't!" Cixi insisted. "I only told her to do as she saw fit. I told her not to worry about anything. I didn't want her decision to be clouded by outside worries. She needed to know that she was free to make her own decision."

"Why didn't you come to me first?" I asked. "She's not only my daughter-in-law, she's my kin. My cousin. I had a right to know."

"I didn't want to worry you."

"I *am* worried! What will I tell her mother if she dies under my care?"

"That's not your responsibility," Cixi said. "That's on her father."

"Please," I said. "I'm begging for your help. If, after her parents arrive and she still chooses to starve herself, then I will accept it. But for now, I cannot have another child's death on my hands. Please, help me."

"Fine," she said. "I'll speak to her."

"Thank you."

I started to leave the room to return to Hailan. I would force the girl to eat if I had to. But as I neared the door, a eunuch met me, falling to his knees.

"My lady, I…I have urgent news."

"What is it?"

"Princess Lifen, she has fallen ill with the smallpox."

"No!" I screamed. I pushed past him into the hallway, but several guards were already there waiting for me. "Let me go! I must go to my daughter at once!"

"I'm sorry, my lady," one of the guards said. "We cannot allow you to leave the palace. There is an outbreak of smallpox in the city. Princess Lifen's whole household has fallen ill."

"No! No! I must go to my daughter! Unhand me!" The eunuchs had to drag me to my palace and lock me inside. I banged on the doors and tried to climb out the windows, but the servants who were trapped inside with me held me back. I screamed and cried for days, praying constantly to the Goddess of Blisters.

But, in the end, my daughter was called to be with the ancestors.

The servants were afraid to tell me. I think they thought I would kill myself when I found out. My heart hurt so much, I did not know why the palsy didn't take me. I was not even permitted to attend Lifen's funeral. Her body and all of her belongings were burned to prevent the disease from spreading.

I took to my bed, not caring what happened to anyone else. All of China could have burned to the ground and I would not have cared. When I learned of Hailan's passing, I did not even weep for her.

FEIYA AND CHONGQI arrived at the Forbidden City only days after Hailan died. I had thought that Feiya and I would mourn the loss of our children together. Instead, Feiya lunged toward me, her hands balled into fists.

"How could you let this happen?" she screamed, servants holding her back.

"I tried to stop her," I said, not admitting that after the death of Lifen, I cared not what happened to Hailan.

"I trusted you to take care of her!" she said.

"I did the best I could," I said.

"You did nothing!" she screamed. "I know what kind of man your son was. How he whored with men and left my daughter a virgin."

"How dare you spread such a vile lie!" I said. "My son was not perfect, but he did not whore with men."

"You are blind, Zhen," she said. "Blind and foolish. Your son was disgusting, and you let my daughter die as vengeance for your own loss."

"That's not true," I said, tears spilling from my eyes. But she was partly correct. I had let Hailan die after I loss Lifen. I shouldn't have done that. I should have done more to protect my daughter-in-law. I might not have ordered Hailan to starve herself, but I didn't stop her. I had failed her, the same way I had failed Ayan.

"I'm sorry," I said, reaching for Feiya. "I'm so sorry."

"Don't touch me!" she screamed. "I will never forgive you for this! I have no cousin."

"What about him?" I asked, pointing to Chongqi. "He was the one who ordered Hailan to starve herself."

"He would never do that," Feiya said. "He loved her."

I turned to Chongqi. "Tell your wife the truth."

He puffed up his chest. "I am proud of the sacrifice my daughter has made. She will be honored above all women. I had no need to tell her what to do. She knew what was expected of her."

"It was that woman," Feiya said. "Cixi did this."

"No," I said. "You heard your husband. Hailan knew his expectations for her. He wanted her to do this. He sent her the basket."

"What basket?" Feiya asked.

"The empty bridal basket, the empty food basket," I said. "It was delivered to her after Zaichun died."

"What?" Feiya asked, turning to her husband. "Did you do that?"

"It matters not," Chongqi said, pulling on his wife's sleeves toward him. "Hailan is gone. We must honor her sacrifice."

"No! *No!*" Feiya said, fighting against her husband's embrace.

"Cixi and Zhen are the empress dowagers again, and we must respect them as we would the emperor."

"Why are you protecting her?" Feiya asked. "Zhen, I understand. She has always been blind where Cixi is concerned. But you? Why, Husband? Why?"

"Enough!" Chongqi finally roared, pushing Feiya away. "Be quiet, Wife. Remember your place. Remember dignity. You will honor the empresses as you honor your husband. Do you understand?"

Feiya collected herself, straightening her gown and wiping her face with her sleeves. She turned to me. "You are my empress, but I will speak to you no more as a friend." She then walked away, toward the room where Hailan's casket had been set up for mourning.

"Feiya," I tried, but she ignored me.

I collapsed to my knees, but two eunuchs caught me and helped me back to my palace. In my bed, I wept until I could weep no more. I begged the palsy to take me, for me to fall into the darkness and never crawl back out again. But this time, it did not come.

CHAPTER THIRTY-EIGHT

"*I* need you," Cixi said as she sat by my bed. Cixi was dressed in an imperial yellow gown, her hair done up with a full liangbatou. I, on the other hand, had not left my bed for days, not even to bathe. My hair had become wiry, graying with age. I had barely eaten for weeks, since Lifen's death. I think my maids had given up caring for my appearance. Why should they bother?

I crossed my arms and rolled my eyes. "You don't need anyone."

Cixi's eyes watered as she placed her hand on mine. "That is unfair, Sister. You know how I miss my son. But someone must rule. If I took to my bed as you have done, then what?"

I had no answer for her because I did not know. Perhaps she was right, and I was acting spoiled. In my grief, I took to my bed, leaving Cixi, who was supposed to be my co-ruler, to govern the country alone.

"I'm sorry," I said. "I simply did not think one lifetime could ever carry so much grief."

"I understand," she said. "But many emperors have lost much more than we have. Emperor Daoguang lost two sons, two empresses, and many daughters before his end came. Perhaps great suffering is the price we must pay for wielding so much power."

"What do you need from me?" I asked.

"We must name an heir," she said. "And I want you by my side when I announce who it is. If there is any doubt as to who the heir should be, people might question his legitimacy."

"Who do you have in mind?" I asked.

"Zaitian," she said. "Prince Chun's son."

I had to laugh at this. "Your sister's son? I assume it is not because you feel any particular affection for the boy. Have you ever even seen him?"

"I have seen him," she said. "Once."

"Prince Chun will not be allowed to stay on the Grand Council," I said.

"He won't be allowed to participate in politics at all," she said. "A father cannot bow to his son, as a councilor would be expected to do, even if that son is an emperor."

"Well, I suppose that's one way to silence an opponent."

"So, will you help me? Will you help Zaitian? His transition to emperor will be much smoother with your support."

"What of Prince Yixin?" I asked. "Don't you think he will expect you to name one of his sons instead, since he was closer in age to Yizhu than Chun is?"

"Prince Yixin already knows," she said. "We have discussed it."

This should not have surprised me. Since I had removed myself from court, it made sense that Cixi and Yixin were working together again. Still, it was jealousy more than any desire to help Cixi or Zaitian that roused me from my bed.

"When will the announcement take place?" I asked.

"Today," she said.

"You could have given me a little more notice."

"I didn't want you to change your mind."

"I would never do that," I told her, squeezing her hand. "You know I would never go back on my word to you. We are sisters, always."

"Will you return to court?" she asked as the maids brought in a copper bathtub and began filling it with water.

"I don't know," I said. "It is difficult for me to rise so early. And listening to all those men chatter on for hours and hours makes my head ache."

"You can return to the reports then," she said. "And oversee Zaitian's education. He will need a mother—"

"I must stop you there," I said. "I understand that we will have to legally adopt Zaitian and raise him here in the Forbidden City. I will not be unkind to the boy, but I have no wish to love him. There is simply no room in my heart for another child."

"I understand," she said. "I will invite his father to oversee his education. And his mother can stay with us from time to time. I would enjoy spending more time with my sister."

I nodded. "I will help you where I can. But it will take time for me to readjust to the life of an empress dowager regent again."

ALL OF THE councilors and high-ranking officials who gathered for the announcement to hear who Cixi and I would be adopting as the new heir seemed surprised to see me when I followed Cixi into the room.

"It is good to see you again," Prince Yixin said, bowing before me. It seemed he had aged a bit since the last time I saw him, with wrinkles forming around his eyes and gray hair dusting his temples. Or, perhaps I had not noticed it before. I was sure my own age was starting to show as well, especially since I had not been taking care of myself as I should have since the deaths of my children.

"Thank you, Brother," I said. His smile wavered. Through the many long years that we had known each other, Prince Yixin and I had walked a thin line between being family, friends, and something more. Now, I had to hold myself together for the sake of the country. I could not risk any further damage to my fractured heart.

The prince bowed and stepped away, standing near Prince Chun and the other councilors. Cixi and I took our usual places behind the yellow screen and the empty throne.

"My lords," Cixi said. "Our country has endured a devastating loss, one that no one in this room, save myself and my fellow empress dowager, can possibly comprehend. To have lost a son and an emperor in one fell swoop is something we could never have foreseen. But we must trust that Heaven has a grand design for us all. A design that will require a new emperor to sit upon the Dragon Throne.

"Empress Dowager Cian and I have come to an agreement. We will adopt Zaitian, son of Prince Chun, son of the Daoguang Emperor, as our own. He will be recognized as the second son of the Xianfeng Emperor, our late husband."

A pained groan escaped from Prince Chun's throat. The men parted, and I saw him grasp for his chest as he crumpled to the floor. Prince Yixin did nothing to aid his brother. At first, I wondered if the man had suffered an apoplexy, but he writhed on the floor, moaning in what can only be described as grief. Zaitian was Prince Chun's only son, thus far. No doubt, he and his wife had held great aspirations for him. Now, the young boy would be lost to them. They would be allowed to see him, as Cixi had promised, but he would not be the son they had hoped he would be.

"The edict has already been signed and stamped by Empress Dowager Cian and myself," Cixi said, ignoring Prince Chun.

"Let the boy be brought to the Forbidden City and his new home immediately. From this moment forth, we have entered the time of Emperor Guangxu, the reign of glorious succession!"

"May the emperor live for ten thousand years!" someone yelled. The rest of the room joined in the cheer, repeating the phrase three times. Prince Chun was practically dragged from the room by guards.

When the audience ended, I went to my palace to undress, relax, and have my evening meal. For some reason, I found it difficult to sleep. For the first time in many months, I allowed thoughts other than grief to creep into my mind. Cixi and I would not be returning to the Summer Palace, so I needed to send servants to collect my things. We could perhaps visit the Summer Palace occasionally, but for now, our primary residence would once again be the Forbidden City. I would have to have the schoolroom cleaned and my desk set up.

I found myself organizing my writing utensils, many of which had fallen into disuse over the last two years and would need to be repaired or replaced, when I heard the arrival of a donkey cart. I looked outside and noticed that it was quite late at night. The cart stopped outside the palace that Zaichun had used when he was a boy, before he moved into the emperor's palace. Some men removed a small child from the cart, took him into the palace, and then left. I saw no lights on in the palace, no maids or nannies bustling about. Had Cixi made no plans at all for the arrival of the child?

I turned away. It was not my concern. I had warned Cixi that I would be unable to care for the boy. I simply couldn't. I didn't know how I could ever look at another child and not feel the sharp pain of loss for my daughter. I tried to busy myself once again with my writing instruments. No doubt, Cixi would expect me to be ready to start receiving reports tomorrow morning.

But then I heard the child cry.

I should not have been able to hear him, with two court-yards and many walls between us. But somehow, his pitiful cries pierced my soul. Almost unable to control myself, I left my palace, alone, in the dead of night, and went to the boy.

I could hardly believe what I saw. The child, merely in his sleeping shirt, was sitting alone, without a fire or blanket to warm him. His face was covered with tears and snot. I had been told that he was four years old, but he seemed much smaller than Zaichun had been at his age.

"Mama?" the little boy cried.

That was all it took to completely tear down the wall I had built around my heart. I gathered the child up into my arms.

"There, there, my boy. I am here now. Mama is here."

CHAPTER THIRTY-NINE

"I am surprised that you sent for me," Tutor Weng said as we walked in the garden together, watching Zaitian play with flowers and blades of grass.

"Why is that?" I asked.

"Zaichun...will not be remembered as a good emperor," he said. "As much as he detested Empress Cixi interfering with his daily business, I dare not say what might have happened if she had not continued to push him to keep to his schedule and duties."

"Hmm. I tried to stay out of ruling as much as possible after Zaichun married. But I know there was much corruption under his watch, or lack of watch, I should say."

"I never before had such a difficult pupil," Tutor Weng said.

"And do you believe that was your fault?" I asked.

"No," he said cautiously. "Not exactly. I never had such troubles with my other pupils. But...I failed to reach him. I was unable to find a method of teaching that spoke to his heart. And that, I fear, was a failure on my part."

"No one is perfect," I said. "Least of all me. And I would be disingenuous if I expected perfection from you. If I asked you to return and teach Zaitian, would you refuse?"

"I think I would be a fool to refuse," he said. "How often does a person get a second opportunity to teach an emperor? But are you sure you want to offer me the role? I still believe a classical education is best for a young man. But many modern thinkers would disagree with me."

"I probably would not hire you to educate a princess again," I said. "But I'm not looking for someone to educate a princess. I need someone to educate an emperor. And I can think of no one better suited than you. So, do you accept?"

Tutor Weng nodded. "I am honored, Your Majesty."

THE NEXT COUPLE of years passed similarly to the years I had spent raising Zaichun and Lifen. The boy brought me a joy I never thought I would experience again. I was indulgent with him, and I knew it. But I could not help it. The boy had lost so much, and at such a young age. He would grow to be an emperor, yes, but he had lost his family in the process. His mother gave birth to two more sons, and both died young. His mother seemed to completely lose her mind to the grief. I compensated by giving Zaitian everything he wanted and more. Nothing brought me greater happiness than seeing him smile.

I oversaw Zaitian's education and personal life and read reports and offered assistance to Cixi when she required it. China once again returned to a more stable state, with few problems and increasing revenue flowing into our coffers every day. But the daily strain of running an empire took its toll on Cixi in ways I did not realize.

It had been the end of another long day for her, and we were talking about a problem with the Russians when she suddenly collapsed. I ran to her side, afraid that, perhaps, a palsy had taken her. But it was not that.

The doctors said that Cixi was simply overcome with exhaustion. She could not sleep, but had no energy. She often vomited and coughed up blood.

"She will recover," one doctor said as Cixi and I anxiously sat together, hoping for a remedy. "But only if she rests. She must not rack her brains so much."

"I know," Cixi said. "But that is impossible. There is simply too much to do."

I looked at my friend and saw how weak she was. She wiped a tear from her eye as she tried to insist she could simply work from her bed. I remembered how Yizhu had done much the same, working from his bed in Rehe Palace. He was dead within a year.

"No," I told her. "You must rest. I will take over for you."

"You?" she asked, skeptically. "But you hate audiences. And what of the Russians?"

"I will figure it out," I said. "I insist that you rest. I cannot lose you too."

"You won't lose me," she said. "I promise."

"Yes, as long as you rest. I will call a meeting of the Grand Council. They can tell me what is going on with the Russians and anything else that needs to be taken care of. If I feel I am not up to the task, I can always ask your advice."

Cixi seemed dubious, but she nodded. She knew she did not have much choice. It was imperative that she take care of her health.

"Take care of the boy for me," I said. "Young people have a way of keeping their parents young."

"I can help you, Baba!" Zaitian, who had been sitting quietly to the side, said, his eyes shining brightly with excitement. For some reason, he often called Cixi Baba, as if she were his father and not his other mother. But Cixi encouraged it, and I saw no reason to correct him.

"You are a dear boy, aren't you?" Cixi said, running her hand down the boy's face. Cixi had not allowed herself to grow particularly close to Zaitian. I think she felt that if she grew to love him too much, she would be betraying her own son. But perhaps now that they would be spending more time together, a love between them would naturally grow.

"Cixi has given much in service to her country," I told the Grand Council the next morning. "Her health has suffered greatly, and she needs time to recover. So, for now, I will be taking over as sole regent. Please, update me on the issue with the Russians."

"Finally, things are as they should be," Prince Yixin said to me later when we were alone.

"What do you mean?" I asked.

"Sole regent," he said. "The position looks good on you. I haven't seen you so confident in decades. You should never have shared the position with Cixi."

"You think I should have shared it with you instead?" I said. "Because that is what would have happened. I would have made you co-regent, if not sole regent, if it had been up to me."

"Would that have been so terrible?" he said. "If not side by side as man and wife, we could have been side by side as we ruled the country for Zaichun."

I did my best to suppress a smile. He was speaking too freely, impudently. I should have had him punished. But I could not. Being able to speak to the prince without restraint made me feel young again.

"I summoned you to talk about the Russians," I said.

"If you insist," he said.

Ever since the Russians took thousands of acres of land from us following the last war with the foreigners, they continued pushing east, into land that had been independent, and then into China proper. I sent troops to hold them back, but I also sent emissaries to the capital of St. Petersburg in order to conduct negotiations.

I had not forgotten the massive loss we experienced after the last war, and that the British, Americans, French, and more had allied with the Russians to do so. Even if we were in the right to declare war against the Russians, I did not trust that the other foreign nations would not take up arms against us if given a chance. I did not trust them the way that Prince Yixin and Cixi did.

The British had been so afraid of China going to war with Russia that they even sent one of their famed military leaders, General Gordon, to advise me. According to Prince Yixin, the British had done so because they thought that if a war between China and Russia were to break out, China would succeed. I had to admit that I enjoyed toying with the British a bit, making them think that I was considering a war just to show them how much China's military might had improved in the last two decades.

But, in the end, I was able to force the Russians to sign the Treaty of Ili, in which the Russians were forced to return the areas they had occupied and reaffirm the borders between our two nations. It was considered a significant win for China, both domestically and on the world stage.

And for the first time in almost thirty years, I felt like an empress.

CHAPTER FORTY

"You have done well, Sister," Cixi said as we walked along the path leading to Yizhu's tomb. It had been twenty years since our husband had died. As such, we were holding a remembrance ceremony. The whole court had traveled to the Western Mausoleums to pay homage to Yizhu and his ancestors. We were surrounded by trees, and colorful flowers had been planted along either side of the path. The sun was shining, and the air was clear. I took a deep breath, relishing the excursion from the Forbidden City, even if it was for a solemn occasion.

"I hardly had to worry about a thing while I was recovering," Cixi went on. "I feel much rested and hope to return to my duties soon."

Her words should have brought me joy. And, indeed, I was glad for the return of her health. But I had become accustomed to my new station, and I had been a success. I had no desire to return to the simple monotony of the Inner Court.

"Do not rush yourself, Sister," I said. "We must make sure you are at optimum health. I have no wish for you to fall ill again."

"You are too kind," she said. "But I am ready to return to my place. And I am sure you are ready to return to yours."

"Of course," I said. "I look forward to sitting at your side behind the yellow screen."

"Oh? You mean—"

"Ladies," Prince Yixin said. I had been so engrossed in our conversation, I had not realized that we had arrived at the tomb.

"Yes, Brother?" I said.

He indicated a position in the center in front of the tomb since he had been the person to organize the event. "You should stand here, Zhen. On this side, Zaitian will stand, as the emperor's son. On your other side should be an empty place for Princess Ayan. Then, further away still, is where the remaining living consorts and concubines should stand."

Ten women from the Inner Court took their place. Lingrong was not among them. I had written to her, asking for her to attend, but she had not replied. She had not replied to any of the letters I had sent to her since the death of her daughter. I had wondered if she was dead herself, so I had sent a messenger to look for her. He returned and told me that the woman was alive, but she was quite dedicated to her new life and would not attend the ceremony. I could have taken offense. I could have forced her to attend. But I knew she was probably still grieving Lifen's death. It was a grief that only she and I shared, so I would leave her to it.

I had expected Cixi to take her place among the other consorts and concubines. After all, when Yizhu died, she still had only been a rank-four consort. But to my shock, Cixi stepped directly next to me, leaving only the smallest space for the ghost of Princess Ayan.

At first, I held my head up, not acknowledging the insult of Cixi putting herself on equal footing as myself at the tomb of our dead husband. After all, we had been equals for all these years. What difference was one day? But I could not ignore the whispers that wafted through the crowd. I made the mistake of glancing at Prince Yixin. He nodded at me, indicating that I should say something to Cixi.

"You should stand with the other consorts," I whispered to her through gritted teeth.

"No," she said.

I felt a white-hot anger that boiled from the soles of my feet travel up my body to my face, which flushed with fury.

"What did you say to me?" I asked, looking at her.

"No," she repeated. "I'm not a lowly consort like them. I'm the empress dowager."

"You were a concubine!" I shrieked, shocking everyone, including myself. Cixi's mouth gaped, and the crowd went deathly silent. In the back of my mind, I knew I was going too far. But now that the frustration of being pushed to the side, to the back of the room, to the top of the table, came rushing out all at once. "I am the empress!"

"I...I...I am sorry, Your Majesty," Cixi stuttered, giving me a bow. She then shuffled to the end of the row of consorts, keeping her face downcast. I could see that she was shaking as she wiped tears from her cheeks. I immediately felt guilty, but I could not apologize now, not with the whole court watching me. As I started to turn around, I glanced down the hill and saw a fox, as bright red as a chrysanthemum flower, dart across the path behind the gathered court. Following her, I saw three little pups. The fox raised her head, sniffed the air, and looked right at me.

Someone in the crowd coughed. The fox yipped, and she and her pups darted away into the woods.

"Mama?" Zaitian said, tugging on my robe. "What are you doing?"

"Nothing," I said, turning and facing the tomb. "Come now,

fold your hands together." I nodded to Prince Yixin for the ceremony to begin.

CIXI DID NOT SPEAK to me on the long journey back to the Forbidden City, and I did not know what to say to her either. I was embarrassed that I had acted so shamefully. Cixi was my sister, my oldest and dearest friend, my co-ruler. How could I speak to her like that? How could I feel jealous? How could I want to take her authority for myself?

I knew I needed to apologize, but I had no idea what to say. I was running through a thousand different apologies in my head, none of them good enough, when I heard a knock on my door.

"Cixi!" I said, standing up as she stepped into the room.

"No need to get up," she said. "I only came to apologize for my behavior today."

"No," I said, going to her and taking her hands in mine and leading her to sit next to me on my bed. "It is I who should apologize. I should not have yelled at you, or called you a concubine."

"You were right," she said. "I was a concubine."

"No, you are an empress. An empress dowager, just like me. The mother of an emperor."

"So are you," she said. "But you were the only one to be an empress while our husband was alive."

"I never really felt like one," I said. "Empress Dowager Jing was the real empress."

"You are a hundred times the empress she ever was!" Cixi said. "At least your son loved you."

"Our son," I said.

"*Our* son. *Our* husband. *Our* regency."

"Exactly," I said. "The only reason I am even a regent is because of you. I would never have had the courage to act the way you did. I shouldn't be jealous. Everything I have is because of you."

"You? Jealous of me? I've always been jealous of you!"

"Stop it," I said.

"I'm serious! You were the better wife, always getting me out of trouble with Yizhu. The better mother. The better regent. You got all that land back without a war. In truth, I don't think the council even wants me back. They just want you."

"That is not true," I said.

"Prince Yixin still wants you," she said playfully.

"Stop it!"

"I see the way he looks at you. The way he *still* looks at you, even after all these years."

I shook my head. "Nothing but a girlish fantasy."

"Well, I will leave you with your naughty thoughts," she said. "And tomorrow, we will do as you said—we will sit behind the yellow screen together."

"I'd like that," I said.

We stood up so I could walk her to the door, but I lost my balance as my head began to spin. I gripped Cixi's hand.

"Zhen?" she said. "Zhen!"

I was seized by a massive pain in my head. It felt like my brain was going to explode. I saw a red flash and crumpled to the floor.

I OPENED my eyes but was unable to move.

"Mama!" Zaitian called out, tears streaming down his cheeks. "Mama! Are you alright?"

I tried to nod, tried to say yes, but the palsy had me in such a grip, I could do nothing.

"Mama," Zaitian cried. "Mama, don't leave me!"

I was able to raise my right hand just at the elbow and touch his cheek. There was so much I wanted to say to this sweet boy. This boy who would be emperor. That I loved him. That he didn't need to be afraid. That he needed to be strong. That he needed to listen to his teachers and his baba. I worked my jaw, trying to speak. To say anything.

"What is it, Mama?" Zaitian asked.

"Fox," was all I could say. "Fox."

"What? Fox? What does that mean?"

My vision blurred and all I could see was the painting of the fox. The painting I had seen as my husband held me down on the table and violated me. The fox lunged toward the bird, his teeth bared.

"Be...ware," I gasped. "Beware the wild fox."

The End

FROM THE AUTHOR

When it comes to the women of the Inner Court of Imperial China, very little is known about them. Empress Cian was the empress of China from 1852-1861, and a regent of China from 1861 to 1881, with only a short two-year break during the rule of the Tongzhi Emperor. Yet even her given name is unknown. In most fictionalized accounts of her better-known counterpart, Empress Cixi, Empress Cian is completely eliminated from the story. I knew there had to be more to this woman, so I was excited to bring her to life here.

I have included a list of sources that I used in researching Empress Cian and the other members of the Qing Dynasty court. If you read nothing else, I highly recommend Jung Chang's *Empress Dowager Cixi: The Concubine Who Launched Modern China*. While it is mostly about Cixi, she also references Cian more than any other source I have found.

If you enjoyed this novel, please visit my website and join my mailing list so you never miss a new release. I have many more books about the women of the Qing Dynasty planned, and I can't wait to share all of them with you!

FROM THE AUTHOR

AmandaRobertsWrites.com

The Qing Dynasty - 1782-1881

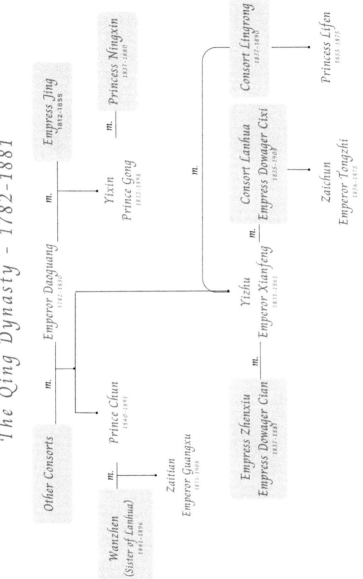

QING DYNASTY TIMELINE

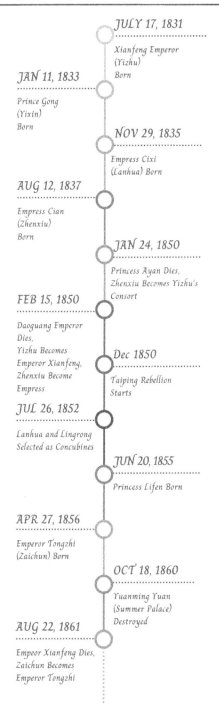

JULY 17, 1831
....
Xianfeng Emperor
(Yizhu)
Born

JAN 11, 1833
....
Prince Gong
(Yixin)
Born

NOV 29, 1835
....
Empress Cixi
(Lanhua) Born

AUG 12, 1837
....
Empress Cian
(Zhenxiu)
Born

JAN 24, 1850
....
Princess Ayan Dies,
Zhenxiu Becomes Yizhu's
Consort

FEB 15, 1850
....
Daoguang Emperor
Dies,
Yizhu Becomes
Emperor Xianfeng,
Zhenxiu Become
Empress

Dec 1850
....
Taiping Rebellion
Starts

JUL 26, 1852
....
Lanhua and Lingrong
Selected as Concubines

JUN 20, 1855
....
Princess Lifen Born

APR 27, 1856
....
Emperor Tongzhi
(Zaichun) Born

OCT 18, 1860
....
Yuanming Yuan
(Summer Palace)
Destroyed

AUG 22, 1861
....
Empeor Xianfeng Dies,
Zaichun Becomes
Emperor Tongzhi

QING DYNASTY TIMELINE

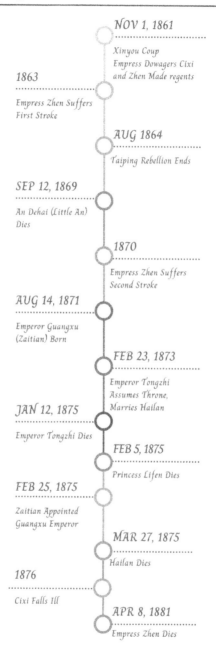

NOV 1, 1861

Xinyou Coup
Empress Dowagers Cixi
and Zhen Made regents

1863

Empress Zhen Suffers
First Stroke

AUG 1864

Taiping Rebellion Ends

SEP 12, 1869

An Dehai (Little An)
Dies

1870

Empress Zhen Suffers
Second Stroke

AUG 14, 1871

Emperor Guangxu
(Zaitian) Born

FEB 23, 1873

Emperor Tongzhi
Assumes Throne,
Marries Hailan

JAN 12, 1875

Emperor Tongzhi Dies

FEB 5, 1875

Princess Lifen Dies

FEB 25, 1875

Zaitian Appointed
Guangxu Emperor

MAR 27, 1875

Hailan Dies

1876

Cixi Falls Ill

APR 8, 1881

Empress Zhen Dies

READER GUIDE/BOOK CLUB DISCUSSION QUESTIONS

1. Zhen was an empress and empress dowager for almost thirty years. So, what is the significance of the book's title?
2. Do you think the characters accurately portrayed the real events upon which the book was based? If not, what would you have changed to make the book more accurate?
3. What did you already know about Empress Cian or the Qing Dynasty before you read this book? Did the story reflect what you already knew? Do you feel the book helped enhance your knowledge and understanding of Imperial China?
4. Describe the relationship between Zhen and Lanhua/Cixi. Does their relationship change throughout the novel or stagnate?
5. Is Zhen a reliable narrator? Is Zhen's view of Lanhua/Cixi trustworthy?
6. Which characters other than Zhen did you find the most interesting? Why?

7. The image of the fox is repeated throughout the novel. Why do you think that was? What does the image represent or hint toward?

8. The Qing Dynasty was the last of Imperial China. How did some of the events in this novel lead toward or foreshadow that end?

9. Yizhu was cruel to Zhen for most of their marriage, yet, as he lay dying, she prayed for him to live. Why?

10. How significant are the differences between Han Chinese and Manchu portrayed in the novel? Do you think those differences will contribute to the fall of the Qing Dynasty?

11. Emperor Tongzhi's name meant "order and prosperity." Emperor Guangxu's name meant "glorious succession." Why do you think these names were chosen?

12. Is the ending satisfying? If so, why? If not, why not, and how would you change it?

13. If you could ask the author a question, what would you ask? Have you read other books by the same author? If so, how does this book compare. If not, does this book inspire you to read others?

14. Has this novel changed you or broadened your perspective? Have you learned something new or been exposed to different ideas about people or a certain part of the world?

BIBLIOGRAPHY

Chang, J. (2013). *Empress Dowager Cixi: The Concubine Who Launched Modern China*. Alfred A. Knopf.

Eastman, L. E. (1988). *Family, Fields, and Ancestors: Constancy and Change in China's Social and Economic History, 1550-1949*. Oxford University Press.

Hayter-Menzies, G. (2011). *The Empress and Mrs. Conger*. Hong Kong University Press.

Headland, I. T. (2017). *Court Life in China*. Pinnacle Press.

Hurd, D. (1967). *The Arrow War: An Anglo-Chinese Confusion, 1856-1860*. The Macmillan Company.

Ling, P. D. (2008). *Two Years in the Forbidden City*. Akasha Classics.

Ling, P. D. (2015). *The True Story of the Empress Dowager: An Insider's Account*. Soul Care Publishing.

M., R. E. J. (2011). *Manchus and Han: Ethnic Relations and Political Power in Late Qing and Early Republican China, 1861-1928*. University of Washington Press.

Mann, S. (1997). *Precious Records: Women in China's Long Eighteenth Century*. Stanford University Press.

McMahon, K. (2020). *Celestial Women*. Rowman & Littlefield.

Rawski, E. S. (2009). *The Last Emperors: A Social History of Qing Imperial Institution*. University of California Press.

Smith, R. J. (1984). *China's Cultural Heritage: The Ch'ing Dynasty, 1644-1912*. Southern Materials Center.

Spence, J. D. (1997). *God's Chinese Son: The Taiping Heavenly Kingdom of Hong Xiuquan*. W. W. Norton.

Wakeman, F. (1975). *The Fall of Imperial China*. Macmillan Publishing Co., Inc. .

Watson, J. L., & Rawski, E. S. (Eds.). (1990). *Death ritual in late Imperial and modern China*. University of California Press.

Watson, R. S., & Ebrey, P. B. (1994). *Marriage and Inequality in Chinese Society*. SMC.

ABOUT THE AUTHOR

 Amanda Roberts is a *USA Today* best-selling author who lived in China for more than a decade. She has a master's degree in English and degrees in history and Chinese language. She has been published in magazines, newspapers, and anthologies around the world. Amanda can be found all over the Internet, but her home is Amanda RobertsWrites.com.

facebook.com/AmandaRobertsWrites

instagram.com/amandarobertswrites

goodreads.com/Amanda_Roberts

bookbub.com/authors/amanda-roberts-2bfe99dd-ea16-4614-a696-84116326dcd1

ABOUT THE PUBLISHER

VISIT OUR WEBSITE
TO SEE ALL OF OUR HIGH QUALITY BOOKS:

http://www.redempresspublishing.com

Quality trade paperbacks, downloads, audio books, and books in foreign languages in genres such as historical, romance, mystery, and fantasy.

CPSIA information can be obtained
at www.ICGtesting.com
Printed in the USA
LVHW040342050523
746132LV00005B/539